813

813

Maurice Leblanc

MINT EDITIONS

813 was first published in 1910.

This edition published by Mint Editions 2021.

ISBN 9781513292373 | E-ISBN 9781513295220

Published by Mint Editions®

MINT
EDITIONS

minteditionbooks.com

Publishing Director: Jennifer Newens
Design & Production: Rachel Lopez Metzger
Project Manager: Micaela Clark
Translated By: Alexander Teixeira De Mottos
Typesetting: Westchester Publishing Services

Contents

Translator's Note

A zealous reader, collating the translation of this book with the original, would hit upon certain differences. These are due to alterations made, in most case, by the author himself, and, in all cases, with his full approval.

A. T. De M.
Chelsea, England, August, 1910

I

The Tragedy at the Palace Hotel

M r. Kesselbach stopped short on the threshold of the sitting-room, took his secretary's arm and, in an anxious voice, whispered:

"Chapman, some one has been here again."

"Surely not, sir," protested the secretary. "You have just opened the hall-door yourself; and the key never left your pocket while we were lunching in the restaurant."

"Chapman, some one has been here again," Mr. Kesselbach repeated. He pointed to a traveling-bag on the mantelpiece. "Look, I can prove it. That bag was shut. It is now open."

Chapman protested.

"Are you quite sure that you shut it, sir? Besides, the bag contains nothing but odds and ends of no value, articles of dress. . ."

"It contains nothing else, because I took my pocket-book out before we went down, by way of precaution. . . But for that. . . No, Chapman, I tell you, some one has been here while we were at lunch."

There was a telephone on the wall. He took down the receiver:

"Hallo! . . . I'm Mr. Kesselbach. . . Suite 415. . . That's right. . . Mademoiselle, would you please put me on to the Prefecture of Police. . . the detective department. . . I know the number. . . one second. . . Ah, here it is! Number 822.48. . . I'll hold the line."

A moment later he continued:

"Are you 822.48? I should like a word with M. Lenormand, the chief of the detective-service. My name's Kesselbach. . . Hullo! . . . Yes, the chief detective knows what it's about. He has given me leave to ring him up. . . Oh, he's not there? . . . To whom am I speaking? . . . Detective-sergeant Gourel? . . . You were there yesterday, were you not, when I called on M. Lenormand? Well, the same thing that I told M. Lenormand yesterday has occurred again to-day. . . Some one has entered the suite which I am occupying. And, if you come at once, you may be able to discover some clues. . . In an hour or two? All right; thanks. . . You have only to ask for suite 415. . . Thank you again."

Rudolf Kesselbach, nicknamed alternatively the King of Diamonds and the Lord of the Cape, possessed a fortune estimated at nearly twenty millions sterling. For the past week, he had occupied suite 415, on the fourth floor of the Palace Hotel, consisting of three rooms, of which the two larger, on the right, the sitting-room and the principal bedroom, faced the avenue; while the other, on the left, in which Chapman, the secretary, slept, looked out on the Rue de Judée.

Adjoining this bedroom, a suite of five rooms had been reserved for Mrs. Kesselbach, who was to leave Monte Carlo, where she was at present staying, and join her husband the moment she heard from him.

Rudolf Kesselbach walked up and down for a few minutes with a thoughtful air. He was a tall man, with a ruddy complexion, and still young; and his dreamy eyes, which showed pale blue through his gold-rimmed spectacles, gave him an expression of gentleness and shyness that contrasted curiously with the strength of the square forehead and the powerfully-developed jaws.

He went to the window: it was fastened. Besides, how could any one have entered that way? The private balcony that ran round the flat broke off on the right and was separated on the left by a stone channel from the balconies in the Rue de Judée.

He went to his bedroom: it had no communication with the neighboring rooms. He went to his secretary's bedroom: the door that led into the five rooms reserved for Mrs. Kesselbach was locked and bolted.

"I can't understand it at all, Chapman. Time after time I have noticed things here. . . funny things, as you must admit. Yesterday, my walking-stick was moved. . . The day before that, my papers had certainly been touched. . . And yet how was it possible? . . .

"It is not possible, sir!" cried Chapman, whose honest, placid features displayed no anxiety. "You're imagining things, that's all. . . You have no proof, nothing but impressions, to go upon. . . Besides, look here: there is no way into this suite except through the entrance-lobby. Very well. You had a special key made on the day of our arrival: and your own man, Edwards, has the only duplicate. Do you trust him?"

"Of course I do! . . . He's been with me for ten years! . . . But Edwards goes to lunch at the same time that we do; and that's a mistake. He must not go down, in future, until we come back."

Chapman gave a slight shrug of the shoulders. There was no doubt about it, the Lord of the Cape was becoming a trifle eccentric, with those incomprehensible fears of his. What risk can you run in an hotel, especially when you carry no valuables, no important sum of money on you or with you?

They heard the hall-door opening. It was Edwards. Mr. Kesselbach called him:

"Are you dressed, Edwards? Ah, that's right! . . . I am expecting no visitors to-day, Edwards. . . or, rather, one visitor only, M. Gourel. Meantime, remain in the lobby and keep an eye on the door. Mr. Chapman and I have some serious work to do."

The serious work lasted for a few minutes, during which Mr. Kesselbach went through his correspondence, read three or four letters and gave instructions how they were to be answered. But, suddenly, Chapman, waiting with pen poised, saw that Mr. Kesselbach was thinking of something quite different from his correspondence. He was holding between his fingers and attentively examining a pin, a black pin bent like a fish-hook:

"Chapman," he said, "look what I've found on the table. This bent pin obviously means something. It's a proof, a material piece of evidence. You can't pretend now that no one has been in the room. For, after all, this pin did not come here of itself."

"Certainly not," replied the secretary. "It came here through me."

"What do you mean?"

"Why, it's a pin which I used to fasten my tie to my collar. I took it out last night, while you were reading, and I twisted it mechanically."

Mr. Kesselbach rose from his chair, with a great air of vexation, took a few steps and stopped.

"You're laughing at me, Chapman, I feel you are. . . and you're quite right. . . I won't deny it, I have been rather. . . odd, since my last journey to the Cape. It's because. . . well. . . you don't know the new factor in my life. . . a tremendous plan. . . a huge thing. . . I can only see it, as yet, in the haze of the future. . . but it's taking shape for all that. . . and it will be something colossal. . . Ah, Chapman, you can't imagine. . . Money I don't care a fig for: I have money, I have too much money. . . But this, this means a great deal more; it means power, might, authority. If the reality comes up to my expectations, I shall be not only Lord of the Cape, but lord of other realms as well. . . Rudolf Kesselbach, the son of the Augsburg ironmonger, will be on a par with many people who till now have looked down upon him. . . He will even take precedence of them, Chapman; he will, take precedence of them, mark my words. . . and, if ever I. . ."

He interrupted himself, looked at Chapman as though he regretted having said too much and, nevertheless, carried away by his excitement, concluded:

"You now understand the reasons of my anxiety, Chapman. . . Here, in this brain, is an idea that is worth a great deal. . . and this idea is suspected perhaps. . . and I am being spied upon. . . I'm convinced of it. . ."

A bell sounded.

"The telephone," said Chapman.

"Could it," muttered Kesselbach, "by any chance be. . . ?" He took down the instrument. "Hullo! . . . Who? The Colonel? Ah, good! Yes, it's I. . . Any news? . . . Good! . . . Then I shall expect you. . . You will come with one of your men? Very well. . . What? No, we shan't be disturbed. . . I will give the necessary orders. . . It's as serious as that, is it? . . . I tell you, my instructions will be positive. . . my secretary and my man shall keep the door; and no one shall be allowed in. . . You know the way, don't you? . . . Then don't lose a minute."

He hung up the receiver and said:

"Chapman, there are two gentlemen coming. Edwards will show them in. . ."

"But M. Gourel. . . the detective-sergeant. . . ?"

"He will come later. . . in an hour. . . And, even then, there's no harm in their meeting. So send Edwards down to the office at once, to tell them. I am at home to nobody. . . except two gentlemen, the Colonel and his friend, and M. Gourel. He must make them take down the names."

Chapman did as he was asked. When he returned to the room, he found Mr. Kesselbach holding in his hand an envelope, or, rather, a little pocket-case, in black morocco leather, apparently empty. He seemed to hesitate, as though he did not know what to do with it. Should he put it in his pocket or lay it down elsewhere? At last he went to the mantelpiece and threw the leather envelope into his traveling-bag:

"Let us finish the mail, Chapman. We have ten minutes left. Ah, a letter from Mrs. Kesselbach! Why didn't you tell me of it, Chapman? Didn't you recognize the handwriting?"

He made no attempt to conceal the emotion which he felt in touching and contemplating that paper which his wife had held in her fingers and to which she had added a look of her eyes, an atom of her scent, a suggestion of her secret thoughts. He inhaled its perfume and, unsealing it, read the letter slowly in an undertone, in fragments that reached Chapman's ears:

> "Feeling a little tired. . . Shall keep my room to-day. . . I feel so bored. . . When can I come to you? I am longing for your wire. . ."

"You telegraphed this morning, Chapman? Then Mrs. Kesselbach will be here to-morrow, Wednesday."

He seemed quite gay, as though the weight of his business had been suddenly relieved and he freed from all anxiety. He rubbed his hands and heaved a deep breath, like a strong man certain of success, like a lucky man who possessed happiness and who was big enough to defend himself.

"There's some one ringing, Chapman, some one ringing at the hall door. Go and see who it is."

But Edwards entered and said:

"Two gentlemen asking for you, sir. They are the ones. . ."

"I know. Are they there, in the lobby?"

"Yes, sir."

"Close the hall-door and don't open it again except to M. Gourel, the detective-sergeant. You go and bring the gentlemen in, Chapman, and tell them that I would like to speak to the Colonel first, to the Colonel alone."

Edwards and Chapman left the room, shutting the door after them. Rudolf Kesselbach went to the window and pressed his forehead against the glass.

Outside, just below his eyes, the carriages and motor-cars rolled along in parallel furrows, marked by the double line of refuges. A bright spring sun made the brass-work and the varnish gleam again. The trees were putting forth their first green shoots; and the buds of the tall chestnuts were beginning to unfold their new-born leaves.

"What on earth is Chapman doing?" muttered Kesselbach. "The time he wastes in palavering! . . ."

He took a cigarette from the table, lit it and drew a few puffs. A faint exclamation escaped him. Close before him stood a man whom he did not know.

He started back:

"Who are you?"

The man—he was a well-dressed individual, rather smart-looking, with dark hair, a dark moustache and hard eyes—the man gave a grin:

"Who am I? Why, the Colonel!"

"No, no. . . The one I call the Colonel, the one who writes to me under that. . . adopted. . . signature. . . is not you!"

"Yes, yes. . . the other was only. . . But, my dear sir, all this, you know, is not of the smallest importance. The essential thing is that I. . . am myself. And that, I assure you, I *am*!"

"But your name, sir? . . ."

"The Colonel. . . until further orders."

Mr. Kesselbach was seized with a growing fear. Who was this man? What did he want with him?

He called out:

"Chapman!"

"What a funny idea, to call out! Isn't my company enough for you?"

"Chapman!" Mr. Kesselbach cried again. "Chapman! Edwards!"

"Chapman! Edwards!" echoed the stranger, in his turn. "What are you doing? You're wanted!"

"Sir, I ask you, I order you to let me pass."

"But, my dear sir, who's preventing you?"

He politely made way. Mr. Kesselbach walked to the door, opened it and gave a sudden jump backward. Behind the door stood another man, pistol in hand. Kesselbach stammered:

"Edwards. . . Chap. . ."

He did not finish. In a corner of the lobby he saw his secretary and his servant lying side by side on the floor, gagged and bound.

Mr. Kesselbach, notwithstanding his nervous and excitable nature, was not devoid of physical courage; and the sense of a definite danger, instead of depressing him, restored all his elasticity and vigor. Pretending dismay and stupefaction, he moved slowly back to the chimneypiece and leant against the wall. His hand felt for the electric bell. He found it and pressed the button without removing his finger.

"Well?" asked the stranger.

Mr. Kesselbach made no reply and continued to press the button.

"Well? Do you expect they will come, that the whole hotel is in commotion, because you are pressing that bell? Why, my dear sir, look behind you and you will see that the wire is cut!"

Mr. Kesselbach turned round sharply, as though he wanted to make

MAURICE LEBLANC

sure; but, instead, with a quick movement, he seized the traveling-bag, thrust his hand into it, grasped a revolver, aimed it at the man and pulled the trigger.

"Whew!" said the stranger. "So you load your weapons with air and silence?"

The cock clicked a second time and a third, but there was no report.

"Three shots more, Lord of the Cape! I shan't be satisfied till you've lodged six bullets in my carcass. What! You give up? That's a pity. . . you were making excellent practice!"

He took hold of a chair by the back, spun it round, sat down a-straddle and, pointing to an arm-chair, said:

"Won't you take a seat, my dear sir, and make yourself at home? A cigarette? Not for me, thanks: I prefer a cigar."

There was a box on the table: he selected an Upmann, light in color and flawless in shape, lit it and, with a bow:

"Thank you! That's a perfect cigar. And now let's have a chat, shall we?"

Rudolf Kesselbach listened to him in amazement. Who could this strange person be? . . . Still, at the sight of his visitor sitting there so quiet and so chatty, he became gradually reassured and began to think that the situation might come to an end without any need to resort to violence or brute force.

He took out a pocket-book, opened it, displayed a respectable bundle of bank-notes and asked:

"How much?"

The other looked at him with an air of bewilderment, as though he found a difficulty in understanding what Kesselbach meant. Then, after a moment, he called:

"Marco!"

The man with the revolver stepped forward.

"Marco, this gentleman is good enough to offer you a few bits of paper for your young woman. Take them, Marco."

Still aiming his revolver with his right hand, Marco put out his left, took the notes and withdrew.

"Now that this question is settled according to your wishes," resumed the stranger, "let us come to the object of my visit. I will be brief and to the point. I want two things. In the first place, a little black morocco pocket-case, shaped like an envelope, which you generally carry on you.

Secondly, a small ebony box, which was in that traveling-bag yesterday. Let us proceed in order. The morocco case?"

"Burnt."

The stranger knit his brows. He must have had a vision of the good old days when there were peremptory methods of making the contumacious speak:

"Very well. We shall see about that. And the ebony box?"

"Burnt."

"Ah," he growled, "you're getting at me, my good man!" He twisted the other's arm with a pitiless hand. "Yesterday, Rudolf Kesselbach, you walked into the Crédit Lyonnais, on the Boulevard des Italiens, hiding a parcel under your overcoat. You hired a safe. . . let us be exact: safe No. 16, in recess No. 9. After signing the book and paying your safe-rent, you went down to the basement; and, when you came up again, you no longer had your parcel with you. Is that correct?"

"Quite."

"Then the box and the pocket-case are at the Crédit Lyonnais?"

"No."

"Give me the key of your safe."

"No."

"Marco!"

Marco ran up.

"Look sharp, Marco! The quadruple knot!"

Before he had even time to stand on the defensive, Rudolf Kesselbach was tied up in a network of cords that cut into his flesh at the least attempt which he made to struggle. His arms were fixed behind his back, his body fastened to the chair and his legs tied together like the legs of a mummy.

"Search him, Marco."

Marco searched him. Two minutes after, he handed his chief a little flat, nickel-plated key, bearing the numbers 16 and 9.

"Capital. No morocco pocket-case?"

"No, governor."

"It is in the safe. Mr. Kesselbach, will you tell me the secret cypher that opens the lock?"

"No."

"You refuse?"

"Yes."

"Marco!"

"Yes, governor."

"Place the barrel of your revolver against the gentleman's temple."

"It's there."

"Now put your finger to the trigger."

"Ready."

"Well, Kesselbach, old chap, do you intend to speak?"

"No."

"I'll give you ten seconds, and not one more. Marco!"

"Yes, governor."

"In ten seconds, blow out the gentleman's brains."

"Right you are, governor."

"Kesselbach, I'm counting. One, two, three, four, five, six. . ."

Rudolph Kesselbach made a sign.

"You want to speak?"

"Yes."

"You're just in time. Well, the cypher. . . the word for the lock?"

"Dolor."

"Dolor. . . Dolor. . . Mrs. Kesselbach's name is Dolores, I believe? You dear boy! . . . Marco, go and do as I told you. . . No mistake, mind! I'll repeat it: meet Jérôme at the omnibus office, give him the key, tell him the word: Dolor. Then, the two of you, go to the Crédit Lyonnais. Jérôme is to walk in alone, sign the name-book, go down to the basement and bring away everything in the safe. Do you quite understand?"

"Yes, governor. But if the safe shouldn't open; if the word Dolor. . ."

"Silence, Marco. When you come out of the Crédit Lyonnais, you must leave Jérôme, go to your own place and telephone the result of the operation to me. Should the word Dolor by any chance fail to open the safe, we (my friend Rudolf Kesselbach and I) will have one. . . *last*. . . interview. Kesselbach, you're quite sure you're not mistaken?"

"Yes."

"That means that you rely upon the futility of the search. We shall see. Be off, Marco!"

"What about you, governor?"

"I shall stay. Oh, I'm not afraid! I've never been in less danger than at this moment. Your orders about the door were positive, Kesselbach, were they not?"

"Yes."

"Dash it all, you seemed very eager to get that said! Can you have been trying to gain time? If so, I should be caught in a trap like a fool. . ." He stopped to think, looked at his prisoner and concluded, "No. . . it's not possible. . . we shall not be disturbed. . ."

He had not finished speaking, when the door-bell rang. He pressed his hand violently on Rudolf Kesselbach's mouth:

"Oh, you old fox, you were expecting some one!"

The captive's eyes gleamed with hope. He could be heard chuckling under the hand that stifled him.

The stranger shook with rage:

"Hold your tongue, or I'll strangle you! Here, Marco, gag him! Quick! . . . That's it!"

The bell rang again. He shouted, as though he himself were Kesselbach and as though Edwards were still there:

"Why don't you open the door, Edwards?"

Then he went softly into the lobby and, pointing to the secretary and the manservant, whispered:

"Marco, help me shift these two into the bedroom. . . over there. . . so that they can't be seen."

He lifted the secretary. Marco carried the servant.

"Good! Now go back to the sitting-room."

He followed him in and at once returned to the lobby and said, in a loud tone of astonishment:

"Why, your man's not here, Mr. Kesselbach. . . No, don't move. . . finish your letter. . . I'll go myself."

And he quietly opened the hall-door.

"Mr. Kesselbach?"

He found himself faced by a sort of jovial, bright-eyed giant, who stood swinging from one foot to the other and twisting the brim of his hat between his fingers. He answered:

"Yes, that's right. Who shall I say. . . ?"

"Mr. Kesselbach telephoned. . . He expects me. . ."

"Oh, it's you. . . I'll tell him. . . Do you mind waiting a minute? . . . Mr. Kesselbach will speak to you."

He had the audacity to leave the visitor standing on the threshold of the little entrance-hall, at a place from which he could see a portion of the sitting-room through the open door, and, slowly, without so much as turning round, he entered the room, went to his confederate by Mr. Kesselbach's side and whispered:

"We're done! It's Gourel, the detective. . ."

The other drew his knife. He caught him by the arm:

"No nonsense! I have an idea. But, for God's sake, Marco, understand me and speak in your turn. Speak *as if you were Kesselbach*. . . You hear, Marco! You *are* Kesselbach."

He expressed himself so coolly, so forcibly and with such authority that Marco understood, without further explanation, that he himself was to play the part of Kesselbach. Marco said, so as to be heard:

"You must apologize for me, my dear fellow. Tell M. Gourel I'm awfully sorry, but I'm over head and ears in work. . . I will see him to-morrow morning, at nine. . . yes, at nine o'clock punctually."

"Good!" whispered the other. "Don't stir."

He went back to the lobby, found Gourel waiting, and said:

"Mr. Kesselbach begs you to excuse him. He is finishing an important piece of work. Could you possibly come back at nine o'clock to-morrow morning?"

There was a pause. Gourel seemed surprised, more or less bothered and undecided. The other man's hand clutched the handle of a knife at the bottom of his pocket. At the first suspicious movement, he was prepared to strike.

At last, Gourel said:

"Very well. . . At nine o'clock to-morrow. . . But, all the same. . . However, I shall be here at nine to-morrow. . ."

And, putting on his hat, he disappeared down the passage of the hotel.

Marco, in the sitting-room, burst out laughing:

"That was jolly clever of you, governor! Oh, how nicely you spoofed him!"

"Look alive, Marco, and follow him. If he leaves the hotel, let him be, meet Jérôme at the omnibus-office as arranged. . . and telephone."

Marco went away quickly.

Then the man took a water-bottle on the chimneypiece, poured himself out a tumblerful, which he swallowed at a draught, wetted his handkerchief, dabbed his forehead, which was covered with perspiration, and then sat down beside his prisoner and, with an affectation of politeness, said:

"But I must really have the honor, Mr. Kesselbach, of introducing myself to you."

And, taking a card from his pocket, he said: "Allow me. . . Arsène Lupin, gentleman-burglar."

THE NAME OF THE FAMOUS adventurer seemed to make the best of impressions upon Mr. Kesselbach. Lupin did not fail to observe the fact and exclaimed:

"Aha, my dear sir, you breathe again! Arsène Lupin is a delicate, squeamish burglar. He loathes bloodshed, he has never committed a more serious crime than that of annexing other people's property. . . a mere peccadillo, eh? And what you're saying to yourself is that he is not going to burden his conscience with a useless murder. Quite so. . . But will your destruction be so useless as all that? Everything depends on the answer. And I assure you that I'm not larking at present. Come on, old chap!"

He drew up his chair beside the arm-chair, removed the prisoner's gag and, speaking very plainly:

"Mr. Kesselbach," he said, "on the day when you arrived in Paris you entered into relations with one Barbareux, the manager of a confidential inquiry agency; and, as you were acting without the knowledge of your secretary, Chapman, it was arranged that the said Barbareux, when communicating with you by letter or telephone, should call himself 'the Colonel.' I hasten to tell you that Barbareux is a perfectly honest man. But I have the good fortune to number one of his clerks among my own particular friends. That is how I discovered the motive of your application to Barbareux and how I came to interest myself in you and to make a search or two here, with the assistance of a set of false keys. . . in the course of which search or two, I may as well tell you, I did not find what I was looking for."

He lowered his voice and, with his eyes fixed on the eyes of his prisoner, watching his expression, searching his secret thoughts, he uttered these words:

"Mr. Kesselbach, your instructions to Barbareux were that he should find a man hidden somewhere in the slums of Paris who bears or used to bear the name of Pierre Leduc. The man answers to this brief description: height, five feet nine inches; hair and complexion, fair; wears a moustache. Special mark: the tip of the little finger of the left hand is missing, as the result of a cut. Also, he has an almost imperceptible scar on the right cheek. You seem to attach enormous importance to this man's discovery, as though it might lead to some great advantage to yourself. Who is the man?"

"I don't know."

The answer was positive, absolute. Did he know or did he not know?

It made little difference. The great thing was that he was determined not to speak.

"Very well," said his adversary, "but you have fuller particulars about him than those with which you furnished Barbareux."

"I have not."

"You lie, Mr. Kesselbach. Twice, in Barbareux's presence, you consulted papers contained in the morocco case."

"I did."

"And the case?"

"Burnt."

Lupin quivered with rage. The thought of torture and of the facilities which it used to offer was evidently passing through his mind again.

"Burnt? But the box? . . . Come, own up. . . confess that the box is at the Crédit Lyonnais."

"Yes."

"And what's inside it?"

"The finest two hundred diamonds in my private collection."

This statement did not seem to displease the adventurer.

"Aha, the finest two hundred diamonds! But, I say, that's a fortune! . . . Yes, that makes you smile. . . It's a trifle to you, no doubt. . . And your secret is worth more than that. . . To you, yes. . . but to me? . . ."

He took a cigar, lit a match, which he allowed to go out again mechanically, and sat for some time thinking, motionless.

The minutes passed.

He began to laugh:

"I dare say you're hoping that the expedition will come to nothing and that they won't open the safe? . . . Very likely, old chap! But, in that case, you'll have to pay me for my trouble. I did not come here to see what sort of figure you cut in an arm-chair. . . The diamonds, since diamonds there appear to be. . . or else the morocco case. . . There's your dilemma." He looked at his watch. "Half an hour. . . Hang it all! . . . Fate is moving very slowly. . . But there's nothing for you to grin at, Mr. Kesselbach. I shall not go back empty-handed, make no mistake about that! . . . At last!"

It was the telephone-bell. Lupin snatched at the receiver and, changing the sound of his voice, imitated the rough accent of his prisoner:

"Yes, Rudolf Kesselbach. . . you're speaking to him. . . Yes, please, mademoiselle, put me on. . . Is that you, Marco? . . . Good. . . Did it go off all right? . . . Excellent! . . . No hitch? . . . My best compliments! . . . Well, what did you pick up? . . . The ebony box? . . . Nothing else? . . . No papers? . . . Tut, tut! . . . And what's in the box? . . . Are they fine diamonds? . . . Capital, capital! . . . One minute, Marco, while I think. . . You see, all this. . . If I were to tell you my opinion. . . Wait, don't go away. . . hold the line. . ."

He turned round.

"Mr. Kesselbach, are you keen on your diamonds?"

"Yes."

"Would you buy them back of me?"

"Possibly."

"For how much? Five hundred thousand francs?"

"Five hundred thousand. . . yes."

"Only, here's the rub: how are we to make the exchange? A cheque? No, you'd swindle me. . . or else I'd swindle you. . . Listen. On the day after to-morrow, go to the Crédit Lyonnais in the morning, draw out your five hundred bank-notes of a thousand each and go for a walk in the Bois, on the Auteuil side. . . I shall have the diamonds in a bag: that's handier. . . The box shows too much. . ."

Kesselbach gave a start:

"No, no. . . the box, too. . . I want everything. . ."

"Ah," cried Lupin, shouting with laughter, "you've fallen into the trap! . . . The diamonds you don't care about. . . they can be replaced. . . But you cling to that box as you cling to your skin. . . Very well, you shall have your box. . . on the word of Arsène. . . you shall have it to-morrow morning, by parcel post!"

He went back to the telephone:

"Marco, have you the box in front of you? . . . Is there anything particular about it? . . . Ebony inlaid with ivory. . . Yes, I know the sort of thing. . . Japanese, from the Faubourg Saint-Antoine. . . No mark? . . . Ah, a little round label, with a blue border and a number! . . . Yes, a shop-mark. . . no importance. And is the bottom of the box thick? . . . Not very thick. . . Bother! No false bottom, then? . . . Look here, Marco: just examine the ivory inlay on the outside. . . or, rather, no, the lid." He reveled with delight. "The lid! That's it, Marco! Kesselbach blinked his eyes just now. . . We're burning! . . . Ah, Kesselbach, old chap, didn't you see me squinting at you? You silly fellow!" And, to Marco, "Well, what do you see? . . . A looking-glass inside the lid? . . . Does it slide? . . . Is it on hinges? . . . No! . . . Well, then, break it. . .

Yes, yes, I tell you to break it. . . That glass serves no purpose there. . . it's been added since!" He lost patience. "Mind your own business, idiot! . . . Do as I say! . . ."

He must have heard the noise which Marco made at the other end of the wire in breaking the glass, for he shouted, in triumph.

"Didn't I tell you, Mr. Kesselbach, that we should find something? . . . Hullo! Have you done it? . . . Well? . . . A letter? Victory! All the diamonds in the Cape and old man Kesselbach's secret into the bargain!"

He took down the second receiver, carefully put the two discs to his ears and continued:

"Read it to me, Marco, read it to me slowly. . . The envelope first. . . Good. . . Now, repeat." He himself repeated, "'Copy of the letter contained in the black morocco case.' And next? Tear the envelope, Marco. . . Have I your permission, Mr. Kesselbach? It's not very good form, but, however. . . Go on, Marco, Mr. Kesselbach gives you leave. . . Done it? . . . Well, then, read it out."

He listened and, with a chuckle:

"The deuce! That's not quite as clear as a pikestaff! Listen. I'll repeat: a plain sheet of paper folded in four, the folds apparently quite fresh. . . Good. . . At the top of the page, on the right, these words: 'Five feet nine, left little finger cut.' And so on. . . Yes, that's the description of Master Pierre Leduc. In Kesselbach's handwriting, I suppose? . . . Good. . . And, in the middle of the page, this word in printed capitals: 'Apoon.' Marco, my lad, leave the paper as it is and don't touch the box or the diamonds. I shall have done with our friend here in ten minutes and I shall be with you in twenty. . . Oh, by the way, did you send back the motor for me? Capital! So long!"

He replaced the instrument, went into the lobby and into the bedroom, made sure that the secretary and the manservant had not unloosed their bonds and, on the other hand, that they were in no danger of being choked by their gags. Then he returned to his chief prisoner.

He wore a determined and relentless look:

"We've finished joking, Kesselbach. If you don't speak, it will be the worse for you. Have you made up your mind?"

"What about?"

"No nonsense, please. Tell me what you know."

"I know nothing."

"You lie. What does this word 'Apoon' mean?"

"If I knew, I should not have written it down."

"Very well; but whom or what does it refer to? Where did you copy it? Where did you get it from?"

Mr. Kesselbach made no reply. Lupin, now speaking in nervous, jerky tones, resumed:

"Listen, Kesselbach, I have a proposal to make to you. Rich man, big man though you may be, there is not so much difference between us. The son of the Augsburg ironmonger and Arsène Lupin, prince of burglars, can come to an understanding without shame on either side. I do my thieving indoors; you do yours on the Stock Exchange. It's all much of a muchness. So here we are, Kesselbach. Let's be partners in this business. I have need of you, because I don't know what it's about. You have need of me, because you will never be able to manage it alone. Barbareux is an ass. I am Lupin. Is it a bargain?"

No answer. Lupin persisted, in a voice shaking with intensity:

"Answer, Kesselbach, is it a bargain? If so, I'll find your Pierre Leduc for you in forty-eight hours. For he's the man you're after, eh? Isn't that the business? Come along, answer! Who is the fellow? Why are you looking for him? What do you know about him?"

He calmed himself suddenly, laid his hand on Kesselbach's shoulder and, harshly:

"One word only. Yes or no?"

"No!"

He drew a magnificent gold watch from Kesselbach's fob and placed it on the prisoner's knees. He unbuttoned Kesselbach's waistcoat, opened his shirt, uncovered his chest and, taking a steel dagger, with a gold-crusted handle, that lay on the table beside him, he put the point of it against the place where the pulsations of the heart made the bare flesh throb:

"For the last time?"

"No!"

"Mr. Kesselbach, it is eight minutes to three. If you don't answer within eight minutes from now, you are a dead man!"

THE NEXT MORNING, SERGEANT GOUREL walked into the Palace Hotel punctually at the appointed hour. Without stopping, scorning to take the lift, he went up the stairs. On the fourth floor he turned to the right, followed the passage and rang at the door of 415.

Hearing no sound, he rang again. After half-a-dozen fruitless attempts, he went to the floor office. He found a head-waiter there:

MAURICE LEBLANC

"Mr. Kesselbach did not sleep here last night. We have not seen him since yesterday afternoon."

"But his servant? His secretary?"

"We have not seen them either."

"Then they also did not sleep in the hotel?"

"I suppose not."

"You suppose not? But you ought to be certain."

"Why? Mr. Kesselbach is not staying in the hotel; he is at home here, in his private flat. He is not waited on by us, but by his own man; and we know nothing of what happens inside."

"That's true. . . That's true. . ."

Gourel seemed greatly perplexed. He had come with positive orders, a precise mission, within the limits of which his mind was able to exert itself. Outside those limits he did not quite know how to act:

"If the chief were here," he muttered, "if the chief were here. . ."

He showed his card and stated his quality. Then he said, on the off-chance:

"So you have not seen them come in?"

"No."

"But you saw them go out?"

"No, I can't say I did."

"In that case, how do you know that they went out?"

"From a gentleman who called yesterday afternoon."

"A gentleman with a dark mustache?"

"Yes. I met him as he was going away, about three o'clock. He said: 'The people in 415 have gone out. Mr. Kesselbach will stay at Versailles to-night, at the Reservoirs; you can send his letters on to him there.'"

"But who was this gentleman? By what right did he speak?"

"I don't know."

Gourel felt uneasy. It all struck him as rather queer.

"Have you the key?"

"No. Mr. Kesselbach had special keys made."

"Let's go and look."

Gourel rang again furiously. Nothing happened. He was about to go when, suddenly, he bent down and clapped his ear to the keyhole:

"Listen. . . I seem to hear. . . Why, yes. . . it's quite distinct. . . I hear moans. . ."

He gave the door a tremendous blow with his fist.

"But, sir, you have not the right. . ."

"Oh, hang the right!"

He struck the door with renewed force, but to so little purpose that he abandoned the attempt forthwith:

"Quick, quick, a locksmith!"

One of the waiters started off at a run. Gourel, blustering and undecided, walked to and fro. The servants from the other floors collected in groups. People from the office, from the manager's department arrived. Gourel cried:

"But why shouldn't we go in though the adjoining rooms? Do they communicate with this suite?"

"Yes; but the communicating doors are always bolted on both sides."

"Then I shall telephone to the detective-office," said Gourel, to whose mind obviously there existed no salvation without his chief.

"And to the commissary of police," observed some one.

"Yes, if you like," he replied, in the tone of a gentleman who took little or no interest in that formality.

When he returned from the telephone, the locksmith had nearly finished trying the keys. The last worked the lock. Gourel walked briskly in.

He at once hastened in the direction from which the moans came and hit against the bodies of Chapman the secretary, and Edwards the manservant. One of them, Chapman, had succeeded, by dint of patience, in loosening his gag a little and was uttering short, stifled moans. The other seemed asleep.

They were released. But Gourel was anxious:

"Where's Mr. Kesselbach?"

He went into the sitting-room. Mr. Kesselbach was sitting strapped to the back of the arm-chair, near the table. His head hung on his chest.

"He has fainted," said Gourel, going up to him. "He must have exerted himself beyond his strength."

Swiftly he cut the cords that fastened the shoulders. The body fell forward in an inert mass. Gourel caught it in his arms and started back with a cry of horror:

"Why, he's dead! Feel. . . his hands are ice-cold! And look at his eyes!"

Some one ventured the opinion:

"An apoplectic stroke, no doubt. . . or else heart-failure."

"True, there's no sign of a wound. . . it's a natural death."

They laid the body on the sofa and unfastened the clothes. But red stains at once appeared on the white shirt; and, when they pushed it back, they saw that, near the heart, the chest bore a little scratch through which had trickled a thin stream of blood.

And on the shirt was pinned a card. Gourel bent forward. It was Arsène Lupin's card, bloodstained like the rest.

Then Gourel drew himself up, authoritatively and sharply:

"Murdered! . . . Arsène Lupin! . . . Leave the flat. . . Leave the flat, all of you! . . . No one must stay here or in the bedroom. . . Let the two men be removed and seen to elsewhere! . . . Leave the flat. . . and don't touch a thing. . .

"The chief is on his way! . . ."

II

The Blue-Edged Label

A rsène Lupin!"

Gourel repeated these two fateful words with an absolutely petrified air. They rang within him like a knell. Arsène Lupin! The great, the formidable Arsène Lupin. The burglar-king, the mighty adventurer! Was it possible?

"No, no," he muttered, "it's not possible, *because he's dead*!"

Only that was just it. . . was he really dead?

Arsène Lupin!

Standing beside the corpse, he remained dull and stunned, turning the card over and over with a certain dread, as though he had been challenged by a ghost. Arsène Lupin! What ought he to do? Act? Take the field with his resources? No, no. . . better not act. . . He was bound to make mistakes if he entered the lists with an adversary of that stamp. Besides, the chief was on his way!

The chief was on his way! All Gourel's intellectual philosophy was summed up in that short sentence. An able, persevering officer, full of courage and experience and endowed with Herculean strength, he was one of those who go ahead only when obeying directions and who do good work only when ordered. And this lack of initiative had become still more marked since M. Lenormand had taken the place of M. Dudouis in the detective-service. M. Lenormand was a chief indeed! With him, one was sure of being on the right track. So sure, even, that Gourel stopped the moment that the chief's incentive was no longer behind him.

But the chief was on his way! Gourel took out his watch and calculated the exact time when he would arrive. If only the commissary of police did not get there first, if only the examining-magistrate, who was no doubt already appointed, or the divisional surgeon, did not come to make inopportune discoveries before the chief had time to fix the essential points of the case in his mind!

"Well, Gourel, what are you dreaming about?"

"The chief!"

M. Lenormand was still a young man, if you took stock only of the expression of his face and his eyes gleaming through his spectacles; but he was almost an old man when you saw his bent back, his skin dry and yellow as wax, his grizzled hair and beard, his whole decrepit, hesitating, unhealthy appearance. He had spent his life laboriously in the colonies as government commissary, in the most dangerous posts. He had there acquired a series of fevers; an indomitable energy, notwithstanding his physical weariness; the habit of living alone, of talking little and acting in silence; a certain misanthropy; and, suddenly, at the age of fifty-five, in consequence of the famous case of the three Spaniards at Biskra, a great and well-earned notoriety.

The injustice was then repaired; and he was straightway transferred to Bordeaux, was next appointed deputy in Paris, and lastly, on the death of M. Dudouis, chief of the detective-service. And in each of these posts he displayed such a curious faculty of inventiveness in his proceedings, such resourcefulness, so many new and original qualities; and above all, he achieved such correct results in the conduct of the last four or five cases with which public opinion had been stirred, that his name was quoted in the same breath with those of the most celebrated detectives.

Gourel, for his part, had no hesitation. Himself a favourite of the chief, who liked him for his frankness and his passive obedience, he set the chief above them all. The chief to him was an idol, an infallible god.

M. Lenormand seemed more tired than usual that day. He sat down wearily, parted the tails of his frock-coat—an old frock-coat, famous for its antiquated cut and its olive-green hue—untied his neckerchief—an equally famous maroon-coloured neckerchief, rested his two hands on his stick, and said:

"Speak!"

Gourel told all that he had seen, and all that he had learnt, and told it briefly, according to the habit which the chief had taught him.

But, when he produced Lupin's card, M. Lenormand gave a start:

"Lupin!"

"Yes, Lupin. The brute's bobbed up again."

"That's all right, that's all right," said M. Lenormand, after a moment's thought.

"That's all right, of course," said Gourel, who loved to add a word of his own to the rare speeches of a superior whose only fault in his eyes was an undue reticence. "That's all right, for at last you will measure your strength with an adversary worthy of you. . . And Lupin will meet his master. . . Lupin will cease to exist. . . Lupin. . ."

"Ferret!" said M. Lenormand, cutting him short.

It was like an order given by a sportsman to his dog. And Gourel ferreted after the manner of a good dog, a lively and intelligent animal, working under his master's eyes. M. Lenormand pointed his stick to a corner, to an easy chair, just as one points to a bush or a tuft of grass, and Gourel beat up the bush or the tuft of grass with conscientious thoroughness.

"Nothing," said the sergeant, when he finished.

"Nothing for you!" grunted M. Lenormand.

"That's what I meant to say. . . I know that, for you, chief, there are things that talk like human beings, real living witnesses. For all that, here is a murder well and duly added to our score against Master Lupin."

"The first," observed M. Lenormand.

"The first, yes. . . But it was bound to come. You can't lead that sort of life without, sooner or later, being driven by circumstances to serious crime. Mr. Kesselbach must have defended himself. . ."

"No, because he was bound."

"That's true," owned Gourel, somewhat disconcertedly, "and it's rather curious too. . . Why kill an adversary who has practically ceased to exist? . . . But, no matter, if I had collared him yesterday, when we were face to face at the hall-door. . ."

M. Lenormand had stepped out on the balcony. Then he went to Mr. Kesselbach's bedroom, on the right, and tried the fastenings of the windows and doors.

"The windows of both rooms were shut when I came in," said Gourel.

"Shut, or just pushed to?"

"No one has touched them since. And they are shut, chief."

A sound of voices brought them back to the sitting-room. Here they found the divisional surgeon, engaged in examining the body, and M. Formerie, the magistrate. M. Formerie exclaimed:

"Arsène Lupin! I am glad that at last a lucky chance has brought me into touch with that scoundrel again! I'll show the fellow the stuff I'm made of! . . . And this time it's a murder! . . . It's a fight between you and me now, Master Lupin!"

M. Formerie had not forgotten the strange adventure of the Princesse de Lamballe's diadem, nor the wonderful way in which Lupin had tricked him a few years before.[1] The thing had remained famous in the annals of the law-courts. People still laughed at it; and in M. Formerie it had left a just feeling of resentment, combined with the longing for a striking revenge.

"The nature of the crime is self-evident," he declared, with a great air of conviction, "and we shall have no difficulty in discovering the motive. So all is well. . . M. Lenormand, how do you do? . . . I am delighted to see you. . ."

M. Formerie was not in the least delighted. On the contrary, M. Lenormand's presence did not please him at all, seeing that the chief detective hardly took the trouble to disguise the contempt in which he held him. However, the magistrate drew himself up and, in his most solemn tones:

"So, doctor, you consider that death took place about a dozen hours ago, perhaps more! . . . That, in fact, was my own idea. . . We are quite agreed. . . And the instrument of the crime?"

"A knife with a very thin blade, Monsieur le Juge d'Instruction," replied the surgeon. "Look, the blade has been wiped on the dead man's own handkerchief. . ."

"Just so. . . just so. . . you can see the mark. . . And now let us go and question Mr. Kesselbach's secretary and man-servant. I have no doubt that their examination will throw some more light on the case."

Chapman, who together with Edwards, had been moved to his own room, on the left of the sitting-room, had already recovered from his experiences. He described in detail the events of the previous day, Mr. Kesselbach's restlessness, the expected visit of the Colonel and, lastly, the attack of which they had been the victims.

"Aha!" cried M. Formerie. "So there's an accomplice! And you heard his name! . . . Marco, you say? . . . This is very important. When we've got the accomplice, we shall be a good deal further advanced. . ."

"Yes, but we've not got him," M. Lenormand ventured to remark.

"We shall see. . . One thing at a time. . . And then, Mr. Chapman, this Marco went away immediately after M. Gourel had rung the bell?"

"Yes, we heard him go."

"And after he went, did you hear nothing else?"

"Yes. . . from time to time, but vaguely. . . The door was shut."

"And what sort of noises did you hear?"

---

1. See *Arsène Lupin*. By Edgar Jepson and Maurice Leblanc. (Doubleday, Page & Co.).

"Bursts of voices. The man. . ."

"Call him by his name, Arsène Lupin."

"Arsène Lupin must have telephoned."

"Capital! We will examine the person of the hotel who has charge of the branch exchange communicating with the outside. And, afterward, did you hear him go out, too?"

"He came in to see if we were still bound; and, a quarter of an hour later, he went away, closing the hall-door after him."

"Yes, as soon as his crime was committed. Good. . . Good. . . It all fits in. . . And, after that?"

"After that, we heard nothing more. . . The night passed. . . I fell asleep from exhaustion. . . So did Edwards. . . And it was not until this morning. . ."

"Yes, I know. . . There, it's not going badly. . . it all fits in. . ."

And, marking off the stages of his investigation, in a tone as though he were enumerating so many victories over the stranger, he muttered thoughtfully:

"The accomplice. . . the telephone. . . the time of the murder. . . the sounds that were heard. . . Good. . . Very good. . . We have still to establish the motive of the crime. . . In this case, as we have Lupin to deal with, the motive is obvious. M. Lenormand, have you noticed the least sign of anything being broken open?"

"No."

"Then the robbery must have been effected upon the person of the victim himself. Has his pocket-book been found?"

"I left it in the pocket of his jacket," said Gourel.

They all went into the sitting-room, where M. Formerie discovered that the pocket-book contained nothing but visiting-cards and papers establishing the murdered man's identity.

"That's odd. Mr. Chapman, can you tell us if Mr. Kesselbach had any money on him?"

"Yes. On the previous day—that is, on Monday, the day before yesterday—we went to the Crédit Lyonnais, where Mr. Kesselbach hired a safe. . ."

"A safe at the Crédit Lyonnais? Good. . . We must look into that."

"And, before we left, Mr. Kesselbach opened an account and drew out five or six thousand francs in bank-notes."

"Excellent. . . that tells us just what we want to know."

Chapman continued:

"There is another point, Monsieur le Juge d'Instruction. Mr. Kesselbach, who for some days had been very uneasy in his mind—I have told you the reason: a scheme to which he attached the utmost importance—Mr. Kesselbach seemed particularly anxious about two things. There was, first, a little ebony box, which he put away safely at the Crédit Lyonnais; and, next, a little black morocco note-case, in which he kept a few papers."

"And where is that?"

"Before Lupin's arrival, he put it, in my presence, into that travelling-bag."

M. Formerie took the bag and felt about in it. The note-case was not there. He rubbed his hands:

"Ah, everything fits in! . . . We know the culprit, the conditions and the motive of the crime. This case won't take long. Are we quite agreed upon everything, M. Lenormand?"

"Upon not one single thing."

There was a moment of stupefaction. The commissary of police had arrived: and, behind him, in spite of the constables keeping the door, a troop of journalists, and the hotel staff had forced their way in and were standing in the entrance-lobby.

Notorious though the old fellow was for his bluntness—a bluntness which was not without a certain discourtesy and which had already procured him an occasional reprimand in high quarters—the abruptness of this reply took every one aback. And M. Formerie in particular appeared utterly nonplussed:

"Still," he said, "I can see nothing that isn't quite simple. Lupin is the thief. . ."

"Why did he commit the murder?" M. Lenormand flung at him.

"In order to commit the theft."

"I beg your pardon; the witnesses' story proves that the theft took place before the murder. Mr. Kesselbach was first bound and gagged, then robbed. Why should Lupin, who has never resorted to murder, choose this time to kill a man whom he had rendered helpless and whom he had already robbed?"

The examining-magistrate stroked his long, fair whiskers, with the gesture customary to him when a question seemed incapable of solution. He replied in a thoughtful tone:

"There are several answers to that. . ."

"What are they?"

"It depends. . . it depends upon a number of facts as yet unknown. . . And, moreover, the objection applies only to the nature of the motives. We are agreed as to the remainder."

"No."

This time, again, the denial was flat, blunt, almost impolite; so much so that the magistrate was absolutely nonplussed, dared not even raise a protest, and remained abashed in the presence of this strange collaborator. At last he said:

"We all have our theories. I should like to know yours."

"I have none."

The chief detective rose and, leaning on his stick, took a few steps through the room. All the people around him were silent. . . And it was rather curious, in a group in which, after all, his position was only that of an auxiliary, a subordinate, to see this ailing, decrepit, elderly man dominate the others by the sheer force of an authority which they had to feel, even though they did not accept it. After a long pause he said:

"I should like to inspect the rooms which adjoin this suite."

The manager showed him the plan of the hotel. The only way out of the right-hand bedroom, which was Mr. Kesselbach's, was through the little entrance-hall of the suite. But the bedroom on the left, the room occupied by the secretary, communicated with another apartment.

"Let us inspect it," said M. Lenormand.

M. Formerie could not help shrugging his shoulders and growling:

"But the communicating door is bolted and the window locked."

"Let us inspect it," repeated M. Lenormand.

He was taken into the apartment, which was the first of the five rooms reserved for Mrs. Kesselbach. Then, at his request, he was taken to the rooms leading out of it. All the communicating doors were bolted on both sides.

"Are not any of these rooms occupied?" he asked.

"No."

"Where are the keys?"

"The keys are always kept in the office."

"Then no one can have got in? . . ."

"No one, except the floor-waiter who airs and dusts the rooms."

"Send for him, please."

The man, whose name was Gustave Beudot, replied that he had closed the windows of five rooms on the previous day in accordance with his general instructions.

"At what time?"

"At six o'clock in the evening."

"And you noticed nothing?"

"No, sir."

"And, this morning. . . ?"

"This morning, I opened the windows at eight o'clock exactly."

"And you found nothing?"

He hesitated. He was pressed with questions and ended by admitting:

"Well, I picked up a cigarette-case near the fireplace in 420. . . I intended to take it to the office this evening."

"Have you it on you?"

"No, it is in my room. It is a gun-metal case. It has a space for tobacco and cigarette-papers on one side and for matches on the other. There are two initials in gold: an L and an M. . ."

"What's that?"

Chapman had stepped forward. He seemed greatly surprised and, questioning the servant:

"A gun-metal cigarette-case, you say?"

"Yes."

"With three compartments—for tobacco, cigarette-papers, and matches. . . Russian tobacco, wasn't it, very fine and light?"

"Yes."

"Go and fetch it. . . I should like to see it for myself. . . to make sure. . ."

At a sign from the chief detective, Gustave Beudot left the room.

M. Lenormand sat down and his keen eyes examined the carpet, the furniture and the curtains. He asked:

"This is room 420, is it not?"

"Yes."

The magistrate grinned:

"I should very much like to know what connection you establish between this incident and the tragedy. Five locked doors separate us from the room in which Mr. Kesselbach was murdered."

M. Lenormand did not condescend to reply.

Time passed. Gustave did not return.

"Where does he sleep?" asked the chief detective.

"On the sixth floor," answered the manager. "The room is on the Rue de Judée side: above this, therefore. It's curious that he's not back yet."

"Would you have the kindness to send some one to see?"

The manager went himself, accompanied by Chapman. A few minutes after, he returned alone, running, with every mark of consternation on his face.

"Well?"

"Dead!"

"Murdered?"

"Yes."

"Oh, by thunder, how clever these scoundrels are!" roared M. Lenormand, "Off with you, Gourel, and have the doors of the hotel locked. . . Watch every outlet. . . And you, Mr. Manager, please take us to Gustave Beudot's room."

The manager led the way. But as they left the room, M. Lenormand stooped and picked up a tiny little round piece of paper, on which his eyes had already fixed themselves.

It was a label surrounded with a blue border and marked with the number 813. He put it in his pocket, on chance, and joined the others. . .

A SMALL WOUND IN THE back, between the shoulder-blades. . .

"Exactly the same wound as Mr. Kesselbach's," declared the doctor.

"Yes," said M. Lenormand, "it was the same hand that struck the blow and the same weapon was used."

Judging by the position of the body, the man had been surprised when on his knees before the bed, feeling under the mattress for the cigarette-case which he had hidden there. His arm was still caught between the mattress and the bed, but the cigarette-case was not to be found.

"That cigarette-case must have been devilish compromising!" timidly suggested M. Formerie, who no longer dared put forward any definite opinion.

"Well, of course!" said the chief detective.

"At any rate, we know the initials: an L and an M. And with that, together with what Mr. Chapman appears to know, we shall easily learn. . ."

M. Lenormand gave a start:

"Chapman! But where is he?"

They looked in the passage among the groups of people crowded together. Chapman was not there.

"Mr. Chapman came with me," said the manager.

"Yes, yes, I know, but he did not come back with you."

"No, I left him with the corpse."

"You left him! . . . Alone?"

"I said to him, 'Stay here. . . don't move.'"

"And was there no one about? Did you see no one?"

"In the passage? No."

"But in the other attics? . . . Or else, look here, round that corner: was there no one hiding there?"

M. Lenormand seemed greatly excited. He walked up and down, he opened the doors of the rooms. And, suddenly, he set off at a run, with an agility of which no one would have thought him capable. He rattled down the six storeys, followed at a distance by the manager and the examining-magistrate. At the bottom, he found Gourel in front of the main door.

"Has no one gone out?"

"No, chief."

"What about the other door, in the Rue Orvieto?"

"I have posted Dieuzy there."

"With firm orders?"

"Yes, chief."

The huge hall of the hotel was crowded with anxious visitors, all commenting on the more or less accurate versions that had reached them of the crime. All the servants had been summoned by telephone and were arriving, one by one. M. Lenormand questioned them without delay. None of them was able to supply the least information. But a fifth-floor chambermaid appeared. Ten minutes earlier, or thereabouts, she had passed two gentlemen who were coming down the servants' staircase between the fifth and the fourth floors.

"They came down very fast. The one in front was holding the other by the hand. I was surprised to see those two gentlemen on the servants' staircase."

"Would you know them again?"

"Not the first one. He had his head turned the other way. He was a thin, fair man. He wore a soft black hat. . . and black clothes."

"And the other?"

"Oh, the other was an Englishman, with a big, clean-shaven face and a check suit. He had no hat on."

The description obviously referred to Chapman.

The woman added:

"He looked. . . he looked quite funny. . . as if he was mad."

Gourel's word was not enough for M. Lenormand. One after the other, he questioned the under-porters standing at the two doors:

"Did you know Mr. Chapman?"

"Yes, sir, he always spoke to us."

"And you have not seen him go out?"

"No, sir. He has not been out this morning."

M. Lenormand turned to the commissary of police: "How many men have you with you, Monsieur le Commissaire?"

"Four."

"That's not sufficient. Telephone to your secretary to send you all the men available. And please be so good as yourself to organize the closest watch at every outlet. The state of siege, Monsieur le Commissaire. . ."

"But I say," protested the manager, "my customers?"

"I don't care a hang, sir, for your customers! My duty comes before everything; and my duty is at all costs to arrest. . ."

"So you believe. . ." the examining-magistrate ventured to interpolate.

"I don't *believe*, monsieur. . . I am sure that the perpetrator of both the murders is still in the hotel."

"But then Chapman. . ."

"At this moment, I cannot guarantee that Chapman is still alive. In any case, it is only a question of minutes, of seconds. . . Gourel, take two men and search all the rooms on the fourth floor. . . Mr. Manager, send one of your clerks with them. . . As for the other floors, I shall proceed as soon as we are reënforced. Come, Gourel, off with you, and keep your eyes open. . . It's big game you're hunting!"

Gourel and his men hurried away. M. Lenormand himself remained in the hall, near the office. This time, he did not think of sitting down, as his custom was. He walked from the main entrance to the door in the Rue Orvieto and returned to the point from which he had started. At intervals he gave instructions:

"Mr. Manager, see that the kitchens are watched. They may try to escape that way. . . Mr. Manager, instruct your young lady at the telephone not to put any of the people in the hotel into communication with outside subscribers. If a call comes from the outside, she can connect the caller with the person asked for, but she must take a note of that person's name. . . Mr. Manager, have a list made out of all your visitors whose name begins with an L or an M."

The tension caught the spectators by the throat, as they stood

MAURICE LEBLANC

clustered in the middle of the hall, silent and gasping for breath, shaking with fear at the least sound, obsessed by the infernal image of the murderer. Where was he hiding? Would he show himself? Was he not one of themselves: this one, perhaps. . . or that one? . . .

And all eyes were turned on the gray-haired gentleman in spectacles, an olive-green frock-coat and a maroon-colored neckerchief, who was walking about, with his bent back, on a pair of shaky legs.

At times, one of the waiters accompanying Sergeant Gourel on his search would come running up.

"Any news?" asked M. Lenormand.

"No, sir, we've found nothing."

The manager made two attempts to induce him to relax his orders regarding the doors. The situation was becoming intolerable. The office was filled with loudly-protesting visitors, who had business outside, or who had arranged to leave Paris.

"I don't care a hang!" said M. Lenormand again.

"But I know them all."

"I congratulate you."

"You are exceeding your powers."

"I know."

"The law will decide against you."

"I'm convinced of that."

"Monsieur le Juge d'Instruction himself. . ."

"M. Formerie had better not interfere. He can mind his own business, which is to examine the servants, as he is doing now. Besides, it has nothing to do with the examining-magistrate, it has to do with the police. It's my affair."

Just then a squad of police burst into the hotel. The chief detective divided them into several sections which he sent up to the third floor. Then, addressing the commissary of police:

"My dear commissary, I leave the task of watching the doors to you. No weakness, I entreat you. I will take the responsibility for anything that happens."

And, turning to the lift, he had himself conveyed to the second floor.

It was a difficult business and a long one, for they had to open the doors of the sixty bedrooms, to inspect all the bathrooms, all the recesses, all the cupboards, every nook and corner.

And it was also fruitless. An hour later, on the stroke of twelve, M. Lenormand had just done the second floor; the other parties had not yet finished the upper floors; and no discovery had been made.

M. Lenormand hesitated: had the murderer retreated to the attics?

He was deciding, however, to go downstairs, when he was told that Mrs. Kesselbach had just arrived with her lady-companion. Edwards, the old confidential man-servant, had accepted the task of informing her of Mr. Kesselbach's death.

M. Lenormand found her in one of the drawing rooms, overcome by the unexpected shock, dry-eyed, but with her features wrung with grief and her body trembling all over, as though convulsed with fever. She was a rather tall, dark woman; and her black and exceedingly beautiful eyes were filled with gold, with little gold spots, like spangles gleaming in the dark. Her husband had met her in Holland, where Dolores was born of an old family of Spanish origin, the Amontis. He fell in love with her at first sight; and for four years the harmony between them, built up of mutual affection and devotion, had never been interrupted.

M. Lenormand introduced himself. She looked at him without replying; and he was silent, for she did not appear, in her stupor, to understand what he said. Then, suddenly, she began to shed copious tears and asked to be taken to her husband.

In the hall, M. Lenormand found Gourel, who was looking for him and who rushed at him with a hat which he held in his hand:

"I picked this up, chief. . . There's no doubt whom it belongs to, is there?"

It was a soft, black felt hat and resembled the description given. There was no lining or label inside it.

"Where did you pick it up?"

"On the second-floor landing of the servants' staircase."

"Nothing on the other floors?"

"Nothing. We've searched everywhere. There is only the first floor left. And this hat shows that the man went down so far. We're burning, chief!"

"I think so."

At the foot of the stairs M. Lenormand stopped:

"Go back to the commissary and give him my orders: he must post two men at the foot of each of the four staircases, revolver in hand. And they are to fire, if necessary. Understand this, Gourel: if Chapman is not saved and if the fellow escapes, it means my resignation. I've been wool-gathering for over two hours."

He went up the stairs. On the first floor he met two policemen leaving a bedroom, accompanied by a servant of the hotel.

The passage was deserted. The hotel staff dared not venture into it. Some of the permanent visitors had locked themselves in their rooms; and the police had to knock for a long time and proclaim who they were before they could get the doors opened.

Farther on, M. Lenormand saw another group of policemen searching the maid's pantry and, at the end of a long passage, he saw some more men who were approaching the turning, that is to say, that part of the passage which contained the rooms overlooking the Rue de Judée.

And, suddenly, he heard these men shouting; and they disappeared at a run.

He hurried after them.

The policemen had stopped in the middle of the passage. At their feet, blocking their way, with its face on the carpet, lay a corpse.

M. Lenormand bent down and took the lifeless head in his hands:

"Chapman," he muttered. "He is dead."

He examined the body. A white knitted silk muffler was tied round the neck. He undid it. Red stains appeared; and he saw that the muffler held a thick wad of cotton-wool in position against the nape of the neck. The wad was soaked with blood.

Once again there was the same little wound, clean, frank and pitiless.

M. Formerie and the commissary were at once told and came hastening up.

"No one gone out?" asked the chief detective. "No surprise?"

"No," said the commissary. "There are two men on guard at the foot of each staircase."

"Perhaps he has gone up again?" said M. Formerie.

"No! . . . No! . . ."

"But some one must have met him. . ."

"No. . . This all happened quite a long time ago. The hands are cold. . . The murder must have been committed almost immediately after the other. . . as soon as the two men came here by the servants' staircase."

"But the body would have been seen! Think, fifty people must have passed this spot during the last two hours. . ."

"The body was not here."

"Then where was it?"

"Why, how can I tell?" snapped the chief detective. "Do as I'm doing, look for yourself! You can't find things by talking."

He furiously patted the knob of his stick with a twitching hand; and he stood there, with his eyes fixed on the body, silent and thoughtful. At last he spoke:

"Monsieur le Commissaire, be so good as to have the victim taken to an empty room. Let them fetch the doctor. Mr. Manager, would you mind opening the doors of all the rooms on this passage for me?"

On the left were three bedrooms and two sitting-rooms, forming an empty suite, which M. Lenormand inspected. On the right were four bedrooms. Two were occupied respectively by a M. Reverdat and an Italian, Baron Giacomini, who were both then out. In the third room they found an elderly English maiden lady still in bed; and, in the fourth, an Englishman who was placidly reading and smoking and who had not been in the least disturbed by the noises in the passage. His name was Major Parbury.

No amount of searching or questioning led to any result. The old maid had heard nothing before the exclamations of the policeman: no noise of a struggle, no cry of pain, no sound of quarreling; and Major Parbury neither.

Moreover, there was no suspicious clue found, no trace of blood, nothing to lead them to suppose that the unfortunate Chapman had been in one of those rooms.

"It's queer," muttered the examining-magistrate, "it's all very queer. . ." And he confessed, ingenuously, "I feel more and more at sea. . . There is a whole series of circumstances that are partly beyond me. What do you make of it, M. Lenormand?"

M. Lenormand was on the point of letting off one of those pointed rejoinders in which he was wont to give vent to his chronic ill-temper, when Gourel appeared upon the scene, all out of breath.

"Chief," he panted, "they've found this. . . downstairs. . . in the office. . . on a chair. . ."

It was a parcel of moderate dimensions, wrapped up in a piece of black serge.

"Did they open it?" asked the chief.

"Yes, but when they saw what the parcel contained, they did it up again exactly as it was. . . fastened very tight, as you can see. . ."

"Untie it."

Gourel removed the wrapper and disclosed a black diagonal jacket and trousers, which had evidently been packed up in a hurry, as the creases in the cloth showed. In the middle was a towel, covered with blood, which had been dipped in water, in order, no doubt, to destroy the marks of the hands that had been wiped on it. Inside the napkin was a steel dagger, with a handle encrusted with gold. This also was red with blood, the blood of three men stabbed within the space of a few hours by an invisible hand, amid the crowd of three hundred people moving about in the huge hotel.

Edwards, the man-servant, at once identified the dagger as belonging to Mr. Kesselbach. He had seen it on the table on the previous day, before the assault committed by Lupin.

"Mr. Manager," said the chief detective, "the restriction is over. Gourel, go and give orders to leave the doors free."

"So you think that Lupin has succeeded in getting out?" asked M. Formerie.

"No. The perpetrator of the three murders which we have discovered is in one of the rooms of the hotel, or, rather, he is among the visitors in the hall or in the reception-rooms. In my opinion, he was staying in the hotel."

"Impossible! Besides, where would he have changed his clothes? And what clothes would he have on now?"

"I don't know, but I am stating a fact."

"And you are letting him go? Why, he'll just walk out quietly, with his hands in his pockets!"

"The one who walks away like that, without his luggage, and who does not return, will be the criminal. Mr. Manager, please come with me to the office. I should like to make a close inspection of your visitors' book."

In the office, M. Lenormand found a few letters addressed to Mr. Kesselbach. He handed them to the examining-magistrate. There was also a parcel that had just come by the Paris parcel-post. The paper in which it was packed was partly torn; and M. Lenormand saw that it held a small ebony box, engraved with the name of Rudolf Kesselbach. Feeling curious, he opened the parcel. The box contained the fragments of a looking-glass which had evidently been fixed to the inside of the lid. It also contained the card of Arsène Lupin.

But one detail seemed to strike the chief detective. On the outside, at the bottom of the box, was a little blue-edged label, similar to the label which he had picked up in the room on the fourth floor where the cigarette-case was found, and this label bore the same number, 813.

III

M. Lenormand Opens His Campaign

A uguste, show M. Lenormand in."

The messenger went out and, a few seconds later, announced the chief of the detective-service.

There were three men in the prime minister's private room on the Place Beauvau: the famous Valenglay, leader of the radical party for the past thirty years and now president of the council and minister of the interior; the attorney-general, M. Testard; and the prefect of police, Delaume.

The prefect of police and the attorney-general did not rise from the chairs which they had occupied during their long conversation with the prime minister. Valenglay, however, stood up and, pressing the chief detective's hand, said, in the most cordial tones:

"I have no doubt, my dear Lenormand, that you know the reason why I asked you to come."

"The Kesselbach case?"

"Yes."

THE KESSELBACH CASE! NOT ONE of us but is able to recall not only the main details of this tragic affair, the tangled skein of which I have set myself to unravel, but even its very smallest incidents, so greatly did the tragedy excite us all during these recent years. Nor is there one of us but remembers the extraordinary stir which it created both in and outside France. And yet there was one thing that upset the public even more than the three murders committed in such mysterious circumstances, more than the detestable atrocity of that butchery, more than anything else; and that was the reappearance—one might almost say the resurrection—of Arsène Lupin.

Arsène Lupin! No one had heard speak of him for over four years, since his incredible, his astounding adventure of the Hollow Needle,[1] since the day when he had slunk away into the darkness before the

---

1. See *The Hollow Needle*. By Maurice Leblanc. Translated by Alexander Teixeira de Mattos and published by Doubleday, Page & Co.

MAURICE LEBLANC

eyes of Holmlock Shears and Isidore Beautrelet, carrying on his back the dead body of the woman whom he loved, and followed by his old servant, Victoire.

From that day onward he had been generally believed to be dead. This was the version put about by the police, who, finding no trace of their adversary, were content purely and simply to bury him.

Some, however, believing him to be saved, described him as leading a placid, Philistine existence. According to them, he was living with his wife and children, growing his small potatoes; whereas others maintained that, bent down with the weight of sorrow and weary of the vanities of this world, he had sought the seclusion of a Trappist monastery.

And here he was once more looming large in the public view and resuming his relentless struggle against society! Arsène Lupin was Arsène Lupin again, the fanciful, intangible, disconcerting, audacious, genial Arsène Lupin! But, this time, a cry of horror arose. Arsène Lupin had taken human life! And the fierceness, the cruelty, the ruthless cynicism of the crime were so great that, then and there, the legend of the popular hero, of the chivalrous and occasionally sentimental adventurer, made way for a new conception of an inhuman, bloodthirsty, and ferocious monster. The crowd now loathed and feared its former idol with more intensity than it had once shown in admiring him for his easy grace and his diverting good-humor.

And, forthwith, the indignation of that frightened crowd turned against the police. Formerly, people had laughed. They forgave the beaten commissary of police for the comical fashion in which he allowed himself to be beaten. But the joke had lasted too long; and, in a burst of revolt and fury, they now called the authorities to account for the unspeakable crimes which these were powerless to prevent.

In the press, at public meetings, in the streets and even in the tribune of the Chamber of Deputies there was such an explosion of wrath that the government grew alarmed and strove by every possible means to allay the public excitement.

It so happened that Valenglay, the premier, took a great interest in all these police questions and had often amused himself by going closely into different cases with the chief of the detective-service, whose good qualities and independent character he valued highly. He sent for the prefect and the attorney-general to see him in his room, talked to them and then sent for M. Lenormand.

"Yes, my dear Lenormand, it's about the Kesselbach case. But, before we discuss it, I must call your attention to a point which more particularly affects and, I may say, annoys Monsieur le Préfet de Police. M. Delaume, will you explain to M. Lenormand. . . ?

"Oh, M. Lenormand knows quite well how the matter stands," said the prefect, in a tone which showed but little good-will toward his subordinate. "We have talked it over already and I have told him what I thought of his improper conduct at the Palace Hotel. People are generally indignant."

M. Lenormand rose, took a paper from his pocket and laid it on the table.

"What is this?" asked Valenglay.

"My resignation, Monsieur le Président du Conseil."

Valenglay gave a jump:

"What! Your resignation! For a well-meaning remark which Monsieur le Préfet thinks fit to address to you and to which, for that matter, he attaches no importance whatever—do you, Delaume? No importance whatever—and there you go, taking offence! You must confess, my dear Lenormand, that you're devilish touchy! Come, put that bit of paper back in your pocket and let's talk seriously."

The chief detective sat down again, and Valenglay, silencing the prefect, who made no attempt to conceal his dissatisfaction, said:

"In two words, Lenormand, the thing is that Lupin's reappearance upon the scene annoys us. The brute has defied us long enough. It used to be funny, I confess, and I, for my part, was the first to laugh at it. But it's no longer a question of that. It's a question of murder now. We could stand Lupin, as long as he amused the gallery. But, when he takes to killing people, no!"

"Then what is it that you ask, Monsieur le Président?"

"What we ask? Oh, it's quite simple! First, his arrest and then his head!"

"I can promise you his arrest, some day or another, but not his head."

"What! If he's arrested, it means trial for murder, a verdict of guilty, and the scaffold."

"No!"

"And why not?"

"Because Lupin has not committed murder."

"Eh? Why, you're mad, Lenormand! The corpses at the Palace Hotel are so many inventions, I suppose! And the three murders were never committed!"

MAURICE LEBLANC

"Yes, but not by Lupin."

The chief spoke these words very steadily, with impressive calmness and conviction. The attorney and the prefect protested.

"I presume, Lenormand," said Valenglay, "that you do not put forward that theory without serious reasons?"

"It is not a theory."

"What proof have you?"

"There are two, to begin with, two proofs of a moral nature, which I at once placed before Monsieur le Juge d'Instruction and which the newspapers have laid stress upon. First and foremost, Lupin does not kill people. Next, why should he have killed anybody, seeing that the object which he set out to achieve, the theft, was accomplished and that he had nothing to fear from an adversary who was gagged and bound?"

"Very well. But the facts?"

"Facts are worth nothing against reason and logic; and, moreover, the facts also are on my side. What would be the meaning of Lupin's presence in the room in which the cigarette-case was discovered? On the other hand, the black clothes which were found and which evidently belonged to the murderer are not in the least of a size to fit Lupin."

"You know him, then, do you?"

"I? No. But Edwards saw him, Gourel saw him; and the man whom they saw is not the man whom the chambermaid saw, on the servants' staircase, dragging Chapman by the hand."

"Then your idea. . ."

"You mean to say, the truth, M. le Président. Here it is, or, at least, here is the truth as far as I know it. On Tuesday, the 16th of April, a man—Lupin—broke into Mr. Kesselbach's room at about two o'clock in the afternoon. . ."

M. Lenormand was interrupted by a burst of laughter. It came from the prefect of police.

"Let me tell you, M. Lenormand, that you are in rather too great a hurry to state your precise facts. It has been shown that, at three o'clock on that day, Mr. Kesselbach walked into the Crédit Lyonnais and went down to the safe deposit. His signature in the register proves it."

M. Lenormand waited respectfully until his superior had finished speaking. Then, without even troubling to reply directly to the attack, he continued:

"At about two o'clock in the afternoon, Lupin, assisted by an accomplice, a man named Marco, bound Mr. Kesselbach hand and foot, robbed him of all the loose cash which he had upon him and compelled him to reveal the cypher of his safe at the Crédit Lyonnais. As soon as the secret was told, Marco left. He joined another accomplice, who, profiting by a certain resemblance to Mr. Kesselbach—a resemblance which he accentuated that day by wearing clothes similar to Mr. Kesselbach's and putting on a pair of gold spectacles—entered the Crédit Lyonnais, imitated Mr. Kesselbach's signature, emptied the safe of its contents and walked off, accompanied by Marco. Marco at once telephoned to Lupin. Lupin, as soon as he was sure that Mr. Kesselbach had not deceived him and that the object of his expedition was attained, went away."

Valenglay seemed to waver in his mind:

"Yes, yes. . . we'll admit that. . . But what surprises me is that a man like Lupin should have risked so much for such a paltry profit: a few bank-notes and the hypothetical contents of a safe."

"Lupin was after more than that. He wanted either the morocco envelope which was in the traveling-bag, or else the ebony box which was in the safe. He had the ebony box, because he has sent it back empty. Therefore, by this time, he knows, or is in a fair way for knowing, the famous scheme which Mr. Kesselbach was planning, and which he was discussing with his secretary a few minutes before his death."

"What was the scheme?"

"I don't exactly know. The manager of Barbareux's agency, to whom he had opened his mind about it, has told me that Mr. Kesselbach was looking for a man who went by the name of Pierre Leduc, a man who had lost caste, it appears. Why and how the discovery of this person was connected with the success of his scheme, I am unable to say."

"Very well," said Valenglay. "So much for Arsène Lupin. His part is played. Mr. Kesselbach is bound hand and foot, robbed, but alive! . . . What happens up to the time when he is found dead?"

"Nothing, for several hours, nothing until night. But, during the night, some one made his way in."

"How?"

"Through room 420, one of the rooms reserved by Mr. Kesselbach. The person in question evidently possessed a false key."

"But," exclaimed the prefect of police, "all the doors between that room and Mr. Kesselbach's flat were bolted; and there were five of them!"

"There was always the balcony."

"The balcony!"

"Yes; the balcony runs along the whole floor, on the Rue de Judée side."

"And what about the spaces in between?"

"An active man can step across them. Our man did. I have found marks."

"But all the windows of the suite were shut; and it was ascertained, after the crime, that they were still shut."

"All except one, the secretary's window, Chapman's, which was only pushed to. I tried it myself."

This time the prime minister seemed a little shaken, so logical did M. Lenormand's version seem, so precise and supported by such sound facts. He asked, with growing interest:

"But what was the man's object in coming?"

"I don't know."

"Ah, you don't know!"

"Any more than I know his name."

"But why did he kill Mr. Kesselbach?"

"I don't know. This all remains a mystery. The utmost that we have the right to suppose is that he did not come with the intention of killing, but with the intention, he too, of taking the documents contained in the morocco note-case and the ebony box; and that, finding himself by accident in the presence of the enemy reduced to a state of helplessness, he killed him."

Valenglay muttered:

"Yes, strictly speaking, that is possible. . . And, according to you, did he find the documents?"

"He did not find the box, because it was not there; but he found the black morocco note-case. So that Lupin and. . . the other are in the same position. Each knows as much as the other about the Kesselbach scheme."

"That means," remarked the premier, "that they will fight."

"Exactly. And the fight has already begun. The murderer, finding a card of Arsène Lupin's, pinned it to the corpse. All the appearances would thus be against Arsène Lupin. . . therefore, Arsène Lupin would be the murderer."

"True. . . true," said Valenglay. "The calculation seemed pretty accurate."

"And the stratagem would have succeeded," continued M. Lenormand, "if in consequence of another and a less favorable accident, the murderer had not, either in coming or going, dropped his cigarette-case in room

420, and if the floor-waiter, Gustave Beudot, had not picked it up. From that moment, knowing himself to be discovered, or on the point of being discovered. . ."

"How did he know it?"

"How? Why, through M. Formerie, the examining-magistrate, himself! The investigation took place with open doors. It is certain that the murderer was concealed among the people, members of the hotel staff and journalists, who were present when Gustave Beudot was giving his evidence; and when the magistrate sent Gustave Beudot to his attic to fetch the cigarette-case, the man followed and struck the blow. Second victim!"

No one protested now. The tragedy was being reconstructed before their eyes with a realism and a probable accuracy which were equally striking.

"And the third victim?" asked Valenglay.

"He himself gave the ruffian his opportunity. When Beudot did not return, Chapman, curious to see the cigarette-case for himself, went upstairs with the manager of the hotel. He was surprised by the murderer, dragged away by him, taken to one of the bedrooms and murdered in his turn."

"But why did he allow himself to be dragged away like that and to be led by a man whom he knew to be the murderer of Mr. Kesselbach and of Gustave Beudot?"

"I don't know, any more than I know the room in which the crime was committed, or the really miraculous way in which the criminal escaped."

"Something has been said about two blue labels."

"Yes, one was found on the box which Lupin sent back; and the other was found by me and doubtless came from the morocco note-case stolen by the murderer."

"Well?"

"I don't think that they mean anything. What does mean something is the number 813, which Mr. Kesselbach wrote on each of them. His handwriting has been recognized."

"And that number 813?"

"It's a mystery."

"Then?"

"I can only reply again that I don't know."

"Have you no suspicions?"

"None at all. Two of my men are occupying one of the rooms in the

Palace Hotel, on the floor where Chapman's body was found. I have had all the people in the hotel watched by these two men. The criminal is not one of those who have left."

"Did no one telephone while the murders were being committed?"

"Yes, some one telephoned from the outside to Major Parbury, one of the four persons who occupied rooms on the first-floor passage."

"And this Major Parbury?"

"I am having him watched by my men. So far, nothing has been discovered against him."

"And in which direction do you intend to seek?"

"Oh, in a very limited direction. In my opinion, the murderer must be numbered among the friends or connections of Mr. and Mrs. Kesselbach. He followed their scent, knew their habits, the reason of Mr. Kesselbach's presence in Paris; and he at least suspected the importance of Mr. Kesselbach's plans."

"Then he was not a professional criminal?"

"No, no, certainly not! The murder was committed with extraordinary cleverness and daring, but it was due to circumstances. I repeat, we shall have to look among the people forming the immediate circle of Mr. and Mrs. Kesselbach. And the proof is that Mr. Kesselbach's murderer killed Gustave Beudot for the sole reason that the waiter had the cigarette-case in his possession; and Chapman for the sole reason that the secretary knew of its existence. Remember Chapman's excitement: at the mere description of the cigarette-case, Chapman received a sudden insight into the tragedy. If he had seen the cigarette-case, we should have been fully informed. The man, whoever he may be, was well aware of that: and he put an end to Chapman. And we know nothing, nothing but the initials L and M."

He reflected for a moment and said:

"There is another proof, which forms an answer to one of your questions, Monsieur le Président: Do you believe that Chapman would have accompanied that man along the passages and staircases of the hotel if he did not already know him?"

The facts were accumulating. The truth or, at least, the probable truth was gaining strength. Many of the points at issue, the most interesting, perhaps, remained obscure. But what a light had been thrown upon the subject! Short of the motives that inspired them, how clearly Lenormand's hearers now perceived the sequence of acts performed on that tragic morning!

There was a pause. Every one was thinking, seeking for arguments, for objections. At last, Valenglay exclaimed:

"My dear Lenormand, this is all quite excellent. You have convinced me. . . But, taking one thing with another, we are no further than we were."

"What do you mean?"

"What I say. The object of our meeting is not to clear up a portion of the mystery, which, one day, I am sure, you will clear up altogether, but to satisfy the public demand as fully as we possibly can. Now whether the murderer is Lupin or another; whether there are two criminals, or three, or only one: all this gives us neither the criminal's name nor his arrest. And the public continues under the disastrous impression that the law is powerless."

"What can I do?"

"Give the public the definite satisfaction which it demands."

"But it seems to me that this explanation ought to be enough. . ."

"Words! The public wants deeds! One thing alone will satisfy it: an arrest."

"Hang it all! Hang it all! We can't arrest the first person that comes along!"

"Even that would be better than arresting nobody," said Valenglay, with a laugh. "Come, have a good look round! Are you sure of Edwards, Kesselbach's servant?"

"Absolutely sure. Besides. . . No, Monsieur le Président, it would be dangerous and ridiculous; and I am sure that Mr. Attorney-General himself. . . There are only two people whom we have the right to arrest: the murderer—I don't know who he is—and Arsène Lupin."

"Well?"

"There is no question of arresting Arsène Lupin, or, at least, it requires time, a whole series of measures, which I have not yet had the leisure to contrive, because I looked upon Lupin as settled down. . . or dead."

Valenglay stamped his foot with the impatience of a man who likes to see his wishes realized on the spot:

"And yet. . . and yet, my dear Lenormand, something must be done. . . if only for your own sake. You know as well as I do that you have powerful enemies. . . and that, if I were not there. . . In short, Lenormand, you can't be allowed to get out of it like this. What are you doing about the accomplices? There are others besides Lupin. There

MAURICE LEBLANC

is Marco; and there's the rogue who impersonated Mr. Kesselbach in order to visit the cellars of the Crédit Lyonnais."

"Would you be satisfied if you got him, Monsieur le Président?"

"Would I be satisfied? Heavens alive, I should think I would!"

"Well, give me seven days."

"Seven days! Why, it's not a question of days, my dear Lenormand! It's a question of hours!"

"How many will you give me, Monsieur le Président?"

Valenglay took out his watch and chuckled:

"I will give you ten minutes, my dear Lenormand!"

The chief took out his, and emphasizing each syllable, said calmly:

"That is four minutes more than I want, Monsieur le Président."

Valenglay looked at him in amazement.

"Four minutes more than you want? What do you mean by that?"

"I mean, Monsieur le Président, that the ten minutes which you allow me are superfluous. I want six, and not one minute more."

"Oh, but look here, Lenormand. . . if you imagine that this is the time for joking. . ."

The chief detective went to the window and beckoned to two men who were walking round the courtyard.

Then he returned:

"Mr. Attorney-General, would you have the kindness to sign a warrant for the arrest of Auguste Maximin Philippe Daileron, aged forty-seven? You might leave the profession open."

He went to the door:

"Come in, Gourel. You, too, Dieuzy."

Gourel entered, accompanied by Inspector Dieuzy.

"Have you the handcuffs, Gourel?"

"Yes, chief."

M. Lenormand went up to Valenglay:

"Monsieur le Président, everything is ready. But I entreat you most urgently to forego this arrest. It upsets all my plans; it may render them abortive; and, for the sake of what, after all, is a very trifling satisfaction, it exposes us to the risk of jeopardizing the whole business."

"M. Lenormand, let me remark that you have only eighty seconds left."

The chief suppressed a gesture of annoyance, strode across the room and, leaning on his stick, sat down angrily, as though he had decided not to speak. Then, suddenly making up his mind:

"Monsieur le Président, the first person who enters this room will be the man whose arrest you asked for. . . against my wish, as I insist on pointing out to you."

"Fifteen seconds, Lenormand!"

"Gourel. . . Dieuzy. . . the first person, do you understand? . . . Mr. Attorney, have you signed the warrant?"

"Ten seconds, Lenormand!"

"Monsieur le Président, would you be so good as to ring the bell?"

Valenglay rang.

The messenger appeared in the doorway and waited.

Valenglay turned to the chief:

"Well, Lenormand, he's waiting for your orders. Whom is he to show in?"

"No one."

"But the rogue whose arrest you promised us? The six minutes are more than past."

"Yes, but the rogue is here!"

"Here? I don't understand. No one has entered the room!"

"I beg your pardon."

"Oh, I say. . . Look here, Lenormand, you're making fun of us. I tell you again that no one has entered the room."

"There were six of us in this room, Monsieur le Président; there are seven now. Consequently, some one has entered the room."

Valenglay started:

"Eh! But this is madness! . . . What! You mean to say. . ."

The two detectives had slipped between the messenger and the door. M. Lenormand walked up to the messenger, clapped his hand on his shoulder and, in a loud voice:

"In the name of the law, Auguste Maximin Philippe Daileron, chief messenger at the Ministry of the Interior, I arrest you."

Valenglay burst out laughing.

"Oh, what a joke! What a joke! That infernal Lenormand! Of all the first-rate notions! Well done, Lenormand! It's long since I enjoyed so good a laugh."

M. Lenormand turned to the attorney-general:

"Mr. Attorney, you won't forget to fill in Master Daileron's profession on the warrant, will you? Chief messenger at the Ministry of the Interior."

"Oh, good! . . . Oh, capital! . . . Chief messenger at the Ministry of the Interior!" spluttered Valenglay, holding his sides. "Oh, this wonderful Lenormand gets hold of ideas that would never occur to anybody else! The public is clamoring for an arrest. . . Whoosh, he flings at its head my chief messenger. . . Auguste. . . the model servant! Well, Lenormand, my dear fellow, I knew you had a certain gift of imagination, but I never suspected that it would go so far as this! The impertinence of it!"

From the commencement of this scene, Auguste had not stirred a limb and seemed to understand nothing of what was going on around him. His face, the typical face of a good, loyal, faithful serving-man, seemed absolutely bewildered. He looked at the gentlemen turn and turn about, with a visible effort to catch the meaning of their words.

M. Lenormand said a few words to Gourel, who went out. Then, going up to Auguste and speaking with great decision, he said:

"There's no way out of it. You're caught. The best thing to do, when the game is lost, is to throw down your cards. What were you doing on Tuesday?"

"I? Nothing. I was here."

"You lie. You were off duty. You went out for the day."

"Oh, yes. . . I remember. . . I had a friend to see me from the country. . . We went for a walk in the Bois."

"Your friend's name was Marco. And you went for a walk in the cellars of the Crédit Lyonnais."

"I? What an idea! . . . Marco! . . . I don't know any one by that name."

"And these? Do you know these?" cried the chief, thrusting a pair of gold-rimmed spectacles under his nose.

"No. . . certainly not. . . I don't wear spectacles. . ."

"Yes, you do; you wear them when you go to the Crédit Lyonnais and when you pass yourself off as Mr. Kesselbach. These come from your room, the room which you occupy, under the name of M. Jérôme, at No. 50 Rue du Colisee."

"My room? *My* room? I sleep here, at the office."

"But you change your clothes over there, to play your parts in Lupin's gang."

A blow in the chest made him stagger back. Auguste reached the window at a bound, climbed over the balcony and jumped into the courtyard.

"Dash it all!" shouted Valenglay. "The scoundrel!"

He rang the bell, ran to the window, wanted to call out. M. Lenormand, with the greatest calm, said:

"Don't excite yourself, Monsieur le Président. . ."

"But that blackguard of an Auguste. . ."

"One second, please. . . I foresaw this ending. . . in fact, I allowed for it. . . It's the best confession we could have. . ."

Yielding in the presence of this coolness, Valenglay resumed his seat. In a moment, Gourel entered, with his hand on the collar of Master Auguste Maximin Philippe Daileron, *alias* Jérôme, chief messenger at the Ministry of the Interior.

"Bring him, Gourel!" said M. Lenormand, as who should say, "Fetch it! Bring it!" to a good retriever carrying the game in its jaws. "Did he come quietly?"

"He bit me a little, but I held tight," replied the sergeant, showing his huge, sinewy hand.

"Very well, Gourel. And now take this chap off to the Dépôt in a cab. Good-bye for the present, M. Jérôme."

Valenglay was immensely amused. He rubbed his hands and laughed. The idea that his chief messenger was one of Lupin's accomplices struck him as a most delightfully ludicrous thing.

"Well done, my dear Lenormand; this is wonderful! But how on earth did you manage it?"

"Oh, in the simplest possible fashion. I knew that Mr. Kesselbach was employing the Barbareux agency and that Lupin had called on him, pretending to come from the agency. I hunted in that direction and discovered that, when the indiscretion was committed to the prejudice of Mr. Kesselbach and of Barbareux, it could only have been to the advantage of one Jérôme, a friend of one of the clerks at the agency. If you had not ordered me to hustle things, I should have watched the messenger and caught Marco and then Lupin."

"You'll catch them, Lenormand, you'll catch them, I assure you. And we shall be assisting at the most exciting spectacle in the world: the struggle between Lupin and yourself. I shall bet on you."

THE NEXT MORNING THE NEWSPAPERS published the following letter:

> "*Open Letter to M. Lenormand, Chief of the Detective-service.*
> "All my congratulations, dear sir and dear friend, on your arrest of Jérôme the messenger. It was a smart piece of work, well executed and worthy of you.

"All my compliments, also, on the ingenious manner in which you proved to the prime minister that I was not Mr. Kesselbach's murderer. Your demonstration was clear, logical, irrefutable and, what is more, truthful. As you know, I do not kill people. Thank you for proving it on this occasion. The esteem of my contemporaries and of yourself, dear sir and dear friend, are indispensable to my happiness.

"In return, allow me to assist you in the pursuit of the monstrous assassin and to give you a hand with the Kesselbach case, a very interesting case, believe me: so interesting and so worthy of my attention that I have determined to issue from the retirement in which I have been living for the past four years, between my books and my good dog Sherlock, to beat all my comrades to arms and to throw myself once more into the fray.

"What unexpected turns life sometimes takes! Here am I, your fellow-worker! Let me assure you, dear sir and dear friend, that I congratulate myself upon it, and that I appreciate this favor of destiny at its true value.

ARSÈNE LUPIN

P.S.—One word more, of which I feel sure that you will approve. As it is not right and proper that a gentleman who has had the glorious privilege of fighting under my banner should languish on the straw of your prisons, I feel it my duty to give you fair warning that, in five weeks' time, on Friday, the 31st of May, I shall set at liberty Master Jérôme, promoted by me to the rank of chief messenger at the Ministry of the Interior. Don't forget the date: Friday, the 31st of May.

A. L.

IV

Prince Sernine at Work

A ground-floor flat, at the corner of the Boulevard Haussmann and the Rue de Courcelles. Here lived Prince Sernine: Prince Sernine, one of the most brilliant members of the Russian colony in Paris, whose name was constantly recurring in the "Arrivals and Departures" column in the newspapers.

Eleven o'clock in the morning. The prince entered his study. He was a man of thirty-eight or forty years of age, whose chestnut hair was mingled with a few silver threads on the temples. He had a fresh, healthy complexion and wore a large mustache and a pair of whiskers cut extremely short, so as to be hardly noticeable against the fresh skin of his cheeks.

He was smartly dressed in a tight-fitting frock-coat and a white drill waistcoat, which showed above the opening.

"Come on!" he said, in an undertone. "I have a hard day's work before me, I expect."

He opened a door leading into a large room where a few people sat waiting, and said:

"Is Varnier there? Come in, Varnier."

A man looking like a small tradesman, squat, solidly built, firmly set upon his legs, entered at the summons. The prince closed the door behind him:

"Well, Varnier, how far are you?"

"Everything's ready for this evening, governor."

"Good. Tell me in a few words."

"It's like this. After her husband's murder, Mrs. Kesselbach, on the strength of the prospectuses which you ordered to be sent to her, selected as her residence the establishment known as the Retreat for Gentlewomen, at Garches. She occupies the last of the four small houses, at the bottom of the garden, which the management lets to ladies who prefer to live quite apart from the other boarders, the house known as the Pavillon de l'Impératrice."

"What servants has she?"

"Her companion, Gertrude, with whom she arrived a few hours after the crime, and Gertrude's sister Suzanne, whom she sent for to Monte Carlo and who acts as her maid. The two sisters are devoted to her."

"What about Edwards, the valet?"

"She did not keep him. He has gone back to his own country."

"Does she see people?"

"No. She spends her time lying on a sofa. She seems very weak and ill. She cries a great deal. Yesterday the examining-magistrate was with her for two hours."

"Very good. And now about the young girl."

"Mlle. Geneviève Ernemont lives across the way. . . in a lane running toward the open country, the third house on the right in the lane. She keeps a free school for backward children. Her grandmother, Mme. Ernemont, lives with her."

"And, according to what you wrote to me, Geneviève Ernemont and Mrs. Kesselbach have become acquainted?"

"Yes. The girl went to ask Mrs. Kesselbach for a subscription for her school. They must have taken a liking to each other, for, during the past four days, they have been walking together in the Parc de Villeneuve, of which the garden of the Retreat is only a dependency."

"At what time do they go out?"

"From five to six. At six o'clock exactly the young lady goes back to her school."

"So you have arranged the thing?"

"For six o'clock to-day. Everything is ready."

"Will there be no one there?"

"There is never any one in the park at that hour."

"Very well. I shall be there. You can go."

He sent him out through the door leading to the hall, and, returning to the waiting-room, called:

"The brothers Doudeville."

Two young men entered, a little overdressed, keen-eyed and pleasant-looking.

"Good morning, Jean. Good morning, Jacques. Any news at the Prefecture?"

"Nothing much, governor."

"Does M. Lenormand continue to have confidence in you?"

"Yes. Next to Gourel, we are his favorite inspectors. A proof is that he has posted us in the Palace Hotel to watch the people who were living on the first-floor passage at the time of Chapman's murder.

Gourel comes every morning, and we make the same report to him that we do to you."

"Capital. It is essential that I should be informed of all that happens and all that is said at the Prefecture of Police. As long as Lenormand looks upon you as his men, I am master of the situation. And have you discovered a trail of any kind in the hotel?"

Jean Doudeville, the elder of the two, replied:

"The Englishwoman who occupied one of the bedrooms has gone."

"That doesn't interest me. I know all about her. But her neighbor, Major Parbury?"

They seemed embarrassed. At last, one of them replied:

"Major Parbury, this morning, ordered his luggage to be taken to the Gare du Nord, for the twelve-fifty train, and himself drove away in a motor. We were there when the train left. The major did not come."

"And the luggage?"

"He had it fetched at the station."

"By whom?"

"By a commissionaire, so we were told."

"Then his tracks are lost?"

"Yes."

"At last!" cried the prince, joyfully.

The others looked at him in surprise.

"Why, of course," he said, "that's a clue!"

"Do you think so?"

"Evidently. The murder of Chapman can only have been committed in one of the rooms on that passage. Mr. Kesselbach's murderer took the secretary there, to an accomplice, killed him there, changed his clothes there; and, once the murderer had got away, the accomplice placed the corpse in the passage. But which accomplice? The manner of Major Parbury's disappearance goes to show that he knows something of the business. Quick, telephone the good news to M. Lenormand or Gourel. The Prefecture must be informed as soon as possible. The people there and I are marching hand in hand."

He gave them a few more injunctions, concerning their double rôle as police-inspectors in the service of Prince Sernine, and dismissed them.

Two visitors remained in the waiting-room. He called one of them in:

"A thousand pardons, Doctor," he said. "I am quite at your orders now. How is Pierre Leduc?"

"He's dead."

"Aha!" said Sernine. "I expected it, after your note of this morning. But, all the same, the poor beggar has not been long. . ."

"He was wasted to a shadow. A fainting-fit; and it was all over."

"Did he not speak?"

"No."

"Are you sure that, from the day when the two of us picked him up under the table in that low haunt at Belleville, are you sure that nobody in your nursing-home suspected that he was the Pierre Leduc whom the police were looking for, the mysterious Pierre Leduc whom Mr. Kesselbach was trying to find at all costs?"

"Nobody. He had a room to himself. Moreover, I bandaged up his left hand so that the injury to the little finger could not be seen. As for the scar on the cheek, it is hidden by the beard."

"And you looked after him yourself?"

"Myself. And, according to your instructions, I took the opportunity of questioning him whenever he seemed at all clear in his head. But I could never get more than an inarticulate stammering out of him."

The prince muttered thoughtfully:

"Dead! . . . So Pierre Leduc is dead? . . . The whole Kesselbach case obviously turned on him, and now he disappears. . . without a revelation, without a word about himself, about his past. . . Ought I to embark on this adventure, in which I am still entirely in the dark? It's dangerous. . . I may come to grief. . ."

He reflected for a moment and exclaimed:

"Oh, who cares? I shall go on for all that. It's no reason, because Pierre Leduc is dead, that I should throw up the game. On the contrary! And the opportunity is too tempting! Pierre Leduc is dead! Long live Pierre Leduc! . . . Go, Doctor, go home. I shall ring you up before dinner."

The doctor went out.

"Now then, Philippe," said Sernine to his last remaining visitor, a little gray-haired man, dressed like a waiter at a hotel, a very tenth-rate hotel, however.

"You will remember, governor," Philippe began, "that last week, you made me go as boots to the Hôtel des Deux-Empereurs at Versailles, to keep my eye on a young man."

"Yes, I know. . . Gérard Baupré. How do things stand with him?"

"He's at the end of his resources."

"Still full of gloomy ideas?"

"Yes. He wants to kill himself."

"Is he serious?"

"Quite. I found this little note in pencil among his papers."

"Ah!" said Sernine, reading the note. "He announces his suicide. . . and for this evening too!"

"Yes, governor, he has bought the rope and screwed the hook to the ceiling. Thereupon, acting on your instructions, I talked to him. He told me of his distress, and I advised him to apply to you: 'Prince Sernine is rich,' I said; 'he is generous; perhaps he will help you.'"

"All this is first-rate. So he is coming?"

"He is here."

"How do you know?"

"I followed him. He took the train to Paris, and he is walking up and down the boulevard at this minute. He will make up his mind from one moment to the other."

Just then the servant brought in a card. The prince glanced at it and said to the man:

"Show M. Gérard Baupré in."

Then, turning to Philippe:

"You go into the dressing-room, here; listen and don't stir."

Left alone, the prince muttered:

"Why should I hesitate? It's fate that sends him my way. . ."

A few minutes later a tall young man entered. He was fair and slender, with an emaciated face and feverish eyes, and he stood on the threshold embarrassed, hesitating, in the attitude of a beggar who would like to put out his hand for alms and dares not.

The conversation was brief:

"Are you M. Gérard Baupré?"

"Yes. . . yes. . . that is my name."

"I have not the honor. . ."

"It's like this, sir. . . Some one told me. . ."

"Who?"

"A hotel servant. . . who said he had been in your service. . ."

"Please come to the point. . ."

"Well! . . ."

The young man stopped, taken aback and frightened by the haughty attitude adopted by the prince, who exclaimed:

"But, sir, there must be some. . ."

"Well, sir, the man told me that you were very rich. . . and very generous. . . And I thought that you might possibly. . ."

He broke off short, incapable of uttering the word of prayer and humiliation.

Sernine went up to him.

"M. Gérard Baupré, did you not publish a volume of poetry called *The Smile of Spring*?"

"Yes, yes," cried the young man, his face lighting up. "Have you read it?"

"Yes. . . Very pretty, your poems, very pretty. . . Only, do you reckon upon being able to live on what they will bring you?"

"Certainly. . . sooner or later. . ."

"Sooner or later? Later rather than sooner, I expect! And, meantime, you have come to ask me for the wherewithal to live?"

"For the wherewithal to buy food, sir."

Sernine put his hand on the young man's shoulder and, coldly:

"Poets do not need food, monsieur. They live on rhymes and dreams. Do as they do. That is better than begging for bread."

The young man quivered under the insult. He turned to the door without a word.

Sernine stopped him:

"One thing more, monsieur. Have you no resources of any kind?"

"None at all."

"And you are not reckoning on anything?"

"I have one hope left: I have written to one of my relations, imploring him to send me something. I shall have his answer to-day. It is my last chance."

"And, if you have no answer, you have doubtless made up your mind, this very evening, to. . ."

"Yes, sir."

This was said quite plainly and simply.

Sernine burst out laughing:

"Bless my soul, what a queer young man you are! And full of artless conviction, too! Come and see me again next year, will you? We will talk about all this. . . it's so curious, so interesting. . . and, above all, so funny! . . . Ha, ha, ha, ha!"

And, shaking with laughter, with affected bows and gestures, he showed him the door.

"Philippe," he said, admitting the hotel-servant, "did you hear?"

"Yes, governor."

"Gérard Baupré is expecting a telegram this afternoon, a promise of assistance. . ."

"Yes, it's his last hope."

"He must not receive that telegram. If it comes, intercept it and tear it up."

"Very well, governor."

"Are you alone at your hotel?"

"Yes, with the cook, who does not sleep in. The boss is away."

"Good. So we are the masters. Till this evening, at eleven. Be off."

Prince Sernine went to his room and rang for his servant:

"My hat, gloves, and stick. Is the car there?"

"Yes, sir."

He dressed, went out, and sank into a large, comfortable limousine, which took him to the Bois de Boulogne, to the Marquis and Marquise de Gastyne's, where he was engaged for lunch.

At half-past two he took leave of his hosts, stopped in the Avenue Kléber, picked up two of his friends and a doctor, and at five minutes to three arrived at the Parc des Princes.

At three o'clock he fought a sword duel with the Italian Major Spinelli, cut his adversary's ear in the first bout, and, at a quarter to four, took a bank at the Rue Cambon Club, from which he retired, at twenty minutes past five, after winning forty-seven thousand francs.

And all this without hurrying, with a sort of haughty indifference, as though the feverish activity that sent his life whizzing through a whirl of tempestuous deeds and events were the ordinary rule of his most peaceful days.

"Octave," he said to his chauffeur, "go to Garches."

And at ten minutes to six he alighted outside the old walls of the Parc de Villeneuve.

ALTHOUGH BROKEN UP NOWADAYS AND spoilt, the Villeneuve estate still retains something of the splendor which it knew at the time when the Empress Eugénie used to stay there. With its old trees, its lake and the leafy horizon of the woods of Saint-Cloud, the landscape has a certain melancholy grace.

An important part of the estate was made over to the Pasteur Institute. A smaller portion, separated from the other by the whole extent of the space reserved for the public, forms a property contained within the walls which is still fairly large, and which comprises the House of Retreat, with four isolated garden-houses standing around it.

"That is where Mrs. Kesselbach lives," said the prince to himself, catching sight of the roofs of the house and the four garden-houses in the distance.

He crossed the park and walked toward the lake.

Suddenly he stopped behind a clump of trees. He had seen two ladies against the parapet of the bridge that crossed the lake:

"Varnier and his men must be somewhere near. But, by Jove, they are keeping jolly well hidden! I can't see them anywhere. . ."

The two ladies were now strolling across the lawns, under the tall, venerable trees. The blue of the sky appeared between the branches, which swayed in the peaceful breeze, and the scent of spring and of young vegetation was wafted through the air.

On the grassy slopes that ran down to the motionless water, daisies, violets, daffodils, lilies of the valley, all the little flowers of April and May stood grouped, and, here and there, formed constellations of every color. The sun was sinking on the horizon.

And, all at once, three men started from a thicket of bushes and made for the two ladies.

They accosted them. A few words were exchanged. The ladies gave visible signs of dread. One of the men went up to the shorter of the two and tried to snatch the gold purse which she was carrying in her hand. They cried out; and the three men flung themselves upon them.

"Now or never!" said the prince.

And he rushed forward. In ten seconds he had almost reached the brink of the water. At his approach, the three men fled.

"Run away, you vagabonds," he chuckled; "run for all you are worth! Here's the rescuer coming!"

And he set out in pursuit of them. But one of the ladies entreated him:

"Oh, sir, I beg of you. . . my friend is ill."

The shorter lady had fallen on the grass in a dead faint.

He retraced his steps and, anxiously:

"She is not wounded?" he asked. "Did those scoundrels. . ."

"No. . . no. . . it's only the fright. . . the excitement. . . Besides you will understand. . . the lady is Mrs. Kesselbach. . ."

"Oh!" he said.

He produced a bottle of smelling-salts, which the younger woman at once applied to her friend's nostrils. And he added:

"Lift the amethyst that serves as a stopper. . . You will see a little box containing some tabloids. Give madame one of them. . . one, no more. . . they are very strong. . ."

He watched the young woman helping her friend. She was fair-haired, very simply dressed; and her face was gentle and grave, with a smile that lit up her features even when she was not smiling.

"That is Geneviève," he thought. And he repeated with emotion, "Geneviève. . . Geneviève. . ."

Meanwhile, Mrs. Kesselbach gradually recovered consciousness. She was astonished at first, seemed not to understand. Then, her memory returning, she thanked her deliverer with a movement of the head.

He made a deep bow and said:

"Allow me to introduce myself. . . I am Prince Sernine. . ."

She said, in a faint voice:

"I do not know how to express my gratitude."

"By not expressing it at all, madame. You must thank chance, the chance that turned my steps in this direction. May I offer you my arm?"

A few minutes later, Mrs. Kesselbach rang at the door of the House of Retreat and said to the prince:

"I will ask one more service of you, monsieur. Do not speak of this assault."

"And yet, madame, it would be the only way of finding out. . ."

"Any attempt to find out would mean an inquiry; and that would involve more noise and fuss about me, examinations, fatigue; and I am worn out as it is."

The prince did not insist. Bowing to her, he asked:

"Will you allow me to call and ask how you are?"

"Oh, certainly. . ."

She kissed Geneviève and went indoors.

Meantime, night was beginning to fall. Sernine would not let Geneviève return alone. But they had hardly entered the path, when a figure, standing out against the shadow, hastened toward them.

"Grandmother!" cried Geneviève.

She threw herself into the arms of an old woman, who covered her with kisses:

"Oh, my darling, my darling, what has happened? How late you are! . . . And you are always so punctual!"

Geneviève introduced the prince:

"Prince Sernine. . . Mme. Ernemont, my grandmother. . ."

Then she related the incident, and Mme. Ernemont repeated:

"Oh, my darling, how frightened you must have been! . . . I shall never forget your kindness, monsieur, I assure you. . . But how frightened you must have been, my poor darling!"

"Come, granny, calm yourself, as I am here. . ."

"Yes, but the fright may have done you harm. . . One never knows the consequences. . . Oh, it's horrible! . . ."

They went along a hedge, through which a yard planted with trees, a few shrubs, a playground and a white house were just visible. Behind the house, sheltered by a clump of elder-trees arranged to form a covered walk, was a little gate.

The old lady asked Prince Sernine to come in and led the way to a little drawing-room or parlor. Geneviève asked leave to withdraw for a moment, to go and see her pupils, whose supper-time it was. The prince and Mme. Ernemont remained alone.

The old lady had a sad and a pale face, under her white hair, which ended in two long, loose curls. She was too stout, her walk was heavy and, notwithstanding her appearance and her dress, which was that of a lady, she had something a little vulgar about her; but her eyes were immensely kind.

Prince Sernine went up to her, took her head in his two hands and kissed her on both cheeks:

"Well, old one, and how are you?"

She stood dumfounded, wild-eyed, open-mouthed. The prince kissed her again, laughing.

She spluttered:

"You! It's you! O mother of God! . . . O mother of God! . . . Is it possible! . . . O mother of God! . . ."

"My dear old Victoire!"

"Don't call me that," she cried, shuddering. "Victoire is dead. . . your old servant no longer exists.[1] I belong entirely to Geneviève." And, lowering her voice, "O mother of God! . . . I saw your name in the papers: then it's true that you have taken to your wicked life again?"

"As you see."

"And yet you swore to me that it was finished, that you were going away for good, that you wanted to become an honest man."

---

1. See *Arsène Lupin*, by Edgar Jepson and Maurice Leblanc, and *The Hollow Needle*, by Maurice Leblanc, translated by Alexander Teixeira de Mattos.

"I tried. I have been trying for four years. . . You can't say that I have got myself talked about during those four years!"

"Well?"

"Well, it bores me."

She gave a sigh and asked:

"Always the same. . . You haven't changed. . . Oh, it's settled, you never will change. . . So you are in the Kesselbach case?"

"Why, of course! But for that, would I have taken the trouble to arrange for an attack on Mrs. Kesselbach at six o'clock, so that I might have the opportunity of delivering her from the clutches of my own men at five minutes past? Looking upon me as her rescuer, she is obliged to receive me. I am now in the heart of the citadel and, while protecting the widow, can keep a lookout all round. Ah, you see, the sort of life which I lead does not permit me to lounge about and waste my time on little questions of politeness and such outside matters. I have to go straight to the point, violently, brutally, dramatically. . ."

She looked at him in dismay and gasped:

"I see. . . I see. . . it's all lies about the attack. . . But then. . . Geneviève. . ."

"Why, I'm killing two birds with one stone! It was as easy to rescue two as one. Think of the time it would have taken, the efforts—useless efforts, perhaps—to worm myself into that child's friendship! What was I to her? What should I be now? An unknown person. . . a stranger. Whereas now I am the rescuer. In an hour I shall be. . . the friend."

She began to tremble:

"So. . . so you did not rescue Geneviève. . . So you are going to mix us up in your affairs. . ." And, suddenly, in a fit of rebellion, seizing him by the shoulders, "No, I won't have it, do you understand? You brought the child to me one day, saying, 'Here, I entrust her to you. . . her father and mother are dead. . . take her under your protection.' Well, she's under my protection now and I shall know how to defend her against you and all your manœuvers!"

Standing straight upright, in a very determined attitude, Mme. Ernemont seemed ready for all emergencies.

Slowly and deliberately Sernine loosened the two hands, one after the other, that held him, and in his turn, took the old lady by the shoulders, forced her into an arm-chair, stooped over and, in a very calm voice, said:

"Rot!"

She began to cry and, clasping her hands together, implored him:

"I beseech you, leave us in peace. We were so happy! I thought that you had forgotten us and I blessed Heaven every time a day had passed. Why, yes. . . I love you just the same. But, Geneviève. . . you see, there's nothing that I wouldn't do for that child. She has taken your place in my heart."

"So I perceive," said he, laughing. "You would send me to the devil with pleasure. Come, enough of this nonsense! I have no time to waste. I must talk to Geneviève."

"You're going to talk to her?"

"Well, is that a crime?"

"And what have you to tell her?"

"A secret. . . a very grave secret. . . and a very touching one. . ."

The old lady took fright:

"And one that will cause her sorrow, perhaps? Oh, I fear everything, I fear everything, where she's concerned! . . ."

"She is coming," he said.

"No, not yet."

"Yes, yes, I hear her. . . Wipe your eyes and be sensible."

"Listen," said she, eagerly, "listen. I don't know what you are going to say, what secret you mean to reveal to this child whom you don't know. But I, who do know her, tell you this: Geneviève has a very plucky, very spirited, but very sensitive nature. Be careful how you choose your words. . . You might wound feelings. . . the existence of which you cannot even suspect. . ."

"Lord bless me! And why not?"

"Because she belongs to another race than you, to a different world. . . I mean, a different moral world. . . There are things which you are forbidden to understand nowadays. Between you and her, the obstacle is insurmountable. . . Geneviève has the most unblemished and upright conscience. . . and you. . ."

"And I?"

"And you are not an honest man!"

Geneviève entered, bright and charming:

"All my babies have gone to bed; I have ten minutes to spare. . . Why, grandmother, what's the matter? You look quite upset. . . Is it still that business with the. . ."

"No, mademoiselle," said Sernine, "I believe I have had the good fortune to reassure your grandmother. Only, we were talking of you, of your childhood; and that is a subject, it seems, which your grandmother cannot touch upon without emotion."

"Of my childhood?" said Geneviève, reddening. "Oh, grandmother!"

"Don't scold her, mademoiselle. The conversation turned in that direction by accident. It so happens that I have often passed through the little village where you were brought up."

"Aspremont?"

"Yes, Aspremont, near Nice. You used to live in a new house, white all over. . ."

"Yes," she said, "white all over, with a touch of blue paint round the windows. . . I was only seven years old when I left Aspremont; but I remember the least things of that period. And I have not forgotten the glare of the sun on the white front of the house, nor the shade of the eucalyptus-tree at the bottom of the garden."

"At the bottom of the garden, mademoiselle, was a field of olive-trees; and under one of those olive-trees stood a table at which your mother used to work on hot days. . ."

"That's true, that's true," she said, quite excitedly, "I used to play by her side. . ."

"And it was there," said he, "that I saw your mother several times. . . I recognized her image the moment I set eyes on you. . . but it was a brighter, happier image."

"Yes, my poor mother was not happy. My father died on the very day of my birth, and nothing was ever able to console her. She used to cry a great deal. I still possess a little handkerchief with which I used to dry her tears at that time."

"A little handkerchief with a pink pattern."

"What!" she exclaimed, seized with surprise. "You know. . ."

"I was there one day when you were comforting her. . . And you comforted her so prettily that the scene remained impressed on my memory."

She gave him a penetrating glance and murmured, almost to herself:

"Yes, yes. . . I seem to. . . The expression of your eyes. . . and then the sound of your voice. . ."

She lowered her eyelids for a moment and reflected as if she were vainly trying to bring back a recollection that escaped her. And she continued:

"Then you knew her?"

"I had some friends living near Aspremont and used to meet her at their house. The last time I saw her, she seemed to me sadder still. . . paler. . . and, when I came back again. . ."

"It was all over, was it not?" said Geneviève. "Yes, she went very quickly. . . in a few weeks. . . and I was left alone with neighbors who sat up with her. . . and one morning they took her away. . . And, on the evening of that day, some one came, while I was asleep, and lifted me up and wrapped me in blankets. . ."

"A man?" asked the prince.

"Yes, a man. He talked to me, quite low, very gently. . . his voice did me good. . . and, as he carried me down the road and also in the carriage, during the night, he rocked me in his arms and told me stories. . . in the same voice. . . in the same voice. . ."

She broke off gradually and looked at him again, more sharply than before and with a more obvious effort to seize the fleeting impression that passed over her at moments. He asked:

"And then? Where did he take you?"

"I can't recollect clearly. . . it is just as though I had slept for several days. . . I can remember nothing before the little town of Montégut, in the Vendée, where I spent the second half of my childhood, with Father and Mother Izereau, a worthy couple who reared me and brought me up and whose love and devotion I shall never forget."

"And did they die, too?"

"Yes," she said, "of an epidemic of typhoid fever in the district. . . but I did not know that until later. . . As soon as they fell ill, I was carried off as on the first occasion and under the same conditions, at night, by some one who also wrapped me up in blankets. . . Only, I was bigger, I struggled, I tried to call out. . . and he had to close my mouth with a silk handkerchief."

"How old were you then?"

"Fourteen. . . it was four years ago."

"Then you were able to see what the man was like?"

"No, he hid his face better and he did not speak a single word to me. . . Nevertheless, I have always believed him to be the same one. . . for I remember the same solicitude, the same attentive, careful movements. . ."

"And after that?"

"After that, came oblivion, sleep, as before. . . This time, I was ill, it appears; I was feverish. . . And I woke in a bright, cheerful room. A white-haired lady was bending over me and smiling. It was grandmother. . . and the room was the one in which I now sleep upstairs."

She had resumed her happy face, her sweet, radiant expression; and she ended, with a smile:

"That was how she became my grandmother and how, after a few trials, the little Aspremont girl now knows the delights of a peaceful life and teaches grammar and arithmetic to little girls who are either naughty or lazy. . . but who are all fond of her."

She spoke cheerfully, in a tone at once thoughtful and gay, and it was obvious that she possessed a reasonable, well-balanced mind. Sernine listened to her with growing surprise and without trying to conceal his agitation:

"Have you never heard speak of that man since?" he asked.

"Never."

"And would you be glad to see him again?"

"Oh, very glad."

"Well, then, mademoiselle. . ."

Geneviève gave a start:

"You know something. . . the truth perhaps. . ."

"No. . . no. . . only. . ."

He rose and walked up and down the room. From time to time, his eyes fell upon Geneviève; and it looked as though he were on the point of giving a more precise answer to the question which she had put to him. Would he speak?

Mme. Ernemont awaited with anguish the revelation of the secret upon which the girl's future peace might depend.

He sat down beside Geneviève, appeared to hesitate, and said at last:

"No. . . no. . . just now. . . an idea occurred to me. . . a recollection. . ."

"A recollection? . . . And. . ."

"I was mistaken. Your story contained certain details that misled me."

"Are you sure?"

He hesitated and then declared:

"Absolutely sure."

"Oh," said she, greatly disappointed. "I had half guessed. . . that that man whom I saw twice. . . that you knew him. . . that. . ."

She did not finish her sentence, but waited for an answer to the question which she had put to him without daring to state it completely.

He was silent. Then, insisting no further, she bent over Mme. Ernemont:

"Good night, grandmother. My children must be in bed by this time, but they could none of them go to sleep before I had kissed them."

She held out her hand to the prince:

"Thank you once more. . ."

"Are you going?" he asked quickly.

"Yes, if you will excuse me; grandmother will see you out."

He bowed low and kissed her hand. As she opened the door, she turned round and smiled. Then she disappeared. The prince listened to the sound of her footsteps diminishing in the distance and stood stock-still, his face white with emotion.

"Well," said the old lady, "so you did not speak?"

"No. . ."

"That secret. . ."

"Later. . . To-day. . . oddly enough. . . I was not able to."

"Was it so difficult? Did not she herself feel that you were the stranger who took her away twice. . . A word would have been enough. . ."

"Later, later," he repeated, recovering all his assurance. "You can understand. . . the child hardly knows me. . . I must first gain the right to her affection, to her love. . . When I have given her the life which she deserves, a wonderful life, such as one reads of in fairy-tales, then I will speak."

The old lady tossed her head:

"I fear that you are making a great mistake. Geneviève does not want a wonderful life. She has simple tastes."

"She has the tastes of all women; and wealth, luxury and power give joys which not one of them despises."

"Yes, Geneviève does. And you would do much better. . ."

"We shall see. For the moment, let me go my own way. And be quite easy. I have not the least intention, as you say, of mixing her up in any of my manœuvers. She will hardly ever see me. . . Only, we had to come into contact, you know. . . That's done. . . Good-bye."

He left the school and walked to where his motor-car was waiting for him. He was perfectly happy:

"She is charming. . . and so gentle, so grave! Her mother's eyes, eyes that soften you. . . Heavens, how long ago that all is! And what a delightful recollection! A little sad, but so delightful!" And he said, aloud, "Certainly I shall look after her happiness! And that at once! This very evening! That's it, this very evening she shall have a sweetheart! Is not love the essential condition of any young girl's happiness?"

He found his car on the high-road:

"Home," he said to Octave.

When Sernine reached home, he rang up Neuilly and telephoned his instructions to the friend whom he called the doctor. Then he dressed, dined at the Rue Cambon Club, spent an hour at the opera and got into his car again:

"Go to Neuilly, Octave. We are going to fetch the doctor. What's the time?"

"Half-past ten."

"Dash it! Look sharp!"

Ten minutes later, the car stopped at the end of the Boulevard Inkerman, outside a villa standing in its own grounds. The doctor came down at the sound of the hooter. The prince asked:

"Is the fellow ready?"

"Packed up, strung up, sealed up."

"In good condition?"

"Excellent. If everything goes as you telephoned, the police will be utterly at sea."

"That's what they're there for. Let's get him on board."

They carried into the motor a sort of long sack shaped like a human being and apparently rather heavy. And the prince said:

"Go to Versailles, Octave, Rue de la Vilaine. Stop outside the Hôtel des Deux-Empereurs."

"Why, it's a filthy hotel," observed the doctor. "I know it well; a regular hovel."

"You needn't tell me! And it will be a hard piece of work, for me, at least. . . But, by Jove, I wouldn't sell this moment for a fortune! Who dares pretend that life is monotonous?"

They reached the Hôtel des Deux-Empereurs. A muddy alley; two steps down; and they entered a passage lit by a flickering lamp.

Sernine knocked with his fist against a little door.

A waiter appeared, Philippe, the man to whom Sernine had given orders, that morning, concerning Gérard Baupré.

"Is he here still?" asked the prince.

"Yes."

"The rope?"

"The knot is made."

"He has not received the telegram he was hoping for?"

"I intercepted it: here it is."

Sernine took the blue paper and read it:

"Gad!" he said. "It was high time. This is to promise him a thousand francs for to-morrow. Come, fortune is on my side. A quarter to twelve. . . In a quarter of an hour, the poor devil will take a leap into eternity. Show me the way, Philippe. You stay here, Doctor."

The waiter took the candle. They climbed to the third floor, and, walking on tip-toe, went along a low and evil-smelling corridor, lined with garrets and ending in a wooden staircase covered with the musty remnants of a carpet.

"Can no one hear me?" asked Sernine.

"No. The two rooms are quite detached. But you must be careful not to make a mistake: he is in the room on the left."

"Very good. Now go downstairs. At twelve o'clock, the doctor, Octave and you are to carry the fellow up here, to where we now stand, and wait till I call you."

The wooden staircase had ten treads, which the prince climbed with definite caution. At the top was a landing with two doors. It took Sernine quite five minutes to open the one of the right without breaking the silence with the least sound of a creaking hinge.

A light gleamed through the darkness of the room. Feeling his way, so as not to knock against one of the chairs, he made for that light. It came from the next room and filtered through a glazed door covered with a tattered hanging.

The prince pulled the threadbare stuff aside. The panes were of ground glass, but scratched in parts, so that, by applying one eye, it was easy to see all that happened in the other room.

Sernine saw a man seated at a table facing him. It was the poet, Gérard Baupré. He was writing by the light of a candle.

Above his head hung a rope, which was fastened to a hook fixed in the ceiling. At the end of the rope was a slip-knot.

A faint stroke sounded from a clock in the street.

"Five minutes to twelve," thought Sernine. "Five minutes more."

The young man was still writing. After a moment, he put down his pen, collected the ten or twelve sheets of paper which he had covered and began to read them over.

What he read did not seem to please him, for an expression of discontent passed across his face. He tore up his manuscript and burnt the pieces in the flame of the candle.

Then, with a fevered hand, he wrote a few words on a clean sheet, signed it savagely and rose from his chair.

But, seeing the rope at ten inches above his head, he sat down again suddenly with a great shudder of alarm.

Sernine distinctly saw his pale features, his lean cheeks, against which he pressed his clenched fists. A tear trickled slowly down his face, a single, disconsolate tear. His eyes gazed into space, eyes terrifying in their unutterable sadness, eyes that already seemed to behold the dread unknown.

And it was so young a face! Cheeks still so smooth, with not a blemish, not a wrinkle! And blue eyes, blue like an eastern sky! . . .

Midnight. . . the twelve tragic strokes of midnight, to which so many a despairing man has hitched the last second of his existence!

At the twelfth stroke, he stood up again and, bravely this time, without trembling, looked at the sinister rope. He even tried to give a smile, a poor smile, the pitiful grimace of the doomed man whom death has already seized for its own.

Swiftly he climbed the chair and took the rope in one hand.

For a moment, he stood there, motionless: not that he was hesitating or lacking in courage. But this was the supreme moment, the one minute of grace which a man allows himself before the fatal deed.

He gazed at the squalid room to which his evil destiny had brought him, the hideous paper on the walls, the wretched bed.

On the table, not a book: all were sold. Not a photograph, not a letter: he had no father, no mother, no relations. What was there to make him cling to life?

With a sudden movement he put his head into the slip-knot and pulled at the rope until the noose gripped his neck.

And, kicking the chair from him with both feet, he leapt into space.

TEN SECONDS, FIFTEEN SECONDS PASSED, twenty formidable, eternal seconds. . .

The body gave two or three jerks. The feet had instinctively felt for a resting-place. Then nothing moved. . .

A few seconds more. . . The little glazed door opened.

Sernine entered.

Without the least haste he took the sheet of paper to which the young man had set his signature, and read:

"Tired of living, ill, penniless, hopeless, I am taking my own life. Let no one be accused of my death.

GÉRARD BAUPRÉ
30 April

He put back the paper on the table where it could be seen, picked up the chair and placed it under the young man's feet. He himself climbed up on the table and, holding the body close to him, lifted it up, loosened the slip-knot and passed the head through it.

The body sank into his arms. He let it slide along the table and, jumping to the floor, laid it on the bed.

Then, with the same coolness, he opened the door on the passage:

"Are you there, all the three of you?" he whispered.

Some one answered from the foot of the wooden staircase near him:

"We are here. Are we to hoist up our bundle?"

"Yes, come along!"

He took the candle and showed them a light.

The three men trudged up the stairs, carrying the sack in which the "fellow" was tied up.

"Put him here," he said, pointing to the table.

With a pocket-knife, he cut the cords round the sack. A white sheet appeared, which he flung back. In the sheet was a corpse, the corpse of Pierre Leduc.

"Poor Pierre Leduc!" said Sernine. "You will never know what you lost by dying so young! I should have helped you to go far, old chap. However, we must do without your services. . . Now then, Philippe, get up on the table; and you, Octave, on the chair. Lift up his head and fasten the slip-knot."

Two minutes later, Pierre Leduc's body was swinging at the end of the rope.

"Capital, that was quite simple! Now you can all of you go. You, Doctor, will call back here to-morrow morning; you will hear of the suicide of a certain Gérard Baupré: you understand, Gérard Baupré. Here is his farewell letter. You will send for the divisional surgeon and the commissary; you will arrange that neither of them notices that the deceased has a cut finger or a scar on one cheek. . ."

"That's easy."

"And you will manage so as to have the report written then and there, to your dictation."

"That's easy."

"Lastly, avoid having the body sent to the Morgue and make them give permission for an immediate burial."

"That's not so easy."

"Try. Have you examined the other one?"

He pointed to the young man lying lifeless on the bed.

"Yes," said the doctor. "The breathing is becoming normal. But it was a big risk to run. . . the carotid artery might have. . ."

"Nothing venture, nothing have. . . How soon will he recover consciousness?"

"In a few minutes."

"Very well. Oh, by the way, don't go yet, Doctor. Wait for me downstairs. There is more for you to do."

The prince, when he found himself alone, lit a cigarette and puffed at it quietly, sending little blue rings of smoke floating up to the ceiling.

A sigh roused him from his thoughts. He went to the bed. The young man was beginning to move; and his chest rose and fell violently, like that of a sleeper under the influence of a nightmare. He put his hands to his throat, as though he felt a pain there; and this action suddenly made him sit up, terrified, panting. . .

Then he saw Sernine in front of him:

"You?" he whispered, without understanding. "You? . . ."

He gazed at him stupidly, as though he had seen a ghost.

He again touched his throat, felt round his neck. . . And suddenly he gave a hoarse cry; a mad terror dilated his eyes, made his hair stand on end, shook him from head to foot like an aspen-leaf! The prince had moved aside; and he saw the man's corpse hanging from the rope.

He flung himself back against the wall. That man, that hanged man, was himself! He was dead and he was looking at his own dead body! Was this a hideous dream that follows upon death? A hallucination that comes to those who are no more and whose distracted brain still quivers with a last flickering gleam of life? . . .

His arms struck at the air. For a moment, he seemed to be defending himself against the squalid vision. Then, exhausted, he fainted away for the second time.

"First-rate," said the prince, with a grin. "A sensitive, impressionable nature. . . At present, the brain is out of gear. . . Come, this is a propitious moment. . . But, if I don't get the business done in twenty minutes. . . he'll escape me. . ."

He pushed open the door between the two garrets, came back to the bed, lifted the young man and carried him to the bed in the other room. Then he bathed his temples with cold water and made him sniff at some salts.

This time, the swoon did not last long.

Gérard timidly opened his eyes and raised them to the ceiling. The vision was gone. But the arrangement of the furniture, the position of the table and the fireplace, and certain other details all surprised him. . . And then came the remembrance of his act, the pain which he felt at his throat. . .

He said to the prince:

"I have had a dream, have I not?"

"No."

"How do you mean, no?" And, suddenly recollecting, "Oh, that's true, I remember. . . I meant to kill myself. . . and I even. . ." Bending forward anxiously, "But the rest, the vision. . ."

"What vision?"

"The man. . . the rope. . . was that a dream? . . ."

"No," said Sernine. "That also was real."

"What are you saying? What are you saying? . . . Oh, no, no! . . . I entreat you! . . . Wake me, if I am asleep. . . or else let me die! . . . But I am dead, am I not? And this is the nightmare of a corpse! . . . Oh, I feel my brain going! . . . I entreat you. . ."

Sernine placed his hand gently on the young man's head and, bending over him:

"Listen to me. . . listen to me carefully and understand what I say. You are alive. Your matter and your mind are as they were and live. But Gérard Baupré is dead. You understand me, do you not? That member of society who was known as Gérard Baupré has ceased to exist. You have done away with that one. To-morrow, the registrar will write in his books, opposite the name you bore, the word 'Dead,' with the date of your decease."

"It's a lie!" stammered the terrified lad. "It's a lie! Considering that I, Gérard Baupré, am here!"

"You are not Gérard Baupré," declared Sernine. And, pointing to the open door, "Gérard Baupré is there, in the next room. Do you wish to see him? He is hanging from the nail to which you hooked him. On the table is a letter in which you certify his death with your signature. It is all quite regular, it is all final. There is no getting away from the irrevocable, brutal fact: Gérard Baupré has ceased to exist!"

The young man listened in despair. Growing calmer, now that facts were assuming a less tragic significance, he began to understand:

"And then. . ." he muttered.

"And then. . . let us talk."

"Yes, yes. . . let us talk. . ."

"A cigarette?" asked the prince. "Will you have one? Ah, I see that you are becoming reconciled to life! So much the better: we shall understand each other; and that quickly."

He lit the young man's cigarette and his own and, at once, in a few words uttered in a hard voice, explained himself:

"You, the late Gérard Baupré, were weary of life, ill, penniless, hopeless. . . Would you like to be well, rich, and powerful?"

"I don't follow you."

"It is quite simple. Accident has placed you on my path. You are young, good-looking, a poet; you are intelligent and—your act of despair shows it—you have a fine sense of conduct. These are qualities which are rarely found united in one person. I value them. . . and I take them for my account."

"They are not for sale."

"Idiot! Who talks of buying or selling? Keep your conscience. It is too precious a jewel for me to relieve you of it."

"Then what do you ask of me?"

"Your life!" And, pointing to the bruises on the young man's throat, "Your life, which you have not known how to employ! Your life, which you have bungled, wasted, destroyed and which, I propose to build up again, in accordance with an ideal of beauty, greatness and dignity that would make you giddy, my lad, if you saw the abyss into which my secret thought plunges. . ." He had taken Gérard's head between his hands and he continued, eagerly: "You are free! No shackles! You have no longer the weight of your name to bear! You have got rid of that number with which society had stamped you as though branding you on the shoulder. You are free! In this world of slaves where each man bears his label you can either come and go unknown, invisible, as if you owned Gyges' ring. . . or else you can choose your own label, the one you like best! Do you understand the magnificent treasure which you represent to an artist. . . to yourself, if you like? A virgin life, a brand-new life! Your life is the wax which you have the right to fashion as you please, according to the whims of your imagination and the counsels of your reason."

MAURICE LEBLANC

The young man made a gesture expressive of weariness:

"Ah, what would you have me do with that treasure? What have I done with it so far? Nothing!"

"Give it to me."

"What can you do with it?"

"Everything. If you are not an artist, I am; and an enthusiastic artist, inexhaustible, indomitable, exuberant. If you have not the Promethean fire, I have! Where you failed, I shall succeed. Give me your life."

"Words, promises!" cried the young man, whose features began to glow with animation. "Empty dreams! I know my own worthlessness! I know my cowardice, my despondency, my efforts that come to nothing, all my wretchedness. To begin life anew, I should need a will which I do not possess. . ."

"I possess mine."

"Friends. . ."

"You shall have them."

"Means. . ."

"I am providing you with means. . . and such means! You will only have to dip, as one would dip into a magic coffer."

"But who are you?" cried the young man, wildly.

"To others, Prince Sernine. . . To you. . . what does it matter? I am more than a prince, more than a king, more than an emperor. . ."

"Who are you? . . . Who are you?" stammered Baupré.

"The Master. . . he who will and who can. . . he who acts. . . There are no bounds to my will, there is none to my power. I am richer than the richest man alive, for his fortune is mine. . . I am more powerful than the mightiest, for their might is at my service!"

He took the other's head in his hands again and, looking deep into his eyes:

"Be rich, too. . . be mighty. . . I offer you happiness. . . and the joy of living. . . and peace for your poet's brain. . . and fame and glory also. . . Do you accept?"

"Yes. . . yes. . ." whispered Gérard, dazzled and overmastered. "What am I to do?"

"Nothing."

"But. . ."

"Nothing, I say. The whole scaffolding of my plans rests on you, but you do not count. You have no active part to play. You are, for the moment, but a silent actor, or not even that, but just a pawn which I move along the board."

"What shall I do?"

"Nothing. Write poetry. You shall live as you please. You shall have money. You shall enjoy life. I will not even bother my head about you. I repeat, you play no part in my venture."

"And who shall I be?"

Sernine stretched out his arm and pointed to the next room:

"You shall take that man's place. *You are that man!*"

Gérard shuddered with revolt and disgust:

"Oh, no, he is dead! . . . And then. . . it is a crime! . . . No, I want a new life, made for me, thought out for me. . . an unknown name. . ."

"That man, I tell you!" cried Sernine, irresistible in his energy and authority. "You shall be that man and none other! That man, because his destiny is magnificent, because his name is illustrious, and because he hands down to you a thrice-venerable heritage of ancestral dignity and pride."

"It is a crime!" moaned Baupré, faltering.

"You shall be that man!" spoke Sernine, with unparalleled vehemence. "You shall be that man! If not, you become Baupré again; and over Baupré I own rights of life and death. Choose."

He drew his revolver, cocked it and took aim at the young man:

"Choose," he repeated.

The expression of his face was implacable. Gérard was frightened and sank down on his bed sobbing:

"I wish to live!"

"You wish it firmly, irrevocably?"

"Yes, a thousand times yes! After the terrible thing which I attempted, death appals me. . . Anything. . . anything rather than death! . . . Anything! . . . Pain. . . hunger. . . illness. . . every torture, every shame. . . crime itself, if need be. . . but not death!"

He shivered with fever and agony, as though the great enemy were still prowling round him and as though he felt himself powerless to escape from its clutches. The prince redoubled his efforts and, in a fervent voice, holding him under him like a prey:

"I will ask nothing impossible of you, nothing wrong. . . If there is anything, I am responsible. . . No, no crime. . . a little pain at most. . . A little of your blood must flow. But what is that, compared with the dread of dying?"

"Pain is indifferent to me."

"Then here and now!" shouted Sernine. "Here and now! Ten seconds of pain and that is all. . . Ten seconds and the other's life is yours. . ."

He had seized him round the body and forced him down on a chair; and he now held the young man's left hand flat on the table, with his five fingers spread out. He swiftly took a knife from his pocket, pressed the blade against the little finger, between the first and second joints, and commanded:

"Strike! Strike your own blow. One blow of the fist and that is all!"

He had taken Gérard's right hand and was trying to bring it down upon the other like a hammer.

Gérard writhed and twisted, convulsed with horror. He understood:

"Never!" he stuttered. "Never!"

"Strike! One blow and it's done! One blow and you will be like that man: no one will recognize you."

"Tell me his name. . ."

"Strike first!"

"Never! Oh, what torture! . . . I beseech you. . . presently. . ."

"Now. . . I insist. . . you must. . ."

"No. . . no. . . I can't do it. . ."

"Strike, you fool! It means fortune, fame, love. . ."

Gérard raised his fist with a sudden movement.

"Love," he said, "yes. . . for that, yes. . ."

"You will love and be loved," said Sernine. "Your betrothed awaits you. I have chosen her myself. She is the purest of the pure, the fairest of the fair. But you must win her. Strike!"

The lad's arm stiffened for the fatal blow; but the instinct of self-preservation was too strong for him. His body was wrung with a superhuman effort. He suddenly released himself from Sernine's hold and fled.

He rushed like a madman to the other room. A yell of terror escaped him, at the sight of the abominable vision, and he came back and fell on his knees before Sernine, beside the table.

"Strike!" said the prince, again spreading out the lad's fingers and fixing the blade of the knife.

What followed was done mechanically. With an automatic movement, with haggard eyes and a livid face, the young man raised his fist and struck:

"Ah!" he cried, with a moan of pain.

A small piece of flesh was separated from the little finger. Blood flowed. For the third time, Gérard fainted.

Sernine looked at him for a second or two and said, gently:

"Poor little chap! . . . There, I'll reward you for what you've done; and a hundred times over. I always pay generously."

He went downstairs and found the doctor waiting below:

"It's done. Go upstairs, you, and make a little cut in his right cheek, similar to Pierre Leduc's. The two scars must be exactly alike. I shall come back for you in an hour."

"Where are you going?"

"To take the air. My heart feels anyhow."

Outside he drew a long breath and lit another cigarette:

"A good day's work," he muttered. "A little over-crowded, a little tiring, but fruitful, really fruitful. I am Dolores Kesselbach's friend. I am Geneviève's friend. I have manufactured a new Pierre Leduc, a very presentable one and entirely at my disposal. Lastly, I have found Geneviève a husband of the sort that you don't find by the dozen. Now my task is done. I have only to gather the fruit of my efforts. It's your turn to work, M. Lenormand. I, for my part, am ready." And he added, thinking of the poor mutilated lad whom he had dazzled with his promises, "Only—for there is an 'only'—I have not the slightest notion who this Pierre Leduc was, whose place I have magnanimously awarded to that good young man. And that's very annoying. . . For when all is said, there's nothing to prove to me that Pierre Leduc was not the son of a pork-butcher! . . ."

V

M. Lenormand at Work

On the morning of the 31st of May, all the newspapers reminded their readers that Lupin, in a letter addressed to M. Lenormand, had announced the escape of the messenger Jérôme for that date. And one of them summed up the situation, as it then stood, in very able terms:

"The horrible carnage at the Palace Hotel took place as far back as the 17th of April. What has been discovered since? Nothing.

"There were three clues: the cigarette-case, the initials L and M and the parcel of clothes left behind in the office of the hotel. What advantage has been taken of these clues? None.

"It appears that the police suspect one of the visitors who was staying on the first floor and who disappeared in a doubtful manner. Have they found him? Have they established his identity? No.

"The tragedy, therefore, remains as mysterious as at the beginning, the gloom is impenetrable.

"To complete the picture, we are told that dissension prevails between the prefect of police and his subordinate, M. Lenormand, and that the latter, finding himself less vigorously supported by the prime minister, virtually sent in his resignation several days ago. According to our information, the conduct of the Kesselbach case is now in the hands of the deputy-chief of the detective-service, M. Weber, a personal enemy of M. Lenormand's.

"In short, disorder and confusion reign; and this in the face of Lupin, who stands for method, energy and steadfastness of mind.

"What conclusion do we draw from these facts? Briefly, this: Lupin will release his accomplice to-day, the 31st of May, as he foretold."

This conclusion, which was echoed in all the other newspapers, was also the conclusion at which the general public had arrived. And we must take it that the threat was not considered devoid of importance in high places, for the prefect of police and, in the absence of M. Lenormand, who was said to be unwell, the deputy-chief of the detective-service, M. Weber, had adopted the most stringent measures, both at the Palais de Justice and at the Santé Prison, where the prisoner was confined.

They did not dare, for sheer reasons of shame, to suspend on that particular day the examinations conducted daily by M. Formerie; but, from the prison to the Boulevard du Palais, a regular mobilization of police-forces guarded the streets along the line.

To the intense astonishment of one and all, the 31st of May passed and the threatened escape did not take place.

One thing did happen, an attempt to execute the plan, as was betrayed by a block of tramway-cars, omnibuses and drays along the road taken by the prison-van and the unaccountable breaking of one of the wheels of the van itself. But the attempt assumed no more definite form.

Lupin, therefore, had met with a check. The public felt almost disappointed and the police triumphed loudly.

On the next day, Saturday, an incredible rumour spread through the Palais and the newspaper-offices: Jérôme the messenger had disappeared.

Was it possible? Although the special editions confirmed the news, people refused to believe it. But, at six o'clock, a note published by the *Dépêche du Soir* made it official:

"We have received the following communication signed by Arsène Lupin. The special stamp affixed to it, in accordance with the circular which Lupin recently sent to the press, guarantees the genuineness of the document:

To the Editor of the Dépêche du Soir
Sir,
"'Pray make my apologies to the public for not keeping my word yesterday. I remembered, at the last moment, that the 31st of May fell on a Friday! Could I set my friend at liberty on a Friday? I did not think it right to assume that responsibility.

"'I must also apologize for not on this occasion explaining, with my customary frankness, how this little event was managed. My process is so ingenious and so simple that I fear lest, if I revealed it, every criminal should be inspired by it. How surprised people will be on the day when I am free to speak! "Is that all?" I shall be asked. That is all; but it had to be thought of.

Permit me to be, Sir,
Your obedient servant,
Arsène Lupin

An hour later, M. Lenormand was rung up on the telephone and informed that Valenglay, the prime minister, wished to see him at the Ministry of the Interior.

"How well you're looking, my dear Lenormand! And I who thought that you were ill and dared not leave your room!"

"I am not ill, Monsieur le Président."

"So you were sulking in your tent! . . . But you were always a bad-tempered fellow."

"I confess to the bad temper, Monsieur le Président, but not to the sulking."

"But you stay at home! And Lupin takes advantage of it to release his friends. . ."

"How could I stop him?"

"How? Why, Lupin's trick was of the plainest. In accordance with his usual method, he announced the date of the escape beforehand; everybody believed in it; an apparent attempt was planned; the escape was not made; and, on the next day, when nobody is thinking about it—whoosh!—the bird takes flight."

"Monsieur le Président," said the chief of the detective-service, solemnly, "Lupin disposes of such means that we are not in a position to prevent what he has decided on. The escape was mathematically certain. I preferred to pass the hand. . . and leave the laughter for others to face."

Valenglay chuckled:

"It's a fact that Monsieur le Préfet de Police and M. Weber cannot be enjoying themselves at the present moment. . . But, when all is said, can you explain to me, M. Lenormand. . ."

"All that we know, Monsieur le Président, is that the escape took place from the Palais de Justice. The prisoner was brought in a prison-van and taken to M. Formerie's room. He left M. Formerie's room, but he did not leave the Palais de Justice. And yet nobody knows what became of him."

"It's most bewildering."

"Most bewildering."

"And has nothing else been discovered?"

"Yes. The inner corridor leading to the examining magistrates' rooms was blocked by an absolutely unprecedented crowd of prisoners, warders, counsel and doorkeepers; and it was discovered that all those people had received forged notices to appear at the same hour. On the other hand, not one of the examining-magistrates who were supposed to have summoned them sat in his room that day; and this because of forged notices from the public prosecutor's office, sending them to every part of Paris. . . and of the outskirts."

"Is that all?"

"No. Two municipal guards and a prisoner were seen to cross the courtyards. A cab was waiting for them outside and all three stepped in.

"And your supposition, Lenormand, your opinion. . ."

"My supposition, Monsieur le Président, is that the two municipal guards were accomplices who, profiting by the disorder in the corridor, took the place of the three warders. And my opinion is that this escape succeeded only through such special circumstances and so strange a combination of facts that we must look upon the most unlikely cases of complicity as absolutely certain. Lupin, for that matter, has connections at the Palais that balk all our calculations. He has agents in your ministry. He has agents at the Prefecture of Police. He has agents around me. It is a formidable organization, a detective-service a thousand times more clever, more daring, more varied and more supple than that under my own orders."

"And you stand this, Lenormand?"

"No, I do not."

"Then why this slackness on your part since the beginning of the case? What have you done against Lupin?"

"I have prepared for the struggle."

"Ah, capital! And, while you were preparing, he was acting."

"So was I."

"And do you know anything?"

"I know a great deal."

"What? Speak!"

Leaning on his stick, M. Lenormand took a little contemplative walk across the spacious room. Then he sat down opposite Valenglay, brushed the facings of his olive-green coat with his finger-tips, settled his spectacles on his nose and said, plainly:

"M. le Président, I hold three trump-cards in my hand. First, I know the name under which Arsène Lupin is hiding at this moment, the name under which he lived on the Boulevard Haussmann, receiving his assistants daily, reconstructing and directing his gang."

"But then why, in heaven's name, don't you arrest him?"

"I did not receive these particulars until later. The prince—let us call him Prince Dash—has disappeared. He is abroad, on other business."

"And, if he does not return. . ."

"The position which he occupies, the manner in which he has flung himself into the Kesselbach case, necessitate his return and under the same name."

"Nevertheless. . ."

"Monsieur le Président, I come to my second trump. I have at last discovered Pierre Leduc."

"Nonsense!"

"Or rather Lupin discovered him, and before disappearing, settled him in a little villa in the neighborhood of Paris."

"By Jove! But how did you know. . ."

"Oh, easily! Lupin has placed two of his accomplices with Pierre Leduc, to watch him and defend him. Now these accomplices are two of my own detectives, two brothers whom I employ in the greatest secrecy and who will hand him over to me at the first opportunity!"

"Well done you! So that. . ."

"So that, as Pierre Leduc, we may say, is the central point of the efforts of all those who are trying to solve the famous Kesselbach secret, I shall, sooner or later, through Pierre Leduc, catch, first, the author of the treble murder, because that miscreant substituted himself for Mr. Kesselbach in the accomplishment of an immense scheme and because Mr. Kesselbach had to find Pierre Leduc in order to be able to accomplish that scheme; and, secondly, Arsène Lupin, because Arsène Lupin is pursuing the same object."

"Splendid! Pierre Leduc is the bait which you are throwing to the enemy."

"And the fish is biting, Monsieur le Président. I have just had word that a suspicious person was seen, a short time ago, prowling round the little villa where Pierre Leduc is living under the protection of my officers. I shall be on the spot in four hours."

"And the third trump, Lenormand?"

"Monsieur le Président, a letter arrived yesterday, addressed to Mr. Rudolf Kesselbach, which I intercepted. . ."

"Intercepted, eh? You're getting on!"

"Yes, I intercepted it, opened it and kept it for myself. Here it is. It is dated two months back. It bears the Capetown postmark and contains these words: 'My dear Rudolf, I shall be in Paris on the 1st of June and in just as wretched a plight as when you came to my assistance. But I have great hopes of this Pierre Leduc affair of which I told you. What a strange story it is! Have you found the man I mean? Where do we stand? I am most anxious to know.' The letter is signed, 'Steinweg.' The first of June," continued M. Lenormand, "is to-day. I have ordered one of my inspectors to hunt me out this Steinweg. I have no doubt that he will succeed."

"Nor I, no doubt at all," cried Valenglay, rising from his chair, "and I make you every apology, my dear Lenormand, and my humble confession: I was on the point of letting you slide. . . for good and all! To-morrow I was expecting the prefect of police and M. Weber."

"I knew that, Monsieur le Président."

"Impossible!"

"But for that, should I have put myself out? You now see my plan of campaign. On the one side, I am setting traps in which the murderer will be caught sooner or later. Pierre Leduc or Steinweg will deliver him into my hands. On the other side, I am on Arsène Lupin's heels. Two of his agents are in my pay and he believes them to be his most devoted helpers. In addition to this, he is working for me, because he is pursuing the perpetrator of the threefold crime as I am. Only, he imagines that he is dishing me, whereas it is I who am dishing him. So I shall succeed, but on one condition. . ."

"What is that?"

"That I am given free scope and allowed to act according to the needs of the moment, without troubling about the public, who are growing impatient, or my superiors, who are intriguing against me."

"I agree."

"In that case, Monsieur le Président, in a few days from this I shall be the victor. . . or I shall be dead."

MAURICE LEBLANC

At Saint-Cloud. A little villa situated on one of the highest points of the upland, in an unfrequented road.

It was eleven o'clock at night. M. Lenormand left his car at Saint-Cloud and walked cautiously along the road. A shadow appeared.

"Is that you, Gourel?"

"Yes, chief."

"Did you tell the brothers Doudeville that I was coming?"

"Yes, your room is ready, you can go to bed and sleep. . . unless they try to carry off Pierre Leduc to-night, which would not surprise me, considering the behavior of the fellow whom the Doudevilles saw."

They walked across the garden, softly entered the house and went up to the first floor. The two brothers, Jean and Jacques Doudeville, were there.

"No news of Prince Sernine?" asked Lenormand.

"No, chief."

"What about Pierre Leduc?"

"He spends the whole day lying flat on his back in his room on the ground-floor, or else in the garden. He never comes up to see us."

"Is he better?"

"Much better. The rest has made a great change in his appearance."

"Is he wholly devoted to Lupin?"

"To Prince Sernine, rather, for he does not suspect that the two are one and the same man. At least, I suppose so. One never knows, with him. He does not speak at all. Oh, he's a queer fish! There's only one person who has the gift of cheering him up, of making him talk and even laugh. That's a young girl from Garches, to whom Prince Sernine introduced him. Geneviève Ernemont her name is. She has been here three times already. . . she was here to-day." He added, jestingly, "I believe there's a little flirting going on. . . It's like his highness Prince Sernine and Mrs. Kesselbach. . . It seems he's making eyes at her! . . . That devil of a Lupin!"

M. Lenormand did not reply. But it was obvious that all these details, to which he seemed to attach no importance, were noted in the recesses of his memory, to be used whenever he might need to draw the logical inferences from them. He lit a cigar, chewed it without smoking it, lit it again and dropped it.

He asked two or three more questions and then, dressed as he was, threw himself on his bed:

"If the least thing happens, let me be awakened. . . If not, I shall sleep through the night. . . Go to your posts, all of you."

The others left the room.

An hour passed, two hours.

Suddenly, M. Lenormand felt some one touch him and Gourel said to him:

"Get up, chief; they have opened the gate."

"One man or two?"

"I only saw one. . . the moon appeared just then. . . he crouched down against a hedge."

"And the brothers Doudeville?"

"I sent them out by the back. They will cut off his retreat when the time comes."

Gourel took M. Lenormand's hand, led him downstairs and then into a little dark room:

"Don't stir, chief; we are in Pierre Leduc's dressing-room. I am opening the door of the recess in which his bed stands. . . Don't be afraid. . . he has taken his veronal as he does every evening. . . nothing can wake him. Come this way. . . It's a good hiding-place, isn't it? . . . These are the curtains of his bed. . . From here you can see the window and the whole side of the room between the window and the bed."

The casement stood open and admitted a vague light, which became very precise at times, when the moon burst through her veil of clouds. The two men did not take their eyes from the empty window-frame, feeling certain that the event which they were awaiting would come from that side.

A slight, creaking noise. . .

"He is climbing the trellis," whispered Gourel.

"Is it high?"

"Six feet or so."

The creaking became more distinct.

"Go, Gourel," muttered M. Lenormand, "find the Doudevilles, bring them back to the foot of the wall and bar the road to any one who tries to get down this way."

Gourel went. At the same moment, a head appeared at the level of the window. Then a leg was flung over the balcony. M. Lenormand distinguished a slenderly-built man, below the middle height, dressed in dark colours and without a hat.

The man turned and, leaning over the balcony, looked for a few seconds into space, as though to make sure that no danger threatened him. Then he stooped down and lay at full length on the floor. He appeared motionless. But soon M. Lenormand realized that the still blacker shadow which he formed against the surrounding darkness was coming forward, nearer.

It reached the bed.

M. Lenormand had an impression that he could hear the man's breathing and, at the same time, that he could just see his eyes, keen, glittering eyes, which pierced the darkness like shafts of fire and which themselves could see through that same darkness.

Pierre Leduc gave a deep sigh and turned over.

A fresh silence. . .

The man had glided along the bed with imperceptible movements and his dark outline now stood out against the whiteness of the sheets that hung down to the floor.

M. Lenormand could have touched him by putting out his arm. This time, he clearly distinguished the breathing, which alternated with that of the sleeper, and he had the illusion that he also heard the sound of a heart beating.

Suddenly, a flash of light. . . The man had pressed the spring of an electric lantern; and Pierre Leduc was lit full in the face, but the man remained in the shade, so that M. Lenormand was unable to see his features.

All that he saw was something that shone in the bright space; and he shuddered. It was the blade of a knife; and that thin, tapering knife, more like a stiletto than a dagger, seemed to him identical with the weapon which he had picked up by the body of Chapman, Mr. Kesselbach's secretary.

He put forth all his will-power to restrain himself from springing upon the man. He wanted first to know what the man had come to do.

The hand was raised. Was he going to strike? M. Lenormand calculated the distance in order to stop the blow. . . But no, it was not a murderous gesture, but one of caution. The hand would only fall if Pierre Leduc stirred or tried to call out. And the man bent over the sleeper, as though he were examining something.

"The right cheek," thought M. Lenormand, "the scar on the right cheek. . . He wants to make sure that it is really Pierre Leduc."

The man had turned a little to one side, so that only his shoulders were visible. But his clothes, his overcoat, were so near that they brushed against the curtains behind which M. Lenormand was hiding.

"One movement on his part," thought the chief detective, "a thrill of alarm; and I shall collar him."

But the man, entirely absorbed in his examination, did not stir. At last, after shifting the dagger to the hand that held the lantern, he raised the sheet, at first hardly at all, then a little more, then more still, until the sleeper's left arm was uncovered and the hand laid bare. The flash of the lantern shone upon the hand. The fingers lay outspread. The little finger was cut on the second joint.

Again Pierre Leduc made a movement. The light was immediately put out; and, for an instant, the man remained beside the bed, motionless, standing straight up. Would he make up his mind to strike? M. Lenormand underwent the agony of the crime which he could so easily prevent, but which he did not want to forestall before the very last second.

A long, a very long silence. Suddenly, he saw or rather fancied that he saw an arm uplifted. Instinctively he moved, stretching his hand above the sleeper. In making this gesture, he hit against the man.

A dull cry. The fellow struck out at space, defended himself at random and fled toward the window. But M. Lenormand had leapt upon him and had his two arms around the man's shoulders.

He at once felt him yielding and, as the weaker of the two, powerless in Lenormand's hands, trying to avoid the struggle and to slip from between his arms. Lenormand, exerting all his strength, held him flat against his chest, bent him in two and stretched him on his back on the floor.

"Ah, I've got him, I've got him!" he muttered triumphantly.

And he felt a singular elation at imprisoning that terrifying criminal, that unspeakable monster, in his irresistible grip. He felt him living and quivering, enraged and desperate, their two lives mingled, their breaths blended:

"Who are you?" he asked. "Who are you? . . . You'll have to speak. . ."

And he clasped the enemy's body with still greater force, for he had an impression that that body was diminishing between his arms, that it was vanishing. He gripped harder. . . and harder. . .

And suddenly he shuddered from head to foot. He had felt, he still felt a tiny prick in the throat. . . In his exasperation, he gripped harder yet: the pain increased! And he observed that the man had succeeded in twisting one arm round, slipping his hand to his chest and holding the dagger on end. The arm, it was true, was incapable of motion; but the closer M. Lenormand tightened his grip, the deeper did the point of the dagger enter the proffered flesh.

He flung back his head a little to escape the point: the point followed the movement and the wound widened.

Then he moved no more, remembering the three crimes and all the alarming, atrocious and prophetic things represented by that same little steel needle which was piercing his skin and which, in its turn, was implacably penetrating. . .

Suddenly, he let go and gave a leap backwards. Then, at once, he tried to resume the offensive. It was too late. The man flung his legs across the window-sill and jumped.

"Look out, Gourel!" he cried, knowing that Gourel was there, ready to catch the fugitive.

He leant out. A crunching of pebbles. . . a shadow between two trees, the slam of the gate. . . And no other sound. . . no interference. . .

Without giving a thought to Pierre Leduc, he called:

"Gourel! . . . Doudeville!"

No answer. The great silence of the countryside at night. . .

In spite of himself, he continued to think of the treble murder, the steel dagger. But no, it was impossible, the man had not had time, had not even had the need to strike, as he had found the road clear.

M. Lenormand jumped out in his turn and, switching on his lantern, recognized Gourel lying on the ground:

"Damn it!" he swore. "If they've killed him, they'll have to pay dearly for it."

But Gourel was not dead, only stunned; and, a few minutes later, he came to himself and growled:

"Only a blow of the fist, chief. . . just a blow of the fist which caught me full in the chest. But what a fellow!"

"There were two of them then?"

"Yes, a little one, who went up, and another, who took me unawares while I was watching."

"And the Doudevilles?"

"Haven't seen them."

One of them, Jacques, was found near the gate, bleeding from a punch in the jaw; the other a little farther, gasping for breath from a blow full on the chest.

"What is it? What happened?" asked M. Lenormand.

Jacques said that his brother and he had knocked up against an individual who had crippled them before they had time to defend themselves.

"Was he alone?"

"No; when he passed near us, he had a pal with him, shorter than himself."

"Did you recognize the man who struck you?"

"Judging by the breadth of his shoulders, I thought he might be the Englishman of the Palace Hotel, the one who left the hotel and whose traces we lost."

"The major?"

"Yes, Major Parbury."

After a moment's reflection, M. Lenormand said:

"There is no doubt possible. There were two of them in the Kesselbach case: the man with the dagger, who committed the murders, and his accomplice, the major."

"That is what Prince Sernine thinks," muttered Jacques Doudeville.

"And to-night," continued the chief detective, "it is they again: the same two." And he added, "So much the better. The chance of catching two criminals is a hundred times greater than the chance of catching one."

M. Lenormand attended to his men, had them put to bed and looked to see if the assailants had dropped anything or left any traces. He found nothing and went back to bed again himself.

In the morning, as Gourel and the Doudevilles felt none the worse for their injuries, he told the two brothers to scour the neighborhood and himself set out with Gourel for Paris, in order to hurry matters on and give his orders.

HE LUNCHED IN HIS OFFICE. At two o'clock, he heard good news. One of his best detectives, Dieuzy, had picked up Steinweg, Rudolf Kesselbach's correspondent, as the German was stepping out of a train from Marseilles.

"Is Dieuzy there?"

"Yes, chief," said Gourel. "He's here with the German."

"Have them brought in to me."

At that moment, the telephone-bell rang. It was Jean Doudeville, speaking from the post-office at Garches. The conversation did not take long:

"Is that you, Jean? Any news?"

"Yes, chief, Major Parbury. . ."

"Well?"

"We have found him. He has become a Spaniard and has darkened his skin. We have just seen him. He was entering the Garches free-school. He was received by that young lady. . . you know, the girl who knows Prince Sernine, Geneviève Ernemont."

"Thunder!"

M. Lenormand let go the receiver, made a grab at his hat, flew into the passage, met Dieuzy and the German, shouted to them to meet him in his office at six o'clock, rushed down the stairs, followed by Gourel and two inspectors whom he picked up on the way, and dived into a taxi-cab:

"Quick as you can to Garches. . . ten francs for yourself!"

He stopped the car a little before the Parc de Villeneuve, at the turn of the lane that led to the school. Jean Doudeville was waiting for him and at once exclaimed:

"He slipped away, ten minutes ago, by the other end of the lane."

"Alone?"

"No, with the girl."

M. Lenormand took Doudeville by the collar:

"Wretch! You let him go! But you ought to have. . . you ought to have. . ."

"My brother is on his track."

"A lot of good that will do us! He'll stick your brother. You're no match for him, either of you!"

He himself took the steering-wheel of the taxi, and resolutely drove into the lane, regardless of the cart-ruts and of the bushes on each side. They soon emerged on a parish-road, which took them to a crossway where five roads met. M. Lenormand, without hesitation chose the one on the left, the Saint-Cucufa Road. As a matter of fact, at the top of the slope that runs down to the lake, they met the other Doudeville brother, who shouted:

"They are in a carriage. . . half a mile away."

The chief did not stop. He sent the car flying down the incline, rushed along the bends, drove round the lake and suddenly uttered an exclamation of triumph. Right at the top of a little hill that stood in front of them, he had seen the hood of a carriage.

Unfortunately, he had taken the wrong road and had to back the machine. When he reached the place where the roads branched, the carriage was still there, stationary. And, suddenly, while he was turning, he saw a girl spring from the carriage. A man appeared on the step. The girl stretched out her arm. Two reports rang out.

She had taken bad aim, without a doubt, for a head looked round the other side of the hood and the man, catching sight of the motor-cab, gave his horse a great lash with the whip and it started off at a gallop. The next moment, a turn of the road hid the carriage from sight.

M. Lenormand finished his tacking in a few seconds, darted straight up the incline, passed the girl without stopping and turned round boldly. He found himself on a steep, pebbly forest road, which ran down between dense woods and which could only be followed very slowly and with the greatest caution. But what did he care! Twenty yards in front of him, the carriage, a sort of two-wheeled cabriolet, was dancing over the stones, drawn, or rather held back, by a horse which knew enough only to go very carefully, feeling its way and taking no risks. There was nothing to fear; escape was impossible.

And the two conveyances went shaking and jolting down-hill. At one moment, they were so close together that M. Lenormand thought of alighting and running with his men. But he felt the danger of putting on the brake on so steep a slope; and he went on, pressing the enemy closely, like a prey which one keeps within sight, within touch. . .

"We've got him, chief, we've got him!" muttered the inspectors, excited by the unexpected nature of the chase.

At the bottom, the way flattened out into a road that ran towards the Seine, towards Bougival. The horse, on reaching level ground, set off at a jog-trot, without hurrying itself and keeping to the middle of the road.

A violent effort shook the taxi. It appeared, instead of rolling, to proceed by bounds, like a darting fawn, and, slipping by the roadside slope, ready to smash any obstacle, it caught up the carriage, came level with it, passed it. . .

An oath from M. Lenormand. . . shouts of fury. . . The carriage was empty!

The carriage was empty. The horse was going along peacefully, with the reins on its back, no doubt returning to the stable of some inn in the neighborhood, where it had been hired for the day. . .

Suppressing his inward rage, the chief detective merely said:

"The major must have jumped out during the few seconds when we lost sight of the carriage, at the top of the descent."

"We have only to beat the woods, chief, and we are sure. . ."

"To return empty-handed. The beggar is far away by this time. He's not one of those who are caught twice in one day. Oh, hang it all, hang it all!"

They went back to the young girl, whom they found in the company of Jacques Doudeville and apparently none the worse for her adventure. M. Lenormand introduced himself, offered to take her back home and at once questioned her about the English major, Parbury.

She expressed astonishment:

"He is neither English nor a major; and his name is not Parbury."

"Then what is his name?"

"Juan Ribeira. He is a Spaniard sent by his government to study the working of the French schools."

"As you please. His name and his nationality are of no importance. He is the man we are looking for. Have you known him long?"

"A fortnight or so. He had heard about a school which I have founded at Garches and he interested himself in my experiment to the extent of proposing to make me an annual grant, on the one condition that he might come from time to time to observe the progress of my pupils. I had not the right to refuse. . ."

"No, of course not; but you should have consulted your acquaintances. Is not Prince Sernine a friend of yours? He is a man of good counsel."

"Oh, I have the greatest confidence in him; but he is abroad at present."

"Did you not know his address?"

"No. And, besides, what could I have said to him? That gentleman behaved very well. It was not until to-day. . . But I don't know if. . ."

"I beg you, mademoiselle, speak frankly. You can have confidence in me also."

"Well, M. Ribeira came just now. He told me that he had been sent by a French lady who was paying a short visit to Bougival, that this lady had a little girl whose education she would like to entrust to me and that she wished me to come and see her without delay. The thing seemed quite natural. And, as this is a holiday and as M. Ribeira had hired a carriage which was waiting for him at the end of the road, I made no difficulty about accepting a seat in it."

"But what was his object, after all?"

She blushed and said:

"To carry me off, quite simply. He confessed it to me after half an hour. . ."

"Do you know nothing about him?"

"No."

"Does he live in Paris?"

"I suppose so."

"Has he ever written to you? Do you happen to have a few lines in his handwriting, anything which he left behind, that may serve us as a clue?"

"No clue at all. . . Oh, wait a minute. . . but I don't think that has any importance. . ."

"Speak, speak. . . please. . ."

"Well, two days ago, the gentleman asked permission to use my typewriting machine; and he typed out—with difficulty, for he evidently had no practice—a letter of which I saw the address by accident."

"What was the address?"

"He was writing to the *Journal* and he put about twenty stamps into the envelope."

"Yes. . . the agony-column, no doubt," said M. Lenormand.

"I have to-day's number with me, chief," said Gourel.

M. Lenormand unfolded the sheet and looked at the eighth page. Presently, he gave a start. He had read the following sentence, printed with the usual abbreviation:[1]

"To any person knowing Mr. Steinweg. Advertiser wishes to know if he is in Paris and his address. Reply through this column."

"Steinweg!" exclaimed Gourel. "But that's the very man whom Dieuzy is bringing to you!"

"Yes, yes," said M. Lenormand, to himself, "it's the man whose letter to Mr. Kesselbach I intercepted, the man who put Kesselbach on the track of Pierre Leduc. . . So they, too, want particulars about Pierre Leduc and his past? . . . They, too, are groping in the dark? . . ."

He rubbed his hands: Steinweg was at his disposal. In less than an hour, Steinweg would have spoken. In less than an hour, the murky veil which oppressed him and which made the Kesselbach case the most agonizing and the most impenetrable that he had ever had in hand: that veil would be torn asunder.

---

1. Personal advertisements in the French newspapers are charged by the line, not by the word; and consequently nearly every word is clipped down to two, three or four letters.—*Translator's Note.*

VI

M. Lenormand Succumbs

M. Lenormand was back in his room at the Prefecture of Police at six o'clock in the evening. He at once sent for Dieuzy:

"Is your man here?"

"Yes, chief."

"How far have you got with him?"

"Not very. He won't speak a word. I told him that, by a new regulation, foreigners were 'bliged to make a declaration at the Prefecture as to the object and the probable length of their stay in Paris; and I brought him here, to your secretary's office."

"I will question him."

But, at that moment, an office-messenger appeared:

"There's a lady asking to see you at once, chief."

"Have you her card?"

"Here, chief."

"Mrs. Kesselbach! Show her in."

He walked across the room to receive the young widow at the door and begged her to take a seat. She still wore the same disconsolate look, the same appearance of illness and that air of extreme lassitude which revealed the distress of her life.

She held out a copy of the *Journal* and pointed to the line in the agony-column which mentioned Steinweg:

"Old Steinweg was a friend of my husband's," she said, "and I have no doubt that he knows a good many things."

"Dieuzy," said M. Lenormand, "bring the person who is waiting. . . Your visit, madame, will not have been useless. I will only ask you, when this person enters, not to say a word."

The door opened. A man appeared, an old man with white whiskers meeting under his chin and a face furrowed with deep wrinkles, poorly clad and wearing the hunted look of those wretches who roam about the world in search of their daily pittance.

He stood on the threshold, blinking his eyelids, stared at M. Lenormand, seemed confused by the silence that greeted him on his entrance and turned his hat in his hands with embarrassment.

But, suddenly, he appeared stupefied, his eyes opened wide and he stammered:

"Mrs. . . Mrs. Kesselbach!"

He had seen the young widow. And, recovering his serenity, smiling, losing his shyness, he went up to her and in a strong German accent:

"Oh, I am glad! . . . At last! . . . I thought I should never. . . I was so surprised to receive no news down there. . . no telegrams. . . And how is our dear Rudolf Kesselbach?"

The lady staggered back, as though she had been struck in the face, and at once fell into a chair and began to sob.

"What's the matter? . . . Why, what's the matter?" asked Steinweg.

M. Lenormand interposed:

"I see, sir, that you know nothing about certain events that have taken place recently. Have you been long travelling?"

"Yes, three months. . . I had been up to the Rand. Then I went back to Capetown and wrote to Rudolf from there. But, on my way home by the East Coast route, I accepted some work at Port Said. Rudolf has had my letter, I suppose?"

"He is away. I will explain the reason of his absence. But, first, there is a point on which we should be glad of some information. It has to do with a person whom you knew and to whom you used to refer, in your intercourse with Mr. Kesselbach, by the name of Pierre Leduc."

"Pierre Leduc! What! Who told you?"

The old man was utterly taken aback.

He spluttered out again:

"Who told you? Who disclosed to you. . . ?"

"Mr. Kesselbach."

"Never! It was a secret which I confided to him and Rudolf keeps his secrets. . . especially this one. . ."

"Nevertheless, it is absolutely necessary that you should reply to our questions. We are at this moment engaged on an inquiry about Pierre Leduc which must come to a head without delay; and you alone can enlighten us, as Mr. Kesselbach is no longer here."

"Well, then," cried Steinweg, apparently making up his mind, "what do you want?"

"Do you know Pierre Leduc?"

"I have never seen him, but I have long been the possessor of a secret which concerns him. Through a number of incidents which I need not relate and thanks to a series of chances, I ended by acquiring the

MAURICE LEBLANC

certainty that the man in whose discovery I was interested was leading a dissolute life in Paris and that he was calling himself Pierre Leduc, which is not his real name."

"But does he know his real name himself?"

"I presume so."

"And you?"

"Yes, I know it."

"Well, tell it to us."

He hesitated; then, vehemently:

"I can't," he said. "No, I can't."

"But why not?"

"I have no right to. The whole secret lies there. When I revealed the secret to Rudolf, he attached so much importance to it that he gave me a large sum of money to purchase my silence and he promised me a fortune, a real fortune, on the day when he should succeed, first, in finding Pierre Leduc and, next, in turning the secret to account." He smiled bitterly. "The large sum of money is already lost. I came to see how my fortune was getting on."

"Mr. Kesselbach is dead," said the chief detective.

Steinweg gave a bound:

"Dead! Is it possible? No, it's a trap. Mrs. Kesselbach, is it true?"

She bowed her head.

He seemed crushed by this unexpected revelation; and, at the same time, it must have been infinitely painful to him, for he began to cry:

"My poor Rudolf, I knew him when he was a little boy. . . He used to come and play at my house at Augsburg. . . I was very fond of him." And, calling Mrs. Kesselbach to witness, "And he of me, was he not, Mrs. Kesselbach? He must have told you. . . His old Daddy Steinweg, he used to call me."

M. Lenormand went up to him and, in his clearest voice:

"Listen to me," he said. "Mr. Kesselbach died murdered. . . Come, be calm. . . exclamations are of no use. . . He died murdered, I say, and all the circumstances of the crime prove that the culprit knew about the scheme in question. Was there anything in the nature of that scheme that would enable you to guess. . . ?"

Steinweg stood dumfounded. He stammered:

"It was my fault. . . If I had not suggested the thing to him. . ."

Mrs. Kesselbach went up to him, entreating him:

"Do you think. . . have you any idea? . . . Oh, Steinweg, I implore you! . . ."

"I have no idea. . . I have not reflected," he muttered. "I must have time to reflect. . ."

"Cast about in Mr. Kesselbach's surroundings," said M. Lenormand. "Did nobody take part in your interviews at that time? Was there nobody in whom he himself could have confided?"

"No."

"Think well."

Both the others, Dolores and M. Lenormand, leant toward him, anxiously awaiting his answer.

"No," he said, "I don't see. . ."

"Think well," repeated the chief detective. "The murderer's Christian name and surname begin with an L and an M."

"An L," he echoed. "I don't see. . . an L. . . an M. . ."

"Yes, the initials are in gold on the corner of a cigarette-case belonging to the murderer."

"A cigarette-case?" asked Steinweg, making an effort of memory.

"A gun-metal case. . . and one of the compartments is divided into two spaces, the smaller for cigarette-papers, the other for tobacco. . ."

"Two spaces, two spaces," repeated Steinweg, whose thoughts seemed stimulated by that detail. "Couldn't you show it to me?"

"Here it is, or rather this is an exact reproduction," said M. Lenormand, giving him a cigarette-case.

"Eh! What!" said Steinweg, taking the case in his hands.

He looked at it with stupid eyes, examined it, turned it over in every direction and, suddenly, gave a cry, the cry of a man struck with a horrible idea. And he stood like that, livid, with trembling hands and wild, staring eyes.

"Speak, come, speak!" said M. Lenormand.

"Oh," he said, as though blinded with light, "now all is explained! . . ."

"Speak, speak!"

He walked across to the windows with a tottering step, then returned and, rushing up to the chief detective:

"Sir, sir. . . Rudolf's murderer. . . I'll tell you. . . Well. . ."

He stopped short.

"Well?"

There was a moment's pause. . . Was the name of the odious criminal about to echo through the great silence of the office, between those walls which had heard so many accusations, so many confessions? M. Lenormand felt as if he were on the brink of the unfathomable abyss and as if a voice were mounting, mounting up to him. . . A few seconds more and he would know. . .

"No," muttered Steinweg, "no, I can't. . ."

"What's that you say?" cried the chief detective, furiously.

"I say that I can't."

"But you have no right to be silent. The law requires you to speak."

"To-morrow. . . I will speak to-morrow. . . I must have time to reflect. . . To-morrow, I will tell you all that I know about Pierre Leduc. . . all that I suppose about that cigarette-case. . . To-morrow, I promise you. . ."

It was obvious that he possessed that sort of obstinacy against which the most energetic efforts are of no avail. M. Lenormand yielded:

"Very well. I give you until to-morrow, but I warn you that, if you do not speak to-morrow, I shall be obliged to go to the examining-magistrate."

He rang and, taking Inspector Dieuzy aside, said:

"Go with him to his hotel. . . and stay there. . . I'll send you two men. . . And mind you keep your eyes about you. Somebody may try to get hold of him."

The inspector went off with Steinweg; and M. Lenormand, returning to Mrs. Kesselbach, who had been violently affected by this scene, made his excuses.

"Pray accept all my regrets, madame. . . I can understand how upset you must feel. . ."

He questioned her as to the period at which Mr. Kesselbach renewed his relations with old Steinweg and as to the length of time for which those relations lasted. But she was so much worn-out that he did not insist.

"Am I to come back to-morrow?" she asked.

"No, it's not necessary. I will let you know all that Steinweg says. May I see you down to your carriage? These three flights are rather steep. . ."

He opened the door and stood back to let her pass. At that moment shouts were heard in the passage and people came running up, inspectors on duty, office-messengers, clerks:

"Chief! Chief!"

"What's the matter?"

"Dieuzy! . . ."

"But he's just left here. . ."

"He's been found on the staircase. . ."

"Not dead? . . ."

"No, stunned, fainting. . ."

"But the man. . . the man who was with him. . . old Steinweg?"

"He's disappeared. . ."

"Damn it!"

He rushed along the passage and down the stairs, where he found Dieuzy lying on the first-floor landing, surrounded by people who were attending to him.

He saw Gourel coming up again:

"Oh, Gourel, have you been downstairs? Did you come across anybody?"

"No, chief. . ."

But Dieuzy was recovering consciousness and, almost before he had opened his eyes, mumbled:

"Here, on the landing, the little door. . ."

"Oh, hang it, the door of Court 7!"[1] shouted the chief detective. "Didn't I say that it was to be kept locked? . . . It was certain that, sooner or later. . ." He seized the door-handle. "Oh, of course! The door is bolted on the other side now!"

The door was partly glazed. He smashed a pane with the butt-end of his revolver, drew the bolt and said to Gourel:

"Run through this way to the exit on the Place Dauphine. . ."

He went back to Dieuzy:

"Come, Dieuzy, tell me about it. How did you come to let yourself be put into this state?"

"A blow in the pit of the stomach, chief. . ."

"A blow? From that old chap? . . . Why, he can hardly stand on his legs! . . ."

"Not the old man, chief, but another, who was walking up and down the passage while Steinweg was with you and who followed us as though he were going out, too. . . When we got as far as this, he asked me for a

---

1. Since M. Lenormand left the detective service, two other criminals have escaped by the same door, after shaking off the officers in charge of them; the police kept both cases dark. Nevertheless, it would be very easy, if this communication is absolutely required, to remove the useless bolt on the other side of the door, which enables the fugitive to cut off all pursuit and to walk away quietly through the passage leading to Civil Court 7 and through the corridor of the Chief President's Court.

MAURICE LEBLANC

light. . . I looked for my matches. . . Then he caught me a punch in the stomach. . . I fell down, and, as I fell, I thought I saw him open that door and drag the old man with him. . ."

"Would you know him again?"

"Oh yes, chief. . . a powerful fellow, very dark-skinned. . . a southerner of sorts, that's certain. . ."

"Ribeira," snarled M. Lenormand. "Always Ribeira! . . . Ribeira, *alias* Parbury. . . Oh, the impudence of the scoundrel! He was afraid of what old Steinweg might say. . . and came to fetch him away under my very nose!" And, stamping his foot with anger, "But, dash it, how did he know that Steinweg was here, the blackguard! It's only four hours since I was chasing him in the Saint-Cucufa woods. . . and now he's here! . . . How did he know? . . . One would think he lived inside my skin! . . ."

He was seized with one of those fits of dreaming in which he seemed to hear nothing and see nothing. Mrs. Kesselbach, who passed at that moment, bowed without his replying.

But a sound of footsteps in the corridor roused him from his lethargy.

"At last, is that you, Gourel?"

"I've found out how it was, chief," said Gourel, panting for breath. "There were two of them. They went this way and out of the Place Dauphine. There was a motor-car waiting for them. There were two people inside: one was a man dressed in black, with a soft hat pulled over his eyes. . ."

"That's he," muttered M. Lenormand, "that's the murderer, the accomplice of Ribeira,—Parbury. And who was the other?"

"A woman, a woman without a hat, a servant-girl, it might be. . . And good-looking, I'm told, with red hair."

"Eh, what! You say she had red hair?"

"Yes."

M. Lenormand turned round with a bound, ran down the stairs four steps at a time, hurried across the courtyard and came out on the Quai des Orfèvres:

"Stop!" he shouted.

A victoria and pair was driving off. It was Mrs. Kesselbach's carriage. The coachman heard and pulled up his horses. M. Lenormand sprang on the step:

"I beg a thousand pardons, madame, but I cannot do without your assistance. I will ask you to let me go with you. . . But we must act swiftly. . . Gourel, where's my taxi?"

"I've sent it away, chief."

"Well then, get another, quick!" . . .

The men all ran in different directions. But ten minutes elapsed before one of them returned with a motor-cab. M. Lenormand was boiling with impatience. Mrs. Kesselbach, standing on the pavement, swayed from side to side, with her smelling-salts in her hand.

At last they were seated.

"Gourel, get up beside the driver and go straight to Garches."

"To my house?" asked Dolores, astounded.

He did not reply. He leant out of the window, waved his pass, explained who he was to the policeman regulating the traffic in the streets. At last, when they reached the Cours-la-Reine, he sat down again and said:

"I beseech you, madame, to give me plain answers to my questions. Did you see Mlle. Geneviève Ernemont just now, at about four o'clock?"

"Geneviève? . . . Yes. . . I was dressing to go out."

"Did she tell you of the advertisement about Steinweg in the *Journal*?"

"She did."

"And it was that which made you come to see me?"

"Yes."

"Were you alone during Mlle. Ernemont's visit?"

"Upon my word, I can't say. . . Why?"

"Recollect. Was one of your servants present?"

"Probably. . . as I was dressing. . ."

"What are their names?"

"Suzanne and Gertrude."

"One of them has red hair, has she not?"

"Yes, Gertrude."

"Have you known her long?"

"Her sister has always been with me. . . and so has Gertrude, for years. . . She is devotion and honesty personified. . ."

"In short, you will answer for her?"

"Oh, absolutely!"

"Very well. . . very well."

It was half-past seven and the daylight was beginning to wane when the taxi-cab reached the House of Retreat. Without troubling about his companion, the chief detective rushed into the porter's lodge:

"Mrs. Kesselbach's maid has just come in, has she not?"

"Whom do you mean, the maid?"

"Why, Gertrude, one of the two sisters."

"But Gertrude can't have been out, sir. We haven't seen her go out."

"Still some one has just come in."

"No, sir, we haven't opened the door to anybody since—let me see—six o'clock this evening."

"Is there no other way out than this gate?"

"No. The walls surround the estate on every side and they are very high. . ."

"Mrs. Kesselbach, we will go to your house, please."

They all three went. Mrs. Kesselbach, who had no key, rang. The door was answered by Suzanne, the other sister.

"Is Gertrude in?" asked Mrs. Kesselbach.

"Yes, ma'am, in her room."

"Send her down, please," said the chief detective.

After a moment, Gertrude came downstairs, looking very attractive and engaging in her white embroidered apron.

She had, in point of fact, a rather pretty face, crowned with red hair.

M. Lenormand looked at her for a long time without speaking, as though he were trying to read what lay behind those innocent eyes.

He asked her no questions. After a minute, he simply said:

"That will do, thank you. Come, Gourel."

He went out with the sergeant and, at once, as they followed the darkling paths of the garden, said:

"That's the one!"

"Do you think so, chief? She looked so placid!"

"Much too placid. Another would have been astonished, would have wanted to know why I sent for her. Not this one! Nothing but the concentrated effort of a face that is determined to smile at all costs. Only, I saw a drop of perspiration trickle from her temple along her ear."

"So that. . . ?

"So that everything becomes plain. Gertrude is in league with the two ruffians who are conspiring round the Kesselbach case, in order either to discover and carry out the famous scheme, or to capture the widow's millions. No doubt, the other sister is in the plot as well. At four o'clock, Gertrude, learning that I know of the advertisement in the *Journal*, takes advantage of her mistress's absence, hastens to Paris, finds Ribeira and the man in the soft hat and drags them off to the Palais, where Ribeira annexes Master Steinweg for his own purposes."

He reflected and concluded:

"All this proves, first, the importance which they attach to Steinweg and their fear of what he may reveal; secondly, that a regular plot is being hatched around Mrs. Kesselbach; thirdly, that I have no time to lose, for the plot is ripe."

"Very well," said Gourel, "but one thing remains unexplained. How was Gertrude able to leave the garden in which we now are and to enter it again, unknown to the porter and his wife?"

"Through a secret passage which the rogues must have contrived to make quite recently."

"And which would end, no doubt," said Gourel, "in Mrs. Kesselbach's house."

"Yes, perhaps," said M. Lenormand, "perhaps. . . But I have another idea."

They followed the circuit of the wall. It was a bright night; and, though their two forms were hardly distinguishable, they themselves could see enough to examine the stones of the walls and to convince themselves that no breach, however skilful, had been effected.

"A ladder, very likely?" suggested Gourel.

"No, because Gertrude is able to get out in broad daylight. A communication of the kind I mean can evidently not end out of doors. The entrance must be concealed by some building already in existence."

"There are only the four garden-houses," objected Gourel, "and they are all inhabited."

"I beg your pardon: the third, the Pavillon Hortense, is not inhabited."

"Who told you so?"

"The porter. Mrs. Kesselbach hired this house, which is near her own, for fear of the noise. Who knows but that, in so doing, she acted under Gertrude's influence?"

He walked round the house in question. The shutters were closed. He lifted the latch of the door, on the off-chance; the door opened.

"Ah, Gourel, I think we've struck it! Let's go in. Light your lantern. . . Oh, the hall. . . the drawing-room. . . the dining-room. . . that's no use. There must be a basement, as the kitchen is not on this floor."

"This way, chief. . . the kitchen-stairs are here."

They went down into a rather large kitchen, crammed full of wicker-work garden-chairs and flower-stands. Beside it was a wash-house, which also served as a cellar, and which presented the same untidy sight of objects piled one on the top of the other.

"What is that shiny thing down there, chief?"

Gourel stooped and picked up a brass pin with a head made of an imitation pearl.

"The pearl is quite bright still," said M. Lenormand, "which it would not be if it had been lying in this cellar long. Gertrude passed this way, Gourel."

Gourel began to demolish a great stack of empty wine-casks, writing desks and old rickety tables.

"You are wasting your time," said M. Lenormand. "If that is the way out, how would she have time first to move all those things and then to replace them behind her? Look, here is a shutter out of use, which has no valid reason for being fastened to the wall by that nail. Draw it back."

Gourel did so. Behind the shutter, the wall was hollowed out. By the light of the lantern they saw an underground passage running downwards.

"I was right," said M. Lenormand. "The communication is of recent date. You see, it's a piece of work hurriedly done, and not intended to last for any length of time. . . No masonry. . . Two planks placed cross-wise at intervals, with a joist to serve as a roof; and that is all. It will hold up as best it may: well enough, in any case, for the object in view, that is to say. . ."

"That is to say what, chief?"

"Well, first to allow of the going backwards and forwards between Gertrude and her accomplices. . . and then, one day, one day soon, of the kidnapping, or rather the total, miraculous, incomprehensible disappearance of Mrs. Kesselbach."

They proceeded cautiously, so as not to knock against certain beams which did not look over-safe. It at once became evident that the tunnel was much longer than the fifty yards at most that separated the house from the boundary of the garden. It must, therefore, end at a fair distance from the walls and beyond the road that skirted the property.

"We are not going in the direction of Villeneuve and the lake are we?" asked Gourel.

"Not at all, the other way about," declared M. Lenormand.

The tunnel descended with a gentle slope. There was a step, then another; and they veered toward the right. They at once knocked up against a door which was fitted into a rubble frame, carefully cemented. M. Lenormand pushed it and it opened.

"One second, Gourel," he said, stopping. "Let us think. . . It might perhaps be wiser to turn back."

"Why?"

"We must reflect that Ribeira will have foreseen the danger and presume that he has taken his precautions, in case the underground passage should be discovered. Now he knows that we are on his track. He knows that we are searching the garden. He no doubt saw us enter the house. How do I know that he is not at this moment laying a trap for us?"

"There are two of us, chief. . ."

"And suppose there were twenty of them?"

He looked in front of him. The tunnel sloped upward again, closed by another door, which was at five or six yards' distance.

"Let us go so far," he said. "Then we shall see."

He passed through, followed by Gourel, whom he told to leave the first door open, and walked to the other door, resolving within himself to go no farther. But this second door was shut; and though the lock seemed to work, he could not succeed in opening it.

"The door is bolted," he said. "Let us make no noise and go back. The more so as, outside, by remembering the position of the tunnel, we can fix the line along which to look for the other outlet."

They therefore retraced their steps to the first door, when Gourel, who was walking ahead, gave an exclamation of surprise:

"Why, it's closed! . . ."

"How is that? When I told you to leave it open!"

"I did leave it open, chief, but the door must have fallen back of its own weight."

"Impossible! We should have heard the sound."

"Then? . . ."

"Then. . . then. . . I don't know. . ." He went up to the door. "Let's see, . . . there's a key. . . does it turn? . . . Yes, it turns. But there seems to be a bolt on the other side."

"Who can have fastened it?"

"They, of course! Behind our backs! . . . Perhaps they have another tunnel that runs above this one, alongside of it. . . or else they were waiting in that empty house. . . In any case, we're caught in a trap. . ."

He grew angry with the lock, thrust his knife into the chink of the door, tried every means and then, in a moment of weariness, said:

"There's nothing to be done!"

"What, chief, nothing to be done? In that case, we're diddled!"

"I dare say!" said M. Lenormand. . .

They returned to the other door and came back again to the first. Both were solid, made of hard wood, strengthened with cross-beams. . . in short, indestructible.

"We should want a hatchet," said the chief of the detective-service, "or at the very least, a serious implement. . . a knife even, with which we might try to cut away the place where the bolt is most likely to be. . . and we have nothing. . ."

He was seized with a sudden fit of rage and flung himself upon the obstacle, as though he hoped to do away with it. Then, powerless, beaten, he said to Gourel:

"Listen, we'll look into this in an hour or two. . . I am tired out. . . I am going to sleep. . . Keep watch so long. . . and if they come and attack us. . ."

"Ah, if they come, we shall be saved, chief!" cried Gourel, who would have been relieved by a fight, however great the odds.

M. Lenormand lay down on the ground. In a minute, he was asleep.

When he woke up, he remained for some seconds undecided, not understanding; and he also asked himself what sort of pain it was that was tormenting him:

"Gourel!" he called. "Come! Gourel!"

Obtaining no reply, he pressed the spring of his lantern and saw Gourel lying beside him, sound asleep.

"What on earth can this pain be?" he thought. "Regular twitchings. . . Oh, why, of course, I am hungry, that's all. . . I'm starving! What can the time be?"

His watch marked twenty minutes past seven, but he remembered that he had not wound it up. Gourel's watch was not going either.

Gourel had awoke under the action of the same inward pangs, which made them think that the breakfast-hour must be long past and that they had already slept for a part of the day.

"My legs are quite numbed," said Gourel, "and my feet feel as if they were on ice. What a funny sensation!" He bent down to rub them and went on: "Why, it's not on ice that my feet were, but in water. . . Look, chief. . . there's a regular pool near the first door. . ."

"Soaked through," M. Lenormand replied. "We'll go back to the second door; you can dry yourself. . ."

"But what are you doing, chief?"

"Do you think I am going to allow myself to be buried alive in this vault? . . . Not if I know it; I haven't reached the age! . . . As the two doors are closed, let us try to pass through the walls."

One by one he loosened the stones that stood out at the height of his hand, in the hope of contriving another gallery that would slope upwards to the level of the soil. But the work was long and painful, for in this part of the tunnel, as he perceived the stones were cemented.

"Chief. . . chief," stammered Gourel, in a stifled voice. . .

"Well?"

"You are standing with your feet in the water."

"Nonsense! . . . Why, so I am! . . . Well, it can't be helped. . . I'll dry them in the sun. . ."

"But don't you see?"

"What?"

"Why, it's rising, chief, it's rising! . . ."

"What's rising?"

"The water! . . ."

M. Lenormand felt a shudder pass over his skin. He suddenly understood. It was not a casual trickling through, as he had thought, but a carefully-prepared flood, mechanically, irresistibly produced by some infernal system.

"Oh, the scoundrel!" he snarled. "If ever I lay hands on him. . . !"

"Yes, yes, chief, but we must first get out of this. . . And, as far as I can see. . ."

Gourel seemed completely prostrated, incapable of having an idea, of proposing a plan.

M. Lenormand knelt down on the ground and measured the rate at which the water was rising. A quarter, or thereabouts, of the first door was covered; and the water was half-way toward the second door.

"The progress is slow, but uninterrupted," he said "In a few hours it will be over our heads."

"But this is terrible, chief, it's horrible!" moaned Gourel.

"Oh, look here, don't come boring me with your lamentations, do you understand? Cry, if it amuses you, but don't let me hear you!"

"It's the hunger that weakens me, chief; my brain's going round."

"Bite your fist!"

As Gourel said, the position was terrible; and, if M. Lenormand had had less energy, he would have abandoned the vain struggle. What was to be done? It was no use hoping that Ribeira would have the charity to let them out. It was no use either hoping that the brothers Doudeville would rescue them, for the inspectors did not know of the existence of the tunnel. So no hope remained. . . no hope but that of an impossible miracle. . .

"Come, come," said M. Lenormand, "this is too silly. We're not going to kick the bucket here! Hang it all, there must be something! . . . Show me a light, Gourel."

Flattening himself against the second door, he examined it from top to bottom, in every corner. There was an enormous bolt on that side, just as there probably was on the other. He unfastened the screws with the blade of his knife; and the bolt came off in his hand.

"And what next?" asked Gourel.

"What next?" he echoed. "Well, this bolt is made of iron, pretty long and very nearly pointed. Certainly, it's not as good as a pick-axe, but it's better than nothing and. . ."

Without finishing his sentence, he drove the implement into the side-wall of the tunnel, a little in front of the pillar of masonry that supported the hinges of the door. As he expected, once he had passed the first layer of cement and stones, he found soft earth:

"To work!" he cried.

"Certainly, chief, but would you explain. . . ?"

"It's quite simple. I want to dig round this pillar a passage, three or four yards long, which will join the tunnel on the other side of the door and allow us to escape."

"But it will take us hours; and meanwhile, the water is rising."

"Show me a light, Gourel."

"In twenty minutes, or half an hour at most, it will have reached our feet."

"Show me a light, Gourel."

M. Lenormand's idea was correct and, with some little exertion, by pulling the earth, which he first loosened with his implement, towards him and making it fall into the tunnel, he was not long in digging a hole large enough to slip into.

"It's my turn, chief!" said Gourel.

"Aha, you're returning to life, I see! Well, fire away! . . . You have only to follow the shape of the pillar."

At that moment, the water was up to their ankles. Would they have time to complete the work begun?

It became more difficult as they went on, for the earth which they disturbed was in their way; and, lying flat on their stomachs in the passage, they were obliged at every instant to remove the rubbish that obstructed them.

After two hours, the work was perhaps three-quarters through, but the water now covered their legs. Another hour and it would reach the opening of the hole which they were digging. And that would mean the end!

Gourel, who was exhausted by the want of food and who was too stout to move with any freedom in that ever-narrower passage, had had to give up. He no longer stirred, trembling with anguish at feeling that icy water which was gradually swallowing him up.

As for M. Lenormand, he worked on with indefatigable ardor. It was a terrible job, this ants' work performed in the stifling darkness. His hands were bleeding. He was fainting with hunger. The insufficiency of the air hampered his breathing; and, from time to time, Gourel's sighs reminded him of the awful danger that threatened him at the bottom of his hole.

But nothing could discourage him, for now he again found opposite him those cemented stones which formed the side-wall of the gallery. It was the most difficult part, but the end was at hand.

"It's rising," cried Gourel, in a choking voice, "it's rising!"

M. Lenormand redoubled his efforts. Suddenly the stem of the bolt which he was using leapt out into space. The passage was dug. He had now only to widen it, which became much easier once he was able to shoot the materials in front of him.

Gourel, mad with terror, was howling like a dying beast. M. Lenormand paid no attention to him. Safety was at hand.

Nevertheless, he had a few seconds of anxiety when he perceived, by the sound of the materials falling, that this part of the tunnel was also under water, which was natural, as the door did not form a sufficiently tight-fitting barrier. But what did it matter! The outlet was free. One last effort. . . he passed through.

"Come, Gourel," he cried, returning to fetch his companion.

He dragged him, half dead, by the wrists:

"Come along, booby, pull yourself together! We are saved."

"Do you really think so, chief? . . . The water's up to our chests. . ."

"Never mind, as long as it's not over our mouths. . . Where's your lantern?"

"It's not working."

"No matter." He gave an exclamation of delight. "One step. . . two steps! . . . A staircase. . . At last!"

They emerged from the water, that accursed water which had almost swallowed them up; and it was a delicious sensation, a release that sent up their spirits.

"Stop!" said M. Lenormand.

His head had knocked against something. With arms outstretched, he pushed against the obstacle, which yielded at once. It was the flap of a trap-door; and, when this trap-door was opened, he found himself in a cellar into which the light of a fine night filtered through an air-hole.

He threw back the flap and climbed the last treads.

Then a veil fell over his eyes. Arms seized upon him. He felt himself as it were wrapped in a sheet, in a sort of sack, and then fastened with cords.

"Now for the other one!" said a voice.

The same operation must have been performed on Gourel; and the same voice said:

"If they call out, kill them at once. Have you your dagger?"

"Yes."

"Come along. You two, take this one. . . you two, that one. . . No light. . . and no noise either. . . It would be a serious matter. They've been searching the garden next door since this morning. . . there are ten or fifteen of them knocking about. . . Go back to the house, Gertrude, and, if the least thing happens, telephone to me in Paris."

M. Lenormand felt that he was being lifted up and carried and, a moment after, that he was in the open air.

"Bring the cart nearer," said a voice.

M. Lenormand heard the sound of a horse and cart.

He was laid out on some boards. Gourel was hoisted up beside him. The horse started at a trot.

The drive lasted about half an hour.

"Halt!" commanded the voice. "Lift them out. Here, driver, turn the cart so that the tail touches the parapet of the bridge. . . Good. . . No boats on the river? Sure? Then let's waste no time. . . Oh, have you fastened some stones to them?"

"Yes, paving-stones."

"Right away, then! Commend your soul to God, M. Lenormand, and pray for me, Parbury-Ribeira, better known by the name of Baron

Altenheim. Are you ready? All right? Well, here's wishing you a pleasant journey, M. Lenormand!"

M. Lenormand was placed on the parapet. Someone gave him a push. He felt himself falling into space and he still heard the voice chuckling:

"A pleasant journey!"

TEN SECONDS LATER IT WAS Sergeant Gourel's turn.

VII

PARBURY-RIBEIRA-ALTENHEIM

The girls were playing in the garden, under the supervision of Mlle. Charlotte, Geneviève's new assistant. Mme. Ernemont came out, distributed some cakes among them and then went back to the room which served as a drawing-room and parlor in one, sat down before a writing-desk and began to arrange her papers and account-books.

Suddenly, she felt the presence of a stranger in the room. She turned round in alarm:

"You!" she cried. "Where have you come from? How did you get in?"

"Hush!" said Prince Sernine. "Listen to me and do not let us waste a minute: Geneviève?"

"Calling on Mrs. Kesselbach."

"When will she be here?"

"Not before an hour."

"Then I will let the brothers Doudeville come. I have an appointment with them. How is Geneviève?"

"Very well."

"How often has she seen Pierre Leduc since I went away, ten days ago?"

"Three times; and she is to meet him to-day at Mrs. Kesselbach's, to whom she introduced him, as you said she must. Only, I may as well tell you that I don't think much of this Pierre Leduc of yours. Geneviève would do better to find some good fellow in her own class of life. For instance, there's the schoolmaster."

"You're mad! Geneviève marry a schoolmaster!"

"Oh, if you considered Geneviève's happiness first. . ."

"Shut up, Victoire. You're boring me with your cackle. I have no time to waste on sentiment. I'm playing a game of chess; and I move my men without troubling about what they think. When I have won the game, I will go into the question whether the knight, Pierre Leduc, and the queen, Geneviève, have a heart or not."

She interrupted him:

"Did you hear? A whistle. . ."

"It's the two Doudevilles. Go and bring them in; and then leave us."

As soon as the two brothers were in the room, he questioned them with his usual precision:

"I know what the newspapers have said about the disappearance of Lenormand and Gourel. Do you know any more?"

"No. The deputy-chief, M. Weber, has taken the case in hand. We have been searching the garden of the House of Retreat for the past week; and nobody is able to explain how they can have disappeared. The whole force is in a flutter. . . No one has ever seen the like. . . a chief of the detective-service disappearing, without leaving a trace behind him!"

"The two maids?"

"Gertrude has gone. She is being looked for."

"Her sister Suzanne?"

"M. Weber and M. Formerie have questioned her. There is nothing against her."

"Is that all you have to tell me?"

"Oh, no, there are other things, all the things which we did not tell the papers."

They then described the incidents that had marked M. Lenormand's last two days: the night visit of the two ruffians to Pierre Leduc's villa; next day, Ribeira's attempt to kidnap Geneviève and the chase through the Saint-Cucufa woods; old Steinweg's arrival, his examination at the detective-office in Mrs. Kesselbach's presence, his escape from the Palais. . .

"And no one knows these details except yourselves?"

"Dieuzy knows about the Steinweg incident: he told us of it."

"And they still trust you at the Prefecture of Police?"

"So much so that they employ us openly. M. Weber swears by us."

"Come," said the prince, "all is not lost. If M. Lenormand has committed an imprudence that has cost him his life, as I suppose he did, at any rate he performed some good work first; and we have only to continue it. The enemy has the start of us, but we will catch him up."

"It won't be an easy job, governor."

"Why not? It is only a matter of finding old Steinweg again, for the answer to the riddle is in his hands."

"Yes, but where has Ribeira got old Steinweg tucked away?"

"At his own place, of course."

"Then we should have to know where Ribeira hangs out."

"Well, of course!"

He dismissed them and went to the House of Retreat. Motor-cars were awaiting outside the door and two men were walking up and down, as though mounting guard.

In the garden, near Mrs. Kesselbach's house, he saw Geneviève sitting on a bench with Pierre Leduc and a thick-set gentleman wearing a single eye-glass. The three were talking and none of them saw him. But several people came out of the house: M. Formerie, M. Weber, a magistrate's clerk, and two inspectors. Geneviève went indoors and the gentleman with the eye-glass went up and spoke to the examining-magistrate and the deputy-chief of the detective-service and walked away with them slowly.

Sernine came beside the bench where Pierre Leduc was sitting and whispered:

"Don't move, Pierre Leduc; it's I."

"You! . . . you! . . ."

It was the third time that the young man saw Sernine since the awful night at Versailles; and each time it upset him.

"Tell me. . . who is the fellow with the eye-glass?"

Pierre Leduc turned pale and jabbered. Sernine pinched his arm:

"Answer me, confound it! Who is he?"

"Baron Altenheim."

"Where does he come from?"

"He was a friend of Mr. Kesselbach's. He arrived from Austria, six days ago, and placed himself at Mrs. Kesselbach's disposal."

The police authorities had, meanwhile, gone out of the garden; Baron Altenheim also.

The prince rose and, turning towards the Pavillon de l'Impératrice, continued:

"Has the baron asked you many questions?"

"Yes, a great many. He is interested in my case. He wants to help me find my family. He appealed to my childhood memories."

"And what did you say?"

"Nothing, because I know nothing. What memories have I? You put me in another's place and I don't even know who that other is."

"No more do I!" chuckled the prince. "And that's just what makes your case so quaint."

"Oh, it's all very well for you to laugh. . . you're always laughing! . . . But I'm beginning to have enough of it. . . I'm mixed up in a heap of nasty matters. . . to say nothing of the danger which I run in pretending to be somebody that I am not."

"What do you mean. . . that you are not? You're quite as much a duke as I am a prince. . . perhaps even more so. . . Besides, if you're not a duke, hurry up and become one, hang it all! Geneviève can't marry any one but a duke! Look at her: isn't she worth selling your soul for?"

He did not even look at Leduc, not caring what he thought. They had reached the house by this time; and Geneviève appeared at the foot of the steps, comely and smiling:

"So you have returned?" she said to the prince. "Ah, that's a good thing! I am so glad. . . Do you want to see Dolores?"

After a moment, she showed him into Mrs. Kesselbach's room. The prince was taken aback. Dolores was paler still and thinner than on the day when he saw her last. Lying on a sofa, wrapped up in white stuffs, she looked like one of those sick people who have ceased to struggle against death. As for her, she had ceased to struggle against life, against the fate that was overwhelming her with its blows.

Sernine gazed at her with deep pity and with an emotion which he did not strive to conceal. She thanked him for the sympathy which he showed her. She also spoke of Baron Altenheim, in friendly terms.

"Did you know him before?" he asked.

"Yes, by name, and through his intimacy with my husband."

"I have met an Altenheim who lives in the Rue de Rivoli. Do you think it's the same?"

"Oh, no, this one lives in. . . As a matter of fact, I don't quite know; he gave me his address, but I can't say that I remember it. . ."

After a few minutes' conversation, Sernine took his leave. Geneviève was waiting for him in the hall:

"I want to speak to you," she said eagerly, "on a serious matter. . . Did you see him?"

"Whom?"

"Baron Altenheim. . . But that's not his name. . . or, at least, he has another. . . I recognized him. . . he does not know it."

She dragged him out of doors and walked on in great excitement.

"Calm yourself, Geneviève. . ."

"He's the man who tried to carry me off. . . But for that poor M. Lenormand, I should have been done for. . . Come, you must know, for you know everything. . ."

"Then his real name is. . ."

"Ribeira."

"Are you sure?"

"It was no use his changing his appearance, his accent, his manner: I knew him at once, by the horror with which he inspires me. But I said nothing. . . until you returned."

"You said nothing to Mrs. Kesselbach either?"

"No. She seemed so happy at meeting a friend of her husband's. But you will speak to her about it, will you not? You will protect her. . . I don't know what he is preparing against her, against myself. . . Now that M. Lenormand is no longer there, he has nothing to fear, he does as he pleases. Who can unmask him?"

"I can. I will be responsible for everything. But not a word to anybody."

They had reached the porter's lodge. The gate was opened. The prince said:

"Good-bye, Geneviève, and be quite easy in your mind. I am there."

He shut the gate, turned round and gave a slight start. Opposite him stood the man with the eye-glass, Baron Altenheim, with his head held well up, his broad shoulders, his powerful frame.

They looked at each other for two or three seconds, in silence. The baron smiled.

Then the baron said:

"I was waiting for you, Lupin."

For all his self-mastery, Sernine felt a thrill pass over him. He had come to unmask his adversary; and his adversary had unmasked him at the first onset. And, at the same time, the adversary was accepting the contest boldly, brazenly, as though he felt sure of victory. It was a swaggering thing to do and gave evidence of no small amount of pluck.

The two men, violently hostile one to the other, took each other's measure with their eyes.

"And what then?" asked Sernine.

"What then? Don't you think we have occasion for a meeting?"

"Why?"

"I want to talk to you."

"What day will suit you?"

"To-morrow. Let us lunch together at a restaurant."

"Why not at your place?"

"You don't know my address."

"Yes, I do."

With a swift movement, the prince pulled out a newspaper protruding from Altenheim's pocket, a paper still in its addressed wrapper, and said:

"No. 29, Villa Dupont."

"Well played!" said the other. "Then we'll say, to-morrow, at my place."

"To-morrow, at your place. At what time?"

"One o'clock."

"I shall be there. Good-bye."

They were about to walk away. Altenheim stopped:

"Oh, one word more, prince. Bring a weapon with you."

"Why?"

"I keep four men-servants and you will be alone."

"I have my fists," said Sernine. "We shall be on even terms."

He turned his back on him and then, calling him back:

"Oh, one word more, baron. Engage four more servants."

"Why?"

"I have thought it over. I shall bring my whip."

AT ONE O'CLOCK THE NEXT day, precisely, a horseman rode through the gate of the so-called Villa Dupont, a peaceful, countrified private road, the only entrance to which is in the Rue Pergolèse, close to the Avenue du Bois.

It is lined with gardens and handsome private houses; and, right at the end, it is closed by a sort of little park containing a large old house, behind which runs the Paris circular railway. It was here, at No. 29, that Baron Altenheim lived.

Sernine flung the reins of his horse to a groom whom he had sent on ahead and said:

"Bring him back at half-past two."

He rang the bell. The garden-gate opened and he walked to the front-door steps, where he was awaited by two tall men in livery who ushered him into an immense, cold, stone hall, devoid of any ornament. The door closed behind him with a heavy thud; and, great and indomitable as his courage was, he nevertheless underwent an unpleasant sensation at feeling himself alone, surrounded by enemies, in that isolated prison.

"Say Prince Sernine."

The drawing-room was near and he was shown straight in.

"Ah, there you are, my dear prince!" said the baron, coming toward him. "Well, will you believe—Dominique, lunch in twenty minutes. Until then, don't let us be interrupted—will you believe, my dear prince, that I hardly expected to see you?"

"Oh, really? Why?"

"Well, your declaration of war, this morning, is so plain that an interview becomes superfluous."

"My declaration of war?"

The baron unfolded a copy of the *Grand Journal* and pointed to a paragraph which ran as follows:

"We are authoritatively informed that M. Lenormand's disappearance has roused Arsène Lupin into taking action. After a brief enquiry and following on his proposal to clear up the Kesselbach case, Arsène Lupin has decided that he will find M. Lenormand, alive or dead, and that he will deliver the author or authors of that heinous series of crimes to justice."

"This authoritative pronouncement comes from you, my dear prince, of course?"

"Yes, it comes from me."

"Therefore, I was right: it means war."

"Yes."

Altenheim gave Sernine a chair, sat down himself and said, in a conciliatory tone:

"Well, no, I cannot allow that. It is impossible that two men like ourselves should fight and injure each other. We have only to come to an explanation, to seek the means: you and I were made to understand each other."

"I think, on the contrary, that two men like ourselves are not made to understand each other."

The baron suppressed a movement of impatience and continued:

"Listen to me, Lupin. . . By the way, do you mind my calling you Lupin?"

"What shall I call you? Altenheim, Ribeira, or Parbury?"

"Oho! I see that you are even better posted than I thought! . . . Hang it all, but you're jolly smart! . . . All the more reason why we should agree." And, bending toward him, "Listen, Lupin, and ponder my words well; I have weighed them carefully, every one. Look here. . . We two are evenly matched. . . Does that make you smile? You are wrong: it may be that you possess resources which I do not; but I have others of which you know nothing. Moreover, as you are aware, I have few scruples, some skill and a capacity for changing my personality which an expert like yourself ought to appreciate. In short, the two adversaries are each as good as the other. But one question remains unanswered: why are we adversaries? We are pursuing the same object, you will say? And what then? Do you know what will come of our rivalry? Each of us will paralyze the efforts and destroy the work of the other; and we shall both miss our aim! And for whose benefit? Some Lenormand or other, a third rogue! . . . It's really too silly."

"It's really too silly, as you say," Sernine admitted. "But there is a remedy."

"What is that?"

"For you to withdraw."

"Don't chaff. I am serious. The proposal which I am going to make is not one to be rejected without examination. Here it is, in two words: let's be partners!"

"I say!"

"Of course, each of us will continue free where his own affairs are concerned. But, for the business in question, let us combine our efforts. Does that suit you? Hand in hand and share alike."

"What do you bring?"

"I?"

"Yes, you know what I'm worth; I've delivered my proofs. In the alliance which you are proposing, you know the figure, so to speak of my marriage-portion. What's yours?"

"Steinweg."

"That's not much."

"It's immense. Through Steinweg, we learn the truth about Pierre Leduc. Through Steinweg, we get to know what the famous Kesselbach plan is all about."

Sernine burst out laughing:

"And you need me for that?"

"I don't understand."

"Come, old chap, your offer is childish. You have Steinweg in your hands. If you wish for my collaboration, it is because you have not succeeded in making him speak. But for that fact, you would do without my services."

"Well, what of it?"

"I refuse."

The two men stood up to each other once more, violent and implacable.

"I refuse," said Sernine. "Lupin requires nobody, in order to act. I am one of those who walk alone. If you were my equal, as you pretend, the idea of a partnership would never have entered your head. The man who has the stature of a leader commands. Union implies obedience. I do not obey."

"You refuse? You refuse?" repeated Altenheim, turning pale under the insult.

"All that I can do for you, old chap, is to offer you a place in my band. You'll be a private soldier, to begin with. Under my orders, you shall see how a general wins a battle. . . and how he pockets the booty, by himself and for himself. Does that suit you. . . Tommy?"

Altenheim was beside himself with fury. He gnashed his teeth:

"You are making a mistake, Lupin," he mumbled, "you are making a mistake. . . I don't want anybody either; and this business gives me no more difficulty than plenty of others which I have pulled off. . . What I said was said in order to effect our object more quickly and without inconveniencing each other."

"You're not inconveniencing me," said Lupin, scornfully.

"Look here! If we don't combine, only one of us will succeed."

"That's good enough for me."

"And he will only succeed by passing over the other's body. Are you prepared for that sort of duel, Lupin? A duel to the death, do you understand? . . . The knife is a method which you despise; but suppose you received one, Lupin, right in the throat?"

"Aha! So, when all is said, that's what you propose?"

"No, I am not very fond of shedding blood. . . Look at my fists: I strike. . . and my man falls. . . I have special blows of my own. . . But *the other one* kills. . . remember. . . the little wound in the throat. . . Ah, Lupin, beware of him, beware of that one! . . . He is terrible, he is implacable. . . Nothing stops him."

He spoke these words in a low voice and with such excitement that Sernine shuddered at the hideous thought of the unknown murderer:

"Baron," he sneered, "one would think you were afraid of your accomplice!"

"I am afraid for the others, for those who bar our road, for you, Lupin. Accept, or you are lost. I shall act myself, if necessary. The goal is too near. . . I have my hand on it. . . Get out of my way, Lupin!"

He was all energy and exasperated will. He spoke forcibly and so brutally that he seemed ready to strike his enemy then and there.

Sernine shrugged his shoulders:

"Lord, how hungry I am!" he said, yawning. "What a time to lunch at!"

The door opened.

"Lunch is served, sir," said the butler.

"Ah, that's good hearing!"

In the doorway, Altenheim caught Sernine by the arm and, disregarding the servant's presence:

"If you take my advice. . . accept. This is a serious moment in your life. . . and you will do better, I swear to you, you will do better. . . to accept. . ."

"Caviare!" cried Sernine. "Now, that's too sweet of you. . . You remembered that you were entertaining a Russian prince!"

They sat down facing each other, with the baron's greyhound, a large animal with long, silver hair, between them.

"Let me introduce Sirius, my most faithful friend."

"A fellow-countryman," said Sernine. "I shall never forget the one which the Tsar was good enough to give me when I had the honor to save his life."

"Ah, you had that honor. . . a terrorist conspiracy, no doubt?"

"Yes, a conspiracy got up by myself. You must know, this dog—its name, by the way, was Sebastopol. . ."

The lunch continued merrily. Altenheim had recovered his good humor and the two men vied with each other in wit and politeness. Sernine told anecdotes which the baron capped with others; and it was a succession of stories of hunting, sport and travel, in which the oldest names in Europe were constantly cropping up: Spanish grandees, English lords, Hungarian magyars, Austrian archdukes.

"Ah," said Sernine, "what a fine profession is ours! It brings us into touch with all the best people. Here, Sirius, a bit of this truffled chicken!"

The dog did not take his eyes off him, and snapped at everything that Sernine gave it.

"A glass of Chambertin, prince?"

"With pleasure, baron."

"I can recommend it. It comes from King Leopold's cellar."

"A present?"

"Yes, a present I made myself."

"It's delicious. . . What a bouquet! . . . With this *pâté de foie gras*, it's simply wonderful! . . . I must congratulate you, baron; you have a first-rate chef."

MAURICE LEBLANC

"My chef is a woman-cook, prince. I bribed her with untold gold to leave Levraud, the socialist deputy. I say, try this hot chocolate-ice; and let me call your special attention to the little dry cakes that go with it. They're an invention of genius, those cakes."

"The shape is charming, in any case," said Sernine, helping himself. "If they taste as good as they look. . . Here, Sirius, you're sure to like this. Locusta herself could not have done better."

He took one of the cakes and gave it to the dog. Sirius swallowed it at a gulp, stood motionless for two or three seconds, as though dazed, then turned in a circle and fell to the floor dead.

Sernine started back from his chair, lest one of the footmen should fall upon him unawares. Then he burst out laughing:

"Look here, baron, next time you want to poison one of your friends, try to steady your voice and to keep your hands from shaking. . . Otherwise, people suspect you. . . But I thought you disliked murder?"

"With the knife, yes," said Altenheim, quite unperturbed. "But I have always had a wish to poison some one. I wanted to see what it was like."

"By Jove, old chap, you choose your subjects well! A Russian prince!"

He walked up to Altenheim and, in a confidential tone, said:

"Do you know what would have happened if you had succeeded, that is to say, if my friends had not seen me return at three o'clock at the latest? Well, at half-past three the prefect of police would have known exactly all that there was to know about the so-called Baron Altenheim; and the said baron would have been copped before the day was out and clapped into jail."

"Pooh!" said Altenheim. "Prison one escapes from. . . whereas one does not come back from the kingdom where I was sending you."

"True, but you would have to send me there first; and that's not so easy."

"I only wanted a mouthful of one of those cakes."

"Are you quite sure?"

"Try."

"One thing's certain, my lad: you haven't the stuff yet which great adventurers are made of; and I doubt if you'll ever have it, considering the sort of traps you lay for me. A man who thinks himself worthy of leading the life which you and I have the honor to lead must also be fit to lead it, and, for that, must be prepared for every eventuality: he must even be prepared not to die if some ragamuffin or other tries to poison him. . . An undaunted soul in an unassailable body: that is the ideal which he must set before himself. . . and attain. Try away, old chap. As for me, I am undaunted and unassailable. Remember King Mithridates!"

He went back to his chair:

"Let's finish our lunch. But as I like proving the virtues to which I lay claim, and as, on the other hand, I don't want to hurt your cook's feelings, just pass me that plate of cakes."

He took one of them, broke it in two and held out one half to the baron:

"Eat that!"

The other gave a movement of recoil.

"Funk!" said Sernine.

And, before the wondering eyes of the baron and his satellites, he began to eat the first and then the second half of the cake, quietly, conscientiously, as a man eats a dainty of which he would hate to miss the smallest morsel.

THEY MET AGAIN.

That same evening, Prince Sernine invited Baron Altenheim to dinner at the Cabaret Vatel, with a party consisting of a poet, a musician, a financier and two pretty actresses, members of the Théâtre Français.

The next day, they lunched together in the Bois and, at night, they met at the Opéra.

They saw each other every day for a week. One would have thought that they could not do without each other and that they were united by a great friendship, built up of mutual confidence, sympathy and esteem.

They had a capital time, drinking good wine, smoking excellent cigars, and laughing like two madmen.

In reality, they were watching each other fiercely. Mortal enemies, separated by a merciless hatred, each feeling sure of winning and longing for victory with an unbridled will, they waited for the propitious moment: Altenheim to do away with Sernine; and Sernine to hurl Altenheim into the pit which he was digging for him.

Each knew that the catastrophe could not be long delayed. One or other of them must meet with his doom; and it was a question of hours, or, at most, of days.

It was an exciting tragedy, and one of which a man like Sernine was bound to relish the strange and powerful zest. To know your adversary

MAURICE LEBLANC

and to live by his side; to feel that death is waiting for you at the least false step, at the least act of thoughtlessness: what a joy, what a delight!

One evening, they were alone together in the garden of the Rue Cambon Club, to which Altenheim also belonged. It was the hour before dusk, in the month of June, at which men begin to dine before the members come in for the evening's card-play. They were strolling round a little lawn, along which ran a wall lined with shrubs. Beyond the shrubs was a small door. Suddenly, while Altenheim was speaking, Sernine received the impression that his voice became less steady, that it was almost trembling. He watched him out of the corner of his eye. Altenheim had his hand in the pocket of his jacket; and Sernine *saw* that hand, through the cloth, clutch the handle of a dagger, hesitating, wavering, resolute and weak by turns.

O exquisite moment! Was he going to strike? Which would gain the day: the timid instinct that dare not, or the conscious will, intense upon the act of killing?

His chest flung out, his arms behind his back, Sernine waited, with alternate thrills of pleasure and of pain. The baron had ceased talking; and they now walked on in silence, side by side.

"Well, why don't you strike?" cried the prince, impatiently. He had stopped and, turning to his companion: "Strike!" he said. "This is the time or never. There is no one to see you. You can slip out through that little door; the key happens to be hanging on the wall; and good-bye, baron. . . unseen and unknown! . . . But, of course, all this was arranged. . . you brought me here. . . And you're hesitating! Why on earth don't you strike?"

He looked him straight in the eyes. The other was livid, quivering with impotent strength.

"You milksop!" Sernine sneered. "I shall never make anything of you. Shall I tell you the truth? Well, you're afraid of me. Yes, old chap, you never feel quite sure what may happen to you when you're face to face with me. You want to act, whereas it's my acts, my possible acts that govern the situation. No, it's quite clear that you're not the man yet to put out my star!"

He had not finished speaking when he felt himself seized round the throat and dragged backward. Some one hiding in the shrubbery, near the little door, had caught him by the head. He saw a hand raised, armed with a knife with a gleaming blade. The hand fell; the point of the knife caught him right in the throat.

At the same moment Altenheim sprang upon him to finish him off; and they rolled over into the flower-borders. It was a matter of twenty or thirty seconds at most. Powerful and experienced wrestler as he was, Altenheim yielded almost immediately, uttering a cry of pain. Sernine rose and ran to the little door, which had just closed upon a dark form. It was too late. He heard the key turn in the lock. He was unable to open it.

"Ah, you scoundrel!" he said. "The day on which I catch you will be the day on which I shed my first blood! That I swear to God! . . ."

He went back, stooped and picked up the pieces of the knife, which had broken as it struck him.

Altenheim was beginning to move. Sernine asked:

"Well, baron, feeling better? You didn't know that blow, eh? It's what I call the direct blow in the solar plexus; that is to say, it snuffs out your vital sun like a candle. It's clean, quick, painless. . . and infallible. Whereas a blow with a dagger. . . ? Pooh! A man has only to wear a little steel-wove gorget, as I do, and he can set the whole world at defiance, especially your little pal in black, seeing that he always strikes at the throat, the silly monster! . . . Here, look at his favorite plaything. . . smashed to atoms!"

He offered him his hand:

"Come, get up, baron. You shall dine with me. And do please remember the secret of my superiority: an undaunted soul in an unassailable body."

He went back to the club rooms, reserved a table for two, sat down on a sofa, and while waiting for dinner, soliloquized, under his breath:

"It's certainly an amusing game, but it's becoming dangerous. I must get it over. . . otherwise those beggars will send me to Paradise earlier than I want to go. The nuisance is that I can't do anything before I find old Steinweg, for, when all is said, old Steinweg is the only interesting factor in the whole business; and my one reason for sticking to the baron is that I keep on hoping to pick up some clue or other. What the devil have they done with him? Altenheim is in daily communication with him: that is beyond a doubt; it is equally beyond a doubt that he is doing his utmost to drag out of him what he knows about the Kesselbach scheme. But where does he see him? Where has he got him shut up? With friends? In his own house, at 29, Villa Dupont?"

He reflected for some time, then lit a cigarette, took three puffs at it and threw it away. This was evidently a signal, for two young men came and sat down beside him. He did not seem to know them, but he conversed with them by stealth. It was the brothers Doudeville, got up that day like men of fashion.

"What is it, governor?"

"Take six of our men, go to 29, Villa Dupont and make your way in."

"The devil! How?"

"In the name of the law. Are you not detective-inspectors? A search. . ."

"But we haven't the right. . ."

"Take it."

"And the servants? If they resist?"

"There are only four of them."

"If they call out?"

"They won't call out."

"If Altenheim returns?"

"He won't return before ten o'clock. I'll see to it. That gives you two hours and a half, which is more than you require to explore the house from top to bottom. If you find old Steinweg, come and tell me."

Baron Altenheim came up. Sernine went to meet him:

"Let's have some dinner, shall we? That little incident in the garden has made me feel hungry. By the way, my dear baron, I have a few bits of advice to give you. . ."

They sat down to table.

After dinner, Sernine suggested a game of billiards. Altenheim accepted. When the game was over, they went to the baccarat-room. The croupier was just shouting:

"There are fifty louis in the bank. Any bids?"

"A hundred louis," said Altenheim.

Sernine looked at his watch. Ten o'clock. The Doudevilles had not returned. The search, therefore, had been fruitless.

"Banco," he said.

Altenheim sat down and dealt the cards:

"I give."

"No."

"Seven."

"Six. I lose," said Sernine. "Shall I double the stakes?"

"Very well," said the baron.

He dealt out the cards.

"Eight," said Sernine.

"Nine," said the baron, laying his cards down.

Sernine turned on his heels, muttering:

"That costs me three hundred louis, but I don't mind; it fixes him here."

Ten minutes later his motor set him down in front of 29, Villa Dupont; and he found the Doudevilles and their men collected in the hall:

"Have you hunted out the old boy?"

"No."

"Dash it! But he must be somewhere or other. Where are the four servants?"

"Over there, in the pantry, tied up, with the cook as well."

"Good. I would as soon they did not see me. Go all you others. Jean, stay outside and keep watch: Jacques, show me over the house."

He quickly ran through the cellar, the ground floor, the first and second floors and the attic. He practically stopped nowhere, knowing that he would not discover in a few minutes what his men had not been able to discover in three hours. But he carefully noted the shape and the arrangement of the rooms, and looked for some little detail which would put him on the scent.

When he had finished, he returned to a bedroom which Doudeville had told him was Altenheim's, and examined it attentively:

"This will do," he said, raising a curtain that concealed a dark closet, full of clothes. "From here I can see the whole of the room."

"But if the baron searches the house?"

"Why should he?"

"He will know that we have been here, through his servants."

"Yes, but he will never dream that one of us is putting up here for the night. He will think that the attempt failed, that is all, so I shall stay."

"And how will you get out?"

"Oh, that's asking me more than I can tell you! The great thing was to get in. Here I am, and here I stay. Go, Doudeville, and shut the doors as you go."

He sat down on a little box at the back of the cupboard. Four rows of hanging clothes protected him. Except in the case of a close investigation, he was evidently quite safe.

Two hours passed. He heard the dull sound of a horse's hoofs and the tinkling of a collar-bell. A carriage stopped, the front door slammed and almost immediately he heard voices, exclamations, a regular outcry that increased, probably, as each of the prisoners was released from his gag.

MAURICE LEBLANC

"They are explaining the thing to him," he thought. "The baron must be in a tearing rage. He now understands the reason for my conduct at the club to-night and sees that I have dished him nicely. . . Dished? That depends. . . After all, I haven't got Steinweg yet. . . That is the first thing that he will want to know: did they get Steinweg? To find this out, he will go straight to the hiding-place. If he goes up, it means that the hiding-place is upstairs. If he goes down, then it is in the basement."

He listened. The sound of voices continued in the rooms on the ground floor, but it did not seem as if any one were moving. Altenheim must be cross-examining his confederates. It was half an hour before Sernine heard steps mounting the staircase.

"Then it must be upstairs," he said to himself. "But why did they wait so long?"

"Go to bed, all of you," said Altenheim's voice.

The baron entered his room with one of his men and shut the door:

"And I am going to bed, too, Dominique. We should be no further if we sat arguing all night."

"My opinion is," said the other, "that he came to fetch Steinweg."

"That is my opinion, too; and that's why I'm really enjoying myself, seeing that Steinweg isn't here."

"But where is he, after all? What have you done with him?"

"That's my secret; and you know I keep my secrets to myself. All that I can tell you is that he is in safe keeping, and that he won't get out before he has spoken."

"So the prince is sold?"

"Sold is the word. And he has had to fork out to attain this fine result! Oh, I've had a good time to-night! . . . Poor prince!"

"For all that," said the other, "we shall have to get rid of him."

"Make your mind easy, old man; that won't take long. Before a week's out you shall have a present of a pocket-book made out of Lupin-skin. But let me go to bed now. I'm dropping with sleep."

There was a sound of the door closing. Then Sernine heard the baron push the bolt, empty his pockets, wind up his watch and undress. He seemed in a gay mood, whistling and singing, and even talking aloud:

"Yes, a Lupin-skin pocket-book. . . in less than a week. . . in less than four days! . . . Otherwise he'll eat us up, the bully! . . . No matter, he missed his shot to-night. . . His calculation was right enough, though. . . Steinweg was bound to be here. . . Only, there you are! . . ."

He got into bed and at once switched off the light.

Sernine had come forward as far as the dividing curtain, which he now lifted slightly, and he saw the vague light of the night filtering through the windows, leaving the bed in profound darkness.

He hesitated. Should he leap out upon the baron, take him by the throat and obtain from him by force and threats what he had not been able to obtain by craft? Absurd? Altenheim would never allow himself to be intimidated.

"I say, he's snoring now," muttered Sernine. "Well, I'm off. At the worst, I shall have wasted a night."

He did not go. He felt that it would be impossible for him to go, that he must wait, that chance might yet serve his turn.

With infinite precautions, he took four or five coats and great-coats from their hooks, laid them on the floor, made himself comfortable and, with his back to the wall, went peacefully to sleep.

The baron was not an early riser. A clock outside was striking nine when he got out of bed and rang for his servant.

He read the letters which his man brought him, splashed about in his tub, dressed without saying a word and sat down to his table to write, while Dominique was carefully hanging up the clothes of the previous day in the cupboard and Sernine asking himself, with his fists ready to strike:

"I wonder if I shall have to stave in this fellow's solar plexus?"

At ten o'clock the baron was ready:

"Leave me," said he to the servant.

"There's just this waistcoat. . ."

"Leave me, I say. Come back when I ring. . . not before."

He shut the door himself, like a man who does not trust others, went to a table on which a telephone was standing and took down the receiver:

"Hullo! . . . Put me on to Garches, please, mademoiselle. . . Very well, I'll wait till you ring me up. . ."

He sat down to the instrument.

The telephone-bell rang.

"Hullo!" said Altenheim. "Is that Garches? . . . Yes, that's right. . . Give me number 38, please, mademoiselle. . ."

A few seconds later, in a lower voice, as low and as distinct as he could make it, he began:

"Are you 38? . . . It's I speaking; no useless words. . . Yesterday? . . . Yes, you missed him in the garden. . . Another time, of course; but the thing's becoming urgent. . . He had the house searched last night. . . I'll tell you about it. . . Found nothing, of course. . . What? . . . Hullo! . . . No, old Steinweg refuses to speak. . . Threats, promises, nothing's any good. . . Hullo! . . . Yes, of course, he sees that we can do nothing. . . We know just a part of the Kesselbach scheme and of the story of Pierre Leduc. . . He's the only one who has the answer to the riddle. . . Oh, he'll speak all right; that I'll answer for. . . this very night, too. . . If not. . . What? . . . Well, what can we do? Anything rather than let him escape! Do you want the prince to bag him from us? As for the prince, we shall have to cook his goose in three days from now. . . You have an idea? . . . Yes, that's a good idea. . . Oh, oh, excellent! I'll see to it. . . When shall we meet? Will Tuesday do? Right you are. I'll come on Tuesday. . . at two o'clock. . . Good-bye."

He replaced the receiver and went out.

A few hours later, while the servants were at lunch, Prince Sernine strolled quietly out of the Villa Dupont, feeling rather faint in the head and weak in the knees, and, while making for the nearest restaurant, he thus summed up the situation:

"So, on Tuesday next, Altenheim and the Palace Hotel murderer have an appointment at Garches, in a house with the telephone number 38. On Tuesday, therefore, I shall hand over the two criminals to the police and set M. Lenormand at liberty. In the evening, it will be old Steinweg's turn; and I shall learn, at last, whether Pierre Leduc is the son of a pork-butcher or not and whether he will make a suitable husband for Geneviève. So be it!"

At eleven o'clock on Tuesday morning Valenglay, the prime minister, sent for the prefect of police and M. Weber, the deputy-chief of the detective-service, and showed them an express letter which he had just received:

"Monsieur Le Président Du Conseil,

"Knowing the interest which you take in M. Lenormand, I am writing to inform you of certain facts which chance has revealed to me.

"M. Lenormand is locked up in the cellars of the Villa des Glycines at Garches, near the House of Retreat.

"The ruffians of the Palace Hotel have resolved to murder him at two o'clock to-day.

"If the police require my assistance, they will find me at half-past one in the garden of the House of Retreat, or at the garden-house occupied by Mrs. Kesselbach, whose friend I have the honor to be.

"I am, Monsieur le Président du Conseil,

Your obedient servant,
PRINCE SERNINE

"This is an exceedingly grave matter, my dear M. Weber," said Valenglay. "I may add that we can have every confidence in the accuracy of Prince Sernine's statements. I have often met him at dinner. He is a serious, intelligent man. . ."

"Will you allow me, Monsieur le Président," asked the deputy-chief detective, "to show you another letter which I also received this morning?"

"About the same case?"

"Yes."

"Let me see it."

He took the letter and read:

SIR,

"This is to inform you that Prince Paul Sernine, who calls himself Mrs. Kesselbach's friend, is really Arsène Lupin.

"One proof will be sufficient: *Paul Sernine* is the anagram of *Arsène Lupin*. Not a letter more, not a letter less.

L. M.

And M. Weber added, while Valenglay stood amazed:

"This time, our friend Lupin has found an adversary who is a match for him. While he denounces the other, the other betrays him to us. And the fox is caught in the trap."

"What do you propose to do?"

"Monsieur le Président, I shall take two hundred men with me!"

MAURICE LEBLANC

VIII

The Olive-Green Frock-Coat

A quarter past twelve, in a restaurant near the Madeleine. The prince is at lunch. Two young men sit down at the next table. He bows to them and begins to speak to them, as to friends whom he has met by chance.

"Are you going on the expedition, eh?"

"Yes."

"How many men altogether?"

"Six, I think. Each goes down by himself. We're to meet M. Weber at a quarter to two, near the House of Retreat."

"Very well, I shall be there."

"What?"

"Am I not leading the expedition? And isn't it my business to find M. Lenormand, seeing that I've announced it publicly?"

"Then you believe that M. Lenormand is not dead, governor?"

"I'm sure of it."

"Do you know anything?"

"Yes, since yesterday I know for certain that Altenheim and his gang took M. Lenormand and Gourel to the bridge at Bougival and heaved them overboard. Gourel sank, but M. Lenormand managed to save himself. I shall furnish all the necessary proofs when the time comes."

"But, then, if he's alive, why doesn't he show himself?"

"Because he's not free."

"Is what you said true, then? Is he in the cellars of the Villa des Glycines?"

"I have every reason to think so."

"But how do you know? . . . What clue? . . ."

"That's my secret. I can tell you one thing: the revelation will be— what shall I say—sensational. Have you finished?"

"Yes."

"My car is behind the Madeleine. Join me there."

At Garches, Sernine sent the motor away, and they walked to the path that led to Geneviève's school. There he stopped:

"Listen to me, lads. This is of the highest importance. You will ring at the House of Retreat. As inspectors, you have your right of entry, have you not? You will then go to the Pavillon Hortense, the empty one. There you will run down to the basement and you will find an old shutter, which you have only to lift to see the opening of a tunnel which I discovered lately and which forms a direct communication with the Villa des Glycines. It was by means of this that Gertrude and Baron Altenheim used to meet. And it was this way that M. Lenormand passed, only to end by falling into the hands of his enemies."

"You think so, governor?"

"Yes, I think so. And now the point is this: you must go and make sure that the tunnel is exactly in the condition in which I left it last night; that the two doors which bar it are open; and that there is still, in a hole near the second door, a parcel wrapped in a piece of black cloth which I put there myself."

"Are we to undo the parcel?"

"No, that's not necessary. It's a change of clothes. Go; and don't let yourselves be seen more than you can help. I will wait for you."

Ten minutes later, they were back:

"The two doors are open," said one of the Doudevilles.

"And the black cloth parcel?"

"In its place near the second door."

"Capital! It is twenty-five past one. Weber will be arriving with his champions. They are to watch the villa. They will surround it as soon as Altenheim is inside. I have arranged with Weber that I shall ring the bell; the door will be opened; and I shall have my foot inside the citadel. Once there, I have my plan. Come, I've an idea that we shall see some fun."

And Sernine, after dismissing them, walked down the path to the school, soliloquizing as he went:

"All bodes well. The battle will be fought on the ground chosen by myself. I am bound to win. I shall get rid of my two adversaries and I shall find myself alone engaged in the Kesselbach case. . . alone, with two whacking trump-cards: Pierre Leduc and Steinweg. . . Besides the king. . . that is to say, Bibi. Only, there's one thing: what is Altenheim up to? Obviously, he has a plan of attack of his own. On which side does he mean to attack me? And how does it come that he has not attacked me yet? It's rather startling. Can he have denounced me to the police?"

He went along the little playground of the school. The pupils were at their lessons. He knocked at the door.

"Ah, is that you?" said Mme. Ernemont, opening the door. "So you have left Geneviève in Paris?"

"For me to do that, Geneviève would have to be in Paris," he replied.

"So she has been, seeing that you sent for her."

"What's that?" he exclaimed catching hold of her arm.

"Why, you know better than I!"

"I know nothing. . . I know nothing. . . Speak! . . ."

"Didn't you write to Geneviève to meet you at the Gare Saint-Lazare?"

"And did she go?"

"Why, of course. . . You were to lunch together at the Hôtel Ritz."

"The letter. . . Show me the letter."

She went to fetch it and gave it to him.

"But, wretched woman, couldn't you see that it was a forgery? The handwriting is a good imitation. . . but it's a forgery. . . Any one can see that." He pressed his clenched hands to his temples with rage. "That's the move I was wondering about. Oh, the dirty scoundrel! He's attacking me through her. . . But how does he know? No, he does not know. . . He's tried it on twice now. . . and it's because of Geneviève, because he's taken a fancy to her. . . Oh, not that! Never! Listen, Victoire, are you sure that she doesn't love him? . . . Oh, I'm losing my head! . . . Wait. . . wait! . . . I must think. . . this isn't the moment. . ."

He looked at his watch:

"Twenty-five minutes to two. . . I have time. . . Idiot that I am! Time to do what? How do I know where she is?"

He walked up and down like a madman; and his old nurse seemed astounded at seeing him so excited, with so little control of himself:

"After all," she said, "there is nothing to prove that she did not suspect the trap at the last moment. . ."

"Where could she be?"

"I don't know. . . perhaps at Mrs. Kesselbach's."

"That's true. . . that's true. . . You're right," he cried, filled with sudden hope.

And he set out at a run for the House of Retreat.

On the way, near the gate, he met the brothers Doudeville, who were entering the porter's lodge. The lodge looked out on the road; and this enabled them to watch the approaches to the Villa des Glycines. Without stopping, he went straight to the Pavillon de l'Impératrice, called Suzanne and told her to take him to Mrs. Kesselbach.

"Geneviève?" he asked.

"Geneviève?"

"Yes; hasn't she been here?"

"No, not for several days. . ."

"But she is to come, is she not?"

"Do you think so?"

"Why, I'm certain of it. Where do you think she is? Can you remember? . . ."

"It's no use my trying. I assure you that Geneviève and I had made no arrangement to see each other." And, suddenly alarmed: "But you're not anxious, are you? Has anything happened to Geneviève?"

"No, nothing."

He had already left the room. An idea had occurred to him. Suppose Altenheim were not at the Villa des Glycines? Suppose the hour of the meeting had been changed!

"I must see him," he said to himself. "I must, at all costs."

And he ran along with a disordered air, indifferent to everything. But, in front of the lodge, he at once recovered his composure: he had caught sight of the deputy-chief of the detective-service talking to the brothers Doudeville in the garden.

Had he commanded his usual acute discernment, he would have perceived the little start which M. Weber gave as he approached; but he saw nothing:

"M. Weber, I believe?" he asked.

"Yes. . . To whom have I the honor. . . ?"

"Prince Sernine."

"Ah, very good! Monsieur le Préfet de Police has told me of the great service which you are doing us, monsieur."

"That service will not be complete until I have handed the ruffians over to you."

"That won't take long. I believe that one of those ruffians has just gone in; a powerful-looking man, with a swarthy complexion. . ."

"Yes, that's Baron Altenheim. Are your men here, M. Weber?"

"Yes, concealed along the road, at two hundred yards from this."

"Well, M. Weber, it seems to me that you might collect them and bring them to this lodge. From here we will go to the villa. As Baron

Altenheim knows me, I presume they will open the door to me and I will go in. . . with you."

"It is an excellent plan," said M. Weber. "I shall come back at once."

He left the garden and walked down the road, in the opposite direction to the Villa des Glycines.

Sernine quickly took one of the brothers Doudeville by the arm:

"Run after him, Jacques. . . keep him engaged. . . long enough for me to get inside the Glycines. . . And then delay the attack as long as you can. . . Invent pretexts. . . I shall want ten minutes. . . Let the villa be surrounded. . . but not entered. And you, Jean, go and post yourself in the Pavillon Hortense, at the entrance to the underground passage. If the baron tries to go out that way, break his head."

The Doudevilles moved away, as ordered. The prince slipped out and ran to a tall gate, barred with iron, which was the entrance to the Glycines.

Should he ring? . . .

There was no one in sight. With one bound, he leapt upon the gate, placing his foot on the lock; and, hanging on to the bars, getting a purchase with his knees and hoisting himself up with his wrists, he managed, at the risk of falling on the sharp points of the bars, to climb over the gate and jump down.

He found a paved courtyard, which he crossed briskly, and mounted the steps of a pillared peristyle, on which the windows looked out. These were all closed to the very top, with full shutters. As he stood thinking how he should make his way into the house, the door was half opened, with a noise of iron that reminded him of the door in the Villa Dupont, and Altenheim appeared:

"I say, prince, is that the way you trespass on private property? I shall be forced to call in the gendarmes, my dear fellow!"

Sernine caught him by the throat and, throwing him down on a bench:

"Geneviève? . . . Where is Geneviève? If you don't tell me what you've done with her, you villain. . ."

"Please observe," stammered the baron, "that you are making it impossible for me to speak."

Sernine released his hold of him:

"To the point! . . . And look sharp! . . . Answer. . . Geneviève?"

"There is one thing," replied the baron, "which is much more urgent, especially where fellows like you and me are concerned, and that is to feel one's self at home. . ."

And he carefully closed the front door, which he barricaded with bolts. Then, leading Sernine to the adjoining drawing-room, a room without furniture or curtains, he said:

"Now I'm your man. What can I do for you, prince?"

"Geneviève?"

"She is in perfect health."

"Ah, so you confess. . . ?"

"Of course! I may even tell you that your imprudence in this respect surprised me. Why didn't you take a few precautions? It was inevitable. . ."

"Enough! Where is she?"

"You are not very polite."

"Where is she?"

"Between four walls, free. . ."

"Free?"

"Yes, free to go from one wall to another."

"Where? Where?"

"Come, prince, do you think I should be fool enough to tell you the secret by which I hold you? You love the little girl. . ."

"Hold your tongue!" shouted Sernine, beside himself. "I forbid you. . ."

"What next? Is there anything to be ashamed of? I love her myself and I have risked. . ."

He did not complete his sentence, frightened by the terrific anger of Sernine, a restrained, dumb anger that distorted the prince's features.

They looked at each other for a long time, each of them seeking for the adversary's weak point. At last, Sernine stepped forward and, speaking very distinctly, like a man who is threatening rather than proposing a compact:

"Listen to me," he said. "You remember the offer of partnership which you made me? The Kesselbach business for the two of us. . . we were to act together. . . we were to share the profits. . . I refused. . . To-day, I accept. . ."

"Too late."

"Wait! I accept more than that: I give the whole business up. . . I shall take no further part in it. . . You shall have it all. . . If necessary, I'll help you."

"What is the condition?"

"Tell me where Geneviève is."

The baron shrugged his shoulders:

"You're driveling, Lupin. I'm sorry for you. . . at your age. . ."

There was a fresh silence between the two enemies, a terrible silence. Then the baron sneered:

"All the same, it's a holy joy to see you like that, sniveling and begging. I say, it seems to me that the private soldier is giving his general a sound beating!"

"You ass!" muttered Sernine.

"Prince, I shall send you my seconds this evening. . . if you are still in this world."

"You ass!" repeated Sernine, with infinite contempt.

"You would rather settle the matter here and now? As you please, prince: your last hour has struck. You can commend your soul to God. You smile! That's a mistake. I have one immense advantage over you! I kill. . . when it's necessary. . ."

"You ass!" said Sernine once more. He took out his watch. "It is two o'clock, baron. You have only a few minutes left. At five past two, ten past at the very latest, M. Weber and half-a-dozen sturdy men, without a scruple amongst them, will lay hands on you. . . Don't you smile, either. The outlet on which you're reckoning is discovered; I know it: it is guarded. So you are thoroughly caught. It means the scaffold, old chap."

Altenheim turned livid. He stammered:

"You did this? . . . You have had the infamy. . ."

"The house is surrounded. The assault is at hand. Speak. . . and I will save you."

"How?"

"The men watching the outlet in the Pavillon Hortense belong to me. I have only to give you a word for them and you are saved. Speak!"

Altenheim reflected for a few seconds and seemed to hesitate; but, suddenly, resolutely, declared:

"This is all bluff. You would never have been simple enough to rush into the lion's mouth."

"You're forgetting Geneviève. But for her, do you think I should be here? Speak!"

"No."

"Very well. Let us wait," said Sernine. "A cigarette?"

"Thank you."

A few seconds passed.

"Do you hear?" asked Sernine.

"Yes. . . yes. . ." said Altenheim, rising.

Blows rang against the gate. Sernine observed:

"Not even the usual summons. . . no preliminaries. . . Your mind is still made up?"

"More so than ever."

"You know that, with the tools they carry, they won't take long?"

"If they were inside this room I should still refuse."

The gate yielded. They heard it creak on its hinges.

"To allow one's self to get nabbed," said Sernine, "is admissible. But to hold out one's own hands to the handcuffs is too silly. Come, don't be obstinate. Speak. . . and bolt!"

"And you?"

"I shall remain. What have I to be afraid of?"

"Look!"

The baron pointed to a chink between the shutters. Sernine put his eye to it and jumped back with a start:

"Oh, you scoundrel, so you have denounced me, too! It's not ten men that Weber's bringing, but fifty men, a hundred, two hundred. . ."

The baron laughed open-heartedly:

"And, if there are so many of them, it's because they're after Lupin; that's obvious! Half-a-dozen would have been enough for me."

"You informed the police?"

"Yes."

"What proof did you give?"

"Your name: *Paul Sernine*, that is to say, *Arsène Lupin*."

"And you found that out all by yourself, did you? . . . A thing which nobody else thought of? . . . Nonsense! It was the other one. Admit it!"

He looked out through the chink. Swarms of policemen were spreading round the villa; and the blows were now sounding on the door. He must, however, think of one of two things: either his escape, or else the execution of the plan which he had contrived. But to go away, even for a moment, meant leaving Altenheim; and who could guarantee that the baron had not another outlet at his disposal to escape by? This thought paralyzed Sernine. The baron free! The baron at liberty to go back to Geneviève and torture her and make her subservient to his odious love!

Thwarted in his designs, obliged to improvise a new plan on the very second, while subordinating everything to the danger which Geneviève

MAURICE LEBLANC

was running, Sernine passed through a moment of cruel indecision. With his eyes fixed on the baron's eyes, he would have liked to tear his secret from him and to go away; and he no longer even tried to convince him, so useless did all words seem to him. And, while pursuing his own thoughts, he asked himself what the baron's thoughts could be, what his weapons, what his hope of safety?

The hall-door, though strongly bolted, though sheeted with iron, was beginning to give way.

The two men stood behind that door, motionless. The sound of voices, the sense of words reached them.

"You seem very sure of yourself," said Sernine.

"I should think so!" cried the other, suddenly tripping him to the floor and running away.

Sernine sprang up at once, dived through a little door under the staircase, through which Altenheim had disappeared, and ran down the stone steps to the basement. . .

A passage led to a large, low, almost pitch-dark room, where he found the baron on his knees, lifting the flap of a trap-door.

"Idiot!" shouted Sernine, flinging himself upon him. "You know that you will find my men at the end of this tunnel and that they have orders to kill you like a dog. . . Unless. . . unless you have an outlet that joins on to this. . . Ah, there, of course, I've guessed it! . . . And you imagine. . ."

The fight was a desperate one. Altenheim, a real colossus, endowed with exceptional muscular force, had caught his adversary round the arms and body and was pressing him against his own chest, numbing his arms and trying to smother him.

"Of course. . . of course," Sernine panted, with difficulty, "of course. . . that's well thought out. . . As long as I can't use my arms to break some part of you, you will have the advantage. . . Only. . . can you. . . ?"

He gave a shudder. The trap-door, which had closed again and on the flap of which they were bearing down with all their weight, the trap-door seemed to move beneath them. He felt the efforts that were being made to raise it; and the baron must have felt them too, for he desperately tried to shift the ground of the contest so that the trap-door might open.

"It's 'the other one'!" thought Sernine, with the sort of unreasoning terror which that mysterious being caused him. "It's the other one. . . If he gets through, I'm done for."

By dint of imperceptible movements, Altenheim had succeeded in shifting his own position; and he tried to drag his adversary after him. But Sernine clung with his legs to the baron's legs and, at the same time, very gradually, tried to release one of his hands.

Above their heads great blows resounded, like the blows of a battering-ram. . .

"I have five minutes," thought Sernine. "In one minute this fellow will have to. . ." Then, speaking aloud, "Look out, old chap. Stand tight!"

He brought his two knees together with incredible force. The baron yelled, with a twisted thigh. Then Sernine, taking advantage of his adversary's pain, made an effort, freed his right arm and seized him by the throat:

"That's capital! . . . We shall be more comfortable like this. . . No, it's not worth while getting out your knife. . . If you do, I'll wring your neck like a chicken's. You see, I'm polite and considerate. . . I'm not pressing too hard. . . just enough to keep you from even wanting to kick about."

While speaking he took from his pocket a very thin cord and, with one hand, with extreme skill, fastened his wrists. For that matter, the baron, now at his last gasp, offered not the least resistance. With a few accurate movements, Sernine tied him up firmly:

"How well you're behaving! What a good thing! I should hardly know you. Here, in case you were thinking of escaping, I have a roll of wire that will finish off my little work. . . The wrists first. . . Now the ankles. . . That's it! . . . By Jove, how nice you look!"

The baron had gradually come to himself again. He spluttered:

"If you give me up, Geneviève will die."

"Really? . . . And how? . . . Explain yourself."

"She is locked up. No one knows where she is. If I'm put away, she will die of starvation."

Sernine shuddered. He retorted:

"Yes, but you will speak."

"Never!"

"Yes, you will speak. Not now; it's too late. But to-night." He bent down over him and, whispering in his ear, said, "Listen, Altenheim, and understand what I say. You'll be caught presently. To-night, you'll sleep at the Dépôt. That is fatal, irrevocable. I myself can do nothing to prevent it now. And, to-morrow, they will take you to the Santé; and later, you know where. . . Well, I'm giving you one more chance of safety. To-night, you understand, I shall come to your cell, at the Dépôt, and you shall tell me where Geneviève is. Two hours later, if you have told the truth, you shall be free. If not. . . it means that you don't attach much value to your head."

The other made no reply. Sernine stood up and listened. There was a great crash overhead. The entrance-door yielded. Footsteps beat the flags of the hall and the floor of the drawing room. M. Weber and his men were searching.

"Good-bye, baron. Think it over until this evening. The prison-cell is a good counsellor."

He pushed his prisoner aside, so as to uncover the trap-door, and lifted it. As he expected, there was no longer any one below on the steps of the staircase.

He went down, taking care to leave the trap-door open behind him, as though he meant to come back.

There were twenty steps, at the bottom of which began the passage through which M. Lenormand and Gourel had come in the opposite direction. He entered it and gave an exclamation. He thought he felt somebody's presence there.

He lit his pocket-lantern. The passage was empty.

Then he cocked his revolver and said aloud:

"All right. . . I'm going to fire."

No reply. Not a sound.

"It's an illusion, no doubt," he thought. "That creature is becoming an obsession. . . Come, if I want to pull off my stroke and win the game, I must hurry. . . The hole in which I hid the parcel of clothes is not far off. I shall take the parcel. . . and the trick is done. . . And what a trick! One of Lupin's best! . . ."

He came to a door that stood open and at once stopped. To the right was an excavation, the one which M. Lenormand had made to escape from the rising water. He stooped and threw his light into the opening:

"Oh!" he said, with a start. "No, it's not possible. . . Doudeville must have pushed the parcel farther along."

But, search and pry into the darkness as he might, the parcel was gone; and he had no doubt but that it was once more the mysterious being who had taken it.

"What a pity! The thing was so neatly arranged! The adventure would have resumed its natural course, and I should have achieved my aim with greater certainty. . . As it is, I must push along as fast as I can. . . Doudeville is at the Pavillon Hortense. . . My retreat is insured. . . No more nonsense. . . I must hurry and set things straight again, if I can. . . And we'll attend to 'him' afterward. . . Oh, he'd better keep clear of my claws, that one!"

But an exclamation of stupor escaped his lips; he had come to the other door; and this door, the last before the garden-house, was shut. He flung himself upon it. What was the good? What could he do?

"This time," he muttered, "I'm badly done!"

And, seized with a sort of lassitude, he sat down. He had a sense of his weakness in the face of the mysterious being. Altenheim hardly counted. But the other, that person of darkness and silence, the other loomed up before him, upset all his plans and exhausted him with his cunning and infernal attacks.

He was beaten.

Weber would find him there, like an animal run to earth, at the bottom of his cave.

"Ah, no!" he cried, springing up with a bound. "No! If there were only myself, well and good! . . . But there is Geneviève, Geneviève, who must be saved to-night. . . After all, the game is not yet lost. . . If the other one vanished just now, it proves that there is a second outlet somewhere near. . . Come, come, Weber and his merry men haven't got me yet. . ."

He had already begun to explore the tunnel and, lantern in hand, was examining the bricks of which the horrible walls were formed, when a yell reached his ears, a dreadful yell that made his flesh creep with anguish.

It came from the direction of the trap-door. And he suddenly remembered that he had left the trap-door open, at the time when he intended to return to the Villa des Glycines.

He hurried back and passed through the first door. His lantern went out on the road; and he felt something, or rather somebody, brush past his knees, somebody crawl along the wall. And, at that same moment, he had a feeling that this being was disappearing, vanishing, he knew not which way.

Just then his foot knocked against a step.

"This is the outlet," he thought, "the second outlet through which 'he' passes."

Overhead, the cry sounded again, less loud, followed by moans, by a hoarse gurgling. . .

He ran up the stairs, came out in the basement room, and rushed to the baron.

Altenheim lay dying, with the blood streaming from his throat! His bonds were cut, but the wire that fastened his wrists and ankles was intact. *His accomplice, being unable to release him, had cut his throat.*

Sernine gazed upon the sight with horror. An icy perspiration covered his whole body. He thought of Geneviève, imprisoned, helpless, abandoned to the most awful of deaths, because the baron alone knew where she was hidden.

He distinctly heard the policemen open the little back door in the hall. He distinctly heard them come down the kitchen stairs.

There was nothing between him and them save one door, that of the basement room in which he was. He bolted the door at the very moment when the aggressors were laying hold of the handle.

The trap-door was open beside him; it meant possible safety, because there remained the second outlet.

"No," he said to himself, "Geneviève first. Afterward, if I have time, I will think of myself."

He knelt down and put his hand on the baron's breast. The heart was still beating.

He stooped lower still:

"You can hear me, can't you?"

The eyelids flickered feebly.

The dying man was just breathing. Was there anything to be obtained from this faint semblance of life?

The policemen were attacking the door, the last rampart.

Sernine whispered.

"I will save you. . . I have infallible remedies. . . One word only. . . Geneviève? . . ."

It was as though this word of hope revived the man's strength. Altenheim tried to utter articulate sounds.

"Answer," said Sernine, persisting. "Answer, and I will save you. . . Answer. . . It means your life to-day. . . your liberty to-morrow. . . Answer! . . ."

The door shook under the blows that rained upon it.

The baron gasped out unintelligible syllables. Leaning over him, affrighted, straining all his energy, all his will to the utmost, Sernine panted with anguish. He no longer gave a thought to the policemen, his inevitable capture, prison. . . But Geneviève. . . Geneviève dying of hunger, whom one word from that villain could set free! . . .

"Answer! . . . You must! . . ."

He ordered and entreated by turns. Altenheim stammered, as though hypnotized and defeated by that indomitable imperiousness:

"Ri. . . Rivoli. . ."

"Rue de Rivoli, is that it? You have locked her up in a house in that street. . . eh? Which number?"

A loud din. . . followed by shouts of triumph. . . The door was down.

"Jump on him, lads!" cried M. Weber. "Seize him. . . seize both of them!"

And Sernine, on his knees:

"The number. . . answer. . . If you love her, answer. . . Why keep silence now?"

"Twenty. . . twenty-seven," whispered the baron.

Hands were laid on Sernine. Ten revolvers were pointed at him.

He rose and faced the policemen, who fell back with instinctive dread.

"If you stir, Lupin," cried M. Weber, with his revolver leveled at him, "I'll blow out your brains."'

"Don't shoot." said Sernine, solemnly. "It's not necessary. I surrender."

"Humbug! This is another of your tricks!"

"No," replied Sernine, "the battle is lost. You have no right to shoot. I am not defending myself."

He took out two revolvers and threw them on the floor.

"Humbug!" M. Weber repeated, implacably. "Aim straight at his heart, lads! At the least movement, fire! At the least word, fire!"

There were ten men there. He placed five more in position. He pointed their fifteen right arms at the mark. And, raging, shaking with joy and fear, he snarled:

"At his heart! At his head! And no pity! If he stirs, if he speaks. . . shoot him where he stands!"

Sernine smiled, impassively, with his hands in his pockets. Death was there, waiting for him, at two inches from his chest, at two inches from his temples. Fifteen fingers were curled round the triggers.

"Ah," chuckled M. Weber, "this is nice, this is very nice! . . . And I think that this time we've scored. . . and it's a nasty look-out for you, Master Lupin! . . ."

He made one of his men draw back the shutters of a large air-hole, which admitted a sudden burst of daylight, and he turned toward Altenheim. But, to his great amazement, the baron, whom he thought dead, opened his eyes, glazed, awful eyes, already filled with all the signs of the coming dissolution. He stared at M. Weber. Then he seemed to look for somebody and, catching sight of Sernine, had a convulsion of anger. He seemed to be waking from his torpor; and his suddenly reviving hatred restored a part of his strength.

He raised himself on his two wrists and tried to speak.

"You know him, eh?" asked M. Weber.

"Yes."

"It's Lupin, isn't it?"

"Yes. . . Lupin. . ."

Sernine, still smiling, listened:

"Heavens, how I'm amusing myself!" he declared.

"Have you anything more to say?" asked M. Weber, who saw the baron's lips making desperate attempts to move.

"Yes."

"About M. Lenormand, perhaps?"

"Yes."

"Have you shut him up? Where? Answer! . . ."

With all his heaving body, with all his tense glance, Altenheim pointed to a cupboard in the corner of the room.

"There. . . there. . ." he said.

"Ah, we're burning!" chuckled Lupin.

M. Weber opened the cupboard. On one of the shelves was a parcel wrapped in black cloth. He opened it and found a hat, a little box, some clothes. . . He gave a start. He had recognized M. Lenormand's olive-green frock-coat.

"Oh, the villains!" he cried. "They have murdered him!"

"No," said Altenheim, shaking his head.

"Then. . . ?"

"It's he. . . he. . ."

"What do you mean by 'he'? . . . Did Lupin kill the chief?"

"No. . ."

Altenheim was clinging to existence with fierce obstinacy, eager to speak and to accuse. . . The secret which he wished to reveal was at the tip of his tongue and he was not able, did not know how to translate it into words.

"Come," the deputy-chief insisted. "M. Lenormand is dead, surely?"

"No."

"He's alive?"

"Yes."

"I don't understand. . . Look here, these clothes? This frock-coat? . . ."

Altenheim turned his eyes toward Sernine. An idea struck M. Weber:

"Ah, I see! Lupin stole M. Lenormand's clothes and reckoned upon using them to escape with. . ."

"Yes. . . yes. . ."

"Not bad," cried the deputy-chief. "It's quite a trick in his style. In this room, we should have found Lupin disguised as M. Lenormand, chained up, no doubt. It would have meant his safety; only he hadn't time. That's it, isn't it?"

"Yes. . . yes. . ."

But, by the appearance of the dying man's eyes, M. Weber felt that there was more, and that the secret was not exactly that. What was it, then? What was the strange and unintelligible puzzle which Altenheim wanted to explain before dying?

He questioned him again:

"And where is M. Lenormand himself?"

"There. . ."

"What do you mean? Here?"

"Yes."

"But there are only ourselves here!"

"There's. . . there's. . ."

"Oh, speak!"

"There's. . . Ser. . . Sernine."

"Sernine! . . . Eh, what?"

"Sernine. . . Lenormand. . ."

M. Weber gave a jump. A sudden light flashed across him.

"No, no, it's not possible," he muttered. "This is madness."

He gave a side-glance at his prisoner. Sernine seemed to be greatly diverted and to be watching the scene with the air of a playgoer who is thoroughly amused and very anxious to know how the piece is going to end.

Altenheim, exhausted by his efforts, had fallen back at full length. Would he die before revealing the solution of the riddle which his strange words had propounded? M. Weber, shaken by an absurd, incredible surmise, which he did not wish to entertain and which persisted in his mind in spite of him, made a fresh, determined attempt:

"Explain the thing to us. . . What's at the bottom of it? What mystery?"

The other seemed not to hear and lay lifeless, with staring eyes.

MAURICE LEBLANC

M. Weber lay down beside him, with his body touching him, and, putting great stress upon his words, so that each syllable should sink down to the very depths of that brain already merged in darkness, said:

"Listen. . . I have understood you correctly, have I not? Lupin and M. Lenormand. . ."

He needed an effort to continue, so monstrous did the words appear to him. Nevertheless, the baron's dimmed eyes seemed to contemplate him with anguish. He finished the sentence, shaking with excitement, as though he were speaking blasphemy:

"That's it, isn't it? You're sure? The two are one and the same? . . ."

The eyes did not move. A little blood trickled from one corner of the man's mouth. . . He gave two or three sobs. . . A last spasm; and all was over. . .

A LONG SILENCE REIGNED IN that basement room filled with people.

Almost all the policemen guarding Sernine had turned round and, stupefied, not understanding or not willing to understand, they still listened to the incredible accusation which the dying scoundrel had been unable to put into words.

M. Weber took the little box which was in the parcel and opened it. It contained a gray wig, a pair of spectacles, a maroon-colored neckerchief and, in a false bottom, a pot or two of make-up and a case containing some tiny tufts of gray hair: in short, all that was needed to complete a perfect disguise in the character of M. Lenormand.

He went up to Sernine and, looking at him for a few seconds without speaking, thoughtfully reconstructing all the phases of the adventure, he muttered:

"So it's true?"

Sernine, who had retained his smiling calmness, replied:

"The suggestion is a pretty one and a bold one. But, before I answer, tell your men to stop worrying me with those toys of theirs."

"Very well," said M. Weber, making a sign to his men. "And now answer."

"What?"

"Are you M. Lenormand?"

"Yes."

Exclamations arose. Jean Doudeville, who was there, while his brother was watching the secret outlet, Jean Doudeville, Sernine's own accomplice, looked at him in dismay. M. Weber stood undecided.

"That takes your breath away, eh?" said Sernine. "I admit that it's rather droll. . . Lord, how you used to make me laugh sometimes, when we were working together, you and I, the chief and the deputy-chief! . . . And the funniest thing is that you thought our worthy M. Lenormand dead. . . as well as poor Gourel. But no, no, old chap: there's life in the old dog yet!" He pointed to Altenheim's corpse. "There, it was that scoundrel who pitched me into the water, in a sack, with a paving-stone round my waist. Only, he forgot to take away my knife. And with a knife one rips open sacks and cuts ropes. So you see, you unfortunate Altenheim: if you had thought of that, you wouldn't be where you are! . . . But enough said. . . Peace to your ashes!"

M. Weber listened, not knowing what to think. At last, he made a gesture of despair, as though he gave up the idea of forming a reasonable opinion.

"The handcuffs," he said, suddenly alarmed.

"If it amuses you," said Sernine.

And, picking out Doudeville in the front row of his assailants, he put out his wrists:

"There, my friend, you shall have the honour. . . and don't trouble to exert yourself. . . I'm playing square. . . as it's no use doing anything else. . ."

He said this in a tone that gave Doudeville to understand that the struggle was finished for the moment and that there was nothing to do but submit.

Doudeville fastened the handcuffs.

Without moving his lips or contracting a muscle of his face, Sernine whispered:

"27, Rue de Rivoli. . . Geneviève. . ."

M. Weber could not suppress a movement of satisfaction at the sight:

"Come along!" he said. "To the detective-office!"

"That's it, to the detective-office!" cried Sernine. "M. Lenormand will enter Arsène Lupin in the jail-book; and Arsène Lupin will enter Prince Sernine."

"You're too clever, Lupin."

"That's true, Weber; we shall never get on, you and I."

During the drive in the motor-car, escorted by three other cars filled with policemen, he did not utter a word.

They did not stay long at the detective office. M. Weber, remembering the escapes effected by Lupin, sent him up at once to the finger-print department and then took him to the Dépôt, whence he was sent on to the Santé Prison.

The governor had been warned by telephone and was waiting for him. The formalities of the entry of commitment and of the searching were soon got over; and, at seven o'clock in the evening, Prince Paul Sernine crossed the threshold of cell 14 in the second division:

"Not half bad, your rooms," he declared, "not bad at all! . . . Electric light, central heating, every requisite. . . capital! Mr. Governor, I'll take this room."

He flung himself on the bed:

"Oh, Mr. Governor, I have one little favor to ask of you!"

"What is that?"

"Tell them not to bring me my chocolate before ten o'clock in the morning. . . I'm awfully sleepy."

He turned his face to the wall. Five minutes later he was sound asleep.

IX

"Santé Palace"

There was one wild burst of laughter over the whole face of the world.

True, the capture of Arsène Lupin made a big sensation; and the public did not grudge the police the praise which they deserved for this revenge so long hoped-for and now so fully obtained. The great adventurer was caught. That extraordinary, genial, invisible hero was shivering, like any ordinary criminal, between the four walls of a prison cell, crushed in his turn by that formidable power which is called the law and which, sooner or later, by inevitable necessity shatters the obstacles opposed to it and destroys the work of its adversaries.

All this was said, printed, repeated and discussed *ad nauseam*. The prefect of police was created a commander, M. Weber an officer of the Legion of Honor. The skill and courage of their humblest coadjutors were extolled to the skies. Cheers were raised and pæans of victory struck up. Articles were written and speeches made.

Very well. But one thing, nevertheless, rose above the wonderful concert of praise, these noisy demonstrations of satisfaction; and that was an immense, spontaneous, inextinguishable and tumultuous roar of laughter.

Arsène Lupin had been chief of the detective-service for four years!!!

He had been chief detective for four years and, really, legally, he was chief detective still, with all the rights which the title confers, enjoying the esteem of his chiefs, the favor of the government and the admiration of the public.

For four years, the public peace and the defence of property had been entrusted to Arsène Lupin. He saw that the law was carried out. He protected the innocent and pursued the guilty.

And what services he had rendered! Never was order less disturbed, never was crime discovered with greater certainty and rapidity. The reader need but take back his mind to the Denizou case, the robbery at the Crédit Lyonnais, the attack on the Orléans express, the murder of Baron Dorf, forming a series of unforeseen and overwhelming triumphs, of magnificent feats of prowess fit to compare with the most famous victories of the most renowned detectives.[1]

Not so very long before, in a speech delivered at the time of the fire at the Louvre and the capture of the incendiaries, Valenglay, the prime minister, had said, speaking in defence of the somewhat arbitrary manner in which M. Lenormand had acted on that occasion:

"With his great powers of discernment, his energy, his qualities of decision and execution, his unexpected methods, his inexhaustible resources, M. Lenormand reminds us of the only man who, if he were still alive, could hope to hold his own against him: I mean Arsène Lupin. M. Lenormand is an Arsène Lupin in the service of society."

And, lo and behold, M. Lenormand was none other than Arsène Lupin!

That he was a Russian prince, who cared! Lupin was an old hand at such changes of personality as that. But chief detective! What a delicious irony! What a whimsical humor in the conduct of that extraordinary life!

M. Lenormand! . . . Arsène Lupin! . . .

People were now able to explain to themselves the apparently miraculous feats of intelligence which had quite recently bewildered the crowd and baffled the police. They understood how his accomplice had been juggled away in the middle of the Palais de Justice itself, in broad daylight and on the appointed day. Had he himself not said:

"My process is so ingenious and so simple. . . How surprised people will be on the day when I am free to speak! 'Is that all?' I shall be asked. That is all; but it had to be thought of."

It was, indeed, childishly simple: all you had to do was to be chief of the detective-service.

Well, Lupin was chief of the detective-service; and every police-officer obeying his orders had made himself the involuntary and unconscious accomplice of Arsène Lupin.

What a comedy! What admirable bluff! It was the monumental and consoling farce of these drab times of ours. Lupin in prison, Lupin irretrievably conquered was, in spite of himself, the great conqueror. From his cell he shone over Paris. He was more than ever the idol, more than ever the master.

---

1. The murder of Baron Dorf, that mysterious and disconcerting affair, will one day be the subject of a story which will give an idea of Arsène Lupin's astonishing qualities as a detective.

When Arsène Lupin awoke next morning, in his room at the "Santé Palace," as he at once nicknamed it, he had a very clear vision of the enormous sensation which would be produced by his arrest under the double name of Sernine and Lenormand and the double title of prince and chief of the detective-service.

He rubbed his hands and gave vent to his thoughts:

"A man can have no better companion in his loneliness than the approval of his contemporaries. O fame! The sun of all living men! . . ."

Seen by daylight, his cell pleased him even better than at night. The window, placed high up in the wall, afforded a glimpse of the branches of a tree, through which peeped the blue of the sky above. The walls were white. There was only one table and one chair, both fastened to the floor. But everything was quite nice and clean.

"Come," he said, "a little rest-cure here will be rather charming. . . But let us see to our toilet. . . Have I all I want? . . . No. . . In that case, ring twice for the chambermaid."

He pressed the button of an apparatus beside the door, which released a signaling-disc in the corridor.

After a moment, bolts and bars were drawn outside, a key turned in the lock and a warder appeared.

"Hot water, please," said Lupin.

The other looked at him with an air of mingled amazement and rage.

"Oh," said Lupin, "and a bath-towel! By Jove, there's no bath-towel!"

The man growled:

"You're getting at me, aren't you? You'd better be careful!"

He was going away, when Lupin caught him roughly by the arm:

"Here! A hundred francs if you'll post a letter for me."

He took out a hundred-franc note, which he had concealed during the search, and offered it to him.

"Where's the letter?" said the warder, taking the money.

"Just give me a moment to write it."

He sat down at the table, scribbled a few words in pencil on a sheet of paper, put it in an envelope and addressed the letter:

"To Monsieur S. B. 42,
"Poste Restante,
*"*Paris.*"*

The warder took the letter and walked away.

"That letter," said Lupin to himself, "will reach destination as safely as if I delivered it myself. I shall have the reply in an hour at latest: just the time I want to take a good look into my position."

He sat down on his chair and, in an undertone, summed up the situation as follows:

"When all is said and done, I have two adversaries to fight at the present moment. There is, first, society, which holds me and which I can afford to laugh at. Secondly, there is a person unknown, who does not hold me, but whom I am not inclined to laugh at in the very least. It is he who told the police that I was Sernine. It was he who guessed that I was M. Lenormand. It was he who locked the door of the underground passage and it was he who had me clapped into prison."

Arsène Lupin reflected for a second and then continued:

"So, at long last, the struggle lies between him and me. And, to keep up that struggle, that is to say, to discover and get to the bottom of the Kesselbach case, here am I, a prisoner, while he is free, unknown, and inaccessible, and holds the two trump-cards which I considered mine: Pierre Leduc and old Steinweg. . . In short, he is near the goal, after finally pushing me back."

A fresh contemplative pause, followed by a fresh soliloquy:

"The position is far from brilliant. On the one side, everything; on the other, nothing. Opposite me, a man of my own strength, or stronger, because he has not the same scruples that hamper me. And I am without weapons to attack him with."

He repeated the last sentence several times, in a mechanical voice, and then stopped and, taking his forehead between his hands, sat for a long time wrapped in thought.

"Come in, Mr. Governor," he said, seeing the door open.

"Were you expecting me?"

"Why, I wrote to you, Mr. Governor, asking you to come! I felt certain that the warder would give you my letter. I was so certain of it that I put your initials, S. B., and your age, forty-two, on the envelope!"

The governor's name, in point of fact, was Stanislas Borély, and he was forty-two years of age. He was a pleasant-looking man, with a very gentle character, who treated the prisoners with all the indulgence possible.

He said to Lupin:

"Your opinion of my subordinate's integrity was quite correct. Here is your money. It shall be handed to you at your release. . . You will now go through the searching-room again."

Lupin went with M. Borély to the little room reserved for this purpose, undressed and, while his clothes were inspected with justifiable suspicion, himself underwent a most fastidious examination.

He was then taken back to his cell and M. Borély said:

"I feel easier. That's done."

"And very well done, Mr. Governor. Your men perform this sort of duty with a delicacy for which I should like to thank them by giving them a small token of my satisfaction."

He handed a hundred-franc note to M. Borély, who jumped as though he had been shot:

"Oh! . . . But. . . where does that come from?"

"No need to rack your brains, Mr. Governor. A man like myself, leading the life that I do, is always prepared for any eventuality: and no mishap, however painful—not even imprisonment—can take him unawares."

Seizing the middle finger of his left hand between the thumb and forefinger of the right, he pulled it off smartly and presented it calmly to M. Borély:

"Don't start like that, Mr. Governor. This is not my finger, but just a tube, made of gold-beater's skin and cleverly colored, which fits exactly over my middle finger and gives the illusion of a real finger." And he added, with a laugh, "In such a way, of course, as to conceal a third hundred-franc note. . . What is a poor man to do? He must carry the best purse he can. . . and must needs make use of it on occasions. . ."

He stopped at the sight of M. Borély's startled face:

"Please don't think, Mr. Governor, that I wish to dazzle you with my little parlor-tricks. I only wanted to show you that you have to do with a. . . client of a rather. . . special nature and to tell you that you must not be surprised if I venture, now and again, to break the ordinary rules and regulations of your establishment."

The governor had recovered himself. He said plainly:

"I prefer to think that you will conform to the rules and not compel me to resort to harsh measures. . ."

"Which you would regret to have to enforce: isn't that it, Mr. Governor? That's just what I should like to spare you, by proving to you in advance that they would not prevent me from doing as I please: from corresponding with my friends, from defending the grave interests confided to me outside these walls, from writing to the newspapers that accept my inspiration, from pursuing the fulfilment of my plans and, lastly, from preparing my escape."

"Your escape!"

Lupin began to laugh heartily:

"But think, Mr. Governor, my only excuse for being in prison is. . . to leave it!"

The argument did not appear to satisfy M. Borély. He made an effort to laugh in his turn:

"Forewarned is forearmed," he said.

"That's what I wanted," Lupin replied. "Take all your precautions, Mr. Governor, neglect nothing, so that later they may have nothing to reproach you with. On the other hand, I shall arrange things in such a way that, whatever annoyance you may have to bear in consequence of my escape, your career, at least, shall not suffer. That is all I had to say to you, Mr. Governor. You can go."

And, while M. Borély walked away, greatly perturbed by his singular charge and very anxious about the events in preparation, the prisoner threw himself on his bed, muttering:

"What cheek, Lupin, old fellow, what cheek! Really, any one would think that you had some idea as to how you were going to get out of this!"

The Santé prison is built on the star plan. In the centre of the main portion is a round hall, upon which all the corridors converge, so that no prisoner is able to leave his cell without being at once perceived by the overseers posted in the glass box which occupies the middle of that central hall.

The thing that most surprises the visitor who goes over the prison is that, at every moment, he will meet prisoners without a guard of any kind, who seem to move about as though they were absolutely free. In reality, in order to go from one point to another—for instance, from their cell to the van waiting in the yard to take them to the Palais de Justice for the magistrate's examination—they pass along straight lines each of which ends in a door that is opened to them by a warder. The sole duty of the warder is to open and shut this door and to watch the two straight lines which it commands. And thus the prisoners, while apparently at liberty to come and go as they please, are sent from door to door, from eye to eye, like so many parcels passed from hand to hand.

Outside, municipal guards receive the object and pack it into one of the compartments of the "salad-basket."[2]

This is the ordinary routine.

In Lupin's case it was disregarded entirely. The police were afraid of that walk along the corridors. They were afraid of the prison-van. They were afraid of everything.

M. Weber came in person, accompanied by twelve constables—the best he had, picked men, armed to the teeth—fetched the formidable prisoner at the door of his cell and took him in a cab, the driver of which was one of his own men, with mounted municipal guards trotting on each side, in front and behind.

"Bravo!" cried Lupin. "I am quite touched by the compliment paid me. A guard of honor. By Jove, Weber, you have the proper hierarchical instinct! You don't forget what is due to your immediate chief." And, tapping him on the shoulder: "Weber, I intend to send in my resignation. I shall name you as my successor."

"It's almost done," said Weber.

"That's good news! I was a little anxious about my escape. Now I am easy in my mind. From the moment when Weber is chief of the detective-service. . . !"

M. Weber did not reply to the gibe. At heart, he had a queer, complex feeling in the presence of his adversary, a feeling made up of the fear with which Lupin inspired him, the deference which he entertained for Prince Sernine and the respectful admiration which he had always shown to M. Lenormand. All this was mingled with spite, envy and satisfied hatred.

They arrived at the Palais de Justice. At the foot of the "mouse-trap," a number of detectives were waiting, among whom M. Weber rejoiced to see his best two lieutenants, the brothers Doudeville.

"Has M. Formerie come?" he asked.

"Yes, chief, Monsieur le Juge d'Instruction is in his room."

M. Weber went up the stairs, followed by Lupin, who had the Doudevilles on either side of him.

"Geneviève?" whispered the prisoner.

"Saved. . ."

---

2. The French slang expression for its prison-van or "black Maria."—*Translator's Note.*

MAURICE LEBLANC

"Where is she?"

"With her grandmother."

"Mrs. Kesselbach?"

"In Paris, at the Bristol."

"Suzanne?"

"Disappeared."

"Steinweg?"

"Released."

"What has he told you?"

"Nothing. Won't make any revelations except to you."

"Why?"

"We told him he owed his release to you."

"Newspapers good this morning?"

"Excellent."

"Good. If you want to write to me, here are my instructions."

They had reached the inner corridor on the first floor and Lupin slipped a pellet of paper into the hand of one of the brothers.

M. Formerie uttered a delicious phrase when Lupin entered his room accompanied by the deputy-chief:

"Ah, there you are! I knew we should lay hands on you some day or other!"

"So did I, Monsieur le Juge d'Instruction," said Lupin, "and I am glad that you have been marked out by fate to do justice to the honest man that I am."

"He's getting at me," thought M. Formerie. And, in the same ironical and serious tone as Lupin, he retorted, "The honest man that you are, sir, will be asked what he has to say about three hundred and forty-four separate cases of larceny, burglary, swindling and forgery, blackmail, receiving and so on. Three hundred and forty-four!"

"What! Is that all?" cried Lupin. "I really feel quite ashamed."

"Don't distress yourself! I shall discover more. But let us proceed in order. Arsène Lupin, in spite of all our inquiries, we have no definite information as to your real name."

"How odd! No more have I!"

"We are not even in a position to declare that you are the same Arsène Lupin who was confined in the Santé a few years back, and from there made his first escape."

"'His first escape' is good, and does you credit."

"It so happens, in fact," continued M. Formerie, "that the Arsène Lupin card in the measuring department gives a description of Arsène Lupin which differs at all points from your real description."

"How more and more odd!"

"Different marks, different measurements, different finger-prints. . . The two photographs even are quite unlike. I will therefore ask you to satisfy us as to your exact identity."

"That's just what I was going to ask you. I have lived under so many distinct names that I have ended by forgetting my own. I don't know where I am."

"So I must enter a refusal to answer?"

"An inability."

"Is this a thought-out plan? Am I to expect the same silence in reply to all my questions?"

"Very nearly."

"And why?"

Lupin struck a solemn attitude and said:

"M. le Juge d'Instruction, my life belongs to history. You have only to turn over the annals of the past fifteen years and your curiosity will be satisfied. So much for my part. As to the rest, it does not concern me: it is an affair between you and the murderers at the Palace Hotel."

"Arsène Lupin, the honest man that you are will have to-day to explain the murder of Master Altenheim."

"Hullo, this is new! Is the idea yours, Monsieur le Juge d'Instruction?"

"Exactly."

"Very clever! Upon my word, M. Formerie, you're getting on!"

"The position in which you were captured leaves no doubt."

"None at all; only, I will venture to ask you this: what sort of wound did Altenheim die of?"

"Of a wound in the throat caused by a knife."

"And where is the knife?"

"It has not been found."

"How could it not have been found, if I had been the assassin, considering that I was captured beside the very man whom I am supposed to have killed?"

"Who killed him, according to you?"

"The same man that killed Mr. Kesselbach, Chapman, and Beudot. The nature of the wound is a sufficient proof."

"How did he get away?"

"Through a trap-door, which you will discover in the room where the tragedy took place."

M. Formerie assumed an air of slyness:

"And how was it that you did not follow that useful example?"

"I tried to follow it. But the outlet was blocked by a door which I could not open. It was during this attempt that 'the other one' came back to the room and killed his accomplice for fear of the revelations which he would have been sure to make. At the same time, he hid in a cupboard, where it was subsequently found, the parcel of clothes which I had prepared."

"What were those clothes for?"

"To disguise myself. When I went to the Glycines my plan was this: to hand Altenheim over to the police, to suppress my own identity as Prince Sernine and to reappear under the features. . ."

"Of M. Lenormand, I suppose?"

"Exactly."

"No."

"What!"

M. Formerie gave a knowing smile and wagged his forefinger from left to right and right to left:

"No," he repeated.

"What do you mean by 'no'?"

"That story about M. Lenormand. . ."

"Well?"

"Will do for the public, my friend. But you won't make M. Formerie swallow that Lupin and Lenormand were one and the same man." He burst out laughing. "Lupin, chief of the detective-service! No, anything you like, but not that! . . . There are limits. . . I am an easy-going fellow. . . I'll believe anything. . . but still. . . Come, between ourselves, what was the reason of this fresh hoax? . . . I confess I can't see. . ."

Lupin looked at him in astonishment. In spite of all that he knew of M. Formerie, he could not conceive such a degree of infatuation and blindness. There was at that moment only one person in the world who refused to believe in Prince Sernine's double personality; and that was M. Formerie! . . .

Lupin turned to the deputy-chief, who stood listening open-mouthed:

"My dear Weber, I fear your promotion is not so certain as I thought. For, you see, if M. Lenormand is not myself, then he exists. . . and, if he exists, I have no doubt that M. Formerie, with all his acumen, will end by discovering him. . . in which case. . ."

"We shall discover him all right, M. Lupin," cried the examining-magistrate. "I'll undertake that, and I tell you that, when you and he are confronted, we shall see some fun." He chuckled and drummed with his fingers on the table. "How amusing! Oh, one's never bored when you're there, that I'll say for you! So you're M. Lenormand, and it's you who arrested your accomplice Marco!"

"Just so! Wasn't it my duty to please the prime minister and save the cabinet? The fact is historical."

M. Formerie held his sides:

"Oh, I shall die of laughing, I know I shall! Lord, what a joke! That answer will travel round the world. So, according to your theory, it was with you that I made the first enquiries at the Palace Hotel after the murder of Mr. Kesselbach? . . ."

"Surely it was with me that you investigated the case of the stolen coronet when I was Duc de Chamerace,"[3] retorted Lupin, in a sarcastic voice.

M. Formerie gave a start. All his merriment was dispelled by that odious recollection. Turning suddenly grave, he asked:

"So you persist in that absurd theory?"

"I must, because it is the truth. It would be easy for you to take a steamer to Cochin-China and to find at Saigon the proofs of the death of the real M. Lenormand, the worthy man whom I replaced and whose death-certificate I can show you."

"Humbug!"

"Upon my word, Monsieur le Juge d'Instruction, I don't care one way or the other. If it annoys you that I should be M. Lenormand, don't let's talk about it. We won't talk about myself; we won't talk about anything at all, if you prefer. Besides, of what use can it be to you? The Kesselbach case is such a tangled affair that I myself don't know where I stand. There's only one man who might help you. I have not succeeded in discovering him. And I don't think that you. . ."

"What's the man's name?"

---

3. See *Arsène Lupin* by Edgar Jepson and Maurice Leblanc.

MAURICE LEBLANC

"He's an old man, a German called Steinweg. . . But, of course, you've heard about him, Weber, and the way in which he was carried off in the middle of the Palais de Justice?"

M. Formerie threw an inquiring glance at the deputy-chief. M. Weber said:

"I undertake to bring that person to you, Monsieur le Juge d'Instruction."

"So that's done," said M. Formerie, rising from his chair. "As you see, Lupin, this was merely a formal examination to bring the two duelists together. Now that we have crossed swords, all that we need is the necessary witness of our fencing-match, your counsel."

"Tut! Is it indispensable?"

"Indispensable."

"Employ counsel in view of such an unlikely trial?"

"You must."

"In that case, I'll choose Maître Quimbel."

"The president of the corporation of the bar. You are wise, you will be well defended."

THE FIRST SITTING WAS OVER. M. Weber led the prisoner away.

As he went down the stairs of the "mouse-trap," between the two Doudevilles, Lupin said, in short, imperative sentences:

"Watch Steinweg. . . Don't let him speak to anybody. . . Be there to-morrow. . . I'll give you some letters. . . one for you. . . important."

Downstairs, he walked up to the municipal guards surrounding the taxi-cab:

"Home, boys," he exclaimed, "and quick about it! I have an appointment with myself for two o'clock precisely."

There were no incidents during the drive. On returning to his cell, Lupin wrote a long letter, full of detailed instructions, to the brothers Doudeville and, two other letters.

One was for Geneviève:

> "Geneviève, you now know who I am and you will understand why I concealed from you the name of him who twice carried you away in his arms when you were a little girl.
>
> "Geneviève, I was your mother's friend, a distant friend, of whose double life she knew nothing, but upon whom she thought that she could rely. And that is why, before dying, she wrote me a few lines asking me to watch over you.

"Unworthy as I am of your esteem, Geneviève, I shall continue faithful to that trust. Do not drive me from your heart entirely.

ARSÈNE LUPIN

The other letter was addressed to Dolores Kesselbach:

"Prince Sernine was led to seek Mrs. Kesselbach's acquaintance by motives of self-interest alone. But a great longing to devote himself to her was the cause of his continuing it.

"Now that Prince Sernine has become merely Arsène Lupin, he begs Mrs. Kesselbach not to deprive him of the right of protecting her, at a distance and as a man protects one whom he will never see again."

There were some envelopes on the table. He took up one and took up a second; then, when he took up the third, he noticed a sheet of white paper, the presence of which surprised him and which had words stuck upon it, evidently cut out of a newspaper. He read:

"You have failed in your fight with the baron. Give up interesting yourself in the case, and I will not oppose your escape.

L. M.

Once more, Lupin had that sense of repulsion and terror with which this nameless and fabulous being always inspired him, a sense of disgust which one feels at touching a venomous animal, a reptile:

"He again," he said. "Even here!"

That also scared him, the sudden vision which he at times received of this hostile power, a power as great as his own and disposing of formidable means, the extent of which he himself was unable to realize.

He at once suspected his warder. But how had it been possible to corrupt that hard-featured, stern-eyed man?

"Well, so much the better, after all!" he cried. "I have never had to do except with dullards... In order to fight myself, I had to chuck myself into the command of the detective-service... This time, I have some one to deal with! ... Here's a man who puts me in his pocket...

by sleight of hand, one might say. . . If I succeed, from my prison cell, in avoiding his blows and smashing him, in seeing old Steinweg and dragging his confession from him, in setting the Kesselbach case on its legs and turning the whole of it into cash, in defending Mrs. Kesselbach and winning fortune and happiness for Geneviève. . . well, then Lupin will be Lupin still! . . ."

Eleven days passed. On the twelfth day, Lupin woke very early and exclaimed:

"Let me see, if my calculations are correct and if the gods are on my side, there will be some news to-day. I have had four interviews with Formerie. The fellow must be worked up to the right point now. And the Doudevilles, on their side, must have been busy. . . We shall have some fun!"

He flung out his fists to right and left, brought them back to his chest, then flung them out again and brought them back again.

This movement, which executed thirty times in succession, was followed by a bending of his body backwards and forwards. Next came an alternate lifting of the legs and then an alternate swinging of the arms.

The whole performance occupied a quarter of an hour, the quarter of an hour which he devoted every morning to Swedish exercises to keep his muscles in condition.

Then he sat down to his table, took up some sheets of white paper, which were arranged in numbered packets, and, folding one of them, made it into an envelope, a work which he continued to do with a series of successive sheets. It was the task which he had accepted and which he forced himself to do daily, the prisoners having the right to choose the labor which they preferred: sticking envelopes, making paper fans, metal purses, and so on. . .

And, in this way, while occupying his hands with an automatic exercise and keeping his muscles supple with mechanical bendings, Lupin was able to have his thoughts constantly fixed on his affairs. . .

And his affairs were complicated enough, in all conscience!

There was one, for instance, which surpassed all the others in importance, and for which he had to employ all the resources of his genius. How was he to have a long, quiet conversation with old Steinweg? The necessity was immediate. In a few days, Steinweg would have recovered from his imprisonment, would receive interviews, might blab. . . to say nothing of the inevitable interference of the enemy, 'the other one.' And it was essential that Steinweg's secret, Pierre Leduc's secret, should be revealed to no one but Lupin. Once published, the secret lost all its value. . .

The bolts grated, the key turned noisily in the lock.

"Ah, it's you, most excellent of jailers! Has the moment come for the last toilet? The hair-cut that precedes the great final cut of all?"

"Magistrate's examination," said the man, laconically.

Lupin walked through the corridors of the prison and was received by the municipal guards, who locked him into the prison-van.

He reached the Palais de Justice twenty minutes later. One of the Doudevilles was waiting near the stairs. As they went up, he said to Lupin:

"You'll be confronted to-day."

"Everything settled?"

"Yes."

"Weber?"

"Busy elsewhere."

Lupin walked into M. Formerie's room and at once recognized old Steinweg, sitting on a chair, looking ill and wretched. A municipal guard was standing behind him.

M. Formerie scrutinized the prisoner attentively, as though he hoped to draw important conclusions from his contemplation of him, and said:

"You know who this gentleman is?"

"Why, Steinweg, of course! . . ."

"Yes, thanks to the active inquiries of M. Weber and of his two officers, the brothers Doudeville, we have found Mr. Steinweg, who, according to you, knows the ins and outs of the Kesselbach case, the name of the murderer and all the rest of it."

"I congratulate you, Monsieur le Juge d'Instruction. Your examination will go swimmingly."

"I think so. There is only one 'but': Mr. Steinweg refuses to reveal anything, except in your presence."

"Well, I never! How odd of him! Does Arsène Lupin inspire him with so much affection and esteem?"

"Not Arsène Lupin, but Prince Sernine, who, he says, saved his life, and M. Lenormand, with whom, he says, he began a conversation. . ."

"At the time when I was chief of the detective-service," Lupin broke in. "So you consent to admit."

"Mr. Steinweg," said the magistrate, "do you recognize M. Lenormand?"

"No, but I know that Arsène Lupin and he are one."

"So you consent to speak?"

"Yes. . . but. . . we are not alone."

"How do you mean? There is only my clerk here. . . and the guard. . ."

"Monsieur le Juge d'Instruction, the secret which I am about to reveal is so important that you yourself would be sorry. . ."

"Guard, go outside, please," said M. Formerie. "Come back at once, if I call. Do you object to my clerk, Steinweg?"

"No, no. . . it might be better. . . but, however. . ."

"Then speak. For that matter, nothing that you reveal will be put down in black on white. One word more, though: I ask you for the last time, is it indispensable that the prisoner should be present at this interview?"

"Quite indispensable. You will see the reason for yourself."

He drew the chair up to the magistrate's desk, Lupin remained standing, near the clerk. And the old man, speaking in a loud voice, said:

"It is now ten years since a series of circumstances, which I need not enter into, made me acquainted with an extraordinary story in which two persons are concerned."

"Their names, please."

"I will give the names presently. For the moment, let me say that one of these persons occupies an exceptional position in France, and that the other, an Italian, or rather a Spaniard. . . yes, a Spaniard. . ."

A bound across the room, followed by two formidable blows of the fist. . . Lupin's two arms had darted out to right and left, as though impelled by springs and his two fists, hard as cannon balls, caught the magistrate and his clerk on the jaw, just below the ear.

The magistrate and the clerk collapsed over their tables, in two lumps, without a moan.

"Well hit!" said Lupin. "That was a neat bit of work."

He went to the door and locked it softly. Then returning:

"Steinweg, have you the chloroform?"

"Are you quite sure that they have fainted?" asks the old man, trembling with fear.

"What do you think! But it will only last for three or four minutes. . . And that is not long enough."

The German produced from his pocket a bottle and two pads of cotton-wool, ready prepared.

Lupin uncorked the bottle, poured a few drops of the chloroform on the two pads and held them to the noses of the magistrate and his clerk.

"Capital! We have ten minutes of peace and quiet before us. That will do, but let's make haste, all the same; and not a word too much, old man, do you hear?" He took him by the arm. "You see what I am able to do. Here we are, alone in the very heart of the Palais de Justice, because I wished it."

"Yes," said the old man.

"So you are going to tell me your secret?"

"Yes, I told it to Kesselbach, because he was rich and could turn it to better account than anybody I knew; but, prisoner and absolutely powerless though you are, I consider you a hundred times as strong as Kesselbach with his hundred millions."

"In that case, speak; and let us take things in their proper order. The name of the murderer?"

"That's impossible."

"How do you mean, impossible? I thought you knew it and were going to tell me everything!"

"Everything, but not that."

"But. . ."

"Later on."

"You're mad! Why?"

"I have no proofs. Later, when you are free, we will hunt together. Besides, what's the good? And then, really, I can't tell you."

"You're afraid of him?"

"Yes."

"Very well," said Lupin. "After all, that's not the most urgent matter. As to the rest, you've made up your mind to speak?"

"Without reserve."

"Well, then, answer. Who is Pierre Leduc?"

"Hermann IV, Grand Duke of Zweibrucken-Veldenz, Prince of Berncastel, Count of Fistingen, Lord of Wiesbaden and other places."

Lupin felt a thrill of joy at learning that his *protégé* was definitely not the son of a pork-butcher!

"The devil!" he muttered. "So we have a handle to our name! . . . As far as I remember, the Grand-duchy of Zweibrucken-Veldenz is in Prussia?"

"Yes, on the Moselle. The house of Veldenz is a branch of the Palatine house of Zweibrucken. The grand-duchy was occupied by the French after the peace of Luneville and formed part of the department of Mont-Tonnerre. In 1814, it was restored in favor of Hermann I, the great grandfather of Pierre Leduc. His son, Hermann II, spent a riotous youth, ruined himself, squandered the finances of his country and made himself impossible to his subjects, who ended by partly burning the old castle at Veldenz and driving their sovereign out of his dominions. The grand-duchy was then administered and governed by three regents, in the name of Hermann II, who, by a curious anomaly, did not abdicate, but retained his title as reigning grand-duke. He lived, rather short of cash, in Berlin; later, he fought in the French war, by the side of Bismarck, of whom he was a friend. He was killed by a shell at the siege of Paris and, in dying, entrusted Bismarck with the charge of his son Hermann, that is, Hermann III."

"The father, therefore, of our Leduc," said Lupin.

"Yes. The chancellor took a liking to Hermann III, and used often to employ him as a secret envoy to persons of distinction abroad. At the fall of his patron Hermann III, left Berlin, travelled about and returned and settled in Dresden. When Bismarck died, Hermann III, was there. He himself died two years later. These are public facts, known to everybody in Germany; and that is the story of the three Hermanns, Grand-dukes of Zweibrucken-Veldenz in the nineteenth century."

"But the fourth, Hermann IV, the one in whom we are interested?"

"We will speak of him presently. Let us now pass on to unknown facts."

"Facts known to you alone," said Lupin.

"To me alone and to a few others."

"How do you mean, a few others? Hasn't the secret been kept?"

"Yes, yes, the secret has been well kept by all who know it. Have no fear; it is very much to their interest, I assure you, not to divulge it."

"Then how do you know it?"

"Through an old servant and private secretary of the Grand-duke Hermann, the last of the name. This servant, who died in my arms in South Africa, began by confiding to me that his master was secretly married and had left a son behind him. Then he told me the great secret."

"The one which you afterwards revealed to Kesselbach."

"Yes."

"One second. . . Will you excuse me? . . ."

Lupin bent over M. Formerie, satisfied himself that all was well and the heart beating normally, and said:

"Go on."

Steinweg resumed:

"On the evening of the day on which Bismarck died, the Grand-duke Hermann III and his faithful manservant—my South African friend—took a train which brought them to Munich in time to catch the express for Vienna. From Vienna, they went to Constantinople, then to Cairo, then to Naples, then to Tunis, then to Spain, then to Paris, then to London, to St. Petersburg, to Warsaw. . . and in none of these towns did they stop. They took a cab, had their two bags put on the top, rushed through the streets, hurried to another station or to the landing-stage, and once more took the train or the steamer."

"In short, they were being followed and were trying to put their pursuers off the scent," Arsène Lupin concluded.

"One evening, they left the city of Treves, dressed in workmen's caps and linen jackets, each with a bundle slung over his shoulder at the end of a stick. They covered on foot the twenty-two miles to Veldenz, where the old Castle of Zweibrucken stands, or rather the ruins of the old castle."

"No descriptions, please."

"All day long, they remained hidden in a neighboring forest. At night, they went up to the old walls. Hermann ordered his servant to wait for him and himself scaled the wall at a breach known as the Wolf's Gap. He returned in an hour's time. In the following week, after more peregrinations, he went back home to Dresden. The expedition was over."

"And what was the object of the expedition?"

"The grand-duke never breathed a word about it to his servant. But certain particulars and the coincidence of facts that ensued enabled the man to build up the truth, at least, in part."

"Quick, Steinweg, time is running short now: and I am eager to know."

"A fortnight after the expedition, Count von Waldemar, an officer in the Emperor's body-guard and one of his personal friends, called on the grand-duke, accompanied by six men. He was there all day, locked up with the grand-duke in his study. There were repeated sounds of altercations, of violent disputes. One phrase even was overheard by the servant, who was passing through the garden, under the windows: 'Those papers were handed to you; His imperial Majesty is sure of it. If you refuse to give them to me of your own free will. . .' The rest of the sentence, the meaning of the threat and, for that matter, the whole scene can be easily guessed by what followed; Hermann's house was ransacked from top to bottom."

"But that is against the law."

"It would have been against the law if the grand-duke had objected; but he himself accompanied the count in his search."

"And what were they looking for? The chancellor's memoirs?"

"Something better than that. They were looking for a parcel of secret documents which were known to exist, owing to indiscretions that had been committed, and which were known for certain to have been entrusted to the Grand-duke Hermann's keeping."

Lupin muttered, excitedly:

"Secret documents. . . and very important ones, no doubt?"

"Of the highest importance. The publication of those papers would lead to results which it would be impossible to foresee, not only from the point of view of home politics, but also from that of Germany's relations with the foreign powers."

"Oh!" said Lupin, throbbing with emotion. "Oh, can it be possible? What proof have you?"

"What proof? The evidence of the grand-duke's wife, the confidences which she made to the servant after her husband's death."

"Yes. . . yes. . ." stammered Lupin. "We have the evidence of the grand-duke himself."

"Better still," said Steinweg.

"What?"

"A document, a document written in his own hand, signed by him and containing. . ."

"Containing what?"

"A list of the secret papers confided to his charge."

"Tell me, in two words. . ."

"In two words? That can't be done. The document is a very long one, scattered all over with annotations and remarks which are sometimes impossible to understand. Let me mention just two titles which obviously refer to two bundles of secret papers: *Original letters of the Crown Prince to Bismarck* is one. The dates show that these letters were written during the three months of the reign of Frederick III. To picture what the letters may contain, you have only to think of the Emperor Frederick's illness, his quarrels with his son. . ."

"Yes, yes, I know. . . And the other title?"

"*Photographs of the letters of Frederick III, and the Empress Victoria to the Queen of England.*"

"Do you mean to say that that's there?" asked Lupin, in a choking voice.

"Listen to the grand-duke's notes: *Text of the treaty with Great Britain and France.* And these rather obscure words: 'Alsace-Lorraine. . . Colonies. . . Limitation of naval armaments. . .'"

"It says that?" blurted Lupin. "And you call that obscure? . . . Why, the words are dazzling with light! . . . Oh, can it be possible? . . . And what next, what next?"

As he spoke there was a noise at the door. Some one was knocking.

"You can't come in," said Lupin. "I am busy. . . Go on, Steinweg."

"But. . ." said the old man, in a great state of alarm.

The door was shaken violently and Lupin recognized Weber's voice. He shouted:

"A little patience, Weber. I shall have done in five minutes."

He gripped the old man's arm and, in a tone of command:

"Be easy and go on with your story. So, according to you, the expedition of the grand duke and his servant to Veldenz Castle had no other object than to hide those papers?"

"There can be no question about that."

"Very well. But the grand-duke may have taken them away since."

"No, he did not leave Dresden until his death."

"But the grand-duke's enemies, the men who had everything to gain by recovering them and destroying them: can't they have tried to find out where the papers were?"

"They have tried."

"How do you know?"

"You can understand that I did not remain inactive and that my first care, after receiving those revelations, was to go to Veldenz and make inquiries for myself in the neighboring villages. Well, I learnt that, on two separate occasions, the castle was invaded by a dozen men, who came from Berlin furnished with credentials to the regents."

"Well?"

"Well, they found nothing, for, since that time, the castle has been found closed to the public."

"But what prevents anybody from getting in?"

"A garrison of fifty soldiers, who keep watch day and night."

"Soldiers of the grand-duchy?"

"No, soldiers drafted from the Emperor's own body-guard."

The din in the passage increased:

"Open the door!" a voice cried. "I order you to open the door!"

"I can't. Weber, old chap; the lock has stuck. If you take my advice, you had better cut the door all round the lock."

"Open the door!"

"And what about the fate of Europe, which we are discussing?"

He turned to the old man:

"So you were not able to enter the castle?"

"No."

"But you are persuaded that the papers in question are hidden there?"

"Look here, haven't I given you proofs enough? Aren't you convinced?"

"Yes, yes," muttered Lupin, "that's where they are hidden. . . there's no doubt about it. . . that's where they are hidden. . ."

He seemed to see the castle. He seemed to conjure up the mysterious hiding-place. And the vision of an inexhaustible treasure, the dream of chests filled with riches and precious stones could not have excited him more than the idea of those few scraps of paper watched over by the Kaiser's guards. What a wonderful conquest to embark upon! And how worthy of his powers! And what a proof of perspicacity and intuition he had once more given by throwing himself at a venture upon that unknown track!

Outside, the men were "working" at the lock.

Lupin asked of old Steinweg:

"What did the grand-duke die of?"

"An attack of pleurisy, which carried him off in a few days. He hardly recovered consciousness before the end; and the horrible thing appears to have been that he was seen to make violent efforts, between his fits of delirium, to collect his thoughts and utter connected words. From time to time, he called his wife, looked at her in a desperate way and vainly moved his lips."

"In a word, he spoke?" said Lupin, cutting him short, for the "working" at the lock was beginning to make him anxious.

"No, he did not speak. But, in a comparatively lucid moment, he summoned up the energy to make some marks on a piece of paper which his wife gave him."

"Well, those marks. . . ?"

"They were illegible, for the most part."

"For the most part? But the others?" asked Lupin, greedily. "The others?"

"There were, first, three perfectly distinct figures: an 8, a 1, and a 3. . ."

"Yes, 813, I know. . . and next?"

"And next, there were some letters. . . several letters, of which all that can be made out for certain are a group of three followed, immediately after, by a group of two letters."

"'Apo On,' is that it?"

"Oh, so you know! . . ."

The lock was yielding; almost all the screws had been taken out. Lupin, suddenly alarmed at the thought of being interrupted, asked:

"So that this incomplete word 'Apo On' and the number 813 are the formulas which the grand-duke bequeathed to his wife and son to enable them to find the secret papers?"

"Yes."

"What became of the grand-duke's wife?"

"She died soon after her husband, of grief, one might say."

"And was the child looked after by the family?"

"What family? The grand-duke had no brothers or sisters. Moreover, he was only morganatically and secretly married. No, the child was taken away by Hermann's old man-servant, who brought him up under the name of Pierre Leduc. He was a bad type of boy, self-willed, capricious and troublesome. One day, he went off and was never seen again."

"Did he know the secret of his birth?"

"Yes; and he was shown the sheet of paper on which Hermann III had written the letters and figures."

"And after that this revelation was made to no one but yourself?"

"That's all."

"And you confided only in Mr. Kesselbach?"

"Yes. But, out of prudence, while showing him the sheet of letters and figures and the list of which I spoke to you, I kept both those documents in my own possession. Events have proved that I was right."

Lupin was now clinging to the door with both hands:

"Weber," he roared, "you're very indiscreet! I shall report you! . . . Steinweg, have you those documents?"

"Yes."

"Are they in a safe place?"

"Absolutely."

"In Paris?"

"No."

"So much the better. Don't forget that your life is in danger and that you have people after you."

"I know. The least false step and I am done for."

"Exactly. So take your precautions, throw the enemy off the scent, go and fetch your papers and await my instructions. The thing is cut and dried. In a month, at latest, we will go to Veldenz Castle together."

"Suppose I'm in prison?"

"I will take you out."

"Can you?"

"The very day after I come out myself. No, I'm wrong: the same evening. . . an hour later."

"You have the means?"

"Since the last ten minutes, an infallible means. You have nothing more to say to me?"

"No."

"Then I'll open the door."

He pulled back the door, and bowing to M. Weber:

"My poor old Weber, I don't know what excuse to make. . ."

He did not finish his sentence. The sudden inrush of the deputy-chief and three policeman left him no time.

M. Weber was white with rage and indignation. The sight of the two men lying outstretched quite unsettled him.

"Dead!" he exclaimed.

"Not a bit of it, not a bit of it," chuckled Lupin, "only asleep! Formerie was tired out. . . so I allowed him a few moments' rest."

"Enough of this humbug!" shouted M. Weber. And, turning to the policemen, "Take him back to the Santé. And keep your eyes open, damn it! As for this visitor. . ."

Lupin learnt nothing more as to Weber's intentions with regard to old Steinweg. A crowd of municipal guards and police constables hustled him down to the prison-van.

On the stairs Doudeville whispered:

"Weber had a line to warn him. It told him to mind the confrontation and to be on his guard with Steinweg. The note was signed 'L. M.'"

But Lupin hardly bothered his head about all this. What did he care for the murderer's hatred or old Steinweg's fate? He possessed Rudolf Kesselbach's secret!

X

Lupin's Great Scheme

C ontrary to his expectations, Lupin had no sort of annoyance to undergo in consequence of his assault on M. Formerie.

The examining-magistrate came to the Santé in person, two days later, and told him, with some embarrassment and with an affectation of kindness, that he did not intend to pursue the matter further.

"Nor I, either," retorted Lupin.

"What do you mean?"

"Well, I mean that I shall send no communication to the press about this particular matter nor do anything that might expose you to ridicule, Monsieur le Juge d'Instruction. The scandal shall not be made public, I promise. That is what you want, is it not?"

M. Formerie blushed and, without replying, continued:

"Only, henceforth, your examinations will take place here."

"It's quite right that the law should put itself out for Lupin!" said that gentleman.

The announcement of this decision, which interrupted his almost daily meetings with the Doudevilles, did not disturb Lupin. He had taken his precautions from the first day, by giving the Doudevilles all the necessary instructions and, now that the preparations were nearly completed, reckoned upon being able to turn old Steinweg's confidences to the best account without delay and to obtain his liberty by one of the most extraordinary and ingenious schemes that had ever entered his brain.

His method of correspondence was a simple one; and he had devised it at once. Every morning he was supplied with sheets of paper in numbered packets. He made these into envelopes; and, every evening, the envelopes, duly folded and gummed, were fetched away. Now Lupin, noticing that his packet always bore the same number, had drawn the inference that the distribution of the numbered packets was always affected in the same order among the prisoners who had chosen that particular kind of work. Experience showed that he was right.

It only remained for the Doudevilles to bribe one of the employees of the private firm entrusted with the supply and dispatch of the envelopes.

This was easily done; and, thenceforward, Lupin, sure of success, had only to wait quietly until the sign agreed upon between him and his friends appeared upon the top sheet of the packet.

On the sixth day, he gave an exclamation of delight:

"At last!" he said.

He took a tiny bottle from a hiding-place, uncorked it, moistened the tip of his forefinger with the liquid which it contained and passed his finger over the third sheet in the packet.

In a moment, strokes appeared, then letters, then words and sentences. He read:

"All well. Steinweg free. Hiding in country. Geneviève
Ernemont good health. Often goes Hôtel Bristol to see
Mrs. Kesselbach, who is ill. Meets Pierre Leduc there every
time. Answer by same means. No danger."

So communications were established with the outside. Once more, Lupin's efforts were crowned with success. All that he had to do now was to execute his plan and lead the press campaign which he had prepared in the peaceful solitude of his prison.

Three days later, these few lines appeared in the *Grand Journal*:

"Quite apart from Prince Bismarck's *Memoirs*, which,
according to well-informed people, contain merely the
official history of the events in which the great chancellor
was concerned, there exists a series of confidential letters of
no little interest.

"These letters have been recently discovered. We hear,
on good authority, that they will be published almost
immediately."

My readers will remember the noise which these mysterious sentences made throughout the civilized world, the comments in which people indulged, the suggestions put forward and, in particular, the controversy that followed in the German press. Who had inspired those lines? What were the letters in question? Who had written them to the chancellor or who had received them from him? Was it an act of posthumous revenge? Or was it an indiscretion committed by one of Bismarck's correspondents?

A second note settled public opinion as to certain points, but, at the same time, worked it up to a strange pitch of excitement. It ran as follows:

To the Editor of the Grand Journal,
SANTÉ PALACE,
Cell 14, Second Division

SIR,

"You inserted in your issue of Tuesday last a paragraph based upon a few words which I let fall, the other evening, in the course of a lecture, which I was delivering at the Santé on foreign politics. Your correspondent's paragraph, although accurate in all essential particulars, requires a slight correction. The letters exist, as stated, and it is impossible to deny their exceptional importance, seeing that, for ten years, they have been the object of an uninterrupted search on the part of the government interested. But nobody knows where they are hidden and nobody knows a single word of what they contain.

"The public, I am convinced, will bear me no ill-will if I keep it waiting for some time before satisfying its legitimate curiosity. Apart from the fact that I am not in possession of all the elements necessary for the pursuit of the truth, my present occupation does not allow me to devote so much time as I could wish to this matter.

"All that I can say for the moment is that the letters were entrusted by the dying statesman to one of his most faithful friends and that this friend had eventually to suffer the serious consequences of his loyalty. Constant spying, domiciliary visits, nothing was spared him.

"I have given orders to two of the best agents of my secret police to take up this scent from the start in a position to get to the bottom of this exciting mystery.

I have the honor to be Sir,
Your obedient servant,
ARSÈNE LUPIN

So it was Arsène Lupin who was conducting the case! It was he who, from his prison cell, was stage-managing the comedy or the tragedy announced in the first note. What luck! Everybody was delighted. With an artist like Lupin, the spectacle could not fail to be both picturesque and startling.

Three days later the *Grand Journal* contained the following letter from Arsène Lupin:

> "The name of the devoted friend to whom I referred has been imparted to me. It was the Grand-Duke Hermann III, reigning (although dispossessed) sovereign of the Grand-duchy of Zweibrucken-Veldenz and a confidant of Prince Bismarck, whose entire friendship he enjoyed.
>
> "A thorough search was made of his house by Count von W——, at the head of twelve men. The result of this search was purely negative, but the grand-duke was nevertheless proved to be in possession of the papers.
>
> "Where had he hidden them? This was a problem which probably nobody in the world would be able to solve at the present moment.
>
> "I must ask for twenty-four hours in which to solve it.
>
> ARSÈNE LUPIN

And, twenty-four hours later, the promised note appeared:

> "The famous letters are hidden in the feudal castle of Veldenz, the capital of the Grand-duchy of Zweibrucken. The castle was partly destroyed in the course of the nineteenth century.
>
> "Where exactly are they hidden? And what are the letters precisely? These are the two problems which I am now engaged in unravelling; and I shall publish the solution in four days' time.
>
> ARSÈNE LUPIN

On the day stated, men scrambled to obtain copies of the *Grand Journal*. To the general disappointment, the promised information was not given. The same silence followed on the next day and the day after.

What had happened?

It leaked out through an indiscretion at the Prefecture of Police. The governor of the Santé, it appeared, had been warned that Lupin was communicating with his accomplices by means of the packets of envelopes which he made. Nothing had been discovered; but it was thought best, in any case, to forbid all work to the insufferable prisoner.

To this the insufferable prisoner replied:

"As I have nothing to do now, I may as well attend to my trial. Please let my counsel, Maître Quimbel, know."

It was true. Lupin, who, hitherto, had refused to hold any intercourse with Maître Quimbel, now consented to see him and to prepare his defence.

On the next day Maître Quimbel, in cheery tones, asked for Lupin to be brought to the barristers' room. He was an elderly man, wearing a pair of very powerful spectacles, which made his eyes seem enormous. He put his hat on the table, spread out his brief-case and at once began to put a series of questions which he had carefully prepared.

Lupin replied with extreme readiness and even volunteered a host of particulars, which Maître Quimbel took down, as he spoke, on slips pinned one to the other.

"And so you say," continued the barrister, with his head over his papers, "that, at that time. . ."

"I say that, at that time. . ." Lupin answered.

Little by little, with a series of natural and hardly perceptible movements, he leant elbows on the table. He gradually lowered his arms, slipped his hand under Maître Quimbel's hat, put his finger into the leather band and took out one of those strips of paper, folded lengthwise, which the hatter inserts between the leather and the lining when the hat is a trifle too large.

He unfolded the paper. It was a message from Doudeville, written in a cipher agreed upon beforehand:

"I am engaged as indoor servant at Maître Quimbel's. You can answer by the same means without fear.

"It was L. M., the murderer, who gave away the envelope trick. A good thing that you foresaw this move!"

Hereupon followed a minute report of all the facts and comments caused by Lupin's revelations.

Lupin took from his pocket a similar strip of paper containing his instructions, quietly substituted it in the place of the other and drew his hand back again. The trick was played.

And Lupin's correspondence with the *Grand Journal* was resumed without further delay.

"I apologize to the public for not keeping my promise. The postal arrangements at the Santé Palace are woefully inadequate.

"However, we are near the end. I have in hand all the documents that establish the truth upon an indisputable basis. I shall not publish them for the moment. Nevertheless, I will say this: among the letters are some that were addressed to the chancellor by one who, at that time, declared himself his disciple and his admirer and who was destined, several years after, to rid himself of that irksome tutor and to govern alone.

"I trust that I make myself sufficiently clear."

And, on the next day:

"The letters were written during the late Emperor's illness. I need hardly add more to prove their importance."

Four days of silence, and then this final note, which caused a stir that has not yet been forgotten:

"My investigation is finished. I now know everything.

"By dint of reflection, I have guessed the secret of the hiding-place.

"My friends are going to Veldenz and, in spite of every obstacle, will enter the castle by a way which I am pointing out to them.

"The newspapers will then publish photographs of the letters, of which I already know the tenor; but I prefer to reproduce the whole text.

"This certain, inevitable publication will take place in a fortnight from to-day precisely, on the 22nd of August next.

"Between this and then I will keep silence. . . and wait."

The communications to the *Grand Journal* did, in fact, stop for a time, but Lupin never ceased corresponding with his friends, "*via* the hat," as they said among themselves. It was so simple! There was no danger. Who could ever suspect that Maître Quimbel's hat served Lupin as a letter-box?

Every two or three mornings, whenever he called, in fact, the celebrated advocate faithfully brought his client's letters: letters from Paris, letters from the country, letters from Germany; all reduced and condensed by Doudeville into a brief form and cipher language. And, an hour later, Maître Quimbel solemnly walked away, carrying Lupin's orders.

Now, one day, the governor of the Santé received a telephone message, signed, "L. M.," informing him that Maître Quimbel was, in all probability, serving Lupin as his unwitting postman and that it would be advisable to keep an eye upon the worthy man's visits. The governor told Maître Quimbel, who thereupon resolved to bring his junior with him.

So, once again, in spite of all Lupin's efforts, in spite of his fertile powers of invention, in spite of the marvels of ingenuity which he renewed after each defeat, once again Lupin found himself cut off from communication with the outside world by the infernal genius of his formidable adversary. And he found himself thus cut off at the most critical moment, at the solemn minute when, from his cell, he was playing his last trump-card against the coalesced forces that were overwhelming him so terribly.

On the 13th of August, as he sat facing the two counsels, his attention was attracted by a newspaper in which some of Maître Quimbel's papers were wrapped up.

He saw a heading in very large type

"813"

The sub-headings were:

"A Fresh Murder
"The Excitement in Germany
"Has the Secret of the 'Apoon' Been Discovered?"

Lupin turned pale with anguish. Below he read the words:

"Two sensational telegrams reach us at the moment of going to press.

"The body of an old man has been found near Augsburg, with his throat cut with a knife. The police have succeeded in identifying the victim: it is Steinweg, the man mentioned in the Kesselbach case.

"On the other hand, a correspondent telegraphs that the famous English detective, Holmlock Shears, has been hurriedly summoned to Cologne. He will there meet the Emperor; and they will both proceed to Veldenz Castle.

"Holmlock Shears is said to have undertaken to discover the secret of the 'Apoon.'

"If he succeeds, it will mean the pitiful failure of the incomprehensible campaign which Arsène Lupin has been conducting for the past month in so strange a fashion."

Perhaps public curiosity was never so much stirred as by the duel announced to take place between Shears and Lupin, an invisible duel in the circumstances, an anonymous duel, one might say, in which everything would happen in the dark, in which people would be able to judge only by the final results, and yet an impressive duel, because of all the scandal that circled around the adventure and because of the stakes in dispute between the two irreconcilable enemies, now once more opposed to each other.

And it was a question not of small private interests, of insignificant burglaries, of trumpery individual passions, but of a matter of really world-wide importance, involving the politics of the three great western nations and capable of disturbing the peace of the world.

People waited anxiously; and no one knew exactly what he was waiting for. For, after all, if the detective came out victorious in the duel, if he found the letters, who would ever know? What proof would any one have of his triumph?

In the main, all hopes were centred on Lupin, on his well-known habit of calling the public to witness his acts. What was he going to do? How could he avert the frightful danger that threatened him? Was he even aware of it?

Those were the questions which men asked themselves.

Between the four walls of his cell, prisoner 14 asked himself pretty nearly the same questions; and he for his part, was not stimulated by idle curiosity, but by real uneasiness, by constant anxiety. He felt himself irrevocably alone, with impotent hands, an impotent will, an impotent brain. It availed him nothing that he was able, ingenious, fearless, heroic. The struggle was being carried on without him. His part was now finished. He had joined all the pieces and set all the springs of the great machine that was to produce, that was, in a manner of speaking, automatically to manufacture his liberty; and it was impossible for him to make a single movement to improve and supervise his handiwork.

At the date fixed, the machine would start working. Between now and then, a thousand adverse incidents might spring up, a thousand obstacles arise, without his having the means to combat those incidents or remove those obstacles.

Lupin spent the unhappiest hours of his life at that time. He doubted himself. He wondered whether his existence would be buried for good in the horror of a jail. Had he not made a mistake in his calculations? Was it not childish to believe that the event that was to set him free would happen on the appointed date?

"Madness!" he cried. "My argument is false... How can I expect such a concurrence of circumstances? There will be some little fact that will destroy all... the inevitable grain of sand..."

Steinweg's death and the disappearance of the documents which the old man was to make over to him did not trouble him greatly. The documents he could have done without in case of need; and, with the few words which Steinweg had told him, he was able, by dint of guess-work and his native genius, to reconstruct what the Emperor's letters contained and to draw up the plan of battle that would lead to victory. But he thought of Holmlock Shears, who was over there now, in the very centre of the battlefield, and who was seeking and who would find the letters, thus demolishing the edifice so patiently built up.

And he thought of "the other one," the implacable enemy, lurking round the prison, hidden in the prison, perhaps, who guessed his most secret plans even before they were hatched in the mystery of his thought.

THE 17TH OF AUGUST! ... The 18th of August! ... The 19th! ... Two more days... Two centuries rather! Oh, the interminable minutes! ...

Lupin, usually so calm, so entirely master of himself, so ingenious at providing matter for his own amusement, was feverish, exultant and depressed by turns, powerless against the enemy, mistrusting everything and everybody, morose.

THE 20TH OF AUGUST! . . .

HE WOULD HAVE WISHED TO act and he could not. Whatever he did, it was impossible for him to hasten the hour of the catastrophe. This catastrophe would take place or would not take place; but Lupin would not know for certain until the last hour of the last day was spent to the last minute. Then—and then alone—he would know of the definite failure of his scheme.

"The inevitable failure," he kept on repeating to himself. "Success depends upon circumstances far too subtle and can be obtained only by methods far too psychological. . . There is no doubt that I am deceiving myself as to the value and the range of my weapons. . . And yet. . ."

Hope returned to him. He weighed his chances. They suddenly seemed to him real and formidable. The fact was going to happen as he had foreseen it happening and for the very reasons which he had expected. It was inevitable. . .

Yes, inevitable. Unless, indeed, Shears discovered the hiding-place. . .

And again he thought of Shears; and again an immense sense of discouragement overwhelmed him.

THE LAST DAY. . .

He woke late, after a night of bad dreams.

He saw nobody that day, neither the examining magistrate nor his counsel.

The afternoon dragged along slowly and dismally, and the evening came, the murky evening of the cells. . . He was in a fever. His heart beat in his chest like the clapper of a bell.

And the minutes passed, irretrievably. . .

At nine o'clock, nothing. At ten o'clock, nothing.

With all his nerves tense as the string of a bow, he listened to the vague prison sounds, tried to catch through those inexorable walls all that might trickle in from the life outside.

Oh, how he would have liked to stay the march of time and to give destiny a little more leisure!

But what was the good? Was everything not finished? . . .

813

"Oh," he cried, "I am going mad! If all this were only over. . . that would be better. I can begin again, differently. . . I shall try something else. . . but I can't go on like this, I can't go on. . ."

He held his head in his hands, pressing it with all his might, locking himself within himself and concentrating his whole mind upon one subject, as though he wished to provoke, as though he wished to create the formidable, stupefying, inadmissible event to which he had attached his independence and his fortune:

"It must happen," he muttered, "it must; and it must, not because I wish it, but because it is logical. And it shall happen. . . it shall happen. . ."

He beat his skull with his fists; and delirious words rose to his lips. . .

The key grated in the lock. In his frenzy, he had not heard the sound of footsteps in the corridor; and now, suddenly, a ray of light penetrated into his cell and the door opened.

Three men entered.

Lupin had not a moment of surprise.

The unheard-of miracle was being worked; and this at once seemed to him natural and normal, in perfect agreement with truth and justice.

But a rush of pride flooded his whole being. At this minute he really received a clear sensation of his own strength and intelligence. . .

"Shall I switch on the light?" asked one of the three men, in whom Lupin recognized the governor of the prison.

"No," replied the taller of his companions, speaking in a foreign accent. "This lantern will do."

"Shall I go?"

"Act according to your duty, sir," said the same individual.

"My instructions from the prefect of police are to comply entirely with your wishes."

"In that case, sir, it would be preferable that you should withdraw."

M. Borély went away, leaving the door half open, and remained outside, within call.

The visitor exchanged a few words with the one who had not yet spoken; and Lupin vainly tried to distinguish his features in the shade. He saw only two dark forms, clad in wide motoring-cloaks and wearing caps with the flaps lowered.

"Are you Arsène Lupin?" asked the man, turning the light of the lantern full on his face.

He smiled:

"Yes, I am the person known as Arsène Lupin, at present a prisoner in the Santé, cell 14, second division."

"Was it you," continued the visitor, "who published in the *Grand Journal* a series of more or less fanciful notes, in which there is a question of a so-called collection of letters. . . ?"

Lupin interrupted him.

"I beg your pardon, sir, but, before pursuing this conversation, the object of which, between ourselves, is none too clear to me, I should be much obliged if you would tell me to whom I have the honour of speaking."

"Absolutely unnecessary," replied the stranger.

"Absolutely essential," declared Lupin.

"Why?"

"For reasons of politeness, sir. You know my name and I do not know yours; this implies a disregard of good form which I cannot suffer."

The stranger lost patience:

"The mere fact that the governor of the prison brought us here shows. . ."

"That M. Borély does not know his manners," said Lupin. "M. Borély should have introduced us to each other. We are equals here, sir: it is no case of a superior and an inferior, of a prisoner and a visitor who condescends to come and see him. There are two men here; and one of those two men has a hat on his head, which he ought not to have."

"Now look here. . ."

"Take the lesson as you please, sir," said Lupin.

The stranger came closer to him and tried to speak.

"The hat first," said Lupin, "the hat. . ."

"You shall listen to me!"

"No."

"Yes."

"No."

Matters were becoming virulent, stupidly. The second stranger, the one who had kept silent, placed his hand on his companion's shoulder and said, in German:

"Leave him to me."

"Why, it was understood. . ."

"Hush. . . and go away!"

"Leaving you alone?"

"Yes."

"But the door?"

"Shut it and walk away."

"But this man. . . you know who he is. . . Arsène Lupin. . ."

"Go away!"

The other went out, cursing under his breath.

"Pull the door!" cried the second visitor. "Harder than that. . . Altogether! . . . That's right. . ."

Then he turned, took the lantern and raised it slowly:

"Shall I tell you who I am?" he asked.

"No," replied Lupin.

"And why?"

"Because I know."

"Ah!"

"You are the visitor I was expecting."

"I?"

"Yes, Sire."

XI

CHARLEMAGNE

S ilence!" said the stranger, sharply. "Don't use that word."
   "Then what shall I call Your. . ."

"Call me nothing."

They were both silent; and this moment of respite was not one of those which go before the struggle of two adversaries ready for the fray. The stranger strode to and fro with the air of a master accustomed to command and to be obeyed. Lupin stood motionless. He had abandoned his usual provocative attitude and his sarcastic smile. He waited, gravely and deferentially. But, down in the depths of his being, he revelled, eagerly, madly, in the marvellous situation in which he found himself placed: here, in his cell, he, a prisoner; he, the adventurer; he, the swindler, the burglar; he, Arsène Lupin. . . face to face with that demi-god of the modern world, that formidable entity, the heir of Cæsar and of Charlemagne.

He was intoxicated for a moment with the sense of his own power. The tears came to his eyes when he thought of his triumph. . .

The stranger stood still.

And at once, with the very first sentence, they came to the immediate point:

"To-morrow is the 22nd of August. The letters are to be published to-morrow, are they not?"

"To-night, in two hours from now, my friends are to hand in to the *Grand Journal*, not the letters themselves, but an exact list of the letters, with the Grand-duke Hermann's annotations."

"That list shall not be handed in."

"It shall not be."

"You will give it to me."

"It shall be placed in the hands of Your. . . in your hands."

"Likewise, all the letters?"

"Likewise, all the letters."

"Without any of them being photographed?"

"Without any of them being photographed."

The stranger spoke in a very calm voice, containing not the least accent of entreaty nor the least inflection of authority. He neither ordered nor requested; he stated the inevitable actions of Arsène Lupin. Things would happen as he said. And they would happen, whatever Arsène Lupin's demands should be, at whatever price he might value the performance of those actions. The conditions were accepted beforehand.

"By Jove," said Lupin to himself, "that's jolly clever of him! If he leaves it to my generosity, I am a ruined man!"

The very way in which the conversation opened, the frankness of the words employed, the charm of voice and manner all pleased him infinitely.

He pulled himself together, lest he should relent and abandon all the advantages which he had conquered so fiercely.

And the stranger continued:

"Have you read the letters?"

"No."

"But some one you know has read them?"

"No."

"In that case. . ."

"I have the grand-duke's list and his notes. Moreover, I know the hiding-place where he put all his papers."

"Why did you not take them before this?"

"I did not know the secret of the hiding-place until I came here. My friends are on the way there now."

"The castle is guarded. It is occupied by two hundred of my most trusty men."

"Ten thousand would not be sufficient."

After a minute's reflection, the visitor asked:

"How do you know the secret?"

"I guessed it."

"But you had other elements of information which the papers did not publish?"

"No, none at all."

"And yet I had the castle searched for four days."

"Holmlock Shears looked in the wrong place."

"Ah!" said the stranger to himself. "It's an odd thing, an odd thing! . . ." And, to Lupin, "You are sure that your supposition is correct?"

"It is not a supposition: it is a certainty."

"So much the better," muttered the visitor. "There will be no rest until those papers cease to exist."

And, placing himself in front of Arsène Lupin:

"How much?"

"What?" said Lupin, taken aback.

"How much for the papers? How much do you ask to reveal the secret?"

He waited for Lupin to name a figure. He suggested one himself:

"Fifty thousand? . . . A hundred thousand?"

And, when Lupin did not reply, he said, with a little hesitation:

"More? Two hundred thousand? Very well! I agree."

Lupin smiled and, in a low voice, said:

"It is a handsome figure. But is it not likely that some sovereign, let us say, the King of England, would give as much as a million? In all sincerity?"

"I believe so."

"And that those letters are priceless to the Emperor, that they are worth two million quite as easily as two hundred thousand francs. . . three million as easily as two?"

"I think so."

"And, if necessary, the Emperor would give that three million francs?"

"Yes."

"Then it will not be difficult to come to an arrangement."

"On that basis?" cried the stranger, not without some alarm.

Lupin smiled again:

"On that basis, no. . . I am not looking for money. I want something else, something that is worth more to me than any number of millions."

"What is that?"

"My liberty."

"What! Your liberty. . . But I can do nothing. . . That concerns your country. . . the law. . . I have no power."

Lupin went up to him and, lowering his voice still more:

"You have every power, Sire. . . My liberty is not such an exceptional event that they are likely to refuse you."

"Then I should have to ask for it?"

"Yes."

"Of whom?"

"Of Valenglay, the prime minister."

"But M. Valenglay himself can do no more than I."

"He can open the doors of this prison for me."

"It would cause a public outcry."

"When I say, open. . . half-open would be enough. . . We should counterfeit an escape. . . The public so thoroughly expects it that it would not so much as ask for an explanation."

"Very well. . . but M. Valenglay will never consent. . ."

"He will consent."

"Why?"

"Because you will express the wish."

"My wishes are not commands. . . to him!"

"No. . . but an opportunity of making himself agreeable to the Emperor by fulfilling them. And Valenglay is too shrewd a politician. . ."

"Nonsense! Do you imagine that the French government will commit so illegal an act for the sole pleasure of making itself agreeable to me?"

"That pleasure will not be the sole one."

"What will be the other?"

"The pleasure of serving France by accepting the proposal which will accompany the request for my release."

"I am to make a proposal? I?"

"Yes, Sire."

"What proposal?"

"I do not know, but it seems to me that there is always a favorable ground on which to come to an understanding. . . there are possibilities of agreement. . ."

The stranger looked at him, without grasping his meaning. Lupin leant forward and, as though seeking his words, as though putting an imaginary case, said:

"Let me suppose that two great countries are divided by some insignificant question. . . that they have different points of view on a matter of secondary importance. . . a colonial matter, for instance, in which their self-esteem is at stake rather than their interest. . . Is it inconceivable that the ruler of one of those countries might come of his own accord to treat this matter in a new spirit of conciliation. . . and give the necessary instructions. . . so that. . ."

"So that I might leave Morocco to France?" said the stranger, with a burst of laughter.

The idea which Lupin was suggesting struck him as the most comical thing that he had ever heard; and he laughed heartily. The disparity was so great between the object aimed at and the means proposed!

"Of course, of course!" he resumed, with a vain attempt to recover his seriousness. "Of course, it's a very original idea: the whole of modern politics upset so that Arsène Lupin may be free! . . . The plans of the Empire destroyed so that Arsène Lupin may continue his exploits! . . . Why not ask me for Alsace and Lorraine at once?"

"I did think of it, Sire," replied Lupin, calmly. The stranger's merriment increased:

"Splendid! And you let me off?"

"This time, yes."

Lupin had crossed his arms. He, too, was amusing himself by exaggerating the part which he was playing; and he continued, with affected seriousness:

"A series of circumstances might one day arise which would put in my hands the power of *demanding* and *obtaining* that restitution. When that day comes, I shall certainly not fail to do so. For the moment, the weapons at my disposal oblige me to be more modest. Peace in Morocco will satisfy me."

"Just that?"

"Just that."

"Morocco against your liberty!"

"Nothing more. . . or, rather—for we must not lose sight entirely of the main object of this conversation—or, rather, a little good will on the part of one of the countries in question. . . and, in exchange, the surrender of the letters which are in my power."

"Those letters, those letters!" muttered the stranger irritably. "After all, perhaps they are not so valuable. . ."

"There are some in your own hand, Sire; and you considered them valuable enough to come to this cell. . ."

"Well, what does it matter?"

"But there are others of which you do not know the authorship and about which I can give you a few particulars."

"Oh, indeed!" said the stranger, rather anxiously.

Lupin hesitated.

"Speak, speak plainly," said the stranger. "Say what you have in your mind."

In the profound silence of the cell, Lupin declared, with a certain solemnity:

"Twenty years ago a draft treaty was prepared between Germany, Great Britain, and France."

"That's not true! It's impossible! Who could have done such a thing?"

"The Emperor's father and the Queen of England, his grandmother, both acting under the influence of the Empress Frederick."

"Impossible! I repeat, it is impossible!"

"The correspondence is in the hiding-place at Veldenz Castle; and I alone know the secret of the hiding-place."

The stranger walked up and down with an agitated step. Then he stopped short:

"Is the text of the treaty included in that correspondence?"

"Yes, Sire. It is in your father's own hand."

"And what does it say?"

"By that treaty, France and Great Britain granted and promised Germany an immense colonial empire, the empire which she does not at present possess and which has become a necessity to her, in these times, to ensure her greatness."

"And what did England demand as a set-off against that empire?"

"The limitation of the German fleet."

"And France?"

"Alsace and Lorraine."

The Emperor leant against the table in silent thought. Lupin continued:

"Everything was ready. The cabinets of Paris and London had been sounded and had consented. The thing was practically done. The great treaty of alliance was on the point of being concluded. It would have laid the foundations of a definite and universal peace. The death of your father destroyed that sublime dream. But I ask Your Imperial Majesty, what will your people think, what will the world think, when it knows that Frederick III, one of the heroes of 1870, a German, a pure and loyal German, respected by all, generally admired for his nobility of character, agreed to the restitution of Alsace-Lorraine and therefore considered that restitution just?"

He was silent for an instant leaving the problem to fix itself in its precise terms before the Emperor's conscience, before his conscience as a man, a son and a sovereign. Then he concluded:

"Your Imperial Majesty yourself must know whether you wish or do not wish history to record the existence of that treaty. As for me, Sire, you can see that my humble personality counts for very little in the discussion."

A long pause followed upon Lupin's words. He waited, with his soul torn with anguish. His whole destiny was at stake, in this minute which he had conceived and, in a manner, produced with such effort and such stubbornness, an historic minute, born of his brain, in which "his humble personality," for all that he might say, weighed heavily upon the fate of empires and the peace of the world.

Opposite him, in the shadow, Cæsar stood meditating.

What answer would he make? What solution would he give to the problem?

He walked across the cell for a few moments, which to Lupin seemed interminable. Then he stopped and asked:

"Are there any other conditions?"

"Yes, Sire, but they are insignificant."

"Name them."

"I have found the son of the Grand-duke of Zweibrucken-Veldenz. The grand-duchy must be restored to him."

"Anything else?"

"He loves a young girl, who loves him in her turn. She is the fairest and the most virtuous of her sex. He must marry her."

"Anything else?"

"That is all."

"There is nothing more?"

"Nothing. Your majesty need only have this letter delivered to the editor of the *Grand Journal*, who will then destroy, unread, the article which he may now receive at any moment."

Lupin held out the letter, with a heavy heart and a trembling hand. If the Emperor took it, that would be a sign of his acceptance.

The Emperor hesitated and then, with an abrupt movement, took the letter, put on his hat, wrapped his cloak round him and walked out without a word.

Lupin remained for a few seconds, staggering, as though dazed. . .

Then, suddenly, he fell into his chair, shouting with joy and pride. . .

"Monsieur le Juge d'Instruction, I am sorry to say good-bye to you to-day."

"Why, M. Lupin, are you thinking of leaving us?"

"With the greatest reluctance, I assure you, Monsieur le Juge d'Instruction. Our relations have been so very pleasant and cordial! But all good things must come to an end. My cure at the Santé Palace is finished. Other duties call me. I have resolved to make my escape to-night."

"Then I wish you good luck, M. Lupin."

"A thousand thanks, M. le Juge d'Instruction."

Arsène Lupin waited patiently for the hour of his escape, not without asking himself how it would be contrived and by what means France and Germany, uniting for the joint performance of this deserving work, would succeed in effecting it without creating too great a scandal.

Late in the afternoon, the warder told him to go to the entrance-yard. He hurried out and was met by the governor, who handed him over to M. Weber. M. Weber made him step into a motor-car in which somebody was already seated.

Lupin had a violent fit of laughter:

"What, you, my poor old Weber! Have they let you in for this tiresome job? Are you to be responsible for my escape? Upon my word, you are an unlucky beggar! Oh, my poor old chap, what hard lines! First made famous through my arrest, you are now to become immortal through my escape!"

He looked at the other man:

"Well, well, Monsieur le Préfet de Police, so you are in the business too! That's a nasty thing for you, what? If you take my advice, you'll stay in the background and leave the honor and glory to Weber! It's his by right! . . . And he can stand a lot, the rascal!"

The car travelled at a fast pace, along the Seine and through Boulogne. At Saint-Cloud, they crossed the river.

"Splendid!" cried Lupin. "We're going to Garches! You want me there, in order to reënact the death of Altenheim. We shall go down into the underground passage, I shall disappear and people will say that I got through another outlet, known to myself alone! Lord, how idiotic!"

He seemed quite unhappy about it:

"Idiotic! Idiotic in the highest degree! I blush for shame! . . . And those are the people who govern us! . . . What an age to live in! . . . But, you poor devils, why didn't you come to me? I'd have invented a beautiful little escape for you, something of a miraculous nature. I had it all ready pigeon-holed in my mind! The public would have yelled with wonder and danced with delight. Instead of which. . . However, it's quite true that you were given rather short notice. . . but all the same. . ."

The programme was exactly as Lupin had foreseen. They walked through the grounds of the House of Retreat to the Pavillon Hortense. Lupin and his two companions went down the stairs and along the underground passage. At the end of the tunnel, the deputy-chief said:

MAURICE LEBLANC

"You are free."

"And there you are!" said Lupin. "Is that all? Well, my dear Weber, thank you very much and sorry to have given you so much trouble. Good-bye, Monsieur le Préfet; kind regards to the missus!"

He climbed the stairs that led to the Villa des Glycines, raised the trap-door and sprang into the room.

A hand fell on his shoulder.

Opposite him stood his first visitor of the day before, the one who had accompanied the Emperor. There were four men with him, two on either side.

"Look here," said Lupin, "what's the meaning of this joke? I thought I was free!"

"Yes, yes," growled the German, in his rough voice, "you are free. . . free to travel with the five of us. . . if that suits you."

Lupin looked at him, for a second, with a mad longing to hit him on the nose, just to teach him. But the five men looked devilish determined. Their leader did not betray any exaggerated fondness for him; and it seemed to him that the fellow would be only too pleased to resort to extreme measures. Besides, after all, what did he care?

He chuckled:

"If it suits me? Why, it's the dream of my life!"

A powerful covered car was waiting in the paved yard outside the villa. Two men got into the driver's seat, two others inside, with their backs to the motor. Lupin and the stranger sat down on the front seat.

"*Vorwarts!*" cried Lupin, in German. "*Vorwarts nach Veldenz!*"

The stranger said:

"Silence! Those men must know nothing. Speak French. They don't know French. But why speak at all?"

"Quite right," said Lupin to himself. "Why speak at all?"

THE CAR TRAVELLED ALL THE evening and all night, without any incident. Twice they stopped to take in petrol at some sleepy little town.

The Germans took it in turns to watch their prisoner, who did not open his eyes until the early morning.

They stopped for breakfast at an inn on a hillside, near which stood a sign-post. Lupin saw that they were at an equal distance from Metz and Luxemburg. From there, they took a road that slanted north-east, in the direction of Treves.

Lupin said to his travelling-companion:

"Am I right in believing that I have the honor of speaking to Count von Waldemar, the Emperor's confidential friend, the one who searched Hermann III's house in Dresden?"

The stranger remained silent.

"You're the sort of chap I can't stand at any price," muttered Lupin. "I'll have some fun with you, one of these days. You're ugly, you're fat, you're heavy; in short, I don't like you." And he added, aloud, "You are wrong not to answer me, Monsieur le Comte. I was speaking in your own interest: just as we were stepping in, I saw a motor come into sight, behind us, on the horizon. Did you see it?"

"No, why?"

"Nothing."

"Still. . ."

"No, nothing at all. . . a mere remark. . . Besides, we are ten minutes ahead. . . and our car is at least a forty-horse-power."

"It's a sixty," said the German, looking at him uneasily from the corner of his eye.

"Oh, then we're all right!"

They were climbing a little slope. When they reached the top, the count leant out of the window:

"Damn it all!" he swore.

"What's the matter?" asked Lupin.

The count turned to him and, in a threatening voice:

"Take care! If anything happens, it will be so much the worse for you."

"Oho! It seems the other's gaining on us! . . . But what are you afraid of, my dear count? It's no doubt a traveller. . . perhaps even some one they are sending to help us."

"I don't want any help," growled the German.

He leant out again. The car was only two or three hundred yards behind.

He said to his men, pointing to Lupin.

"Bind him. If he resists. . ."

He drew his revolver.

"Why should I resist, O gentle Teuton?" chuckled Lupin. And he added, while they were fastening his hands, "It is really curious to see how people take precautions when they need not and don't when they ought to. What the devil do you care about that motor? Accomplices of mine? What an idea!"

Without replying, the German gave orders to the driver:

"To the right! . . . Slow down! . . . Let them pass. . . If they slow down also, stop!"

But, to his great surprise, the motor seemed, on the contrary, to increase its speed. It passed in front of the car like a whirlwind, in a cloud of dust. Standing up at the back, leaning over the hood, which was lowered, was a man dressed in black.

He raised his arm.

Two shots rang out.

The count, who was blocking the whole of the left window, fell back into the car.

Before even attending to him, the two men leapt upon Lupin and finished securing him.

"Jackasses! Blockheads!" shouted Lupin, shaking with rage. "Let me go, on the contrary! There now, we're stopping! But go after him, you silly fools, catch him up! . . . It's the man in black, I tell you, the murderer! . . . Oh, the idiots! . . ."

They gagged him. Then they attended to the count. The wound did not appear to be serious and was soon dressed. But the patient, who was in a very excited state, had an attack of fever and became delirious.

It was eight o'clock in the morning. They were in the open country, far from any village. The men had no information as to the exact object of the journey. Where were they to go? Whom were they to send to?

They drew up the motor beside a wood and waited. The whole day went by in this way. It was evening before a squad of cavalry arrived, dispatched from Treves in search of the motor-car.

Two hours later, Lupin stepped out of the car, and still escorted by his two Germans, by the light of a lantern climbed the steps of a staircase that led to a small room with iron-barred windows.

Here he spent the night.

THE NEXT MORNING, AN OFFICER led him, through a courtyard filled with soldiers, to the centre of a long row of buildings that ran round the foot of a mound covered with monumental ruins.

He was shown into a large, hastily-furnished room. His visitor of two days back was sitting at a writing-table, reading newspapers and reports, which he marked with great strokes of red pencil:

"Leave us," he said to the officer.

And, going up to Lupin:

"The papers."

The tone was no longer the same. It was now the harsh and imperious tone of the master who is at home and addressing an inferior. . . and such an inferior! A rogue, an adventurer of the worst type, before whom he had been obliged to humiliate himself!

"The papers," he repeated.

Lupin was not put out of countenance. He said, quite calmly:

"They are in Veldenz Castle."

"We are in the out-buildings of the castle. Those are the ruins of Veldenz, over there."

"The papers are in the ruins."

"Let us go to them. Show me the way."

Lupin did not budge.

"Well?"

"Well, Sire, it is not as simple as you think. It takes some time to bring into play the elements which are needed to open that hiding-place."

"How long do you want?"

"Twenty-four hours."

An angry movement, quickly suppressed:

"Oh, there was no question of that between us!"

"Nothing was specified, neither that nor the little trip which Your Imperial Majesty made me take in the charge of half a dozen of your body-guard. I am to hand over the papers, that is all."

"And I am not to give you your liberty until you do hand over those papers."

"It is a question of confidence, Sire. I should have considered myself quite as much bound to produce the papers if I had been free on leaving prison; and Your Imperial Majesty may be sure that I should not have walked off with them. The only difference is that they would now be in your possession. For we have lost a day, Sire. And a day, in this business. . . is a day too much. . . Only, there it is, you should have had confidence."

The Emperor gazed with a certain amazement at that outcast, that vagabond, who seemed vexed that any one should doubt his word.

He did not reply, but rang the bell:

"The officer on duty," he commanded.

Count von Waldemar appeared, looking very white.

"Ah, it's you, Waldemar? So you're all right again?"

"At your service, Sire."

　　　　　　　　　　　　　　MAURICE LEBLANC

"Take five men with you. . . the same men, as you're sure of them. Don't leave this. . . gentleman until to-morrow morning." He looked at his watch. "Until to-morrow morning at ten o'clock. No, I will give him till twelve. You will go wherever he thinks fit to go, you will do whatever he tells you to do. In short, you are at his disposal. At twelve o'clock, I will join you. If, at the last stroke of twelve, he has not handed me the bundle of letters, you will put him back in your car and, without losing a second, take him straight to the Santé Prison."

"If he tries to escape. . ."

"Take your own course."

He went out.

Lupin helped himself to a cigar from the table and threw himself into an easy chair:

"Good! I just love that way of going to work. It is frank and explicit."

The count had brought in his men. He said to Lupin:

"March!"

Lupin lit his cigar and did not move.

"Bind his hands," said the count.

And, when the order was executed, he repeated:

"Now then, march!"

"No."

"What do you mean by no?"

"I'm wondering."

"What about?"

"Where on earth that hiding-place can be!"

The count gave a start and Lupin chuckled:

"For the best part of the story is that I have not the remotest idea where that famous hiding-place is nor how to set about discovering it. What do you say to that, my dear Waldemar, eh? Funny, isn't it? . . . Not the very remotest idea! . . ."

XII

The Emperor's Letters

The ruins of Veldenz are well known to all who visit the banks of the Rhine and the Moselle. They comprise the remains of the old feudal castle, built in 1377 by the Archbishop of Fistingen, an enormous dungeon-keep, gutted by Turenne's troops, and the walls, left standing in their entirety, of a large Renascence palace, in which the grand-dukes of Zweibrucken lived for three centuries.

It was this palace that was sacked by Hermann II's rebellious subjects. The empty windows display two hundred yawning cavities on the four frontages. All the wainscoting, the hangings and most of the furniture were burnt. You walk on the scorched girders of the floors; and the sky can be seen at intervals through the ruined ceilings.

Lupin, accompanied by his escort, went over the whole building in two hours' time:

"I am very pleased with you, my dear count. I don't think I ever came across a guide so well posted in his subject, nor—which is rare—so silent. And now, if you don't mind, we will go to lunch."

As a matter of fact, Lupin knew no more than at the first moment and his perplexity did nothing but increase. To obtain his release from prison and to strike the imagination of his visitor, he had bluffed, pretending to know everything; and he was still seeking for the best place at which to begin to seek.

"Things look bad," he said to himself, from time to time. "Things are looking about as bad as they can look."

His brain, moreover, was not as clear as usual. He was obsessed by an idea, the idea of "the other one," the murderer, the assassin, whom he knew to be still clinging to his footsteps.

How did that mysterious personality come to be on his tracks? How had he heard of Lupin's leaving prison and of his rush to Luxemburg and Germany? Was it a miraculous intuition? Or was it the outcome of definite information? But, if so, at what price, by means of what promises or threats was he able to obtain it?

All these questions haunted Lupin's mind.

At about four o'clock, however, after a fresh walk through the ruins, in the course of which he had examined the stones, measured the thickness of the walls, investigated the shape and appearance of things, all to no purpose, he asked the count:

"Is there no one left who was in the service of the last grand-duke who lived in the castle?"

"All the servants of that time went different ways. Only one of them continued to live in the district."

"Well?"

"He died two years ago."

"Any children?"

"He had a son, who married and who was dismissed, with his wife, for disgraceful conduct. They left their youngest child behind, a little girl, Isilda."

"Where does she live?"

"She lives here, at the end of these buildings. The old grandfather used to act as a guide to visitors, in the days when the castle was still open to the public. Little Isilda has lived in the ruins ever since. She was allowed to remain out of pity. She is a poor innocent, who is hardly able to talk and does not know what she says."

"Was she always like that?"

"It seems not. Her reason went gradually, when she was about ten years old."

"In consequence of a sorrow, of a fright?"

"No, for no direct cause, I am told. The father was a drunkard and the mother committed suicide in a fit of madness."

Lupin reflected and said:

"I should like to see her."

The count gave a rather curious smile:

"You can see her, by all means."

She happened to be in one of the rooms which had been set apart for her. Lupin was surprised to find an attractive little creature, too thin, too pale, but almost pretty, with her fair hair and her delicate face. Her sea-green eyes had the vague, dreamy look of the eyes of blind people.

He put a few questions to which Isilda gave no answer and others to which she replied with incoherent sentences, as though she understood neither the meaning of the words addressed to her nor those which she herself uttered.

He persisted, taking her very gently by the hand and asking her in an affectionate tone about the time when she still had her reason, about her grandfather, about the memories which might be called up by her life as a child playing freely among the majestic ruins of the castle.

She stood silent, with staring eyes; impassive, any emotion which she might have felt was not enough to rouse her slumbering intelligence.

Lupin asked for a pencil and paper and wrote down the number 813. The count smiled again.

"Look here, what are you laughing at?" cried Lupin, irritably.

"Nothing. . . nothing. . . I'm very much interested, that's all. . ."

Isilda looked at the sheet of paper, when he showed it to her, and turned away her head, with a vacant air.

"No bite!" said the count, satirically.

Lupin wrote the letters "Apoon."

Isilda paid no more attention than before.

He did not give up the experiment, but kept on writing the same letters, each time watching the girl's face.

She did not stir, but kept her eyes fixed on the paper with an indifference which nothing seemed to disturb. Then, all at once, she seized the pencil, snatched the last sheet out of Lupin's hands and, as though acting under a sudden inspiration, wrote two "L's" in the middle of a space left open by Lupin.

He felt a thrill.

A word had been formed: "Apollon."

Meanwhile, Isilda clung to both pencil and paper and, with clutching fingers and a strained face, was struggling to make her hand submit to the hesitating orders of her poor little brain.

Lupin waited, feverishly.

She rapidly wrote another word, the word "Diane."

"Another word! . . . Another word!" shouted Lupin.

She twisted her fingers round the pencil, broke the lead, made a big "J" with the stump and, now utterly exhausted, dropped the pencil.

"Another word! I must have another word!" said Lupin, in a tone of command, catching her by the arm.

But he saw by her eyes, which had once more become indifferent, that that fleeting gleam of intelligence could not shine out again.

"Let us go," he said.

He was walking away, when she ran after him and stood in his path. He stopped:

"What is it?"

She held out the palm of her hand.

"What? Money? . . . Is she in the habit of begging?" he asked the count.

"No," said Waldemar, "and I can't understand."

Isilda took two gold coins from her pocket and chinked them together, gleefully.

Lupin looked at them. They were French coins, quite new, bearing the date of that year.

"Where did you get these?" asked Lupin, excitedly.

"French money! . . . Who gave it you? . . . And when? . . . Was it to-day? Speak! . . . Answer! . . ." He shrugged his shoulders. "Fool that I am! As though she could answer! . . . My dear count, would you mind lending me forty marks? . . . Thanks. . . Here, Isilda, that's for you."

She took the two coins, jingled them with the others in the palm of her hand and then, putting out her arm, pointed to the ruins of the Renascence palace, with a gesture that seemed to call attention more particularly to the left wing and to the top of that wing.

Was it a mechanical movement? Or must it be looked upon as a grateful acknowledgment for the two gold coins?

He glanced at the count. Waldemar was smiling again.

"What makes the brute keep on grinning like that?" said Lupin to himself. "Any one would think that he was having a game with me."

He went to the palace on the off-chance, attended by his escort.

THE GROUND-FLOOR CONSISTED OF A number of large reception-rooms, running one into the other and containing the few pieces of furniture that had escaped the fire.

On the first floor, on the north side, was a long gallery, out of which twelve handsome rooms opened all exactly alike.

There was a similar gallery on the second floor, but with twenty-four smaller rooms, also resembling one another. All these apartments were empty, dilapidated, wretched to look at.

Above, there was nothing. The attics had been burnt down.

For an hour, Lupin walked, ran, rushed about indefatigably, with his eyes on the look-out.

When it began to grow dusk, he hurried to one of his twelve rooms on the first floor, as if he were selecting it for special reasons known to himself alone. He was rather surprised to find the Emperor there, smoking and seated in an arm-chair which he had sent for.

Taking no notice of his presence, Lupin began an inspection of the room, according to the methods which he was accustomed to employ in such cases, dividing the room into sections, each of which he examined in turn.

After twenty minutes of this work, he said:

"I must beg you, Sire, to be good enough to move. There is a fireplace here. . ."

The Emperor tossed his head:

"Is it really necessary for me to move?"

"Yes, Sire, this fireplace. . ."

"The fireplace is just the same as the others and the room is no different from its fellows."

Lupin looked at the Emperor without understanding. The Emperor rose and said, with a laugh:

"I think, M. Lupin, that you have been making just a little fun of me."

"How do you mean, Sire?"

"Oh, it's hardly worth mentioning! You obtained your release on the condition of handing me certain papers in which I am interested and you have not the smallest notion as to where they are. I have been thoroughly—what do you call it, in French?—*roulé* 'done'!"

"Do you think so, Sire?"

"Why, what a man knows he doesn't have to hunt for! And you have been hunting for ten good hours! Doesn't it strike you as a case for an immediate return to prison?"

Lupin seemed thunderstruck:

"Did not Your Imperial Majesty fix twelve o'clock to-morrow as the last limit?"

"Why wait?"

"Why? Well, to allow me to complete my work!"

"Your work? But it's not even begun, M. Lupin."

"There Your Imperial Majesty is mistaken."

"Prove it. . . and I will wait until to-morrow."

Lupin reflected and, speaking in a serious tone:

"Since Your Imperial Majesty requires proofs in order to have confidence in me, I will furnish them. The twelve rooms leading out of this gallery each bear a different name, which is inscribed in French— obviously by a French decorative artist—over the various doors. One of the inscriptions, less damaged by the fire than the others, caught my eye as I was passing along the gallery. I examined the other doors: all of them bore hardly legible traces of names caned over the pediments. Thus I found a 'D' and an 'E' the first and last letters of 'Diane.' I found an 'A' and 'Lon' which pointed to 'Apollon.' These are the French equivalents of Diana and Apollo, both of them mythological deities. The other inscriptions presented similar characteristics. I discovered traces of such names as Jupiter, Venus, Mercury, Saturn and so on. This part of the problem was solved: each of the twelve rooms bears the name of an Olympian god or goddess; and the letters APOON, completed by Isilda, point to the Apollo Room or Salle d'Apollon. So it is here, in the room in which we now are, that the letters are hidden. A few minutes, perhaps, will suffice in which to discover them."

"A few minutes or a few years. . . or even longer!" said the Emperor, laughing.

He seemed greatly amused; and the count also displayed a coarse merriment.

Lupin asked:

"Would Your Imperial Majesty be good enough to explain?"

"M. Lupin, the exciting investigation which you have conducted to-day and of which you are telling us the brilliant results has already been made by me. . . yes, a fortnight ago, in the company of your friend Holmlock Shears. Together we questioned little Isilda; together, we employed the same method in dealing with her that you did; and together we observed the names in the gallery and got as far as this room, the Apollo Room."

Lupin turned livid. He spluttered:

"Oh, did Shears get. . . as far as. . . this?"

"Yes, after four days' searching. True, it did not help us, for we found nothing. All the same, I know that the letters are not here."

Trembling with rage, wounded in his innermost pride, Lupin fired up under the gibe, as though he had been lashed with a whip. He had never felt humiliated to such a degree as this. In this fury, he could have strangled the fat Waldemar, whose laughter incensed him. Containing himself with an effort, he said:

"It took Shears four days, Sire, and me only four hours. And I should have required even less, if I had not been thwarted in my search."

"And by whom, bless my soul? By my faithful count? I hope he did not dare. . . !"

"No, Sire, but by the most terrible and powerful of my enemies, by that infernal being who killed his own accomplice Altenheim."

"Is he here? Do you think so?" exclaimed the Emperor, with an agitation which showed that he was familiar with every detail of the dramatic story.

"He is wherever I am. He threatens me with his constant hatred. It was he who guessed that I was M. Lenormand, the chief of the detective-service; it was he who had me put in prison; it was he, again, who pursued me, on the day when I came out. Yesterday, aiming at me in the motor, he wounded Count von Waldemar."

"But how do you know, how can you be sure that he is at Veldenz?"

"Isilda has received two gold coins, two French coins!"

"And what is he here for? With what object?"

"I don't know, Sire, but he is the very spirit of evil. Your Imperial Majesty must be on your guard: he is capable of anything and everything."

"It is impossible! I have two hundred men in the ruins. He cannot have entered. He would have been seen."

"Some one has seen him, beyond a doubt."

"Who?"

"Isilda."

"Let her be questioned! Waldemar, take your prisoner to where the girl is."

Lupin showed his bound hands:

"It will be a tough battle. Can I fight like this?"

The Emperor said to the count:

"Unfasten him. . . And keep me informed."

In this way, by a sudden effort, bringing the hateful vision of the murder into the discussion, boldly, without evidence, Arsène Lupin gained time and resumed the direction of the search:

"Sixteen hours still," he said to himself, "it's more than I want."

HE REACHED THE PREMISES OCCUPIED by Isilda, at the end of the old out-buildings. These buildings served as barracks for the two hundred soldiers guarding the ruins; and the whole of this, the left wing, was reserved for the officers.

Isilda was not there. The count sent two of his men to look for her. They came back. No one had seen the girl.

Nevertheless, she could not have left the precincts of the ruins. As for the Renascence palace, it was, so to speak, invested by one-half of the troops; and no one was able to obtain admittance.

At last, the wife of a subaltern who lived in the next house declared that she had been sitting at her window all day and that the girl had not been out.

"If she hadn't gone out," said Waldemar, "she would be here now: and she is not here."

Lupin observed:

"Is there a floor above?"

"Yes, but from this room to the upper floor there is no staircase."

"Yes, there is."

He pointed to a little door opening on a dark recess. In the shadow, he saw the first treads of a staircase as steep as a ladder.

"Please, my dear count," he said to Waldemar, who wanted to go up, "let me have the honor."

"Why?"

"There's danger."

He ran up and at once sprang into a low and narrow loft. A cry escaped him:

"Oh!"

"What is it?" asked the count, emerging in his turn.

"Here. . . on the floor. . . Isilda. . ."

He knelt down beside the girl, but, at the first glance, saw that she was simply stunned and that she bore no trace of a wound, except a few scratches on the wrists and hands. A handkerchief was stuffed into her mouth by way of a gag.

"That's it," he said. "The murderer was here with her. When we came, he struck her a blow with his fist and gagged her so that we should not hear her moans."

"But how did he get away?"

"Through here. . . look. . . there is a passage connecting all the attics on the first floor."

"And from there?"

"From there, he went down the stairs of one of the other dwellings."

"But he would have been seen!"

"Pooh, who knows? The creature's invisible. Never mind! Send your men to look. Tell them to search all the attics and all the ground-floor lodgings."

He hesitated. Should he also go in pursuit of the murderer?

But a sound brought him back to the girl's side. She had got up from the floor and a dozen pieces of gold money had dropped from her hands. He examined them. They were all French.

"Ah," he said, "I was right! Only, why so much gold? In reward for what?"

Suddenly, he caught sight of a book on the floor and stooped to pick it up. But the girl darted forward with a quicker movement, seized the book and pressed it to her bosom with a fierce energy, as though prepared to defend it against any attempt to take hold of it.

"That's it," he said. "The money was offered her for the book, but she refused to part with it. Hence the scratches on the hands. The interesting thing would be to know why the murderer wished to possess the book. Was he able to look through it first?"

He said to Waldemar:

"My dear count, please give the order."

Waldemar made a sign to his men. Three of them threw themselves on the girl and, after a hard tussle, in which the poor thing stamped, writhed and screamed with rage, they took the volume from her.

"Gently, child," said Lupin, "be calm. . . It's all in a good cause. . . Keep an eye on her, will you? Meanwhile, I will have a look at the object in dispute."

It was an odd volume of Montesquieu's *Voyage au temple de Guide*, in a binding at least a century old. But Lupin had hardly opened it before he exclaimed:

"I say, I say, this is queer! There is a sheet of parchment stuck on each right hand page; and those sheets are covered with a very close, small handwriting."

He read, at the beginning:

"*Diary of the Chevalier GILLES DE MALRÊCHE, French servant to His Royal Highness the Prince of ZWEIBRUCKENVELDENZ, begun in the Year of Our Lord 1794.*"

"What! Does it say that?" asked the count.

"What surprises you?"

"Isilda's grandfather, the old man who died two years ago, was called Malreich, which is the German form of the same name."

"Capital! Isilda's grandfather must have been the son or the grandson of the French servant who wrote his diary in an odd volume of Montesquieu's works. And that is how the diary came into Isilda's hands."

He turned the pages at random:

"*15 September, 1796.* His Royal Highness went hunting.

"*20 September, 1796.* His Royal Highness went out riding. He was mounted on Cupidon."

"By Jove!" muttered Lupin. "So far, it's not very exciting."
He turned over a number of pages and read:

"*12 March, 1803.* I have remitted ten crowns to Hermann. He is giving music-lessons in London."

Lupin gave a laugh:
"Oho! Hermann is dethroned and our respect comes down with a rush!"
"Yes," observed Waldemar, "the reigning grand-duke was driven from his dominions by the French troops."
Lupin continued:

"*1809. Tuesday.* Napoleon slept at Veldenz last night. I made His Majesty's bed and this morning I emptied his slops."

"Oh, did Napoleon stop at Veldenz?"
"Yes, yes, on his way back to the army, at the time of the Austrian campaign, which ended with the battle of Wagram. It was an honor of which the grand-duchal family were very proud afterwards."
Lupin went on reading:

"*28 October, 1814.* His Royal Highness returned to his dominions.

"*29 October, 1814.* I accompanied His Royal Highness to the hiding-place last night and was happy to be able to show him that no one had guessed its existence. For that matter, who would have suspected that a hiding-place could be contrived in. . ."

Lupin stopped, with a shout. Isilda had suddenly escaped from the men guarding her, made a grab at him and taken to flight, carrying the book with her.
"Oh, the little mischief! Quick, you! . . . Go round by the stairs below. I'll run after her by the passage."

813

But she had slammed the door behind her and bolted it. He had to go down and run along the buildings with the others, looking for a staircase which would take them to the first floor.

The fourth house was the only one open. He went upstairs. But the passage was empty and he had to knock at doors, force locks and make his way into unoccupied rooms, while Waldemar, showing as much ardor in the pursuit as himself, pricked the curtains and hangings with the point of his sword.

A voice called out from the ground-floor, towards the right wing. They rushed in that direction. It was one of the officers' wives, who beckoned to them at the end of a passage and told them that the girl must be in her lodging.

"How do you know?" asked Lupin.

"I wanted to go to my room. The door was shut and I could not get in."

Lupin tried and found the door locked:

"The window!" he cried. "There must be a window!"

He went outside, took the count's sword and smashed the panes. Then, helped up by two men, he hung on to the wall, passed his arm through the broken glass, turned the latch and stumbled into the room.

He saw Isilda huddled before the fireplace, almost in the midst of the flames:

"The little beast!" he said. "She has thrown it into the fire!"

He pushed her back savagely, tried to take the book and burnt his hands in the attempt. Then, with the tongs, he pulled it out of the grate and threw the table cloth over it to stifle the blaze.

But it was too late. The pages of the old manuscript, all burnt up, were falling into ashes.

Lupin gazed at her in silence. The count said:

"One would think that she knew what she was doing."

"No, she does not know. Only, her grandfather must have entrusted her with that book as a sort of treasure, a treasure which no one was ever to set eyes on, and, with her stupid instinct, she preferred to throw it into the fire rather than part with it."

"Well then. . ."

"Well then what?"

"You won't find the hiding-place."

"Aha, my dear count, so you did, for a moment, look upon my success as possible? And Lupin does not strike you as quite a charlatan? Make your mind easy, Waldemar: Lupin has more than one string to his bow. I shall succeed."

"Before twelve o'clock to-morrow?"

"Before twelve o'clock to-night. But, for the moment, I am starving with hunger. And, if your kindness would go so far. . ."

He was taken to the sergeants' mess and a substantial meal prepared for him, while the count went to make his report to the Emperor.

Twenty minutes later, Waldemar returned and they sat down and dined together, opposite each other, silent and pensive.

"Waldemar, a good cigar would be a treat. . . I thank you. . . Ah, this one crackles as a self-respecting Havana should!"

He lit his cigar and, after a minute or two:

"You can smoke, count; I don't mind in the least; in fact, I rather like it."

An hour passed. Waldemar dozed and, from time to time, swallowed a glass of brandy to wake himself up.

Soldiers passed in and out, waiting on them.

"Coffee," asked Lupin.

They brought him some coffee.

"What bad stuff!" he grumbled. "If that's what Cæsar drinks! . . . Give me another cup all the same, Waldemar. We may have a long night before us. Oh, what vile coffee!"

He lit a second cigar and did not say another word. Ten minutes passed. He continued not to move or speak.

Suddenly, Waldemar sprang to his feet and said to Lupin, angrily:

"Hi! Stand up, there!"

Lupin was whistling a tune at the moment. He kept on whistling, peacefully.

"Stand up, I say!"

Lupin turned round. His Imperial Majesty had just entered. Lupin rose from his chair.

"How far are we?" asked the Emperor.

"I think, Sire, that I shall be able to satisfy Your Imperial Majesty soon."

"What? Do you know. . ."

"The hiding-place? Very nearly, Sire. . . A few details still escape me. . . but everything will be cleared up, once we are on the spot: I have no doubt of it."

"Are we to stay here?"

"No, Sire, I will beg you to go with me to the Renascence palace. But we have plenty of time; and, if Your Imperial Majesty will permit me, I should like first to think over two or three points."

Without waiting for the reply, he sat down, to Waldemar's great indignation.

In a few minutes, the Emperor, who had walked away and was talking to the count, came up to him:

"Are you ready now, M. Lupin?"

Lupin kept silence. A fresh question. His head fell on his chest.

"But he's asleep; I really believe that he's asleep!"

Waldemar, beside himself with rage, shook him violently by the shoulder. Lupin fell from his chair, sank to the floor, gave two or three convulsive movements and then lay quite still.

"What's the matter with him?" exclaimed the Emperor. "He's not dead, I hope!"

He took a lamp and bent over him:

"How pale he is! A face like wax! . . . Look, Waldemar. . . Feel his heart. . . He's alive, is he not?"

"Yes, Sire," said the count, after a moment, "the heart is beating quite regularly."

"Then what is it? I don't understand. . . What happened?"

"Shall I go and fetch the doctor?"

"Yes, run. . ."

The doctor found Lupin in the same state, lying inert and quiet. He had him put on a bed, subjected him to a long examination and asked what he had had to eat.

"Do you suspect a case of poisoning, doctor?"

"No, Sire, there are no traces of poisoning. But I am thinking. . . what's on that tray and in that cup?"

"Coffee," said the count.

"For you?"

"No, for him. I did not have any."

The doctor poured out some coffee, tasted it and said:

"I was right. He has been put to sleep with a narcotic."

"But by whom?" cried the Emperor, angrily. "Look here, Waldemar; it's exasperating, the way things happen in this place!"

"Sire? . . ."

"Well, yes, I've had enough of it! . . . I am really beginning to believe that the man's right and that there is some one in the castle. . . That French money, that narcotic. . ."

"If any one had got into this enclosure, Sire, it would be known by this time. . . We've been hunting in every direction for three hours."

"Still, I didn't make the coffee, I assure you. . . And, unless you did. . ."

"Oh, Sire!"

"Well, then, hunt about. . . search. . . You have two hundred men at your disposal; and the out-houses are not so large as all that! For, after all, the ruffian is prowling round here, round these buildings. . . near the kitchen. . . somewhere or other! Go and bustle about!"

The fat Waldemar bustled about all night, conscientiously, because it was the master's order, but without conviction, because it was impossible for a stranger to hide among ruins which were so well-watched. And, as a matter of fact, the event proved that he was right: the investigations were fruitless; and no one was able to discover the mysterious hand that had prepared the narcotic drink.

Lupin spent the night lifeless on his bed. In the morning, the doctor, who had not left his side, told a messenger of the Emperor's that he was still asleep.

At nine o'clock, however, he made his first movement, a sort of effort to wake up.

Later on, he stammered:

"What time is it?"

"Twenty-five to ten."

He made a fresh effort; and it was evident that, in the midst of his torpor, his whole being was intent upon returning to life.

A clock struck ten.

He started and said:

"Let them carry me; let them carry me to the palace."

With the doctor's approval, Waldemar called his men and sent word to the Emperor. They laid Lupin on a stretcher and set out for the palace.

"The first floor," he muttered.

They carried him up.

"At the end of the corridor," he said. "The last room on the left."

They carried him to the last room, which was the twelfth, and gave him a chair, on which he sat down, exhausted.

The Emperor arrived: Lupin did not stir, sat looking, unconscious, with no expression in his eyes.

813

Then, in a few minutes, he seemed to wake, looked round him, at the walls, the ceilings, the people, and said:

"A narcotic, I suppose?"

"Yes," said the doctor.

"Have they found. . . the man?"

"No."

He seemed to be meditating and several times jerked his head with a thoughtful air: but they soon saw that he was asleep.

The Emperor went up to Waldemar:

"Order your car round."

"Oh? . . . But then, Sire. . . ?"

"Well, what? I am beginning to think that he is taking us in and that all this is merely play-acting, to gain time."

"Possibly. . . yes. . ." said Waldemar, agreeing.

"It's quite obvious! He is making the most of certain curious coincidences, but he knows nothing; and his story about gold coins and his narcotic are so many inventions! If we lend ourselves to his little game any longer, he'll slip out of your fingers. Your car, Waldemar."

The count gave his orders and returned. Lupin had not woke up. The Emperor, who was looking round the room, said to Waldemar:

"This is the Minerva room, is it not?"

"Yes, Sire."

"But then why is there an 'N' in two places?"

There were, in fact, two "N's," one over the chimneypiece, the other over an old dilapidated clock fitted into the wall and displaying a complicated set of works, with weights hanging lifeless at the end of their cords.

"The two 'N's' . . ." said Waldemar.

The Emperor did not listen to the answer. Lupin had moved again, opening his eyes and uttering indistinct syllables. He stood up, walked across the room and fell down from sheer weakness.

Then came the struggle, the desperate struggle of his brain, his nerves, his will against that hideous, paralyzing torpor, the struggle of a dying man against death, the struggle of life against extinction. And the sight was one of infinite sadness.

"He is suffering," muttered Waldemar.

"Or at least, he is pretending to suffer," declared the Emperor, "and pretending very cleverly at that. What an actor!"

Lupin stammered:

"An injection, doctor, an injection of caffeine. . . at once. . ."

"May I, Sire?" asked the doctor.

"Certainly. . . Until twelve o'clock, do all that he asks. He has my promise."

"How many minutes. . . before twelve o'clock?" asked Lupin.

"Forty," said somebody.

"Forty? . . . I shall do it. . . I am sure to do it. . . I've got to do it. . ." He took his head in his two hands. "Oh, if I had my brain, the real brain, the brain that thinks! It would be a matter of a second! There is only one dark spot left. . . but I cannot. . . my thoughts escape me. . . I can't grasp it. . . it's awful."

His shoulders shook. Was he crying?

They heard him repeating:

"813. . . 813. . ." And, in a lower voice, "813. . . an '8' . . . a '1' . . . a '3' . . . yes, of course. . . But why? . . . That's not enough. . ."

The Emperor muttered:

"He impresses me. I find it difficult to believe that a man can play a part like that. . ."

Half-past eleven struck. . . a quarter to twelve. . .

Lupin remained motionless, with his fists glued to his temples.

The Emperor waited, with his eyes fixed on a chronometer which Waldemar held in his hand.

Ten minutes more. . . five minutes more. . .

"Is the car there, Waldemar? . . . Are your men ready?"

"Yes, Sire."

"Is that watch of yours a repeater, Waldemar?"

"Yes, Sire."

"At the last stroke of twelve, then. . ."

"But. . ."

"At the last stroke of twelve, Waldemar."

There was really something tragic about the scene, that sort of grandeur and solemnity which the hours assume at the approach of a possible miracle, when it seems as though the voice of fate itself were about to find utterance.

The Emperor did not conceal his anguish. This fantastic adventurer who was called Arsène Lupin and whose amazing life he knew, this man troubled him. . . and, although he was resolved to make an end of all this dubious story, he could not help waiting. . . and hoping.

Two minutes more. . . one minute more. . .

813

Then they counted by seconds.

Lupin seemed asleep.

"Come, get ready," said the Emperor to the count.

The count went up to Lupin and placed his hand on his shoulder.

The silvery chime of the repeater quivered and struck. . . one, two, three, four, five. . .

"Waldemar, old chap, pull the weights of the old clock."

A moment of stupefaction. It was Lupin's voice, speaking very calmly.

Waldemar, annoyed at the familiarity of the address, shrugged his shoulders.

"Do as he says, Waldemar," said the Emperor.

"Yes, do as I say, my dear count," echoed Lupin, recovering his powers of chaff. "You know the ropes so well. . . all you have to do is to pull those of the clock. . . in turns. . . one, two. . . capital! . . . That's how they used to wind it up in the old days."

The pendulum, in fact, was started; and they heard its regular ticking.

"Now the hands," said Lupin. "Set them at a little before twelve. . . Don't move. . . Let me. . ."

He rose and walked to the face of the clock, standing two feet away, at most, with his eyes fixed, with every nerve attentive.

The twelve strokes sounded, twelve heavy, deep strokes.

A long silence. Nothing happened. Nevertheless, the Emperor waited, as though he were sure that something was going to happen. And Waldemar did not move, stood with wide-open eyes.

Lupin, who had stooped over the clock-face, now drew himself up, muttering:

"That's it. . . I have it. . ."

He went back to his chair and commanded:

"Waldemar, set the hands at two minutes to twelve again. Oh, no, old chap, not backwards! The way the hands go! . . . Yes, I know, it will take rather long. . . but it can't be helped."

All the hours struck and the half hours, up to half-past eleven.

"Listen, Waldemar," said Lupin.

And he spoke seriously, without jesting, as though himself excited and anxious:

"Listen, Waldemar. Do you see on the face of the clock a little round dot marking the first hour? That dot is loose, isn't it? Put the fore-finger of your left hand on it and press. Good. Do the same with your thumb on the dot marking the third hour. Good. With your right hand, push

MAURICE LEBLANC

in the dot at the eighth hour. Good. Thank you. Go and sit down, my dear fellow."

The minute-hand shifted, moved to the twelfth dot and the clock struck again.

Lupin was silent and very white. The twelve strokes rang out in the silence.

At the twelfth stroke, there was a sound as of a spring being set free. The clock stopped dead. The pendulum ceased swinging.

And suddenly, the bronze ornament representing a ram's head, which crowned the dial, fell forwards, uncovering a sort of little recess cut out of the stone wall.

In this recess was a chased silver casket.

Lupin took it and carried it to the Emperor:

"Would Your Imperial Majesty be so good as to open it yourself? The letters which you instructed me to look for are inside."

The Emperor raised the lid and seemed greatly astonished.

The casket was empty.

The casket was empty.

It was an enormous, unforeseen sensation. After the success of the calculation made by Lupin, after the ingenious discovery of the secret of the clock, the Emperor, who had no doubt left as to the ultimate success, appeared utterly confounded.

Opposite him was Lupin, pallid and wan, with drawn jaws and bloodshot eyes, gnashing his teeth with rage and impotent hate.

He wiped the perspiration from his forehead, then snatched up the casket, turned it over, examined it, as though he hoped to find a false bottom. At last, for greater certainty, in a fit of fury, he crushed it, with an irresistible grip.

That relieved him. He breathed more easily.

The Emperor said:

"Who has done this?"

"Still the same man, Sire, the one who is following the same road as I and pursuing the same aim: Mr. Kesselbach's murderer."

"When?"

"Last night. Ah, Sire, why did you not leave me free when I came out of prison! Had I been free, I should have come here without losing an hour. I should have arrived before him! I should have given Isilda money before he did! I should have read Malreich, the old French servant's diary, before he did!"

"So you think that it was through the revelations in the diary. . . ?"

"Why, yes, Sire! He had time to read them. And, lurking I don't know where, kept informed of all our movements by I don't know whom, he put me to sleep last night, in order to get rid of me."

"But the palace was guarded."

"Guarded by your soldiers, Sire. Does that count with a man like him? Besides, I have no doubt that Waldemar concentrated his search upon the out-buildings, thus thinning the posts in the palace."

"But the sound of the clock! Those twelve strokes in the night!"

"It was mere child's play, Sire, mere child's play, to him, to prevent the clock from striking!"

"All this seems very impossible to my mind."

"It all seems monstrous clear to mine, Sire! If it were possible to feel in every one of your soldiers' pockets here and now, or to know how much money they will each of them spend during the next twelve months, we should be sure to find two or three who are, at this moment, in possession of a few bank-notes: French bank-notes, of course."

"Oh!" protested Waldemar.

"But yes, my dear count, it is a question of price; and that makes no difference to 'him.' If 'he' wished, I am sure that you yourself. . ."

The Emperor, wrapped up in his own thoughts, was not listening. He walked across the room from left to right and right to left, then beckoned to one of the officers standing in the gallery:

"My car. . . And tell them to get ready. . . We're starting."

He stopped, watched Lupin for a moment and, going up to the count:

"You too, Waldemar, be off. . . Straight to Paris, without a break. . ."

Lupin pricked up his ears. He heard Waldemar reply:

"I should like to have a dozen additional guards. . . With that devil of a man. . ."

"Take them. And look sharp. You must get there to-night."

Lupin stamped his foot violently on the floor:

"Well, no, Sire! No, no, no! It shan't be, I swear it shan't! No, no never!"

"What do you mean?"

"And the letters, Sire? The stolen letters?"

"Upon my word! . . ."

"So!" cried Lupin, indignantly folding his arms. "So your Imperial Majesty gives up the struggle? You look upon the defeat as irretrievable?

You declare yourself beaten? Well, I do not, Sire. I have begun and I mean to finish."

The Emperor smiled at this display of mettle:

"I do not give up, but my police will set to work."

Lupin burst out laughing:

"Excuse me, Sire! It is so funny! Your police! Your Imperial Majesty's police! Why, they're worth just about as much as any other police, that is to say, nothing, nothing at all! No, Sire, I will not return to the Santé! Prison I can afford to laugh at. But time enough has been wasted as it is. I need my freedom against that man and I mean to keep it."

The Emperor shrugged his shoulders:

"You don't even know who the man is."

"I shall know, Sire. And I alone can know. And he knows that I am the only one who can know. I am his only enemy. I am the only one whom he attacks. It was I whom he meant to hit, the other day, when he fired his revolver. He considered it enough to put me and me only to sleep, last night, to be free to do as he pleased. The fight lies between him and me. The outside world has nothing to say to it. No one can help me and no one can help him. There are two of us; and that is all. So far, chance has favored him. But, in the long run, it is inevitable, it is doomed that I should gain the day."

"Why?"

"Because I am the better man."

"Suppose he kills you?"

"He will not kill me. I shall draw his claws, I shall make him perfectly harmless. And you shall have the letters, Sire. They are yours. There is no power on earth than can prevent me from restoring them to you."

He spoke with a violent conviction and a tone of certainty that gave to the things which he foretold the real appearance of things already accomplished.

The Emperor could not help undergoing a vague, inexplicable feeling in which there was a sort of admiration combined with a good deal of that confidence which Lupin was demanding in so masterful a manner. In reality, he was hesitating only because of his scruples against employing this man and making him, so to speak, his ally. And, anxiously, not knowing what decision to take, he walked from the gallery to the windows without saying a word.

At last, he asked:

"And who says that the letters were stolen last night?"

"The theft is dated, Sire."

"What do you say?"

"Look at the inner side of the pediment which concealed the hiding-place. The date is written in white chalk: 'Midnight, 24 August.' . . ."

"So it is," muttered the Emperor, nonplussed. "How was it that I did not see?" And he added, betraying his curiosity, "Just as with those two 'N's' painted on the wall. . . I can't understand. This is the Minerva Room."

"This is the room in which Napoleon, the Emperor of the French slept," said Lupin.

"How do you know?"

"Ask Waldemar, Sire. As for myself, when I was turning over the old servants' diary, it came upon me as a flash of light. I understood that Shears and I had been on the wrong scent. Apoon, the imperfect word written by the Grand-duke Hermann on his death-bed, is a contraction not of Apollon, but of Napoleon."

"That's true. . . you are right," said the Emperor. "The same letters occur in both words and in the same order. The grand-duke evidently meant to write 'Napoleon.' But that figure 813? . . ."

"Ah, that was the point that gave me most trouble. I always had an idea that we must add up the three figures 8, 1 and 3; and the number 12, thus obtained, seemed to me at once to apply to this room, which is the twelfth leading out of the gallery. But that was not enough for me. There must be something else, something which my enfeebled brain could not succeed in translating into words. The sight of that clock, situated precisely in the Napoleon Room, was a revelation to me. The number 12 evidently meant twelve o'clock. The hour of noon! The hour of midnight! Is this not the solemn moment which a man most readily selects? But why those three figures 8, 1 and 3, rather than any others which would have given the same total? . . . It was then that I thought of making the clock strike for the first time, by way of experiment. And it was while making it strike that I saw the dots of the first, third and eighth hour were movable and that they alone were movable. I therefore obtained three figures, 1, 3 and 8, which, placed in a more prophetic order, gave the number 813. Waldemar pushed the three dots, the spring was released and Your Imperial Majesty knows the result. . . This, Sire, is the explanation of that mysterious word and of those three figures 8, 1, 3 which the grand-duke wrote with his dying hand and by the aid of which he hoped that his son would one day recover the secret of Veldenz and become the possessor of the famous letters which he had hidden there."

The Emperor listened with eager attention, more and more surprised at the ingenuity, perspicacity, shrewdness and intelligent will which he observed in the man.

"Waldemar," he said, when Lupin had finished.

"Sire?"

But, just as he was about to speak, shouts were heard in the gallery outside.

Waldemar left the room and returned:

"It's the mad girl, Sire. They won't let her pass."

"Let her come in." cried Lupin, eagerly. "She must come in, Sire."

At a sign from the Emperor, Waldemar went out to fetch Isilda.

Her entrance caused a general stupefaction. Her pale face was covered with dark blotches. Her distorted features bore signs of the keenest suffering. She panted for breath, with her two hands clutched against her breast.

"Oh!" cried Lupin, struck with horror.

"What is it?" asked the Emperor.

"Your doctor, Sire. There is not a moment to lose."

He went up to her:

"Speak, Isilda. . . Have you seen anything? Have you anything to say?"

The girl had stopped; her eyes were less vacant, as though lighted up by the pain. She uttered sounds. . . but not a word.

"Listen," said Lupin. "Answer yes or no. . . make a movement of the head. . . Have you seen him? Do you know where he is? . . . You know who he is. . . Listen! if you don't answer. . ."

He suppressed a gesture of anger. But, suddenly, remembering the experiment of the day before and that she seemed rather to have retained a certain optical memory of the time when she enjoyed her full reason, he wrote on the white wall a capital "L" and "M."

She stretched out her arm toward the letters and nodded her head as though in assent.

"And then?" said Lupin. "What then? . . . Write something yourself."

But she gave a fearful scream and flung herself to the ground, yelling.

Then, suddenly, came silence, immobility. One last convulsive spasm. And she moved no more.

"Dead?" asked the Emperor.

"Poisoned, Sire."

"Oh, the poor thing! . . . And by whom?"

"By 'him,' Sire. She knew him, no doubt. He must have been afraid of what she might tell."

The doctor arrived. The Emperor pointed to the girl. Then, addressing Waldemar:

"All your men to turn out. . . Make them go through the houses. . . telegraph to the stations on the frontier. . ."

He went up to Lupin:

"How long do you want to recover the letters?"

"A month, Sire. . . two months at most."

"Very well. Waldemar will wait for you here. He shall have my orders and full powers to grant you anything you wish."

"What I should like, Sire, is my freedom."

"You are free."

Lupin watched him walk away and said, between his teeth:

"My freedom first. . . And afterward, when I have given you back the letters, O Majesty, one little shake of the hand! Then we shall be quits! . . ."

XIII

The Seven Scoundrels

"Will you see this gentleman, ma'am?"

Dolores Kesselbach took the card from the footman and read:

"André Beauny. . . No," she said, "I don't know him."

"The gentleman seems very anxious to see you, ma'am. He says that you are expecting him."

"Oh. . . possibly. . . Yes, bring him here."

Since the events which had upset her life and pursued her with relentless animosity, Dolores, after staying at the Hôtel Bristol had taken up her abode in a quiet house in the Rue des Vignes, down at Passy. A pretty garden lay at the back of the house and was surrounded by other leafy gardens. On days when attacks more painful than usual did not keep her from morning till night behind the closed shutters of her bedroom, she made her servants carry her under the trees, where she lay stretched at full length, a victim to melancholy, incapable of fighting against her hard fate.

Footsteps sounded on the gravel-path and the footman returned, followed by a young man, smart in appearance and very simply dressed, in the rather out-of-date fashion adopted by some of our painters, with a turn-down collar and a flowing necktie of white spots on a blue ground.

The footman withdrew.

"Your name is André Beauny, I believe?" said Dolores.

"Yes, madame."

"I have not the honor. . ."

"I beg your pardon, madame. Knowing that I was a friend of Mme. Ernemont, Geneviève's grandmother, you wrote to her, at Garches, saying that you wished to speak to me. I have come."

Dolores rose in her seat, very excitedly:

"Oh, you are. . ."

"Yes."

She stammered:

"Really? . . . Is it you? . . . I do not recognize you."

"You don't recognize Prince Paul Sernine?"

"No. . . everything is different. . . the forehead. . . the eyes. . . And that is not how the. . ."

"How the newspapers represented the prisoner at the Santé?" he said, with a smile. "And yet it is I, really."

A long silence followed, during which they remained embarrassed and ill at ease.

At last, he asked:

"May I know the reason. . . ?"

"Did not Geneviève tell you? . . ."

"I have not seen her. . . but her grandmother seemed to think that you required my services. . ."

"That's right. . . that's right. . ."

"And in what way. . . ? I am so pleased. . ."

She hesitated a second and then whispered:

"I am afraid."

"Afraid?" he cried.

"Yes," she said, speaking in a low voice, "I am afraid, afraid of everything, afraid of to-day and of to-morrow. . . and of the day after. . . afraid of life. I have suffered so much. . . I can bear no more."

He looked at her with great pity in his eyes. The vague feeling that had always drawn him to this woman took a more precise character now that she was asking for his protection. He felt an eager need to devote himself to her, wholly, without hope of reward.

She continued:

"I am alone now, quite alone, with servants whom I have picked up on chance, and I am afraid. . . I feel that people are moving about me."

"But with what object?"

"I do not know. But the enemy is hovering around and coming closer."

"Have you seen him? Have you noticed anything?"

"Yes, the other day two men passed several times in the street and stopped in front of the house."

"Can you describe them?"

"I saw one of them better than the other. He was tall and powerful, clean-shaven and wore a little black cloth jacket, cut quite short."

"A waiter at a café, perhaps?"

"Yes, a head-waiter. I had him followed by one of my servants. He went down the Rue de la Pompe and entered a common-looking house. The ground-floor is occupied by a wine-shop: it is the first house in the street, on the left. Then, a night or two ago, I saw a shadow in the garden from my bedroom window."

"Is that all?"

"Yes."

He thought and then made a suggestion:

"Would you allow two of my men to sleep downstairs, in one of the ground-floor rooms?"

"Two of your men? . . ."

"Oh, you need not be afraid! They are decent men, old Charolais and his son,[1] and they don't look in the least like what they are. . . You will be quite safe with them. . . As for me. . ."

He hesitated. He was waiting for her to ask him to come again. As she was silent, he said:

"As for me, it is better that I should not be seen here. . . Yes, it is better. . . for your sake. My men will let me know how things go on. . ."

He would have liked to say more and to remain and to sit down beside her and comfort her. But he had a feeling that they had said all that they had to say and that a single word more, on his side, would be an insult.

Then he made her a very low bow and went away.

He went up the garden, walking quickly, in his haste to be outside and master his emotion. The footman was waiting for him at the hall-door. As he passed out into the street, somebody rang, a young woman.

He gave a start:

"Geneviève!"

She fixed a pair of astonished eyes upon him and at once recognized him, although bewildered by the extreme youthfulness of his appearance; and this gave her such a shock that she staggered and had to lean against the door for support. He had taken off his hat and was looking at her without daring to put out his hand. Would she put out hers? He was no longer Prince Sernine: he was Arsène Lupin. And she knew that he was Arsène Lupin and that he had just come out of prison.

It was raining outside. She gave her umbrella to the footman and said:

"Please open it and put it somewhere to dry."

Then she walked straight in.

---

1. See *Arsène Lupin*, by Edgar Jepson and Maurice Leblanc.

"My poor old chap!" said Lupin to himself, as he walked away. "What a series of blows for a sensitive and highly-strung creature like yourself! You must keep a watch on your heart or. . . Ah, what next? Here are my eyes beginning to water now! That's a bad sign. M. Lupin: you're growing old!"

He gave a tap on the shoulder to a young man who was crossing the Chaussee de la Muette and going toward the Rue des Vignes. The young man stopped, stared at him and said:

"I beg your pardon, monsieur, but I don't think I have the honor. . ."

"Think again, my dear M. Leduc. Or has your memory quite gone? Don't you remember Versailles? And the little room at the Hôtel des Trois-Empereurs?"

The young man bounded backwards:

"You!"

"Why, yes, I! Prince Sernine, or rather Lupin, since you know my real name! Did you think that Lupin had departed this life? . . . Oh, yes, I see, prison. . . You were hoping. . . Get out, you baby!" He patted him gently on the shoulder. "There, there, young fellow, don't be frightened: you have still a few nice quiet days left to write your poems in. The time has not yet come. Write your verses. . . poet!"

Then he gripped Leduc's arm violently and, looking him full in the face, said:

"But the time is drawing near. . . poet! Don't forget that you belong to me, body and soul. And prepare to play your part. It will be a hard and magnificent part. And, as I live, I believe you're the man to play it!"

He burst out laughing, turned on one foot and left young Leduc astounded.

A little further, at the corner of the Rue de la Pompe, stood the wine-shop of which Mrs. Kesselbach had spoken to him. He went in and had a long talk with the proprietor.

Then he took a taxi and drove to the Grand Hotel, where he was staying under the name of André Beauny, and found the brothers Doudeville waiting for him.

Lupin, though used to that sort of pleasure, nevertheless enjoyed the marks of admiration and devotion with which his friends overwhelmed him:

"But, governor, tell us. . . what happened? We're accustomed to all sorts of wonders with you; but still, there are limits. . . So you are free? And here you are, in the heart of Paris, scarcely disguised. . . !"

"Have a cigar," said Lupin.

"Thank you, no."

"You're wrong, Doudeville. These are worth smoking. I have them from a great connoisseur, who is good enough to call himself my friend."

"Oh, may one ask. . . ?"

"The Kaiser! Come, don't look so flabbergasted, the two of you! And tell me things: I haven't seen the papers. What effect did my escape have on the public?"

"Tremendous, governor!"

"What was the police version?"

"Your flight took place at Garches, during an attempt to reënact the murder of Altenheim. Unfortunately, the journalists have proved that it was impossible."

"After that?"

"After that, a general fluster. People wondering, laughing and enjoying themselves like mad."

"Weber?"

"Weber is badly let in."

"Apart from that, no news at the detective-office? Nothing discovered about the murderer? No clue to help us to establish Altenheim's identity?"

"No."

"What fools they are! And to think that we pay millions a year to keep those people. If this sort of thing goes on, I shall refuse to pay my rates. Take a seat and a pen. I will dictate a letter which you must hand in to the *Grand Journal* this evening. The world has been waiting for news of me long enough. It must be gasping with impatience. Write."

He dictated:

To the Editor of the *Grand Journal*:

Sir,

"I must apologize to your readers for disappointing their legitimate impatience.

"I have escaped from prison and I cannot possibly reveal how I escaped. In the same way, since my escape, I have discovered the famous secret and I cannot possibly disclose what the secret is nor how I discovered it.

"All this will, some day or other, form the subject of a rather original story which my biographer-in-ordinary will publish from my notes. It will form a page of the history of France which our grandchildren will read with interest.

"For the moment, I have more important matters to attend to. Disgusted at seeing into what hands the functions which I once exercised have fallen, tired of finding the Kesselbach-Altenheim case still dragging along, I am discharging M. Weber and resuming the post of honor which I occupied with such distinction and to the general satisfaction under the name of M. Lenormand.

I am, Sir,
Your obedient servant
ARSÈNE LUPIN,
Chief of the Detective-service

At eight o'clock in the evening, Arsène Lupin and Jean Doudeville walked into Caillard's, the fashionable restaurant, Lupin in evening-clothes, but dressed like an artist, with rather wide trousers and a rather loose tie, and Doudeville in a frock-coat, with the serious air and appearance of a magistrate.

They sat down in that part of the restaurant which is set back and divided from the big room by two columns.

A head-waiter, perfectly dressed and supercilious in manner, came to take their orders, note-book in hand. Lupin selected the dinner with the nice thought of an accomplished epicure:

"Certainly," he said, "the prison ordinary was quite acceptable; but, all the same, it is nice to have a carefully-ordered meal."

He ate with a good appetite and silently, contenting himself with uttering, from time to time, a short sentence that marked his train of thought:

"Of course, I shall manage. . . but it will be a hard job. . . Such an adversary! . . . What staggers me is that, after six months' fighting, I don't even know what he wants! . . . His chief accomplice is dead, we are near the end of the battle and yet, even now, I can't understand his game. . . What is the wretch after? . . . My own plan is quite clear: to lay hands on the grand-duchy, to shove a grand-duke of my own making on the throne, to give him Geneviève for a wife. . . and to reign. That is what I call lucid, honest and fair. But he, the low fellow, the ghost in the dark: what is he aiming at?"

He called:

MAURICE LEBLANC

"Waiter!"

The head-waiter came up:

"Yes, sir?"

"Cigars."

The head-waiter stalked away, returned and opened a number of boxes.

"Which do you recommend?"

"These Upmanns are very good, sir."

Lupin gave Doudeville an Upmann, took one for himself and cut it. The head-waiter struck a match and held if for him. With a sudden movement, Lupin caught him by the wrist:

"Not a word. . . I know you. . . Your real name is Dominique Lecas!"

The man, who was big and strong, tried to struggle away. He stifled a cry of pain: Lupin had twisted his wrist.

"Your name is Dominique. . . you live in the Rue de la Pompe, on the fourth floor, where you retired with a small fortune acquired in the service—listen to me, you fool, will you, or I'll break every bone in your body!—acquired in the service of Baron Altenheim, at whose house you were butler."

The other stood motionless, his face pallid with fear. Around them, the small room was empty. In the restaurant beside it, three gentlemen sat smoking and two couples were chatting over their liquors.

"You see, we are quiet. . . we can talk."

"Who are you? Who are you?"

"Don't you recollect me? Why, think of that famous luncheon in the Villa Dupont! . . . You yourself, you old flunkey, handed me the plate of cakes. . . and such cakes!"

"Prince. . . Prince. . ." stammered the other.

"Yes, yes, Prince Arsène, Prince Lupin in person. . . Aha, you breathe again! . . . You're saying to yourself that you have nothing to fear from Lupin, isn't that it? Well, you're wrong, old chap, you have everything to fear." He took a card from his pocket and showed it to him. "There, look, I belong to the police now. Can't be helped: that's what we all come to in the end, all of us robber-kings and emperors of crime."

"Well?" said the head-waiter, still greatly alarmed.

"Well, go to that customer over there, who's calling you, get him what he wants and come back to me. And no nonsense, mind you: don't go trying to get away. I have ten men outside, with orders to keep their eyes on you. Be off."

The head-waiter obeyed. Five minutes after, he returned and, standing in front of the table, with his back to the restaurant, as though discussing the quality of the cigars with his customers, he said:

"Well? What is it?"

Lupin laid a number of hundred-franc notes in a row on the table:

"One note for each definite answer to my questions."

"Done!"

"Now then. How many of you were there with Baron Altenheim?"

"Seven, without counting myself."

"No more?"

"No. Once only, we picked up some workmen in Italy to make the underground passage from the Villa des Glycines, at Garches."

"Were there two underground passages?"

"Yes, one led to the Pavillon Hortense and the other branched off from the first and ran under Mrs. Kesselbach's house."

"What was the object?"

"To carry off Mrs. Kesselbach."

"Were the two maids, Suzanne and Gertrude, accomplices?"

"Yes."

"Where are they?"

"Abroad."

"And your seven pals, those of the Altenheim gang?"

"I have left them. They are still going on."

"Where can I find them?"

Dominique hesitated. Lupin unfolded two notes of a thousand francs each and said:

"Your scruples do you honor, Dominique. There's nothing for it but to swallow them like a man and answer."

Dominique replied:

"You will find them at No. 3, Route de la Revolte, Neuilly. One of them is called the Broker."

"Capital. And now the name, the real name of Altenheim. Do you know it?"

"Yes, Ribeira."

"Dominique, Dominique, you're asking for trouble. Ribeira was only an assumed name. I asked you the real name."

"Parbury."

"That's another assumed name."

The head-waiter hesitated. Lupin unfolded three hundred franc notes.

"Pshaw, what do I care!" said the man. "After all, he's dead, isn't he? Quite dead."

"His name," said Lupin.

"His name? The Chevalier de Malreich."

Lupin gave a jump in his chair:

"What? What do you say? The Chevalier—say it again—the Chevalier. . . ?"

"Raoul de Malreich."

A long pause. Lupin, with his eyes fixed before him, thought of the mad girl at Veldenz, who had died by poison: Isilda bore the same name, Malreich. And it was the name borne by the small French noble who came to the court of Veldenz in the eighteenth century.

He resumed his questions:

"What country did this Malreich belong to?"

"He was of French origin, but born in Germany. . . I saw some papers once. . . that was how I came to know his name. . . Oh, if he had found it out, he would have wrung my neck, I believe!"

Lupin reflected and said:

"Did he command the lot of you?"

"Yes."

"But he had an accomplice, a partner?"

"Oh hush. . . hush. . . !"

The head-waiter's face suddenly expressed the most intense alarm. Lupin noticed the same sort of terror and repulsion which he himself felt when he thought of the murderer.

"Who is he? Have you seen him?"

"Oh, don't let us talk of that one. . . it doesn't do to talk of him."

"Who is he, I'm asking you."

"He is the master. . . the chief. . . Nobody knows him."

"But you've seen him, you. Answer me. Have you seen him?"

"Sometimes, in the dark. . . at night. Never by daylight. His orders come on little scraps of paper. . . or by telephone."

"His name?"

"I don't know it. We never used to speak of him. It was unlucky."

"He dresses in black, doesn't he?"

"Yes, in black. He is short and slender. . . with fair hair. . ."

"And he kills, doesn't he?"

"Yes, he kills. . . he kills where another might steal a bit of bread."

His voice shook. He entreated:

"Let us stop this. . . it won't do to talk of him. . . I tell you. . . it's unlucky."

Lupin was silent, impressed, in spite of himself, by the man's anguish. He sat long thinking and then rose and said to the head-waiter:

"Here, here's your money; but, if you want to live in peace, you will do well not to breathe a word of our conversation to anybody."

He left the restaurant with Doudeville and walked to the Porte Saint-Denis without speaking, absorbed in all that he had heard. At last, he seized his companion's arm and said:

"Listen to me, Doudeville, carefully. Go to the Gare du Nord. You will get there in time to catch the Luxemburg express. Go to Veldenz, the capital of the grand-duchy of Zweibrucken-Veldenz. At the town-hall, you will easily obtain the birth-certificate of the Chevalier de Malreich and further information about the family. You will be back on the day after to-morrow: that will be Saturday."

"Am I to let them know at the detective-office?"

"I'll see to that. I shall telephone that you are ill. Oh, one word more: on Saturday, meet me at twelve o'clock in a little café on the Route de la Revolte, called the Restaurant Buffalo. Come dressed as a workman."

THE NEXT DAY, LUPIN, WEARING a short smock and a cap, went down to Neuilly and began his investigations at No. 3, Route de la Revolte. A gateway opened into an outer yard; and here he found a huge block of workmen's dwellings, a whole series of passages and workshops, with a swarming population of artisans, women and brats. In a few minutes, he had won the good-will of the portress, with whom he chatted for an hour on the most varied topics. During this hour, he saw three men pass, one after the other, whose manner struck him:

"That's game," he thought, "and gamy game at that! . . . They follow one another by scent! . . . Look quite respectable, of course, but with the eye of the hunted deer which knows that the enemy is all around and that every tuft, every blade of grass may conceal an ambush."

That afternoon and on the Saturday morning, he pursued his inquiries and made certain that Altenheim's seven accomplices all lived on the premises. Four of them openly followed the trade of second-hand clothes-dealers. Two of the others sold newspapers; and the third described himself as a broker and was nicknamed accordingly.

They went in and out, one after the other, without appearing to know one another. But, in the evening, Lupin discovered that they met in a sort of coach-house situated right at the back of the last of the yards, a place in which the Broker kept his wares piled up: old iron, broken kitchen-ranges, rusty stove-pipes. . . and also, no doubt, the best part of the stolen goods.

"Come," he said, "the work is shaping nicely. I asked my cousin of Germany for a month and I believe a fortnight will be enough for my purpose. And what I like about it is that I shall start operations with the scoundrels who made me take a header in the Seine. My poor old Gourel, I shall revenge you at last. And high time too!"

At twelve o'clock on Saturday, he went to the Restaurant Buffalo, a little low-ceilinged room to which brick-layers and cab-drivers resorted for their mid-day meal. Some one came and sat down beside him:

"It's done, governor."

"Ah, is it you, Doudeville? That's right! I'm dying to know. Have you the particulars? The birth-certificate? Quick, tell me."

"Well, it's like this: Altenheim's father and mother died abroad."

"Never mind about them."

"They left three children."

"Three?"

"Yes. The eldest would have been thirty years old by now. His name was Raoul de Malreich."

"That's our man, Altenheim. Next?"

"The youngest of the children was a girl, Isilda. The register has an entry, in fresh ink, 'Deceased.'"

"Isilda. . . Isilda," repeated Lupin. "That's just what I thought: Isilda was Altenheim's sister. . . I saw a look in her face which I seemed to recognize. . . So that was the link between them. . . But the other, the third child, or rather the second?"

"A son. He would be twenty-six by now."

"His name?"

"Louis de Malreich."

Lupin gave a little start:

"That's it! Louis de Malreich. . . The initials L. M. . . The awful and terrifying signature! . . . The murderer's name is Louis de Malreich. . . He was the brother of Altenheim and the brother of Isilda and he killed both of them for fear of what they might reveal."

Lupin sat long, silent and gloomy, under the obsession, no doubt, of the mysterious being.

Doudeville objected:

"What had he to fear from his sister Isilda? She was mad, they told me."

"Mad, yes, but capable of remembering certain details of her childhood. She must have recognized the brother with whom she grew up. . . and that recollection cost her her life." And he added, "Mad! But all those people were mad. . . The mother was mad. . . The father a dipsomaniac. . . Altenheim a regular brute beast. . . Isilda, a poor innocent. . . As for the other, the murderer, he is the monster, the crazy lunatic. . ."

"Crazy? Do you think so, governor?"

"Yes, crazy! With flashes of genius, of devilish cunning and intuition, but a crack-brained fool, a madman, like all that Malreich family. Only madmen kill and especially madmen of his stamp. For, after all. . ."

He interrupted himself; and his face underwent so great a change that Doudeville was struck by it:

"What's the matter, governor?"

"Look."

A man had entered and hung his hat—a soft, black felt hat—on a peg. He sat down at a little table, examined the bill of fare which a waiter brought him, gave his order and waited motionless, with his body stiff and erect and his two arms crossed over the table-cloth.

And Lupin saw him full-face.

He had a lean, hard visage, absolutely smooth and pierced with two sockets in the depths of which appeared a pair of steel-gray eyes. The skin seemed stretched from bone to bone, like a sheet of parchment, so stiff and so thick that not a hair could have penetrated through it.

And the face was dismal and dull. No expression enlivened it. No thought seemed to abide under that ivory forehead; and the eye-lids, entirely devoid of lashes, never flickered, which gave the eyes the fixed look of the eyes in a statue.

Lupin beckoned to one of the waiters:

"Who is that gentleman?"

"The one eating his lunch over there?"

"Yes."

"He is a customer. He comes here two or three times a week."

"Can you tell me his name?"

"Why, yes. . . Leon Massier."

"Oh!" blurted Lupin, very excitedly. "L. M. . . the same two letters. . . could it be Louis de Malreich?"

He watched him eagerly. Indeed, the man's appearance agreed with

Lupin's conjectures, with what he knew of him and of his hideous mode of existence. But what puzzled him was that look of death about him: where he anticipated life and fire, where he would have expected to find the torment, the disorder, the violent facial distortion of the great accursed, he beheld sheer impassiveness.

He asked the waiter:

"What does he do?"

"I really can't say. He's a rum cove. . . He's always quite alone. . . He never talks to anybody. . . We here don't even know the sound of his voice. . . He points his finger at the dishes on the bill of fare which he wants. . . He has finished in twenty minutes; then he pays and goes. . ."

"And he comes back again?"

"Every three or four days. He's not regular."

"It's he, it cannot be any one else," said Lupin to himself. "It's Malreich. There he is. . . breathing. . . at four steps from me. There are the hands that kill. There is the brain that gloats upon the smell of blood. There is the monster, the vampire! . . ."

And, yet, was it possible? Lupin had ended by looking upon Malreich as so fantastic a being that he was disconcerted at seeing him in the flesh, coming, going, moving. He could not explain to himself how the man could eat bread and meat like other men, drink beer like any one else: this man whom he had pictured as a foul beast, feeding on live flesh and sucking the blood of his victims.

"Come away, Doudeville."

"What's the matter with you, governor? You look quite white!"

"I want air. Come out."

Outside, he drew a deep breath, wiped the perspiration from his forehead and muttered:

"That's better. I was stifling." And, mastering himself, he added, "Now we must play our game cautiously and not lose sight of his tracks."

"Hadn't we better separate, governor? Our man saw us together. He will take less notice of us singly."

"Did he see us?" said Lupin, pensively. "He seems to me to see nothing, to hear nothing and to look at nothing. What a bewildering specimen!"

And, in fact, ten minutes later, Leon Massier appeared and walked away, without even looking to see if he was followed. He had lit a cigarette and smoked, with one of his hands behind his back, strolling along like a saunterer enjoying the sunshine and the fresh air and never suspecting that his movements could possibly be watched.

He passed through the toll-gates, skirted the fortifications, went out again through the Porte Champerret and retraced his steps along the Route de la Revolte.

Would he enter the buildings at No. 3? Lupin eagerly hoped that he would, for that would have been a certain proof of his complicity with the Altenheim gang; but the man turned round and made for the Rue Delaizement, which he followed until he passed the Velodrome Buffalo.

On the left, opposite the cycling-track, between the public tennis-court and the booths that line the Rue Delaizement, stood a small detached villa, surrounded by a scanty garden. Leon Massier stopped, took out his keys, opened first the gate of the garden and then the door of the house and disappeared.

Lupin crept forward cautiously. He at once noticed that the block in the Route de la Revolte stretched back as far as the garden-wall. Coming still nearer, he saw that the wall was very high and that a coach-house rested against it at the bottom of the garden. The position of the buildings was such as to give him the certainty that his coach-house stood back to back with the coach-house in the inner yard of No. 3, which served as a lumber-room for the Broker.

Leon Massier, therefore, occupied a house adjoining the place in which the seven members of the Altenheim gang held their meetings. Consequently, Leon Massier was, in point of fact, the supreme leader who commanded that gang; and there was evidently a passage between the two coach-houses through which he communicated with his followers.

"I was right," said Lupin. "Leon Massier and Louis de Malreich are one and the same man. The situation is much simpler than it was."

"There is no doubt about that," said Doudeville, "and everything will be settled in a few days."

"That is to say, I shall have been stabbed in the throat."

"What are you saying, governor? There's an idea!"

"Pooh, who knows? I have always had a presentiment that that monster would bring me ill-luck."

THENCEFORTH IT BECAME A MATTER of watching Malreich's life in such a way that none of his movements went unobserved. This life was of the oddest, if one could believe the people of the neighborhood whom Doudeville questioned. "The bloke from the villa," as they called him, had been living there for a few months only. He saw and received nobody.

He was not known to keep a servant of any kind. And the windows, though they were left wide open, even at night, always remained dark and were never lit with the glow of a lamp or candle.

Moreover, Leon Massier most often went out at the close of day and did not come in again until very late. . . at dawn, said people who had come upon him at sunrise.

"And does any one know what he does?" asked Lupin of his companion, when they next met.

"No, he leads an absolutely irregular existence. He sometimes disappears for several days together. . . or, rather, he remains indoors. When all is said, nobody knows anything."

"Well, we shall know; and that soon."

He was wrong. After a week of continuous efforts and investigations, he had learnt no more than before about that strange individual. The extraordinary thing that constantly happened was this, that, suddenly, while Lupin was following him, the man, who was ambling with short steps along the streets, without ever turning round or ever stopping, the man would vanish as if by a miracle. True, he sometimes went through houses with two entrances. But, at other times, he seemed to fade away in the midst of the crowd, like a ghost. And Lupin was left behind, petrified, astounded, filled with rage and confusion.

He at once hurried to the Rue Delaizement and stood on guard outside the villa. Minutes followed upon minutes, half-hour upon half-hour. A part of the night slipped away. Then, suddenly, the mysterious man hove in sight. What could he have been doing?

"AN EXPRESS MESSAGE FOR YOU, governor," said Doudeville, at eight o'clock one evening, as he joined him in the Rue Delaizement.

Lupin opened the envelope. Mrs. Kesselbach implored him to come to her aid. It appeared that two men had taken up their stand under her windows, at night, and one of them had said:

"What luck, we've dazzled them completely this time! So it's understood; we shall strike the blow to-night."

Mrs. Kesselbach thereupon went downstairs and discovered that the shutter in the pantry did not fasten, or, at least, that it could be opened from the outside.

"At last," said Lupin, "it's the enemy himself who offers to give battle. That's a good thing! I am tired of marching up and down under Malreich's windows."

"Is he there at this moment?"

"No, he played me one of his tricks again in Paris, just as I was about to play him one of mine. But, first of all, listen to me, Doudeville. Go and collect ten of our men and bring them to the Rue des Vignes. Look here, bring Marco and Jérôme, the messenger. I have given them a holiday since the business at the Palace Hotel: let them come this time. Daddy Charolais and his son ought to be mounting guard by now. Make your arrangements with them, and at half-past eleven, come and join me at the corner of the Rue des Vignes and the Rue Raynouard. From there we will watch the house."

Doudeville went away. Lupin waited for an hour longer, until that quiet thoroughfare, the Rue Delaizement, was quite deserted, and then, seeing that Leon Massier did not return, he made up his mind and went up to the villa.

There was no one in sight. . . He took a run and jumped on the stone ledge that supported the railings of the garden. A few minutes later, he was inside.

His plan was to force the door of the house and search the rooms in order to find the Emperor's letters which Malreich had stolen from Veldenz. But he thought a visit to the coach-house of more immediate importance.

He was much surprised to see that it was open and, next, to find, by the light of his electric lantern, that it was absolutely empty and that there was no door in the back wall. He hunted about for a long time, but met with no more success. Outside, however, he saw a ladder standing against the coach-house and obviously serving as a means of reaching a sort of loft contrived under the slate roof.

The loft was blocked with old packing-cases, trusses of straw and gardener's frames, or rather it seemed to be blocked, for he very soon discovered a gangway that took him to the wall. Here, he knocked up against a cucumber-frame, which he tried to move. Failing to effect his purpose, he examined the frame more closely and found, first, that it was fixed to the wall and, secondly, that one of the panes was missing. He passed his arm through and encountered space. He cast the bright light of the lantern through the aperture and saw a big shed, a coach-house larger than that of the villa and filled with old iron-work and objects of every kind.

"That's it," said Lupin to himself. "This window has been contrived in the Broker's lumber-room, right up at the top, and from here Louis de Malreich sees, hears and watches his accomplices, without being seen or heard by them. I now understand how it is that they do not know their leader."

Having found out what he wanted, he put out his light and was on the point of leaving, when a door opened opposite him, down below. Some one came in and lit a lamp. He recognized the Broker. He thereupon resolved to stay where he was, since the expedition, after all, could not be done so long as that man was there.

The Broker took two revolvers from his pocket. He tested the triggers and changed the cartridges, whistling a music-hall tune as he did so.

An hour elapsed in this way. Lupin was beginning to grow restless, without, however, making up his mind to go.

More minutes passed, half an hour, an hour. . .

At last, the man said aloud:

"Come in."

One of the scoundrels slipped into the shed; and, one after the other, a third arrived and a fourth. . .

"We are all here," said the Broker. "Dieudonne and Chubby will meet us down there. Come, we've no time to lose. . . Are you armed?"

"To the teeth."

"That's all right. It'll be hot work."

"How do you know, Broker?"

"I've seen the chief. . . When I say that I've seen him, no. . . but he spoke to me. . ."

"Yes," said one of the men, "in the dark, at a street-corner, as usual. Ah, Altenheim's ways were better than that. At least, one knew what one was doing."

"And don't you know?" retorted the Broker. "We're breaking in at the Kesselbach woman's."

"And what about the two watchers? The two coves whom Lupin posted there?"

"That's their look-out: there's seven of us. They had better give us as little trouble as possible."

"What about the Kesselbach?"

"Gag her first, then bind her and bring her here. . . There, on that old sofa. . . And then wait for orders."

"Is the job well paid?"

"The Kesselbach's jewels to begin with."

"Yes, if it comes off. . . but I'm speaking of the certainty."

"Three hundred-franc notes apiece, beforehand, and twice as much again afterwards."

"Have you the money?"

"Yes."

"That's all right. You can say what you like, but, as far as paying goes, there's no one to equal that bloke." And, in a voice so low that Lupin could hardly hear, "I say, Broker, if we're obliged to use the knife, is there a reward?"

"The same as usual, two thousand."

"If it's Lupin?"

"Three thousand."

"Oh, if we could only get him!"

One after the other, they left the lumber-room. Lupin heard the Broker's parting words:

"This is the plan of attack. We divide into three lots. A whistle; and every one runs forward. . ."

Lupin hurriedly left his hiding-place, went down the ladder, ran round the house, without going in, and climbed back over the railings:

"The Broker's right; it'll be hot work. . . Ah, it's my skin they're after! A reward for Lupin! The rascals!"

He passed through the toll-gate and jumped into a taxi:

"Rue Raynouard."

He stopped the cab at two hundred yards from the Rue des Vignes and walked to the corner of the two streets. To his great surprise, Doudeville was not there.

"That's funny," said Lupin. "It's past twelve. . . This business looks suspicious to me."

He waited ten minutes, twenty minutes. At half-past twelve, nobody had arrived. Further delay was dangerous. After all, if Doudeville and his men were prevented from coming, Charolais, his son and he, Lupin, himself were enough to repel the attack, without counting the assistance of the servants.

He therefore went ahead. But he caught sight of two men who tried to hide in the shadow of a corner wall.

"Hang it!" he said. "That's the vanguard of the gang, Dieudonné and Chubby. I've allowed myself to be out-distanced, like a fool."

Here he lost more time. Should he go straight up to them, disable them and then climb into the house through the pantry-window, which he knew to be unlocked? That would be the most prudent course and would enable him, moreover, to take Mrs. Kesselbach away at once and to remove her to a place of safety.

Yes, but it also meant the failure of his plan; it meant missing this glorious opportunity of trapping the whole gang, including Louis de Malreich himself, without doubt.

Suddenly a whistle sounded from somewhere on the other side of the house. Was it the rest of the gang, so soon? And was an offensive movement to be made from the garden?

But, at the preconcerted signal, the two men climbed through the window and disappeared from view.

Lupin scaled the balcony at a bound and jumped into the pantry. By the sound of their footsteps, he judged that the assailants had gone into the garden; and the sound was so distinct that he felt easy in his mind: Charolais and his son could not fail to hear the noise.

He therefore went upstairs. Mrs. Kesselbach's bedroom was on the first landing. He walked in without knocking.

A night-light was burning in the room; and he saw Dolores, on a sofa, fainting. He ran up to her, lifted her and, in a voice of command, forcing her to answer:

"Listen. . . Charolais? His son. . . Where are they?"

She stammered:

"Why, what do you mean? . . . They're gone, of course! . . ."

"What, gone?"

"You sent me word. . . an hour ago. . . a telephone-message. . ."

He picked up a piece of blue paper lying beside her and read:

"Send the two watchers away at once. . . and all my men. . . Tell them to meet me at the Grand Hotel. Have no fear."

"Thunder! And you believed it? . . . But your servants?"

"Gone."

He went up to the window. Outside, three men were coming from the other end of the garden.

From the window in the next room, which looked out on the street, he saw two others, on the pavement.

And he thought of Dieudonné, of Chubby, of Louis de Malreich, above all, who must now be prowling around, invisible and formidable.

"Hang it!" he muttered. "I half believe they've done me this time!"

XIV

The Man in Black

At that moment, Arsène Lupin felt the impression, the certainty, that he had been drawn into an ambush, by means which he had not the time to perceive, but of which he guessed the prodigious skill and address. Everything had been calculated, everything ordained; the dismissal of his men, the disappearance or treachery of the servants, his own presence in Mrs. Kesselbach's house.

Clearly, the whole thing had succeeded, exactly as the enemy wished, thanks to circumstances almost miraculously fortunate; for, after all, he might have arrived before the false message had sent his friends away. But then there would have been a battle between his own gang and the Altenheim gang. And Lupin, remembering Malreich's conduct, the murder of Altenheim, the poisoning of the mad girl at Veldenz, Lupin asked himself whether the ambush was aimed at him alone or whether Malreich had not contemplated the possibility of a general scuffle, involving the killing of accomplices who had by this time become irksome to him.

It was an intuition, rather, a fleeting idea, that just passed through his mind. The hour was one for action. He must defend Dolores, the abduction of whom was, in all likelihood, the first and foremost reason of the attack.

He half-opened the casement window on the street and levelled his revolver. A shot, rousing and alarming the neighborhood, and the scoundrels would take to their heels.

"Well, no," he muttered, "no! It shall not be said that I shirked the fight. The opportunity is too good. . . And, then, who says that they would run away! . . . There are too many of them to care about the neighbors."

He returned to Dolores' room. There was a noise downstairs. He listened and, finding that it came from the staircase, he locked the door.

Dolores was crying and throwing herself about the sofa.

He implored her:

"Are you strong enough? We are on the first floor. I could help you down. We can lower the sheets from the window. . ."

"No, no, don't leave me... I am frightened... I haven't the strength... they will kill me... Oh, protect me!"

He took her in his arms and carried her to the next room. And, bending over her:

"Don't move; and keep calm. I swear to you that not one of those men shall touch you, as long as I am alive."

The door of the first room was tried. Dolores, clinging to him with all her might, cried:

"Oh, there they are! There they are! . . . They will kill you. . . you are alone! . . ."

Eagerly, he said:

"No, I am not alone. . . You are here. . . You are here beside me. . ."

He tried to release himself. She took his head in her two hands, looked him deep in the eyes and whispered:

"Where are you going? What are you going to do? No. . . you must not die. . . I won't have it. . . you must live. . . you must."

She stammered words which he did not catch and which she seemed to stifle between her lips lest he should hear them; and, having spent all her energy, exhausted, she fell back unconscious.

He leant over her and gazed at her for a moment. Softly, lightly, he pressed a kiss upon her hair.

Then he went back to the first room, carefully closed the door between the two and switched on the electric light.

"One second, my lads!" he cried. "You seem in a great hurry to get yourselves smashed to pieces! . . . Don't you know that Lupin's here? I'll make you dance!"

While speaking, he unfolded a screen in such a way as to hide the sofa on which Mrs. Kesselbach had been lying; and he now spread dresses and coverings over it. The door was on the point of giving way under the blows of the men outside.

"Here I am! Coming! Are you ready? Now, gentlemen, one at a time! . . ."

He briskly turned the key and drew the bolt.

Shouts, threats, a roar of infuriated animals came through the open doorway.

Yet none of them dared come forward. Before rushing at Lupin, they hesitated, seized with alarm, with fear. . .

This was what he had reckoned on.

Standing in the middle of the room, full in the light, with outstretched arm, he held between his fingers a sheaf of bank-notes, which he divided, counting them one by one, into seven equal shares. And he calmly said:

"Three thousand francs' reward for each of you, if Lupin is sent to his last account? That's what you were promised, isn't it? Here's double the money!"

He laid the bundles on the table, within reach of the scoundrels.

The Broker roared:

"Humbug! He's trying to gain time. Shoot him down!"

He raised his arm. His companions held him back.

And Lupin continued:

"Of course, this need not affect your plan of campaign. You came here, first, to kidnap Mrs. Kesselbach and, secondly, to lay hands on her jewels. Far be it from me to interfere with your laudable intentions!"

"Look here, what are you driving at?" growled the Broker, listening in spite of himself.

"Aha, Broker, I'm beginning to interest you, am I? . . . Come in, old chap. . . Come in, all of you. . . There's a draught at the top of those stairs. . . and such pretty fellows as you mustn't run the risk of catching cold. . . What, are we afraid? Why, I'm all by myself! . . . Come, pull yourselves together, my lambs!"

They entered the room, puzzled and suspicious.

"Shut the door, Broker. . . we shall be more comfortable. Thanks, old man. Oh, by the way, I see the notes are gone. Therefore we're agreed. How easy it is for honest men to come to terms!"

"Well. . . and next?"

"Next? Well, as we're partners. . ."

"Partners?"

"Why, haven't you accepted my money? We're working together, old man, and we will carry off the young woman together first and carry off the jewels after."

The Broker grinned:

"Don't want you for that."

"Yes, you do, old man."

"Why?"

"Because you don't know where the jewels are hidden and I do."

"We'll find out."

"To-morrow. Not to-night."

"Well, let's hear. What do you want?"

"My share of the jewels."

"Why didn't you take the lot, as you know where they are?"

"Can't get at them by myself. There's a way of doing it, but I don't know it. You're here, so I'm making use of you."

The Broker hesitated:

"Share the jewels. . . Share the jewels. . . A few bits of glass and brass, most likely. . ."

"You fool! . . . There's more than a million's worth."

The men quivered under the impression made upon them.

"Very well," said the Broker. "But suppose the Kesselbach gets away? She's in the next room, isn't she?"

"No, she's in here."

Lupin for a moment pulled back one of the leaves of the screen, revealing the heap of dresses and bed-clothes which he had laid out on the sofa:

"She's here, fainting. But I shan't give her up till we've divided."

"Still. . ."

"You can take it or leave it. I don't care if I am alone. You know what I'm good for. So please yourselves. . ."

The men consulted with one another and the Broker said:

"Where is the hiding-place you're talking of?"

"Under the fireplace. But, when you don't know the secret, you must first lift up the whole chimneypiece, looking-glass, marble and all in a lump, it seems. It's no easy job."

"Pooh, we're a smart lot, we are! Just you wait and see. In five minutes. . ."

He gave his orders and his pals at once set to work with admirable vigor and discipline. Two of them, standing on chairs, tried to lift the mirror. The four others attacked the fireplace itself. The Broker, on his knees, kept his eyes on the hearth and gave the word of command:

"Cheerily, lads! . . . Altogether, if you please! . . . Look out! . . . One, two. . . ah, there, it's moving! . . ."

Standing behind them, with his hands in his pockets, Lupin watched them affectionately and, at the same time, revelled with all his pride, as an artist and master, in this striking proof of his authority, of his might, of the incredible sway which he wielded over others. How could those scoundrels for a second accept that improbable story and lose all sense of things, to the point of relinquishing every chance of the fight in his favor?

He took from his pockets two great massive and formidable revolvers and, calmly, choosing the first two men whom he would bring down and the two who would fall next, he aimed as he might have aimed at a pair of targets in a rifle-gallery.

Two shots together and two more. . .

Loud yells of pain. . . Four men came tumbling down, one after the other, like dolls at a cockshy.

"Four from seven leaves three," said Lupin. "Shall I go on?"

His arms remained outstretched, levelled at the Broker and his two pals.

"You swine!" growled the Broker, feeling for a weapon.

"Hands up," cried Lupin, "or I fire! . . . That's it. . . Now, you two, take away his toys. . . If not. . . !"

The two scoundrels, shaking with fear, caught hold of their leader and compelled him to submit.

"Bind him! . . . Bind him, confound it! . . . What difference does it make to you? . . . Once I'm gone, you're all free. . . Come along, have you finished? The wrists first. . . with your belts. . . And the ankles. . . Hurry up! . . ."

The Broker, beaten and disabled, made no further resistance. While his pals were binding him, Lupin stooped over them and dealt them two terrific blows on the head with the butt-end of his revolver. They sank down in a heap.

"That's a good piece of work," he said, taking breath. "Pity there are not another fifty of them. I was just in the mood. . . And all so easily done. . . with a smile on one's face. . . What do you think of it, Broker?"

The scoundrel lay cursing. Lupin said:

"Cheer up, old man! Console yourself with the thought that you are helping in a good action, the rescue of Mrs. Kesselbach. She will thank you in person for your gallantry."

He went to the door of the second room and opened it:

"What's this?" he said, stopping on the threshold, taken aback, dumfounded.

The room was empty.

He went to the window, saw a ladder leaning against the balcony, a telescopic steel ladder, and muttered:

"Kidnapped. . . kidnapped. . . Louis de Malreich. . . Oh, the villain! . . ."

He reflected for a minute, trying to master his anguish of mind, and said to himself that, after all, as Mrs. Kesselbach seemed to be in no immediate danger, there was no cause for alarm.

But he was seized with a sudden fit of rage and flew at the seven scoundrels, gave a kick or two to those of the wounded who stirred, felt for his bank-notes and put them back in his pocket, then gagged the men's mouths and tied their hands with anything that he could find—blind-cords, curtain-loops, blankets and sheets reduced to strips—and, lastly, laid in a row on the carpet, in front of the sofa, seven bundles of humanity, packed tight together and tied up like so many parcels:

"Mummies on toast!" he chuckled. "A dainty dish for those who like that sort of thing! . . . You pack of fools, how does this suit you, eh? There you are, like corpses at the Morgue. . . Serves you right for attacking Lupin, Lupin the protector of the widow and orphan! . . . Are you trembling? Quite unnecessary, my lambs! Lupin never hurt a fly yet! . . . Only, Lupin is a decent man, he can't stand vermin; and the Lupin knows his duty. I ask you, is life possible with a lot of scamps like you about? Think of it: no respect for other people's lives; no respect for property, for laws, for society; no conscience; no anything! What are we coming to? Lord, what are we coming to?"

Without even taking the trouble to lock them in, he left the room, went down the street and walked until he came to his taxi. He sent the driver in search of another and brought both cabs back to Mrs. Kesselbach's house.

A good tip, paid in advance, avoided all tedious explanations. With the help of the two men, he carried the seven prisoners down and plumped them anyhow, on one another's knees, into the cabs. The wounded men yelled and moaned. He shut the doors, shouting:

"Mind your hands!"

He got up beside the driver of the front cab.

"Where to?" asked the man.

"36, Quai des Orfevers: the detective-office."

The motors throbbed, the drivers started the gear and the strange procession went scooting down the slopes of the Trocadero.

In the streets, they passed a few vegetable-carts. Men carrying long poles were turning out the street-lamps.

There were stars in the sky. A cool breeze was wafted through the air.

Lupin sang aloud:

The Place de la Concorde, the Louvre. . . In the distance, the dark bulk of Notre Dame. . .

He turned round and half opened the door:

"Having a good time, mates? So am I, thank you. It's a grand night for a drive and the air's delicious! . . ."

They were now bumping over the ill-paved quays. And soon they arrived at the Palais de Justice and the door of the detective-office.

"Wait here," said Lupin to the two drivers, "and be sure you look after your seven fares."

He crossed the outer yard and went down the passage on the right leading to the rooms of the central office. He found the night inspectors on duty.

"A bag, gentlemen," he said, as he entered, "a fine bag too. Is M. Weber here? I am the new commissary of police for Auteuil."

"M. Weber is in his flat. Do you want him sent for?"

"Just one second. I'm in a hurry. I'll leave a line for him."

He sat down at a table and wrote:

My Dear Weber,

"I am bringing you the seven scoundrels composing Altenheim's gang, the men who killed Gourel (and plenty of others) and who killed me as well, under the name of M. Lenormand.

"That only leaves their leader unaccounted for. I am going to effect his arrest this minute. Come and join me. He lives in the Rue Delaizement, at Neuilly and goes by the name of Leon Massier.

Kind regards
Yours,
Arsène Lupin,
Chief of the Detective-service

He sealed the letter:

"Give that to M. Weber. It's urgent. Now I want seven men to receive the goods. I left them on the quay."

On going back to the taxis, he was met by a chief inspector:

"Ah, it's you M. Lebœuf!" he said. "I've made a fine haul. . . The whole of Altenheim's gang. . . They're there in the taxi-cabs."

"Where did you find them?"

"Hard at work kidnapping Mrs. Kesselbach and robbing her house. But I'll tell you all about it when the time comes."

The chief inspector took him aside and, with the air of surprise:

"I beg your pardon, monsieur, but I was sent for to see the commissary of police for Auteuil. And I don't seem to. . . Whom have I the honor of addressing?"

"Somebody who is making you a handsome present of seven hooligans of the finest quality."

"Still, I should like to know. . ."

"My name?"

"Yes."

"Arsène Lupin."

He nimbly tripped the chief inspector up, ran to the Rue de Rivoli, jumped into a passing taxi-cab and drove to the Porte des Ternes.

The Route de la Revolte was close by. He went to No. 3.

For all his coolness and self-command, Arsène Lupin was unable to control his excitement. Would he find Dolores Kesselbach? Had Louis de Malreich taken her either to his own place or to the Broker's shed?

Lupin had taken the key of the shed from the Broker, so that it was easy for him, after ringing and walking across the different yards, to open the door and enter the lumber-shop.

He switched on his lantern and took his bearings. A little to the right was the free space in which he had seen the accomplices hold their last confabulation. On the sofa mentioned by the Broker he saw a black figure, Dolores lay wrapped in blankets and gagged.

He helped her up.

"Ah, it's you, it's you!" she stammered. "They haven't touched you!"

And, rising and pointing to the back of the shop:

"There. . . he went out that side. . . I heard him. . . I am sure. . . You must go. . . please!"

"I must get you away first," he said.

"No, never mind me. . . go after him. . . I entreat you. . . Strike him!"

Fear, this time, instead of dejecting her, seemed to be giving her unwonted strength; and she repeated, with an immense longing to place her terrible enemy in his power:

"Go after him first. . . I can't go on living like this. . . You must save me from him. . . I can't go on living. . ."

He unfastened her bonds, laid her carefully on the sofa and said:

"You are right. . . Besides, you have nothing to fear here. . . Wait for me, I shall come back."

As he was going away, she caught hold of his hand:

"But you yourself?"

"Well?"

"If that man. . ."

It was as though she dreaded for Lupin the great, final contest to which she was exposing him and as though, at the last moment, she would have been glad to hold him back.

He said:

"Thank you, have no fear. What have I to be afraid of? He is alone."

And, leaving her, he went to the back of the shed. As he expected, he found a ladder standing against the wall which brought him to the level of the little window through which he had watched the scoundrels hold their meeting. It was the way by which Malreich had returned to his house in the Rue Delaizement.

He, therefore, took the same road, just as he had done a few hours earlier, climbed into the loft of the other coach-house and down into the garden. He found himself at the back of the villa occupied by Malreich.

Strange to say, he did not doubt, for a moment that Malreich was there. He would meet him inevitably; the formidable battle which they were waging against each other was nearing its end. A few minutes more and, one way or another, all would be over.

He was amazed, on grasping the handle of a door, to find that the handle turned and the door opened under his pressure. The villa was not even locked.

He passed through a kitchen, a hall and up a staircase; and he walked deliberately, without seeking to deaden the sound of his footsteps.

On the landing, he stopped. The perspiration streamed from his forehead; and his temples throbbed under the rush of his blood. Nevertheless, he remained calm, master of himself and conscious of his least thoughts. He laid two revolvers on a stair:

"No weapons," he said to himself. "My hands only, just the effort of my two hands. . . That's quite enough. . . That will be better. . ."

Opposite him were three doors. He chose the middle one, turned the handle and encountered no obstacle. He went in. There was no light in the room, but the rays of the night entered through the wide-open window and, amid the darkness, he saw the sheets and the white curtains of the bed.

And somebody was standing beside it.

He savagely cast the gleam of his lantern upon that form.

Malreich!

The pallid face of Malreich, his dim eyes, his cadaverous cheek-bones, his scraggy neck. . .

And all this stood motionless, opposite him, at five steps' distance; and he could not have said whether that dull face, that death-face, expressed the least terror or even a grain of anxiety.

Lupin took a step forward. . . and a second. . . and a third. . .

The man did not move.

Did he see? Did he understand? It was as though the man's eyes were gazing into space and that he thought himself possessed by an hallucination, rather than looking upon a real image.

One more step. . .

"He will defend himself," thought Lupin, "he is bound to defend himself."

And Lupin thrust out his arms.

The man did not make a movement. He did not retreat; his eyelids did not blink.

The contact took place.

And it was Lupin, scared and bewildered, who lost his head. He knocked the man back upon his bed, stretched him at full length, rolled him in the sheets, bound him in the blankets and held him under his knee, like a prey. . . whereas the man had not made the slightest movement of resistance.

"Ah!" shouted Lupin, drunk with delight and satisfied hatred. "At last I have crushed you, you odious brute! At last I am the master!"

He heard a noise outside, in the Rue Delaizement; men knocking at the gate. He ran to the window and cried:

"Is that you, Weber? Already? Well done! You are a model servant! Break down the gate, old chap, and come up here; delighted to see you!"

In a few minutes, he searched his prisoner's clothes, got hold of his pocket-book, cleared the papers out of the drawers of the desk and the davenport, flung them on the table and went through them.

He gave a shout of joy: the bundle of letters was there, the famous bundle of letters which he had promised to restore to the Emperor.

He put back the papers in their place and went to the window:

"It's all finished, Weber! You can come in! You will find Mr. Kesselbach's murderer in his bed, all ready tied up... Good-bye, Weber!"

And Lupin, tearing down the stairs, ran to the coach-house and went back to Dolores Kesselbach, while Weber was breaking into the villa.

Single-handed, he had arrested Altenheim's seven companions!

And he had delivered to justice the mysterious leader of the gang, the infamous monster, Louis de Malreich!

A young man sat writing at a table on a wide wooden balcony.

From time to time, he raised his head and cast a vague glance toward the horizon of hills, where the trees, stripped by the autumn, were shedding their last leaves over the red roofs of the villas and the lawns of the gardens. Then he went on writing.

Presently he took up his paper and read aloud:

> *Nos jours s'en vont à la dérive,*
> *Comme emportés par un courant*
> *Qui les pousse vers une rive*
> *Où l'on n'aborde qu'en mourant.*[1]

"Not so bad," said a voice behind him. "Mme. Amable Tastu might have written that, or Mrs. Felicia Hemans. However, we can't all be Byrons or Lamartines!"

"You! ... You! ...." stammered the young man, in dismay.

"Yes, I, poet, I myself, Arsène Lupin come to see his dear friend Pierre Leduc."

Pierre Leduc began to shake, as though shivering with fever. He asked, in a low voice:

"Has the hour come?"

"Yes, my dear Pierre Leduc: the hour has come for you to give up, or rather to interrupt the slack poet's life which you have been leading for months at the feet of Geneviève Ernemont and Mrs. Kesselbach and to perform the part which I have allotted to you in my play... oh, a

---

1. *Our days go by, adrift, adrift,*
   Borne along by current swift
   That urges them toward the strand
   Where not until we die, we land.

MAURICE LEBLANC

fine play, I assure you, thoroughly well-constructed, according to all the canons of art, with top notes, comic relief and gnashing of teeth galore! We have reached the fifth act; the grand finale is at hand; and you, Pierre Leduc, are the hero. There's fame for you!"

The young man rose from his seat:

"And suppose I refuse?"

"Idiot!"

"Yes, suppose I refuse? After all, what obliges me to submit to your will? What obliges me to accept a part which I do not know, but which I loathe in advance and feel ashamed of?"

"Idiot!" repeated Lupin.

And forcing Pierre Leduc back into his chair, he sat down beside him and, in the gentlest of voices:

"You quite forget, my dear young man, that you are not Pierre Leduc, but Gérard Baupré. That you bear the beautiful name of Pierre Leduc is due to the fact that you, Gérard Baupré, killed Pierre Leduc and robbed him of his individuality."

The young man bounded with indignation:

"You are mad! You know as well as I do that you conceived the whole plot. . ."

"Yes, I know that, of course; but the law doesn't know it; and what will the law say when I come forward with proof that the real Pierre Leduc died a violent death and that you have taken his place?"

The young man, overwhelmed with consternation, stammered:

"No one will believe you. . . Why should I have done that? With what object?"

"Idiot! The object is so self-evident that Weber himself could have perceived it. You lie when you say that you will not accept a part which you do not know. You know your part quite well. It is the part which Pierre Leduc would have played were he not dead."

"But Pierre Leduc, to me, to everybody, was only a name. Who was he? Who am I?"

"What difference can that make to you?"

"I want to know. I want to know what I am doing!"

"And, if you know, will you go straight ahead?"

"Yes, if the object of which you speak is worth it."

"If it were not, do you think I would take all this trouble?"

"Who am I? Whatever my destiny, you may be sure that I shall prove worthy of it. But I want to know. Who am I?"

Arsène Lupin took off his hat, bowed and said: "Hermann IV, Grand-duke of Zweibrucken-Veldenz, Prince of Berncastel, Elector of Treves and lord of all sorts of places."

THREE DAYS LATER, ARSÈNE LUPIN took Mrs. Kesselbach away in a motor-car in the direction of the frontier. The journey was accomplished in silence, Lupin remembered with emotion Dolores's terrified conduct and the words which she spoke in the house in the Rue des Vignes, when he was about to defend her against Altenheim's accomplices. And she must have remembered also, for she remained embarrassed and evidently perturbed in his presence.

In the evening they reached a small castle, all covered with creepers and flowers, roofed with an enormous slate cap and standing in a large garden full of ancestral trees.

Here Mrs. Kesselbach found Geneviève already installed, after a visit to the neighboring town, where she had engaged a staff of servants from among the country-people.

"This will be your residence, madame," said Lupin. "You are at Bruggen Castle. You will be quite safe here, while waiting the outcome of these events. I have written to Pierre Leduc and he will be your guest from to-morrow."

He started off again at once, drove to Veldenz and handed over to Count von Waldemar the famous letters which he had recaptured:

"You know my conditions, my dear Waldemar," said Lupin. "The first and most important thing is to restore the House of Zweibrucken-Veldenz and to reinstate the Grand-duke Hermann IV, in the grand-duchy."

"I shall open negotiations with the Council of Regency to-day. According to my information, it will not be a difficult matter. But this Grand-duke Hermann. . ."

"His Royal Highness is at present staying at Bruggen Castle, under the name of Pierre Leduc. I will supply all the necessary proofs of his identity."

That same evening, Lupin took the road back to Paris, with the intention of actively hurrying on the trial of Malreich and the seven scoundrels.

IT WOULD BE WEARISOME TO recapitulate the story of the case: the facts, down to the smallest details, are in the memory of one and all.

It was one of those sensational events which still form a subject of conversation and discussion among the weather-beaten laborers in the remotest villages.

But what I wish to recall is the enormous part played by Lupin in the conduct of the case and in the incidents appertaining to the preliminary inquiry. As a matter of fact, it was he who managed the inquiry. From the very start, he took the place of the authorities, ordering police-searches, directing the measures to be taken, prescribing the questions to be put to the prisoners, assuming the responsibility for everything.

We can all remember the universal amazement when, morning after morning, we read in the papers those letters, so irresistible in their masterly logic, signed, by turns:

> "ARSÈNE LUPIN, *Examining-magistrate*."
> "ARSÈNE LUPIN, *Public Prosecutor*."
> "ARSÈNE LUPIN, *Minister of Justice*."
> "ARSÈNE LUPIN, *Copper*."

He flung himself into the business with a spirit, an ardor, a violence, even, that was astonishing in one usually so full of light-hearted chaff and, when all was said, so naturally disposed by temperament to display a certain professional indulgence.

No, this time he was prompted by hatred.

He hated Louis de Malreich, that bloodthirsty scoundrel, that foul brute, of whom he had always been afraid and who, even beaten, even in prison, still gave him that sensation of dread and repugnance which one feels at the sight of a reptile.

Besides, had not Malreich had the audacity to persecute Dolores?

"He has played and lost," said Lupin. "He shall pay for it with his head."

That was what he wanted for his terrible enemy: the scaffold, the bleak, dull morning when the blade of the guillotine slides down and kills. . .

It was a strange prisoner whom the examining-magistrate questioned for months on end between the four walls of his room, a strange figure, that bony man, with the skeleton face and the lifeless eyes!

He seemed quite out of himself. His thoughts were not there, but elsewhere. And he cared so little about answering!

"My name is Leon Massier."

That was the one sentence to which he confined himself.

And Lupin retorted.

"You lie. Leon Massier, born at Perigueux, left fatherless at the age of ten, died seven years ago. You took his papers. But you forgot his death-certificate. Here it is."

And Lupin sent a copy of the document to the public prosecutor.

"I am Leon Massier," declared the prisoner, once again.

"You lie," replied Lupin. "You are Louis de Malreich, the last surviving descendant of a small French noble who settled in Germany in the eighteenth century. You had a brother who called himself Parbury, Ribeira and Altenheim, by turns: you killed your brother. You had a sister, Isilda de Malreich: you killed your sister."

"I am Leon Massier."

"You lie. You are Malreich. Here is your birth-certificate. Here are your brother's and your sister's."

And Lupin sent the three certificates.

Apart from the question of his identity, Malreich, crushed, no doubt, by the accumulation of proofs brought up against him, did not defend himself. What could he say? They had forty notes written in his own hand—a comparison of the handwritings established the fact—written in his own hand to the gang of his accomplices, forty notes which he had omitted to tear up after taking them back. And all these notes were orders relating to the Kesselbach case, the capture of M. Lenormand and Gourel, the pursuit of old Steinweg, the construction of the underground passages at Garches and so on. What possibility was there of a denial?

One rather odd thing baffled the law officers. The seven scoundrels, when confronted with their leader, all declared that they did not know him, because they had never seen him. They received his instructions either by telephone, or else in the dark, by means of those same little notes which Malreich slipped into their hands without a word.

But, for the rest, was not the existence of the communication between the villa in the Rue Delaizement and the Broker's shed an ample proof of complicity? From that spot, Malreich saw and heard. From that spot, the leader watched his men.

Discrepancies? Apparently irreconcilable facts? Lupin explained them all away. In a celebrated article, published on the morning of the trial, he took up the case from the start, revealed what lay beneath it, unravelled its web, showed Malreich, unknown to all, living in the room of his brother, the sham Major Parbury, passing unseen along the passages of the Palace Hotel and murdering Mr. Kesselbach, murdering Beudot the floor-waiter, murdering Chapman the secretary.

The trial lingers in the memory. It was both terrifying and gloomy: terrifying because of the atmosphere of anguish that hung over the crowd of onlookers and the recollection of crime and blood that obsessed their minds: gloomy, heavy, darksome, stifling because of the tremendous silence observed by the prisoner.

Not a protest, not a movement, not a word. A face of wax that neither saw nor heard. An awful vision of impassive calmness! The people in court shuddered. Their distraught imaginations conjured up a sort of supernatural being rather than a man, a sort of genie out of the Arabian Nights, one of those Hindu gods who symbolize all that is ferocious, cruel, sanguinary and pernicious.

As for the other scoundrels, the people did not even look at them, treated them as insignificant supers overshadowed by that stupendous leader.

The most sensational evidence was that given by Mrs. Kesselbach. To the general astonishment and to Lupin's own surprise, Dolores, who had answered none of the magistrate's summonses and who had retired to an unknown spot, Dolores appeared, a sorrow-stricken widow, to give damning evidence against her husband's murderer.

She gazed at him for many seconds and then said, simply:

"That is the man who entered my house in the Rue des Vignes, who carried me off and who locked me up in the Broker's shed. I recognize him."

"On your oath?"

"I swear it before God and man."

Two days later, Louis de Malreich, *alias* Leon Massier was sentenced to death. And his overpowering personality may be said to have absorbed that of his accomplices to such an extent that they received the benefit of extenuating circumstances.

"Louis de Malreich have you nothing to say?" asked the presiding judge.

He made no reply.

One question alone remained undecided in Lupin's eyes: why had Malreich committed all those crimes? What did he want? What was his object?

Lupin was soon to understand; and the day was not far off when, gasping with horror, struck, mortally smitten with despair, he would know the awful truth.

For the moment, although the thought of it constantly hovered over his mind, he ceased to occupy himself with the Malreich case. Resolved to get a new skin, as he put it; reassured, on the other hand, as to the fate of Mrs. Kesselbach and Geneviève, over whose peaceful existence he watched from afar; and, lastly, kept informed by Jean Doudeville, whom he had sent to Veldenz, of all the negotiations that were being pursued between the court of Berlin and the regent of Zweibrucken-Veldenz, he employed all his time in winding up the past and preparing for the future.

The thought of the different life which he wished to lead under the eyes of Mrs. Kesselbach filled him with new ambitions and unexpected sentiments, in which the image of Dolores played a part, without his being able to tell exactly how or why.

In a few weeks, he got rid of all the proofs that could have compromised him sooner or later, all the traces that could have led to his ruin. He gave each of his old companions a sum of money sufficient to keep them from want for the rest of their lives and said good-bye to them, saying that he was going to South America.

One morning, after a night of careful thought and a deep study of the situation, he cried:

"It's done. There's nothing to fear now. The old Lupin is dead. Make way for the young one."

His man brought him a telegram from Germany. It contained the news for which he had been waiting. The Council of Regency, greatly influenced by the Court of Berlin, had referred the question to the electors; and the electors, greatly influenced by the Council of Regency, had declared their unshaken attachment to the old dynasty of the Veldenz. Count von Waldemar was deputed, together with three delegates selected from the nobility, the army and the law, to go to Bruggen Castle, carefully to establish the identity of the Grand-duke Hermann IV and to make all the arrangements with His Royal Highness for his triumphal entry into the principality of his fathers, which was to take place in the course of the following month.

"This time, I've pulled it off," said Lupin to himself. "Mr. Kesselbach's great scheme is being realized. All that remains for me to do is to make Waldemar swallow Pierre Leduc; and that is child's play. The banns between Geneviève and Pierre shall be published to-morrow. And it shall be the grand-duke's affianced bride that will be presented to Waldemar."

Full of glee, he started in his motor for Bruggen Castle.

He sang in the car, he whistled, he chatted to his chauffeur:

"Octave, do you know whom you have the honor of driving? The master of the world! . . . Yes, old man, that staggers you, eh? Just so, but it's the truth. I am the master of the world."

He rubbed his hands and went on soliloquizing:

"All the same, it was a long job. It's a year since the fight began. True, it was the most formidable fight I ever stood to win or lose. . . By Jupiter, what a war of giants!" And he repeated, "But this time, I've pulled it off! The enemies are in the water. There are no obstacles left between the goal and me. The site is free: let us build upon it! I have the materials at hand, I have the workmen: let us build, Lupin! And let the palace be worthy of you!"

He stopped the car at a few hundred yards from the castle, so that his arrival might create as little fuss as possible, and said to Octave:

"Wait here for twenty minutes, until four o'clock, and then drive in. Take my bags to the little chalet at the end of the park. That's where I shall sleep."

At the first turn of the road, the castle appeared in sight, standing at the end of a dark avenue of lime trees. From the distance, he saw Geneviève passing on the terrace.

His heart was softly stirred:

"Geneviève, Geneviève," he said, fondly. "Geneviève. . . the vow which I made to the dying mother is being fulfilled as well. . . Geneviève a grand-duchess! . . . And I, in the shade, watching over her happiness. . . and pursuing the great schemes of Arsène Lupin!"

He burst out laughing, sprang behind a cluster of trees that stood to the left of the avenue and slipped along the thick shrubberies. In this way, he reached the castle without the possibility of his being seen from the windows of the drawing-room or the principal bedrooms.

He wanted to see Dolores before she saw him and pronounced her name several times, as he had pronounced Geneviève's, but with an emotion that surprised himself:

"Dolores. . . Dolores. . ."

He stole along the passages and reached the dining-room. From this room, through a glass panel, he could see half the drawing-room.

He drew nearer.

Dolores was lying on a couch; and Pierre Leduc, on his knees before her, was gazing at her with eyes of ecstasy. . .

XV

THE MAP OF EUROPE

Pierre Leduc loved Dolores!

Lupin felt a keen, penetrating pain in the depths of his being, as though he had been wounded in the very source of life; a pain so great that, for the first time, he had a clear perception of what Dolores had gradually, unknown to himself, become to him.

Pierre Leduc loved Dolores! And he was looking at her as a man looks at the woman he loves.

Lupin felt a murderous instinct rise up within him, blindly and furiously. That look, that look of love cast upon Dolores, maddened him. He received an impression of the great silence that enveloped Dolores and Pierre Leduc; and in silence, in the stillness of their attitude there was nothing living but that look of love, that dumb and sensuous hymn in which the eyes told all the passion, all the desire, all the transport, all the yearning that one being can feel for another.

And he saw Mrs. Kesselbach also. Dolores' eyes were invisible under their lowered lids, the silky eyelids with the long black lashes. But how she seemed to feel that look of love which sought for hers! How she quivered under that impalpable caress!

"She loves him. . . she loves him," thought Lupin, burning with jealousy.

And, when Pierre made a movement:

"Oh, the villain! If he dares to touch her, I will kill him!"

Then, realizing the disorder of his reason and striving to combat it, he said to himself:

"What a fool I am! What, you, Lupin, letting your self go like this! . . . Look here, it's only natural that she should love him. . . Yes, of course, you expected her to show a certain emotion at your arrival. . . a certain agitation. . . You silly idiot, you're only a thief, a robber. . . whereas he is a prince and young. . ."

Pierre had not stirred further. But his lips moved and it seemed as though Dolores were waking. Softly, slowly, she raised her lids, turned her head a little and her eyes met the young man's eyes with the look that offers itself and surrenders itself and is more intense than the most intense of kisses.

What followed came suddenly and unexpectedly, like a thunderclap. In three bounds, Lupin rushed into the drawing-room, sprang upon the young man, flung him to the ground and, with one hand on his rival's chest, beside himself with anger, turning to Mrs. Kesselbach, he cried:

"But don't you know? Hasn't he told you, the cheat? . . . And you love him, you love that! Does he look like a grand-duke? Oh, what a joke!"

He grinned and chuckled like a madman, while Dolores gazed at him in stupefaction:

"He, a grand-duke! Hermann IV, Grand-duke of Zweibrucken-Veldenz! A reigning sovereign! Elector of Treves! But it's enough to make one die of laughing! He! Why, his name is Baupré, Gérard Baupré, the lowest of ragamuffins. . . a beggar, whom I picked up in the gutter! . . . A grand-duke? But it's I who made him a grand-duke! Ha, ha, ha, what a joke! . . . If you had seen him cut his little finger. . . he fainted three times. . . the milksop! . . . Ah, you allow yourself to lift your eyes to ladies. . . and to rebel against the master! . . . Wait a bit, Grand-duke of Zweibrucken-Veldenz, I'll show you!"

He took him in his arms, like a bundle, swung him to and fro for a moment and pitched him through the open window:

"Mind the rose trees, grand-duke! There are thorns!"

When he turned round, Dolores was close to him and looking at him with eyes which he had never seen in her before, the eyes of a woman who hates and who is incensed with rage. Could this possibly be Dolores, the weak, ailing Dolores?

She stammered:

"What are you doing? . . . How dare you? . . . And he. . . Then it's true? . . . lied to me? . . ."

"Lied to you?" cried Lupin, grasping the humiliation which she had suffered as a woman. "Lied to you? He, a grand-duke! A puppet, that's all, a puppet of which I pulled the string. . . an instrument which I tuned, to play upon as I chose! Oh, the fool, the fool!"

Overcome with renewed rage, he stamped his foot and shook his fist at the open window. And he began to walk up and down the room, flinging out phrases in which all the pent-up violence of his secret thought burst forth:

"The fool! Then he didn't see what I expected of him? He did not suspect the greatness of the part he was to play? Oh, I shall have to drive it into his noddle by force, I see! Lift up your head, you idiot! You shall be grand-duke by the grace of Lupin! And a reigning sovereign! With a civil list! And subjects to fleece! And a palace which Charlemagne shall rebuild for you! And a master that shall be I, Lupin! Do you understand, you numskull? Lift up your head, dash it! Higher than that! Look up at the sky, remember that a Zweibrucken was hanged for cattle-lifting before the Hohenzollerns were ever heard of. And you are a Zweibrucken, by Jove, no less; and I am here, I, I, Lupin! And you shall be grand-duke, I tell you! A paste-board grand-duke? Very well! But a grand-duke all the same, quickened with my breath and glowing with my ardor. A puppet? Very well. But a puppet that shall speak *my* words and make *my* movements and perform *my* wishes and realize *my* dreams. . . yes. . . my dreams."

He stood motionless, as though dazzled by the glory of his conception. Then he went up to Dolores and, sinking his voice, with a sort of mystic exaltation, he said:

"On my left, Alsace-Lorraine. . . On my right, Baden, Wurtemburg, Bavaria. . . South Germany. . . all those disconnected, discontented states, crushed under the heel of the Prussian Charlemagne, but restless and ready to throw off the yoke at any moment. . . Do you understand all that a man like myself can do in the midst of that, all the aspirations that he can kindle, all the hatred that he can produce, all the angry rebellion that he can inspire?"

In a still lower voice, he repeated:

"And, on my left, Alsace-Lorraine! . . . Do you fully understand? . . . Dreams? Not at all! It is the reality of the day after to-morrow, of to-morrow! . . . Yes. . . I wish it. . . I wish it. . . Oh, all that I wish and all that I mean to do is unprecedented! . . . Only think, at two steps from the Alsatian frontier! In the heart of German territory! Close to the old Rhine! . . . A little intrigue, a little genius will be enough to change the surface of the earth. Genius I have. . . and to spare. . . And I shall be the master! I shall be the man who directs. The other, the puppet can have the title and the honors. . . I shall have the power! . . . I shall remain in the background. No office: I will not be a minister, nor even a chamberlain. Nothing. I shall be one of the servants in the palace, the gardener perhaps. . . Yes, the gardener. . . Oh, what a tremendous life! To grow flowers and alter the map of Europe!"

She looked at him greedily, dominated, swayed by the strength of that man. And her eyes expressed an admiration which she did not seek to conceal.

He put his hands on Dolores' shoulders and said:

"That is my dream. Great as it is, it will be surpassed by the facts: that I swear to you. The Kaiser has already seen what I am good for. One day, he will find me installed in front of him, face to face. I hold all the trumps. Valenglay will act at my bidding. . . England also. . . The game is played and won. . . That is my dream. . . There is another one. . ."

He stopped suddenly. Dolores did not take her eyes from him; and an infinite emotion changed every feature of her face.

A vast joy penetrated him as he once more felt, and clearly felt, that woman's confusion in his presence. He no longer had the sense of being to her. . . what he was, a thief, a robber; he was a man, a man who loved and whose love roused unspoken feelings in the depths of a friendly soul.

Then he said no more, but he lavished upon her, unuttered, every known word of love and admiration; and he thought of the life which he might lead somewhere, not far from Veldenz, unknown and all-powerful. . .

A long silence united them. Then she rose and said, softly:

"Go away, I entreat you to go. . . Pierre shall marry Geneviève, I promise you that, but it is better that you should go. . . that you should not be here. . . Go. Pierre shall marry Geneviève."

He waited for a moment. Perhaps he would rather have had more definite words, but he dared not ask for anything. And he withdrew, dazed, intoxicated and happy to obey, to subject his destiny to hers!

On his way to the door, he came upon a low chair, which he had to move. But his foot knocked against something. He looked down. It was a little pocket-mirror, in ebony, with a gold monogram.

Suddenly, he started and snatched up the mirror. The monogram consisted of two letters interlaced, an "L" and an "M."

An "L" and an "M!"

"Louis de Malreich," he said to himself, with a shudder.

He turned to Dolores:

"Where does this mirror come from? Whose is it? It is important that I should. . ."

She took it from him and looked at it:

"I don't know. . . I never saw it before. . . a servant, perhaps. . ."

"A servant, no doubt," he said, "but it is very odd. . . it is one of those coincidences. . ."

At that moment, Geneviève entered by the other door, and without seeing Lupin, who was hidden by a screen, at once exclaimed:

"Why, there's your glass, Dolores! . . . So you have found it, after making me hunt for it all this time! . . . Where was it?" And the girl went away saying, "Oh, well, I'm very glad it's found! . . . How upset you were! . . . I will go and tell them at once to stop looking for it. . ."

Lupin had not moved. He was confused, and tried in vain to understand. Why had Dolores not spoken the truth? Why had she not at once said whose the mirror was?

An idea flashed across his mind; and he asked, more or less at random:

"Do you know Louis de Malreich?"

"Yes," she said, watching him, as though striving to guess the thoughts that beset him.

He rushed toward her, in a state of intense excitement:

"You know him? Who was he? Who is he? Who is he? And why did you not tell me? Where have you known him? Speak. . . answer. . . I implore you. . ."

"No," she said.

"But you must, you must. . . Think! Louis de Malreich! The murderer! The monster! . . . Why did you not tell me?"

She, in turn, placed her hands on Lupin's shoulders and, in a firm voice, declared:

"Listen, you must never ask me, because I shall never tell. . . It is a secret which I shall take with me to the grave. . . Come what may, no one will ever know, no one in the wide world, I swear it!"

He stood before her for some minutes, anxiously, with a confused brain.

He remembered Steinweg's silence and the old man's terror when Lupin asked him to reveal the terrible secret. Dolores also knew and she also refused to speak.

He went out without a word.

THE OPEN AIR, THE SENSE of space, did him good. He passed out through the park-wall and wandered long over the country. And he soliloquized aloud:

"What does it mean? What is happening? For months and months, fighting hard and acting, I have been pulling the strings of all the characters that are to help me in the execution of my plans; and, during this time, I have completely forgotten to stoop over them and see what is going on in their hearts and brains. I do not know Pierre Leduc, I do not know Geneviève, I do not know Dolores. . . And I have treated them as so many jumping-jacks, whereas they are live persons. And to-day I am stumbling over obstacles."

He stamped his foot and cried:

"Over obstacles that do not exist! What do I care for the psychological state of Geneviève, of Pierre? . . . I will study that later, at Veldenz, when I have secured their happiness. But Dolores. . . she knew Malreich and said nothing! . . . Why? What relation united them? Was she afraid of him? Is she afraid that he will escape from prison and come to revenge himself for an indiscretion on her part?"

At night, he went to the chalet which he had allotted to his own use at the end of the park and dined in a very bad temper, storming at Octave, who waited on him and who was always either too slow or too fast:

"I'm sick of it, leave me alone. . . You're doing everything wrong to-day. . . And this coffee. . . It's not fit to drink."

He pushed back his cup half-full and, for two hours, walked about the park, sifting the same ideas over and over again. At last, one suggestion took definite shape within his mind:

"Malreich has escaped from prison. He is terrifying Mrs. Kesselbach. By this time, he already knows the story of the mirror from her. . ."

Lupin shrugged his shoulders:

"And to-night he's coming to pull my leg, I suppose! I'm talking nonsense. The best thing I can do is to go to bed."

He went to his room, undressed and got into bed. He fell asleep at once, with a heavy sleep disturbed by nightmares. Twice he woke and tried to light his candle and twice fell back, as though stunned by a blow.

Nevertheless, he heard the hours strike on the village clock, or rather he thought that he heard them strike, for he was plunged in a sort of torpor in which he seemed to retain all his wits.

And he was haunted by dreams, dreams of anguish and terror. He plainly heard the sound of his window opening. He plainly, through his closed eyelids, through the thick darkness, *saw* a form come toward the bed.

And the form bent over him.

He made the incredible effort needed to raise his eyelids and look. . . or, at least, he imagined that he did. Was he dreaming? Was he awake? He asked himself the question in despair.

A further sound. . .

He took up the box of matches by his bedside:

"Let's have a light on it," he said, with a great sense of elation.

He struck a match and lit the candle.

Lupin felt the perspiration stream over his skin, from head to foot, while his heart ceased beating, stopped with terror. *The man was there.*

Was it possible? No, no. . . and yet he *saw*. . . Oh, the fearsome sight! . . . The man, the monster, was there. . .

"He shall not. . . he shall not," stammered Lupin madly.

The man, the monster was there, dressed in black, with a mask on his face and with his felt hat pulled down over his fair hair.

"Oh, I am dreaming. . . I am dreaming!" said Lupin, laughing. "It's a nightmare! . . ."

Exerting all his strength and all his will-power, he tried to make a movement, one movement, to drive away the vision.

He could not.

And, suddenly, he remembered: the coffee! The taste of it. . . similar to the taste of the coffee which he had drunk at Veldenz!

He gave a cry, made a last effort and fell back exhausted. But, in his delirium, he felt that the man was unfastening the top button of his pajama-jacket and baring his neck, felt that the man was raising his arm, saw that the hand was clutching the handle of a dagger, a little steel dagger similar to that which had struck Kesselbach, Chapman, Altenheim and so many others. . .

A FEW HOURS LATER, LUPIN woke up, shattered with fatigue, with a scorched palate.

He lay for several minutes collecting his thoughts and, suddenly, remembering, made an instinctive defensive movement, as though he were being attacked:

"Fool that I am!" he cried, jumping out of bed. "It was a nightmare, an hallucination. It only needs a little reflection. Had it been 'he,' had it really been a man, in flesh and blood, who lifted his hand against me last night, he would have cut my throat like a rabbit's. 'He' doesn't hesitate. Let's be logical. Why should he spare me? For the sake of my good looks? No, I have been dreaming, that's all. . ."

He began to whistle and dressed himself, assuming the greatest calmness, but his brain never ceased working and his eyes sought about. . .

On the floor, on the window-ledge, not a trace. As his room was on the ground-floor and as he slept with his window open, it was evident that his assailant would have entered that way.

Well, he discovered nothing; and nothing either at the foot of the wall outside, or on the gravel of the path that ran round the chalet.

"Still. . . still. . ." he repeated, between his teeth. . .

He called Octave:

"Where did you make the coffee which you gave me last night?"

"At the castle, governor, like the rest of the things. There is no range here."

"Did you drink any of it?"

"No."

"Did you throw away what was left in the coffee-pot?"

"Why, yes, governor. You said it was so bad. You only took a few mouthfuls."

"Very well. Get the motor ready. We're leaving."

Lupin was not the man to remain in doubt. He wanted to have a decisive explanation with Dolores. But, for this, he must first clear up certain points that seemed to him obscure and see Jean Doudeville who had sent him some rather curious information from Veldenz.

He drove, without stopping, to the grand-duchy, which he reached at two o'clock. He had an interview with Count de Waldemar, whom he asked, upon some pretext, to delay the journey of the delegates of the Regency to Bruggen. Then he went in search of Doudeville, in a tavern at Veldenz.

Doudeville took him to another tavern, where he introduced him to a shabbily-dressed little gentleman, Herr Stockli, a clerk in the department of births, deaths and marriages. They had a long conversation. They went out together and all three passed stealthily through the offices of the town-hall. At seven o'clock, Lupin dined and set out again. At ten o'clock he arrived at Bruggen Castle and asked for Geneviève, so that she might take him to Mrs. Kesselbach's room.

He was told that Mlle. Ernemont had been summoned back to Paris by a telegram from her grandmother.

"Ah!" he said. "Could I see Mrs. Kesselbach?"

"Mrs. Kesselbach went straight to bed after dinner. She is sure to be asleep."

"No, I saw a light in her boudoir. She will see me."

He did not even wait for Mrs. Kesselbach to send out an answer. He walked into the boudoir almost upon the maid's heels, dismissed her and said to Dolores:

"I have to speak to you, madame, on an urgent matter. . . Forgive me. . . I confess that my behavior must seem importunate. . . But you will understand, I am sure. . ."

He was greatly excited and did not seem much disposed to put off the explanation, especially as, before entering the room, he thought he heard a sound.

Yet Dolores was alone and lying down. And she said, in her tired voice:

"Perhaps we might. . . to-morrow. . ."

He did not answer, suddenly struck by a smell that surprised him in that boudoir, a smell of tobacco. And, at once, he had the intuition, the certainty, that there was a man there, at the moment when he himself arrived, and that perhaps the man was there still, hidden somewhere. . .

Pierre Leduc? No, Pierre Leduc did not smoke. Then who?

Dolores murmured:

"Be quick, please."

"Yes, yes, but first. . . would it be possible for you to tell me. . . ?"

He interrupted himself. What was the use of asking her? If there were really a man in hiding, would she be likely to tell?

Then he made up his mind and, trying to overcome the sort of timid constraint that oppressed him at the sense of a strange presence, he said, in a very low voice, so that Dolores alone should hear:

"Listen, I have learnt something. . . which I do not understand. . . and which perplexes me greatly. You will answer me, will you not, Dolores?"

He spoke her name with great gentleness and as though he were trying to master her by the note of love and affection in his voice.

"What have you learnt?" she asked.

"The register of births at Veldenz contains three names which are those of the last descendants of the family of Malreich, which settled in Germany. . ."

"Yes, you have told me all that. . ."

"You remember, the first name is Raoul de Malreich, better known under his *alias* of Altenheim, the scoundrel, the swell hooligan, now dead. . . murdered."

"Yes."

"Next comes Louis de Malreich, the monster, this one, the terrible murderer who will be beheaded in a few days from now."

"Yes."

"Then, lastly, Isilda, the mad daughter. . ."

"Yes."

"So all that is quite positive, is it not?"

"Yes."

"Well," said Lupin, leaning over her more closely than before, "I have just made an investigation which showed to me that the second of the three Christian names, or rather a part of the line on which it is written, has at some time or other, been subjected to erasure. The line is written over, in a new hand, with much fresher ink; but the writing below is not quite effaced, so that. . ."

"So that. . . ?" asked Mrs. Kesselbach, in a low voice.

"So that, with a good lens and particularly with the special methods which I have at my disposal, I was able to revive some of the obliterated syllables and, without any possibility of a mistake, in all certainty, to reconstruct the old writing. I then found not Louis de Malreich, but. . ."

"Oh, don't, don't! . . ."

Suddenly shattered by the strain of her prolonged effort of resistance, she lay bent in two and, with her head in her hands, her shoulders shaken with convulsive sobs, she wept.

Lupin looked for long seconds at this weak and listless creature, so pitifully helpless. And he would have liked to stop, to cease the torturing questions which he was inflicting upon her. But was it not to save her that he was acting as he did? And, to save her, was it not necessary that he should know the truth, however painful?

He resumed:

"Why that forgery?"

"It was my husband," she stammered, "it was my husband who did it. With his fortune, he could do everything; and he bribed a junior clerk to have the Christian name of the second child altered for him on the register."

"The Christian name and the sex," said Lupin.

"Yes," she said.

"Then," he continued, "I am not mistaken: the original Christian name, the real one, was Dolores?"

"Yes."

"But why did your husband. . . ?"

She whispered in a shame-faced manner, while the tears streamed down her cheeks.

"Don't you understand?"

"No."

"But think," she said, shuddering, "I was the sister of Isilda, the mad woman, the sister of Altenheim, the ruffian. My husband—or rather my affianced husband—would not have me remain that. He loved me. I loved him too, and I consented. He suppressed Dolores de Malreich on the register, he bought me other papers, another personality, another birth-certificate; and I was married in Holland under another maiden name, as Dolores Amonti."

Lupin reflected for a moment and said, thoughtfully:

"Yes. . . yes. . . I understand. . . But then Louis de Malreich does not exist; and the murderer of your husband, the murderer of your brother and sister, does not bear that name. . . His name. . ."

She sprang to a sitting posture and, eagerly:

"His name! Yes, that is his name. . . yes, it is his name nevertheless. . . Louis de Malreich. . . L. M. . . Remember. . . Oh, do not try to find out. . . it is the terrible secret. . . Besides, what does it matter? . . . They have the criminal. . . He is the criminal. . . I tell you he is. Did he defend himself when I accused him, face to face? Could he defend himself, under that name or any other? It is he. . . it is he. . . He committed the murders. . . He struck the blows. . . The dagger. . . The steel dagger. . . Oh, if I could only tell all I know! . . . Louis de Malreich. . . If I could only. . ."

She fell back on the sofa in a fit of hysterical sobbing; and her hand clutched Lupin's and he heard her stammering, amid inarticulate words:

"Protect me. . . protect me. . . You alone, perhaps. . . Oh, do not forsake me. . . I am so unhappy! . . . Oh, what torture. . . what torture! . . . It is hell! . . ."

With his free hand, he stroked her hair and forehead with infinite gentleness; and, under his caress, she gradually relaxed her tense nerves and became calmer and quieter.

Then he looked at her again and long, long asked himself what there could be behind that fair, white brow, what secret was ravaging that mysterious soul. She also was afraid. But of whom? Against whom was she imploring him to protect her?

Once again, he was obsessed by the image of the man in black, by that Louis de Malreich, the sinister and incomprehensible enemy, whose attacks he had to ward off without knowing whence they came or even if they were taking place.

He was in prison, watched day and night. Tush! Did Lupin not know by his own experience that there are beings for whom prison does not exist and who throw off their chains at the given moment? And Louis de Malreich was one of those.

Yes, there was some one in the Santé prison, in the condemned man's cell. But it might be an accomplice or some victim of Malreich. . . while Malreich himself prowled around Bruggen Castle, slipped in under cover of the darkness, like an invisible spectre, made his way into the chalet in the park and, at night, raised his dagger against Lupin asleep and helpless.

And it was Louis de Malreich who terrorized Dolores, who drove her mad with his threats, who held her by some dreadful secret and forced her into silence and submission.

And Lupin imagined the enemy's plan: to throw Dolores, scared and trembling, into Pierre Leduc's arms, to make away with him, Lupin, and to reign in his place, over there, with the grand-duke's power and Dolores's millions.

It was a likely supposition, a certain supposition, which fitted in with the facts and provided a solution of all the problems.

"Of all?" thought Lupin. "Yes. . . But then, why did he not kill me, last night, in the chalet? He had but to wish. . . *and he did not wish*. One movement and I was dead. He did not make that movement. Why?"

Dolores opened her eyes, saw him and smiled, with a pale smile:

"Leave me," she said:

He rose, with some hesitation. Should he go and see if the enemy was behind the curtain or hidden behind the dresses in a cupboard?

She repeated, gently:

"Go. . . I am so sleepy. . ."

He went away.

But, outside, he stopped behind some trees that formed a dark cluster in front of the castle. He saw a light in Dolores' boudoir. Then the light passed into the bedroom. In a few minutes, all was darkness.

He waited. If the enemy was there, perhaps he would come out of the castle. . .

An hour elapsed. . . Two hours. . . Not a sound. . .

"There's nothing to be done," thought Lupin. "Either he is burrowing in some corner of the castle. . . or else he has gone out by a door which

I cannot see from here. Unless the whole thing is the most ridiculous supposition on my part. . ."

He lit a cigarette and walked back to the chalet.

As he approached it, he saw, at some distance from him, a shadow that appeared to be moving away.

He did not stir, for fear of giving the alarm.

The shadow crossed a path. By the light of the moon, he seemed to recognize the black figure of Malreich.

He rushed forward.

The shadow fled and vanished from sight.

"Come," he said, "it shall be for to-morrow. And, this time. . ."

Lupin went to Octave's, his chauffeur's, room, woke him and said:

"Take the motor and go to Paris. You will be there by six o'clock in the morning. See Jacques Doudeville and tell him two things: first, to give me news of the man under sentence of death; and secondly, as soon as the post-offices open, to send me a telegram which I will write down for you now. . ."

He worded the telegram on a scrap of paper and added:

"The moment you have done that, come back, but this way, along the wall of the park. Go now. No one must suspect your absence."

Lupin went to his own room, pressed the spring of his lantern and began to make a minute inspection. "It's as I thought," he said presently. "Some one came here to-night, while I was watching beneath the window. And, if he came, I know what he came for. . . I was certainly right: things are getting warm. . . The first time, I was spared. This time, I may be sure of my little stab."

For prudence's sake, he took a blanket, chose a lonely spot in the park and spent the night under the stars.

Octave was back by ten o'clock in the morning:

"It's all right, governor. The telegram has been sent."

"Good. And is Louis de Malreich still in prison?"

"Yes. Doudeville passed his cell at the Santé last night as the warder was coming out. They talked together. Malreich is just the same, it appears: silent as the grave. He is waiting."

"Waiting for what?"

"The fatal hour of course. They are saying, at headquarters, that the execution will take place on the day after to-morrow."

"That's all right, that's all right," said Lupin. "And one thing is quite plain: he has not escaped."

He ceased to understand or even to look for the explanation of the riddle, so clearly did he feel that the whole truth would soon be revealed to him. He had only to prepare his plan, for the enemy to fall into the trap.

"Or for me to fall into it myself," he thought, laughing.

He felt very gay, very free from care; and no fight had ever looked more promising to him.

A footman came from the castle with the telegram which he had told Doudeville to send him and which the postman had just brought. He opened it and put it in his pocket.

A LITTLE BEFORE TWELVE O'CLOCK, he met Pierre Leduc in one of the avenues and said, off-hand:

"I am looking for you. . . things are serious. . . You must answer me frankly. Since you have been at the castle, have you ever seen a man there, besides the two German servants whom I sent in?"

"No."

"Think carefully. I'm not referring to a casual visitor. I mean a man who hides himself, a man whose presence you might have discovered or, less than that, whose presence you might have suspected from some clue or even by some intuition?"

"No. . . Have you. . . ?"

"Yes. Some one is hiding here. . . some one is prowling about. . . Where? And who is it? And what is his object? I don't know. . . but I shall know. I already have a suspicion. Do you, on your side, keep your eyes open and watch. And, above all, not a word to Mrs. Kesselbach. . . It is no use alarming her. . ."

He went away.

Pierre Leduc, taken aback and upset, went back to the castle. On his way, he saw a piece of blue paper on the edge of the lawn. He picked it up. It was a telegram, not crumpled, like a piece of paper that had been thrown away, but carefully folded: obviously lost.

It was addressed to "Beauny," the name by which Lupin was known at Bruggen. And it contained these words:

"We know the whole truth. Revelations impossible by letter. Will take train to-night. Meet me eight o'clock to-morrow morning Bruggen station."

"Excellent!" said Lupin, who was watching Pierre Leduc's movements from a neighboring coppice. "Excellent! In two minutes from now, the young idiot will have shown Dolores the telegram and told her all my fears. They will talk about it all day. And 'the other one' will hear, 'the other one' will know, because he knows everything, because he lives in Dolores' own shadow and because Dolores is like a fascinated prey in his hands. . . And, to-night. . ."

He walked away humming to himself:

"To-night. . . to-night. . . we shall dance. . . Such a waltz, my boys! The waltz of blood, to the tune of the little nickel-plated dagger! . . . We shall have some fun, at last! . . ."

He reached the chalet, called to Octave, went to his room, flung himself on his bed, and said to the chauffeur:

"Sit down in that chair, Octave, and keep awake. Your master is going to take forty winks. Watch over him, you faithful servant."

He had a good sleep.

"Like Napoleon on the morning of Austerlitz," he said, when he woke up.

It was dinner-time. He made a hearty meal and then, while he smoked a cigarette, inspected his weapons and renewed the charges of his two revolvers:

"Keep your powder dry and your sword sharpened, as my chum the Kaiser says. Octave!"

Octave appeared.

"Go and have your dinner at the castle, with the servants. Tell them you are going to Paris to-night, in the motor."

"With you, governor?"

"No, alone. And, as soon as dinner is over, make a start, ostensibly."

"But I am not to go to Paris. . ."

"No, remain outside the park, half a mile down the road, until I come. You will have a long wait."

He smoked another cigarette, went for a stroll, passed in front of the castle, saw a light in Dolores' rooms and then returned to the chalet.

There he took up a book. It was *The Lives of Illustrious Men*.

"There is one missing: the most illustrious of all. But the future will put that right; and I shall have my Plutarch some day or other."

He read the life of Cæsar and jotted down a few reflections in the margin.

At half-past eleven, he went to his bedroom.

Through the open window, he gazed into the immense, cool night, all astir with indistinct sounds. Memories rose to his lips, memories of fond phrases which he had read or uttered; and he repeatedly whispered Dolores's name, with the fervor of a stripling who hardly dares confide to the silence the name of his beloved.

He left the window half open, pushed aside a table that blocked the way, and put his revolvers under his pillow. Then, peacefully, without evincing the least excitement, he got into bed, fully dressed as he was, and blew out the candle.

And his fear began.

It was immediate. No sooner did he feel the darkness around him than his fear began!

"Damn it all!" he cried.

He jumped out of bed, took his weapons and threw them into the passage:

"My hands, my hands alone! Nothing comes up to the grip of my hands!"

He went to bed again. Darkness and silence, once more. And, once more, his fear. . .

The village clock struck twelve. . .

Lupin thought of the foul monster who, outside, at a hundred yards, at fifty yards from where he lay, was trying the sharp point of his dagger:

"Let him come, let him come?" whispered Lupin, shuddering. "Then the ghosts will vanish. . ."

One o'clock, in the village. . .

And minutes passed, endless minutes, minutes of fever and anguish. . . Beads of perspiration stood at the roots of his hair and trickled down his forehead; and he felt as though his whole frame were bathed in a sweat of blood. . .

Two o'clock. . .

And now, somewhere, quite close, a hardly perceptible sound stirred, a sound of leaves moving. . . but different from the sound of leaves moving in the night breeze. . .

As Lupin had foreseen, he was at once pervaded by an immense calm. All his adventurous being quivered with delight. The struggle was at hand, at last!

Another sound grated under the window, more plainly this time, but still so faint that it needed Lupin's trained ear to distinguish it.

Minutes, terrifying minutes. . . The darkness was impenetrable. No light of star or moon relieved it.

And, suddenly, without hearing anything, he *knew* that the man was in the room.

And the man walked toward the bed. He walked as a ghost walks, without displacing the air of the room, without shaking the objects which he touched.

But, with all his instinct, with all his nervous force, Lupin saw the movements of the enemy and guessed the very sequence of his ideas.

He himself did not budge, but remained propped against the wall, almost on his knees, ready to spring.

He felt that the figure was touching, feeling the bed-clothes, to find the spot at which it must strike. Lupin heard its breath. He even thought that he heard the beating of its heart. And he noticed with pride that his own heart beat no louder than before. . . whereas the heart of the other. . . oh, yes, he could hear it now, that disordered, mad heart, knocking, like a clapper of a bell, against the cavity of the chest!

The hand of the other rose. . .

A second, two seconds. . .

Was he hesitating? Was he once more going to spare his adversary?

And Lupin, in the great silence, said:

"But strike! Why don't you strike?"

A yell of rage. . . The arm fell as though moved by a spring.

Then came a moan.

Lupin had caught the arm in mid-air at the level of the wrist. . . And, leaping out of bed, tremendous, irresistible, he clutched the man by the throat and threw him.

THAT WAS ALL. THERE WAS no struggle. There was no possibility even of a struggle. The man lay on the floor, nailed, pinned by two steel rivets, which were Lupin's hands. And there was not a man in the world strong enough to release himself from that grip.

And not a word. Lupin uttered none of those phrases in which his mocking humor usually delighted. He had no inclination to speak. The moment was too solemn.

He felt no vain glee, no victorious exaltation. In reality, he had but one longing, to know who was there: Louis de Malreich, the man sentenced to death, or another? Which was it?

At the risk of strangling the man, he squeezed the throat a little more. . . and a little more. . . and a little more still. . .

And he felt that all the enemy's strength, all the strength that remained to him, was leaving him. The muscles of the arm relaxed and became lifeless. The hand opened and dropped the dagger.

Then, free to move as he pleased, with his adversary's life hanging in the terrible clutch of his fingers, he took his pocket-lantern with one hand, laid his finger on the spring, without pressing, and brought it close to the man's face.

He had only to press the spring to wish to know and he would know.

For a second, he enjoyed his power. A flood of emotion upheaved him. The vision, of his triumph dazzled him. Once again, superbly, heroically, he was the master.

He switched on the light. The face of the monster came into view.

Lupin gave a shriek of terror.

Dolores Kesselbach!

XVI

ARSÈNE LUPIN'S THREE MURDERS

A cyclone passed through Lupin's brain, a hurricane in which roars of thunder, gusts of wind, squalls of all the distraught elements were tumultuously unchained in the chaotic night.

And great flashes of lightning shot through the darkness. And, by the dazzling gleam of those lightning-flashes, Lupin, scared, shaken with thrills, convulsed with horror, saw and tried to understand.

He did not move, clinging to the enemy's throat, as if his stiffened fingers were no longer able to release their grip. Besides, although he now *knew*, he had not, so to speak, the exact feeling that it was Dolores. It was still the man in black, Louis de Malreich, the foul brute of the darkness; and that brute he held and did not mean to let go.

But the truth rushed upon the attack of his mind and of his consciousness; and, conquered, tortured with anguish, he muttered:

"Oh, Dolores! . . . Dolores! . . ."

He at once saw the excuse: it was madness. She was mad. The sister of Altenheim and Isilda, the daughter of the last of the Malreichs, of the demented mother, of the drunken father, was herself mad. A strange madwoman, mad with every appearance of sanity, but mad nevertheless, unbalanced, brain-sick, unnatural, truly monstrous.

That he most certainly understood! It was homicidal madness. Under the obsession of an object toward which she was drawn automatically, she killed, thirsting for blood, unconsciously, infernally.

She killed because she wanted something, she killed in self-defence, she killed because she had killed before. But she killed also and especially for the sake of killing. Murder satisfied sudden and irresistible appetites that arose in her. At certain seconds in her life, in certain circumstances, face to face with this or that being who had suddenly become the foe, her arm had to strike.

And she struck, drunk with rage, ferociously, frenziedly.

A strange madwoman, not answerable for her murders, and yet so lucid in her blindness, so logical in her mental derangement, so intelligent in her absurdity! What skill, what perseverance, what cunning contrivances, at once abominable and admirable!

813

And Lupin, in a rapid view, with prodigious keenness of outlook, saw the long array of bloodthirsty adventures and guessed the mysterious paths which Dolores had pursued.

He saw her obsessed and possessed by her husband's scheme, a scheme which she evidently understood only in part. He saw her, on her side, looking for that same Pierre Leduc whom her husband was seeking, looking for him in order to marry him and to return, as queen, to that little realm of Veldenz from which her parents had been ignominiously driven.

And he saw her at the Palace Hotel, in the room of her brother, Altenheim, at the time when she was supposed to be at Monte Carlo. He saw her, for days together, spying upon her husband, creeping along the walls, one with the darkness, undistinguishable and unseen in her shadowy disguise.

And, one night, she found Mr. Kesselbach fastened up. . . and she stabbed him.

And, in the morning, when on the point of being denounced by the floor-waiter. . . she stabbed him.

And, an hour later, when on the point of being denounced by Chapman, she dragged him to her brother's room. . . and stabbed him.

All this pitilessly, savagely, with diabolical skill.

And, with the same skill, she communicated by telephone with her two maids, Gertrude and Suzanne, both of whom had arrived from Monte Carlo, where one of them had enacted the part of her mistress. And Dolores, resuming her feminine attire, discarding the fair wig that altered her appearance beyond recognition, went down to the ground-floor, joined Gertrude at the moment when the maid entered the hotel and pretended herself to have just arrived, all ignorant of the tragedy that awaited her.

An incomparable actress, she played the part of the wife whose life is shattered. Every one pitied her. Every one wept for her. Who could have suspected her?

And then came the war with him, Lupin, that barbarous contest, that unparalleled contest which she waged, by turns, against M. Lenormand and Prince Sernine, spending her days stretched on her sofa, ill and fainting, but her nights on foot, scouring the roads indefatigable and terrible.

And the diabolical contrivances: Gertrude and Suzanne, frightened and subdued accomplices, both of them serving her as emissaries, disguising themselves to represent her, perhaps, as on the day when old Steinweg was carried off by Baron Altenheim, in the middle of the Palais de Justice.

And the series of murders: Gourel drowned; Altenheim, her brother, stabbed. Oh, the implacable struggle in the underground passages of the Villa des Glycines, the invisible work performed by the monster in the dark: how clear it all appeared to-day!

And it was she who tore off his mask as Prince Sernine, she who betrayed him to the police, she who sent him to prison, she who thwarted all his plans, spending her millions to win the battle.

And then events followed faster: Suzanne and Gertrude disappeared, dead, no doubt! Steinweg, assassinated! Isilda, the sister, assassinated!

"Oh, the ignominy, the horror of it!" stammered Lupin, with a start of revulsion and hatred.

He execrated her, the abominable creature. He would have liked to crush her, to destroy her. And it was a stupefying sight, those two beings, clinging to each other, lying motionless in the pale dawn that began to mingle with the shades of the night.

"Dolores. . . Dolores. . ." he muttered, in despair.

He leapt back, terror-stricken, wild-eyed. What was it? What was that? What was that hideous feeling of cold which froze his hands?

"Octave! Octave?" he shouted, forgetting that the chauffeur was not there.

Help, he needed help, some one to reassure him and assist him. He shivered with fright. Oh, that coldness, that coldness of death which he had felt! Was it possible? . . . Then, during those few tragic minutes, with his clenched fingers, he had. . .

Violently, he forced himself to look. Dolores did not stir.

He flung himself on his knees and drew her to him.

She was dead.

HE REMAINED FOR SOME SECONDS a prey to a sort of numbness in which his grief seemed to be swallowed up. He no longer suffered. He no longer felt rage nor hatred nor emotion of any kind. . . nothing but a stupid prostration, the sensation of a man who has received a blow with a club and who does not know if he is still alive, if he is thinking, or if he is the sport of a nightmare.

Nevertheless, it seemed to him that an act of justice had taken place, and it did not for a second occur to him that it was he who had taken life. No, it was not he. It was outside him and his will. It was destiny, inexorable destiny that had accomplished the work of equity by slaying the noxious beast.

Outside, the birds were singing. Life was recommencing under the old trees, which the spring was preparing to bring into bud. And Lupin, waking from his torpor, felt gradually welling up within him an indefinable and ridiculous compassion for the wretched woman, odious, certainly, abject and twenty times criminal, but so young still and now. . . dead.

And he thought of the tortures which she must have undergone in her lucid moments, when reason returned to the unspeakable madwoman and brought the sinister vision of her deeds.

"Protect me. . . I am so unhappy!" she used to beg.

It was against herself that she asked to be protected, against her wild-beast instincts, against the monster that dwelt within her and forced her to kill, always to kill.

"Always?" Lupin asked himself.

And he remembered the night, two days since, when, standing over him, with her dagger raised against the enemy who had been harassing her for months, against the indefatigable enemy who had run her to earth after each of her crimes, he remembered that, on that night, she had not killed. And yet it would have been easy: the enemy lay lifeless and powerless. One blow and the implacable struggle was over. No, she had not killed, she too had given way to feelings stronger than her own cruelty, to mysterious feelings of pity, of sympathy, of admiration for the man who had so often mastered her.

No, she had not killed, that time. And now, by a really terrifying vicissitude of fate, it was he who had killed her.

"I have taken life!" he thought, shuddering from head to foot. "These hands have killed a living being; and that creature is Dolores! . . . Dolores! . . . Dolores! . . ."

He never ceased repeating her name, her name of sorrow, and he never ceased staring at her, a sad, lifeless thing, harmless now, a poor hunk of flesh, with no more consciousness than a little heap of withered leaves or a little dead bird by the roadside.

Oh! how could he do other than quiver with compassion, seeing that of those two, face to face, he was the murderer, and she, who was no more, the victim?

"Dolores! . . . Dolores! . . . Dolores! . . ."

THE DAYLIGHT FOUND LUPIN SEATED beside the dead woman, remembering and thinking, while his lips, from time to time, uttered the disconsolate syllables:

"Dolores! . . . Dolores! . . ."

He had to act, however, and, in the disorder of his ideas, he did not know how to act nor with what act to begin:

"I must close her eyes first," he said.

The eyes, all empty, filled only with death, those beautiful gold-spangled eyes, had still the melancholy softness that gave them their charm. Was it possible that those eyes were the eyes of a monster? In spite of himself and in the face of the implacable reality, Lupin was not yet able to blend into one single being those two creatures whose images remained so distinct at the back of his brain.

He stooped swiftly, lowered the long, silky eyelids, and covered the poor distorted face with a veil.

Then it seemed to him that Dolores was farther away and that the man in black was really there, this time, in his dark clothes, in his murderer's disguise.

He now ventured to touch her, to feel in her clothes. In an inside pocket were two pocket-books. He took one of them and opened it. He found first a letter signed by Steinweg, the old German. It contained the following lines:

"Should I die before being able to reveal the terrible secret, let it be known that the murderer of my friend Kesselbach is his wife, whose real name is Dolores de Malreich, sister to Altenheim and sister to Isilda.

"The initials L. and M. relate to her. Kesselbach never, in their private life, called his wife Dolores, which is the name of sorrow, but Letitia, which denotes joy. L. M.—Letitia de Malreich—were the initials inscribed on all the presents which he used to give her, for instance, on the cigarette-case which was found at the Palace Hotel and which belonged to Mrs. Kesselbach. She had contracted the smoking-habit on her travels.

"Letitia! She was indeed the joy of his life for four years, four years of lies and hypocrisy, in which she prepared the death of the man who loved her so well and who trusted her so whole-heartedly.

"Perhaps I ought to have spoken at once. I had not the courage, in memory of my old friend Kesselbach, whose name she bore.

"And then I was afraid. . . On the day when I unmasked her, at the Palais de Justice, I read my doom in her eyes.

"Will my weakness save me?"

"Him also," thought Lupin, "him also she killed! . . . Why, of course, he knew too much! . . . The initials. . . that name, Letitia. . . the secret habit of smoking!"

And he remembered the previous night, that smell of tobacco in her room.

He continued his inspection of the first pocket-book. There were scraps of letters, in cipher, no doubt handed to Dolores by her accomplices, in the course of their nocturnal meetings. There were also addresses on bits of paper, addresses of milliners and dressmakers, but addresses also of low haunts, of common hotels. . . And names. . . twenty, thirty names. . . queer names: Hector the Butcher, Armand of Grenelle, the Sick Man. . .

But a photograph caught Lupin's eye. He looked at it. And, at once, as though shot from a spring, dropping the pocket-book, he bolted out of the room, out of the chalet and rushed into the park.

He had recognized the portrait of Louis de Malreich, the prisoner at the Santé!

Not till then, not till that exact moment did he remember: the execution was to take place next day.

And, as the man in black, as the murderer was none other than Dolores Kesselbach, Louis de Malreich's name was really and truly Leon Massier and he was innocent!

Innocent? But the evidence found in his house, the Emperor's letters, all, all the things that accused him beyond hope of denial, all those incontrovertible proofs?

Lupin stopped for a second, with his brain on fire:

"Oh," he cried, "I shall go mad, I, too! Come, though, I must act. . . the sentence is to be executed. . . to-morrow. . . to-morrow at break of day."

He looked at his watch:

"Ten o'clock. . . How long will it take me to reach Paris? Well. . . I shall be there presently. . . yes, presently, I must. . . And this very evening I shall take measures to prevent. . . But what measures? How can I prove his innocence? . . . How prevent the execution? Oh, never mind! Once I am there, I shall find a way. My name is not Lupin for nothing! . . . Come on! . . ."

He set off again at a run, entered the castle and called out:

"Pierre! Pierre! . . . Has any one seen M. Pierre Leduc? . . . Oh, there you are! . . . Listen. . ."

He took him on one side and jerked out, in imperious tones:

"Listen, Dolores is not here. . . Yes, she was called away on urgent business. . . she left last night in my motor. . . I am going too. . . Don't interrupt, not a word! . . . A second lost means irreparable harm. . . You, send away all the servants, without any explanation. Here is money. In half an hour from now, the castle must be empty. And let no one enter it until I return. . . Not you either, do you understand? . . . I forbid you to enter the castle. . . I'll explain later. . . serious reasons. Here, take the key with you. . . Wait for me in the village. . ."

And once more, he darted away.

Five minutes later, he was with Octave. He jumped into the car:

"Paris!"

THE JOURNEY WAS A REAL race for life or death. Lupin, thinking that Octave was not driving fast enough, took the steering-wheel himself and drove at a furious, break-neck speed. On the road, through the villages, along the crowded streets of the towns they rushed at sixty miles an hour. People whom they nearly upset roared and yelled with rage: the meteor was far away, was out of sight.

"G—governor," stammered Octave, livid with dismay, "we shall be stuck!"

"You, perhaps, the motor, perhaps; but I shall arrive!" said Lupin.

He had a feeling as though it were not the car that was carrying him, but he carrying the car and as though he were cleaving space by dint of his own strength, his own will-power. Then what miracle could prevent his arriving, seeing that his strength was inexhaustible, his will-power unbounded?

"I shall arrive because I have got to arrive," he repeated.

And he thought of the man who would die, if he did not arrive in time to save him, of the mysterious Louis de Malreich, so disconcerting with his stubborn silence and his expressionless face.

And amid the roar of the road, under the trees whose branches made a noise as of furious waves, amid the buzzing of his thoughts, Lupin, all the same, strove to set up an hypothesis. And this hypothesis became gradually more defined, logical, probable, certain, he said to himself, now that he knew the hideous truth about Dolores and saw all the resources and all the odious designs of that crazy mind:

"Yes, it was she who contrived that most terrible plot against Malreich. What was it she wanted? To marry Pierre Leduc, whom she had bewitched, and to become the sovereign of the little principality from which she had been banished. The object was attainable, within reach of her hand. There was one sole obstacle. . . I, Lupin, who, for weeks and weeks, persistently barred her road; I, whom she encountered after every murder; I, whose perspicacity she dreaded; I, who would never lay down my arms before I had discovered the culprit and found the letters stolen from the Emperor. . . Well, the culprit should be Louis de Malreich, or rather, Leon Massier. Who was this Leon Massier? Did she know him before her marriage? Had she been in love with him? It is probable; but this, no doubt, we shall never know. One thing is certain, that she was struck by the resemblance to Leon Massier in figure and stature which she might attain by dressing up like him, in black clothes, and putting on a fair wig. She must have noticed the eccentric life led by that lonely man, his nocturnal expeditions, his manner of walking in the streets and of throwing any who might follow him off the scent. And it was in consequence of these observations and in anticipation of possible eventualities that she advised Mr. Kesselbach to erase the name of Dolores from the register of births and to replace it by the name of Louis, so that the initials might correspond with those of Leon Massier. . . The moment arrived at which she must act; and thereupon she concocted her plot and proceeded to put it into execution. Leon lived in the Rue Delaizement. She ordered her accomplices to take up their quarters in the street that backed on to it. And she herself told me the address of Dominique the head-waiter, and put me on the track of the seven scoundrels, knowing perfectly well that, once on the track, I was bound to follow it to the end, that is to say, beyond the seven scoundrels, till I came up with their leader, the man who watched them and who commanded them, the man in black, Leon Massier, Louis de Malreich. . . As a matter of fact, I came up with the seven scoundrels first. Then what would happen? Either I should be beaten or we should all destroy one another, as she must have hoped, that night in the Rue des Vignes. In either case Dolores would have been rid of me. But what really happened was this: I captured the seven scoundrels. Dolores fled from the Rue des Vignes. I found her in the Broker's shed. She sent me after Leon Massier, that is to say, Louis de Malreich. I found in his house the Emperor's letters, *which she herself had placed there*, and I delivered him to justice and I revealed the secret communication, *which she herself had caused to be made*, between the two coach-houses, and I produced all the evidence *which she herself had prepared*, and I proved, by means of documents *which she herself had forged*, that Leon Massier had stolen the social status of Leon Massier and that his real name was Louis de Malreich. . . And Louis de Malreich was sentenced to death. . . And Dolores de Malreich, victorious at last, safe from all suspicion once the culprit was discovered, released from her infamous and criminal past, her husband dead, her brother dead, her sister dead, her two maids dead, Steinweg dead, delivered by me from her accomplices, whom I handed over to Weber all packed up, delivered, lastly, from herself by me, who was sending the innocent man whom she had substituted for herself to the scaffold, Dolores de Malreich, triumphant, rich with the wealth of her millions and loved by Pierre Leduc, Dolores de Malreich would sit upon the throne of her native grand-duchy. . . Ah," cried Lupin, beside himself with excitement, "that man shall not die! I swear it as I live: he shall not die!"

"Look out, governor," said Octave, scared, "we are near the town now. . . the outskirts. . . the suburbs. . ."

"What shall I care?"

"But we shall topple over. . . And the pavement is greasy. . . we are skidding. . ."

"Never mind."

"Take care. . . Look ahead. . ."

"What?"

"A tram-car, at the turn. . ."

"Let it stop!"

"Do slow down, governor!"

"Never!"

"But we have no room to pass!"

"We shall get through."

"We can't get through."

"Yes, we can."

"Oh, Lord!"

A crash. . . outcries. . . The motor had run into the tram-car, cannoned against a fence, torn down ten yards of planking and, lastly, smashed itself against the corner of a slope.

"Driver, are you disengaged?"

Lupin, lying flat on the grass of the slope, had hailed a taxi-cab.

He scrambled to his feet, gave a glance at his shattered car and the people crowding round to Octave's assistance and jumped into the cab:

"Go to the Ministry of the Interior, on the Place Beauvau. . . Twenty francs for yourself. . ."

He settled himself in the taxi and continued:

"No, no, he shall not die! No, a thousand times no, I will not have that on my conscience! It is bad enough to have been tricked by a woman and to have fallen into the snare like a schoolboy. . . That will do! No more blunders for me! I have had that poor wretch arrested. . . I have had him sentenced to death. . . I have brought him to the foot of the scaffold. . . but he shall not mount it! . . . Anything but that! If he mounts the scaffold, there will be nothing left for me but to put a bullet through my head."

They were approaching the toll-house. He leant out:

"Twenty francs more, driver, if you don't stop."

And he shouted to the officials:

"Detective-service!"

They passed through.

"But don't slow down, don't slow down, hang it!" roared Lupin. "Faster! . . . Faster still! Are you afraid of running over the old ladies? Never mind about them! I'll pay the damage!"

In a few minutes, they were at the Ministry of the Interior. Lupin hurried across the courtyard and ran up the main staircase. The waiting-room was full of people. He scribbled on a sheet of paper, "Prince Sernine," and, hustling a messenger into a corner, said:

"You know me, don't you? I'm Lupin. I procured you this berth; a snug retreat for your old age, eh? Only, you've got to show me in at once. There, take my name through. That's all I ask of you. The premier will thank you, you may be sure of that. . . and so I will. . . But, hurry you fool! Valenglay is expecting me. . ."

Ten seconds later, Valenglay himself put his head through the door of his room and said:

"Show the prince in."

Lupin rushed into the room, slammed the door and, interrupting the premier, said:

"No, no set phrases, you can't arrest me. . . It would mean ruining yourself and compromising the Emperor. . . No, it's not a question of

MAURICE LEBLANC

that. Look here. Malreich is innocent. . . I have discovered the real criminal. . . It's Dolores Kesselbach. She is dead. Her body is down there. I have undeniable proofs. There is no doubt possible. It was she. . ."

He stopped. Valenglay seemed not to understand.

"But, look here, Monsieur le President, we must save Malreich. . . Only think. . . a judicial error! . . . An innocent man guillotined! . . . Give your orders. . . say you have fresh information. . . anything you please. . . but, quick, there is no time to lose. . ."

Valenglay looked at him attentively, then went to a table, took up a newspaper and handed it to him, pointing his finger at an article as he did so.

Lupin cast his eye at the head-line and read:

"Execution of the Monster"
"Louis de Malreich underwent the death-penalty this morning. . ."

He read no more. Thunderstruck, crushed, he fell into the premier's chair with a moan of despair. . .

How long he remained like that he could not say. When he was outside again, he remembered a great silence and then Valenglay bending over him and sprinkling water on his forehead. He remembered, above all, the premier's hushed voice whispering:

"Listen. . . you won't say anything about this will you? Innocent, perhaps, I don't say not. . . But what is the use of revelations, of a scandal? A judicial error can have serious consequences. Is it worth while? . . . A rehabilitation? For what purpose? He was not even sentenced under his own name. It is the name of Malreich which is held up to public execration. . . the name of the real criminal, as it happens. . . So. . ."

And, pushing Lupin gradually toward the door, he said:

"So go. . . Go back there. . . Get rid of the corpse. . . And let not a trace remain, eh? Not the slightest trace of all this business. . . I can rely on you, can I not?"

And Lupin went back. He went back like a machine, because he had been told to do so and because he had no will left of his own.

He waited for hours at the railway-station. Mechanically, he ate his dinner, took a ticket and settled down in a compartment.

He slept badly. His brain was on fire between nightmares and half-waking intervals in which he tried to make out why Malreich had not defended himself:

"He was a madman. . . surely. . . half a madman. . . He must have known her formerly. . . and she poisoned his life. . . she drove him crazy. . . So he felt he might as well die. . . Why defend himself?"

The explanation only half satisfied him, and he promised himself sooner or later to clear up the riddle and to discover the exact part which Massier had played in Dolores' life. But what did it matter for the moment? One fact alone stood out clearly, which was Massier's madness, and he repeated, persistently:

"He was a madman. . . Massier was undoubtedly mad. Besides, all those Massiers. . . a family of madmen. . ."

He raved, mixing up names in his enfeebled brain.

But, on alighting at Bruggen Station, in the cool, moist air of the morning, his consciousness revived. Things suddenly assumed a different aspect. And he exclaimed:

"Well, after all, it was his own look-out! He had only to protest. . . I accept no responsibility. . . It was he who committed suicide. . . He was only a dumb actor in the play. . . He has gone under. . . I am sorry. . . But it can't be helped!"

The necessity for action stimulated him afresh. Wounded, tortured by that crime of which he knew himself to be the author for all that he might say, he nevertheless looked to the future:

"Those are the accidents of war," he said. "Don't let us think about it. Nothing is lost. On the contrary! Dolores was the stumbling-block, since Pierre Leduc loved her. Dolores is dead. Therefore Pierre Leduc belongs to me. And he shall marry Geneviève, as I have arranged! And he shall reign! And I shall be the master! And Europe, Europe is mine!"

He worked himself up, reassured, full of sudden confidence, and made feverish gestures as he walked along the road, whirling an imaginary sword, the sword of the leader whose will is law, who commands and triumphs:

"Lupin, you shall be king! You shall be king, Arsène Lupin!"

He inquired in the village of Bruggen and heard that Pierre Leduc had lunched yesterday at the inn. Since then, he had not been seen.

"Oh?" asked Lupin. "Didn't he sleep here?"

"No."

"But where did he go after his lunch?"

"He took the road to the castle."

Lupin walked away in some surprise. After all, he had told the young man to lock the doors and not to return after the servants had gone.

He at once received a proof that Pierre had disobeyed him: the park gates were open.

He went in, hunted all over the castle, called out. No reply.

Suddenly, he thought of the chalet. Who could tell? Perhaps Pierre Leduc, worrying about the woman he loved and driven by an intuition, had gone to look for her in that direction. And Dolores' corpse was there!

Greatly alarmed, Lupin began to run.

At first sight, there seemed to be no one in the chalet.

"Pierre! Pierre!" he cried.

Hearing no sound, he entered the front passage and the room which he had occupied.

He stopped short, rooted to the threshold.

Above Dolores' corpse, hung Pierre Leduc, with a rope round his neck, dead.

LUPIN IMPATIENTLY PULLED HIMSELF TOGETHER from head to foot. He refused to yield to a single gesture of despair. He refused to utter a single violent word. After the cruel blows which fate had dealt him, after Dolores' crimes and death, after Massier's execution, after all those disturbances and catastrophes, he felt the absolute necessity of retaining all his self-command. If not, his brain would undoubtedly give way. . .

"Idiot!" he said, shaking his fist at Pierre Leduc. "You great idiot, couldn't you wait? In ten years we should have had Alsace-Lorraine again!"

To relieve his mind, he sought for words to say, for attitudes; but his ideas escaped him and his head seemed on the point of bursting.

"Oh, no, no!" he cried. "None of that, thank you! Lupin mad too! No, old chap! Put a bullet through your head, if you like; and, when all is said, I don't see any other way out. But Lupin drivelling, wheeled about in a bath-chair. . . no! Style, old fellow, finish in style!"

He walked up and down, stamping his feet and lifting his knees very high, as certain actors do when feigning madness. And he said:

"Swagger, my lad, swagger! The eyes of the gods are upon you! Lift up your head! Pull in your stomach, hang it! Throw out your chest! . . .

Everything is breaking up around you. What do you care? . . . It's the final disaster, I've played my last card, a kingdom in the gutter, I've lost Europe, the whole world ends in smoke. . . Well. . . and what of it? Laugh, laugh! Be Lupin, or you're in the soup. . . Come, laugh! Louder than that, louder, louder! That's right! . . . Lord, how funny it all is! Dolores, old girl, a cigarette!"

He bent down with a grin, touched the dead woman's face, tottered for a second and fell to the ground unconscious.

AFTER LYING FOR AN HOUR, he came to himself and stood up. The fit of madness was over; and, master of himself, with relaxed nerves, serious and silent, he considered the position.

He felt that the time had come for the irrevocable decisions that involve a whole existence. His had been utterly shattered, in a few days, under the assault of unforeseen catastrophes, rushing up, one after the other, at the very moment when he thought his triumph assured. What should he do? Begin again? Build up everything again? He had not the courage for it. What then?

The whole morning, he roamed tragically about the park and gradually realized his position in all its slightest details. Little by little, the thought of death enforced itself upon him with inflexible rigor.

But, whether he decided to kill himself or to live, there was first of all a series of definite acts which he was obliged to perform. And these acts stood out clearly in his brain, which had suddenly become quite cool.

The mid-day Angelus rang from the church-steeple.

"To work!" he said, firmly.

He returned to the chalet in a very calm frame of mind, went to his room, climbed on a stool, and cut the rope by which Pierre Leduc was hanging:

"You poor devil!" he said. "You were doomed to end like that, with a hempen tie around your neck. Alas, you were not made for greatness: I ought to have foreseen that and not hooked my fortune to a rhymester!"

He felt in the young man's clothes and found nothing. But, remembering Dolores' second pocket-book, he took it from the pocket where he had left it.

He gave a start of surprise. The pocket-book contained a bundle of letters whose appearance was familiar to him; and he at once recognized the different writings.

"The Emperor's letters!" he muttered, slowly. "The old chancellor's letters! The whole bundle which I myself found at Leon Massier's and which I handed to Count von Waldemar! . . . How did it happen? . . . Did she take them in her turn from that blockhead of a Waldemar?" And, suddenly, slapping his forehead, "Why, no, the blockhead is myself. These are the real letters! She kept them to blackmail the Emperor when the time came. And the others, the ones which I handed over, are copies, forged by herself, of course, or by an accomplice, and placed where she knew that I should find them. . . And I played her game for her, like a mug! By Jove, when women begin to interfere. . . !"

There was only a piece of pasteboard left in the pocket-book, a photograph. He looked at it. It was his own.

"Two photographs. . . Massier and I. . . the two she loved best, no doubt. . . For she loved me. . . A strange love, built up of admiration for the adventurer that I am, for the man who, by himself, put away the seven scoundrels whom she had paid to break my head! A strange love! I felt it throbbing in her the other day, when I told her my great dream of omnipotence. Then, really, she had the idea of sacrificing Pierre Leduc and subjecting her dream to mine. If the incident of the mirror had not taken place, she would have been subdued. But she was afraid. I had my hand upon the truth. My death was necessary for her salvation and she decided upon it." He repeated several times, pensively, "And yet she loved me. . . Yes, she loved me, as others have loved me. . . others to whom I have brought ill-luck also. . . Alas, all those who love me die! . . . And this one died too, strangled by my hand. . . What is the use of living? . . . What is the use of living?" he asked again, in a low voice. "Is it not better to join them, all those women who have loved me. . . and who have died of their love. . . Sonia, Raymonde, Clotilde, Destange, Miss Clarke? . . ."

He laid the two corpses beside each other, covered them with the same sheet, sat down at a table and wrote:

"I have triumphed over everything and I am beaten. I have reached the goal and I have fallen. Fate is too strong for me. . . And she whom I loved is no more. I shall die also."

And he signed his name:

"ARSÈNE LUPIN."

He sealed the letter and slipped it into a bottle which he flung through the window, on the soft ground of a flower-border.

Next, he made a great pile on the floor with old newspapers, straw and shavings, which he went to fetch in the kitchen. On the top of it he emptied a gallon of petrol. Then he lit a candle and threw it among the shavings.

A flame at once arose and other flames leapt forth, quick, glowing, crackling.

"Let's clear out," said Lupin. "The chalet is built of wood, it will all flare up like a match. And, by the time they come from the village, break down the gates and run to this end of the park, it will be too late. They will find ashes, the remains of two charred corpses and, close at hand, my farewell letter in a bottle. . . Good-bye, Lupin! Bury me simply, good people, without superfluous state. . . a poor man's funeral. . . No flowers, no wreaths. . . Just a humble cross and a plain epitaph; 'Here lies Arsène Lupin, adventurer.'"

He made for the park wall, climbed over it, and turning round, saw the flames soaring up to the sky. . .

HE WANDERED BACK TOWARD PARIS on foot, bowed down by destiny, with despair in his heart. And the peasants were amazed at the sight of this traveller who paid with bank-notes for his fifteen-penny meals.

Three foot-pads attacked him one evening in the forest. He defended himself with his stick and left them lying for dead. . .

He spent a week at an inn. He did not know where to go. . . What was he to do? What was there for him to cling to? He was tired of life. He did not want to live. . .

"IS THAT YOU?"

Mme. Ernemont stood in her little sitting-room in the villa at Garches, trembling, scared and livid, staring at the apparition that faced her.

Lupin! . . . It was Lupin.

"You!" she said. "You! . . . But the papers said. . ."

He smiled sadly:

"Yes, I am dead."

"Well, then. . . well, then. . ." she said, naïvely.

"You mean that, if I am dead, I have no business here. Believe me, I have serious reasons, Victoire."

"How you have changed!" she said, in a voice full of pity.

"A few little disappointments. . . However, that's over. . . Tell me, is Geneviève in?"

She flew at him, in a sudden rage:

"You leave her alone, do you hear? Geneviève? You want to see Geneviève, to take her back? Ah, this time I shall not let her out of my sight! She came back tired, white as a sheet, nervous; and the color has hardly yet returned to her cheeks. You shall leave her alone, I swear you shall."

He pressed his hand hard on the old woman's shoulder:

"I *will*—do you understand?—I *will* speak to her."

"No."

"I mean to speak to her."

"No."

He pushed her about. She drew herself up and, crossing her arms:

"You shall pass over my dead body first, do you hear? The child's happiness lies in this house and nowhere else. . . With all your ideas of money and rank, you would only make her miserable. Who is this Pierre Leduc of yours? And that Veldenz of yours? Geneviève a grand-duchess! You are mad. That's no life for her! . . . You see, after all, you have thought only of yourself in this matter. It was your power, your fortune you wanted. The child you don't care a rap about. Have you so much as asked yourself if she loved your rascally grand-duke? Have you asked yourself if she loved anybody? No, you just pursued your object, that is all, at the risk of hurting Geneviève and making her unhappy for the rest of her life. . . Well, I won't have it! What she wants is a simple, honest existence, led in the broad light of day; and that is what you can't give her. Then what are you here for?"

He seemed to waver, but, nevertheless, he murmured in a low voice and very sadly:

"It is impossible that I should never see her again, it is impossible that I should not speak to her. . ."

"She believes you dead."

"That is exactly what I do not want! I want her to know the truth. It is a torture to me to think that she looks upon me as one who is no more. Bring her to me, Victoire."

He spoke in a voice so gentle and so distressed that she was utterly moved, and said:

"Listen. . . First of all, I want to know. . . It depends upon what you intend to say to her. . . Be frank, my boy. . . What do you want with Geneviève?"

He said, gravely:

"I want to say this: 'Geneviève, I promised your mother to give you wealth, power, a fairy-like existence. And, on the day when I had attained my aim, I would have asked you for a little place, not very far from you. Rich and happy, you would have forgotten—yes, I am sure of it—you would have forgotten who I am, or rather who I was. Unfortunately, fate has been too strong for me. I bring you neither wealth nor power. And it is I, on the contrary, who have need of you. Geneviève, will you help me?'"

"To do what?" asked the old woman, anxiously.

"To live. . ."

"Oh!" she said. "Has it come to that, my poor boy? . . ."

"Yes," he answered, simply, without any affectation of sorrow, "yes, it has come to that. Three human beings are just dead, killed by me, killed by my hands. The burden of the memory is more than I can bear. I am alone. For the first time in my life, I need help. I have the right to ask that help of Geneviève. And her duty is to give it to me. . . If not. . ."

"If not. . . ?"

"Then all is over."

The old woman was silent, pale and quivering with emotion. She once more felt all her affection for him whom she had fed at her breast and who still and in spite of all remained "her boy." She asked:

"What do you intend to do with her?"

"We shall go abroad. We will take you with us, if you like to come. . ."

"But you forget. . . you forget. . ."

"What?"

"Your past. . ."

"She will forget it too. She will understand that I am no longer the man I was, that I do not wish to be."

"Then, really, what you wish is that she should share your life, the life of Lupin?"

"The life of the man that I shall be, of the man who will work so that she may be happy, so that she may marry according to her inclination. We will settle down in some nook or other. We will struggle together, side by side. And you know what I am capable of. . ."

She repeated, slowly, with her eyes fixed on his:

"Then, really, you wish her to share Lupin's life?"

He hesitated a second, hardly a second, and declared, plainly:

"Yes, yes, I wish it, I have the right."

"You wish her to abandon all the children to whom she has devoted herself, all this life of work which she loves and which is essential to her happiness?"

"Yes, I wish it, it is her duty."

The old woman opened the window and said:

"In that case, call her."

Geneviève was in the garden, sitting on a bench. Four little girls were crowding round her. Others were playing and running about.

He saw her full-face. He saw her grave, smiling eyes. She held a flower in her hand and plucked the petals one by one and gave explanations to the attentive and eager children. Then she asked them questions. And each answer was rewarded with a kiss to the pupil.

Lupin looked at her long, with infinite emotion and anguish. A whole leaven of unknown feelings fermented within him. He had a longing to press that pretty girl to his breast, to kiss her and tell her how he respected and loved her. He remembered the mother, who died in the little village of Aspremont, who died of grief.

"Call her," said Victoire. "Why don't you call her?"

He sank into a chair and stammered:

"I can't. . . I can't do it. . . I have not the right. . . It is impossible. . . Let her believe me dead. . . That is better. . ."

He wept, his shoulders shaking with sobs, his whole being overwhelmed with despair, swollen with an affection that arose in him, like those backward flowers which die on the very day of their blossoming.

The old woman knelt down beside him and, in a trembling voice, asked:

"She is your daughter, is she not?"

"Yes, she is my daughter."

"Oh, my poor boy!" she said, bursting into tears. "My poor boy! . . ."

Epilogue

THE SUICIDE

To horse!" said the Emperor.

He corrected himself, on seeing the magnificent ass which they brought him:

"To donkey, rather! Waldemar, are you sure this animal is quiet to ride and drive?"

"I will answer for him as I would for myself, Sire," declared the count.

"In that case, I feel safe," said the Emperor, laughing. And, turning to the officers with him, "Gentlemen, to horse!"

The market-place of the village of Capri was crowded with sight-seers, kept back by a line of Italian carabiniers, and, in the middle, all the donkeys of the place, which had been requisitioned to enable the Emperor to go over that island of wonders.

"Waldemar," said the Emperor, taking the head of the cavalcade, "what do we begin with?"

"With Tiberius's Villa, Sire."

They rode under a gateway and then followed a roughly-paved path, rising gradually to the eastern promontory of the island.

The Emperor laughed and enjoyed himself and good-humoredly chaffed the colossal Count von Waldemar, whose feet touched the ground on either side of the unfortunate donkey borne down under his weight.

In three-quarters of an hour, they arrived first at Tiberius's Leap, an enormous rock, a thousand feet high, from which the tyrant caused his victims to be hurled into the sea. . .

The Emperor dismounted, walked up to the hand-rail and took a glance at the abyss. Then he went on foot to the ruins of Tiberius's Villa, where he strolled about among the crumbling halls and passages.

He stopped for a moment.

There was a glorious view of the point of Sorrento and over the whole island of Capri. The glowing blue of the sea outlined the beautiful curve of the bay; and cool perfumes mingled with the scent of the citron-trees.

"The view is finer still, Sire," said Waldemar, "from the hermit's little chapel, at the summit."

"Let us go to it."

But the hermit himself descended by a steep path. He was an old man, with a hesitating gait and a bent back. He carried the book in which travellers usually write down their impressions.

He placed the book on a stone seat.

"What am I write?" asked the Emperor.

"Your name, Sire, and the date of your visit. . . and anything you please."

The Emperor took the pen which the hermit handed him and bent down to write.

"Take care, Sire, take care!"

Shouts of alarm. . . a great crash from the direction of the chapel. . . The Emperor turned round. He saw a huge rock come rolling down upon him like a whirlwind.

At the same moment, he was seized round the body by the hermit and flung to a distance of ten yards away.

The rock struck against the stone seat where the Emperor had been standing a quarter of a second before and smashed the seat into fragments. But for the hermit, the Emperor would have been killed.

He gave him his hand and said, simply:

"Thank you."

The officers flocked round him.

"It's nothing, gentlemen. . . We have escaped with a fright. . . though it was a fine fright, I confess. . . All the same, but for the intervention of this worthy man. . ."

And, going up to the hermit:

"What is your name, my friend?"

The hermit had kept his head concealed in his hood. He pushed it back an inch or so and, in a very low voice, so as to be heard by none but the Emperor, he said:

"The name of a man, Sire, who is very pleased that you have shaken him by the hand."

The Emperor gave a start and stepped back. Then, at once controlling himself:

"Gentlemen," he said to the officers, "I will ask you to go up to the chapel. More rocks can break loose; and it would perhaps be wise to warn the authorities of the island. You will join me later. I want to thank this good man."

He walked away, accompanied by the hermit. When they were alone, he said:

"You! Why?"

"I had to speak to you, Sire. If I had asked for an audience. . . would you have granted my request? I preferred to act directly and I intended to make myself known while Your Imperial Majesty was signing the book, when that stupid accident. . ."

"Well?" said the Emperor.

"The letters which I gave Waldemar to hand to you, Sire, are forgeries."

The Emperor made a gesture of keen annoyance:

"Forgeries? Are you sure?"

"Absolutely sure, Sire."

"Yet that Malreich. . ."

"Malreich was not the culprit."

"Then who was?"

"I must beg Your Imperial Majesty to treat my answer as secret and confidential. The real culprit was Mrs. Kesselbach."

"Kesselbach's own wife?"

"Yes, Sire. She is dead now. It was she who made or caused to be made the copies which are in your possession. She kept the real letters."

"But where are they?" exclaimed the Emperor. "That is the important thing! They must be recovered at all costs! I attach the greatest value to those letters. . ."

"Here they are, Sire."

The Emperor had a moment of stupefaction. He looked at Lupin, looked at the letters, then at Lupin again and pocketed the bundle without examining it.

Clearly, this man was puzzling him once more. Where did this scoundrel spring from who, possessing so terrible a weapon, handed it over like that, generously, unconditionally? It would have been so easy for him to keep the letters and to make such use of them as he pleased! No, he had given his promise and he was keeping his word.

And the Emperor thought of all the astounding things which that man had done.

"The papers said that you were dead," he said.

"Yes, Sire. In reality, I am dead. And the police of my country, glad to be rid of me, have buried the charred and unrecognizable remains of my body."

"Then you are free?"

"As I always have been."

"And nothing attaches you to anything?"

"Nothing, Sire."

"In that case. . ."

The Emperor hesitated and then, explicitly:

"In that case, enter my service. I offer you the command of my private police. You shall be the absolute master. You shall have full power, even over the other police."

"No, Sire."

"Why not?"

"I am a Frenchman."

There was a pause. The Emperor was evidently pleased with the answer. He said:

"Still, as you say that no link attaches you. . ."

"That is, one, Sire, which nothing can sever." And he added, laughing, "I am dead as a man, but alive as a Frenchman. I am sure that Your Imperial Majesty will understand."

The Emperor took a few steps up and down. Then he said:

"I should like to pay my debt, however. I heard that the negotiations for the grand-duchy of Veldenz were broken off. . ."

"Yes, Sire, Pierre Leduc was an imposter. He is dead."

"What can I do for you? You have given me back those letters. . . You have saved my life. . . What can I do?"

"Nothing, Sire."

"You insist upon my remaining your debtor?"

"Yes, Sire."

The Emperor gave a last glance at that strange man who set himself up in his presence as his equal. Then he bowed his head slightly and walked away without another word.

"Aha, Majesty, I've caught you this time!" said Lupin, following him with his eyes. And, philosophically, "No doubt it's a poor revenge. . . and would rather have recovered Alsace-Lorraine. . . But still. . ."

He interrupted himself and stamped his foot on the ground:

"You confounded Lupin! Will you never change, will you always remain hateful and cynical to the last moment of your existence? Be serious, hang it all! The time has come, now or never, to be serious!"

He climbed the path that leads to the chapel and stopped at the place where the rock had broken loose. He burst out laughing:

"It was a good piece of work and His Imperial Majesty's officers did not know what to make of it. But how could they guess that I myself loosened that rock, that, at the last moment, I gave the decisive blow of the pick-axe and that the aforesaid rock rolled down the path which I had made between it and. . . an emperor whose life I was bent on saving?"

He sighed:

"Ah, Lupin, what a complex mind you have! All that trouble because you had sworn that this particular Majesty should shake you by the hand! A lot of good it has done you! 'An Emperor's hand five fingers has, no more,' as Victor Hugo might have said."

He entered the chapel and, with a special key, opened the low door of a little sacristy. On a heap of straw, lay a man, with his hands and legs bound and a gag in his mouth.

"Well, my friend, the hermit," said Lupin, "it wasn't so very long, was it? Twenty-four hours at the most. . . But I have worked jolly hard on your behalf! Just think, you have saved the Emperor's life! Yes, old chap. You are the man who saved the Emperor's life. I have made your fortune, that's what I've done. They'll build a cathedral for you and put up a statue to you when you're dead and gone. Here, take your things."

The hermit, nearly dead with hunger, staggered to his feet. Lupin quickly put on his own clothes and said:

"Farewell, O worthy and venerable man. Forgive me for this little upset. And pray for me. I shall need it. Eternity is opening its gate wide to me. Farewell."

He stood for a few moments on the threshold of the chapel. It was the solemn moment at which one hesitates, in spite of everything, before the terrible end of all things. But his resolution was irrevocable and, without further reflection, he darted out, ran down the slope, crossed the level ground of Tiberius's Leap and put one leg over the hand-rail:

"Lupin, I give you three minutes for play-acting. 'What's the good?' you will say. 'There is nobody here.' Well. . . and what about you? Can't you act your last farce for yourself? By Jove, the performance is worth it. . . *Arsène Lupin*, heroic comedy in eighty scenes. . . The curtain rises on the death-scene. . . and the principal part is played by Lupin in person. . . 'Bravo, Lupin!' . . . Feel my heart, ladies and gentlemen. . . seventy beats to the minute. . . And a smile on my lips. . . 'Bravo, Lupin! Oh, the rogue, what cheek he has!' . . . Well, jump, my lord. . . Are you ready? It's the last adventure, old fellow. No regrets? Regrets? What for, heavens above? My life was splendid. Ah, Dolores, Dolores, if you had not come into it, abominable monster that you were!. . . . And you, Malreich, why did you not speak? . . . And you, Pierre Leduc. . . Here I am! . . . My three dead friends, I am about to join you. . . Oh, Geneviève, my dear Geneviève! . . . Here, have you done, you old play-actor? . . . Right you are! Right you are! I'm coming. . ."

He pulled his other leg over, looked down the abyss at the dark and motionless sea and, raising his head:

"Farewell, immortal and thrice-blessed nature! *Moriturus te salutat!* Farewell, all that is beautiful on earth! Farewell, splendor of things. Farewell, life!"

He flung kisses to space, to the sky, to the sun. . . Then, folding his arms, he took the leap.

SIDI-BEL-ABBES. THE BARRACKS OF THE Foreign Legion. An adjutant sat smoking and reading his newspaper in a small, low-ceilinged room.

Near him, close to the window opening on the yard, two great devils of non-commissioned officers were jabbering in guttural French, mixed with Teutonic phrases.

The door opened. Some one entered. It was a slightly-built man, of medium height, smartly-dressed.

The adjutant rose, glared angrily at the intruder and growled:

"I say, what on earth is the orderly up to? . . . And you, sir, what do you want?"

"Service."

This was said frankly, imperiously.

The two non-coms burst into a silly laugh. The man looked at them askance.

"In other words, you wish to enlist in the Legion?" asked the adjutant.

"Yes, but on one condition."

"Conditions, by Jove! What conditions?"

"That I am not left mouldering here. There is a company leaving for Morocco. I'll join that."

One of the non-coms gave a fresh chuckle and was heard to say:

"The Moors are in for a bad time. The gentleman's enlisting."

"Silence!" cried the man, "I don't stand being laughed at."

His voice sounded harsh and masterful.

The non-com, a brutal-looking giant, retorted:

"Here, recruity, you'd better be careful how you talk to me, or. . ."

"Or what?"

"You'll get something you won't like, that's all!"

The man went up to him, took him round the waist, swung him over the ledge of the window and pitched him into the yard.

Then he said to the other:

"Go away."

The other went away.

The man at once returned to the adjutant and said:

"Lieutenant, pray be so good as to tell the major that Don Luis Perenna, a Spanish grandee and a Frenchman at heart, wishes to take service in the Foreign Legion. Go, my friend."

The flabbergasted adjutant did not move.

"Go, my friend, and go at once. I have no time to waste."

The adjutant rose, looked at his astounding visitor with a bewildered eye and went out in the tamest fashion.

Then Lupin lit a cigarette and, sitting down in the adjutant's chair, said, aloud:

"As the sea refused to have anything to say to me, or rather as I, at the last moment, refused to have anything to say to the sea, we'll go and see if the bullets of the Moors are more compassionate. And, in any case, it will be a smarter finish. . . Face the enemy, Lupin, and all for France! . . ."

THE END

A Note About the Author

Maurice Leblanc (1864–1941) was a French novelist and short story writer. Born and raised in Rouen, Normandy, Leblanc attended law school before dropping out to pursue a writing career in Paris. There, he made a name for himself as a leading author of crime fiction, publishing critically acclaimed stories and novels with moderate commercial success. On July 15th, 1905, Leblanc published a story in *Je sais tout*, a popular French magazine, featuring Arsène Lupin, gentleman thief. The character, inspired by Sir Arthur Conan Doyle's Sherlock Holmes stories, brought Leblanc both fame and fortune, featuring in 21 novels and short story collections and defining his career as one of the bestselling authors of the twentieth century. Appointed to the *Légion d'Honneur*, France's highest order of merit, Leblanc and his works remain cultural touchstones for generations of devoted readers. His stories have inspired numerous adaptations, including *Lupin,* a smash-hit 2021 television series.

A Note from the Publisher

Spanning many genres, from non-fiction essays to literature classics to children's books and lyric poetry, Mint Edition books showcase the master works of our time in a modern new package. The text is freshly typeset, is clean and easy to read, and features a new note about the author in each volume. Many books also include exclusive new introductory material. Every book boasts a striking new cover, which makes it as appropriate for collecting as it is for gift giving. Mint Edition books are only printed when a reader orders them, so natural resources are not wasted. We're proud that our books are never manufactured in excess and exist only in the exact quantity they need to be read and enjoyed.

bookfinity™

Discover more of your favorite classics with Bookfinity™.

- Track your reading with custom book lists.
- Get great book recommendations for your personalized Reader Type.
- Add reviews for your favorite books.
- AND MUCH MORE!

Visit **bookfinity.com** and take the fun Reader Type quiz to get started.

Enjoy our classic and modern companion pairings!

Printed in the USA
CPSIA information can be obtained
at www.ICGtesting.com
JSHW022209140824
68134JS00018B/959